THE LITTLE OLD LADY WHO BROKE ALL THE RULES

CATHARINA INGELMAN-SUNDBERG

Translated from the Swedish
by Rod Bradbury

PAN BOOKS

First published in 2012 by Bokförlaget Forum, Sweden, under the title *Kaffe med Rån*

This edition published 2014 by Pan Books
an imprint of Pan Macmillan, a division of Macmillan Publishers Limited
Pan Macmillan, 20 New Wharf Road, London N1 9RR
Basingstoke and Oxford
Associated companies throughout the world
www.panmacmillan.com

ISBN 978-1-4472-5061-6

7 9 8 6

A CIP catalogue record for this book is available from the British Library.

Typeset by Ellipsis Digital Limited, Glasgow
Printed and bound by CPI Group (UK) Ltd, Croydon, CR0 4YY

*To my nephews and nieces, Fredrik, Isabella, Simon,
Hanna, Maria, Henrik, Catrin, Hampus, Susanne, Christian,
Catharina, Helena, Fredrika, Anna and Sophia*

A crime a day keeps the doctor away.

Christina, aged seventy-seven

Prologue

The little old lady gripped the handles of her Zimmer frame, hung her walking stick next to the shopping basket and did her best to look assertive. After all, a woman of seventy-nine about to commit her first bank robbery needed to project an air of authority. She straightened her back, pulled her hat down over her forehead and thrust open the door. Supported by her frame, she walked slowly and determinedly into the bank. It was five minutes before closing time and three customers were waiting in the queue. The Zimmer frame squeaked faintly. She had greased it with olive oil, but one of the wheels had been wobbly ever since she had collided with the cleaning trolley at the retirement home. Not that it really mattered. The most important thing was that it had a large basket with room for a lot of money.

Martha Andersson from Södermalm, Stockholm, walked with a slight stoop, wearing a plain coat of nondescript colour, chosen especially to avoid attracting attention. She was smaller than average and solidly built, but not fat. She wore sensible dark walking shoes which would be perfect for a quick escape if it was necessary. That was assuming she was still able to pick up the speed to run. It wasn't something she had attempted in a number of years, so she might have to settle with a brisk trot. Her heavily veined hands were hidden inside a pair of well-used leather gloves and her short white hair was concealed under a wide-brimmed brown hat. She had wrapped a neon-coloured scarf around her neck, so if a photo was taken of her with a flash, it would automatically overexpose the rest of the picture and her facial features would disappear. The scarf was mainly an extra safety measure, since her mouth and nose were shadowed by her hat. But if she had to be old, she might as well be wise, too.

The bank's little branch on Götgatan looked like most banks in Sweden these days. There was just one cashier standing behind the solitary service counter; bland and boring walls; a highly polished floor and a small table brimming with brochures about advantageous loans and investment advice. *Dear brochure-writers*, Martha thought, *I know of much better ways of making lots of money!* Martha intended to laugh all the way to the bank, and all the way back out again, too.

She sat down on the customers' sofa and pretended to study the posters advertising savings accounts but found it hard to keep her hands still. She discreetly slipped one hand into her pocket for a fruit pastille. One of those unhealthy sweets that the doctors warned her against and dentists secretly loved. She tried to be good; she tried not to give in to the sugary treats. But if she was going to be rebellious, then today was the day. Surely she was allowed one guilty pleasure?

The queue number changed with a buzz and a man in his forties hurried up to the counter. His business was soon dealt with and then a teenage girl was served almost as quickly. However, the last in line was an elderly gentleman who took much longer as he was mumbling and fumbling with bits of paper. Martha was growing impatient. She mustn't be in the bank too long. Somebody might notice her body language or some other detail which might give her away. So she tried her best just to look like an old lady getting some cash out of the bank. Ironically, that was exactly what she was going to do, although the cashier was going to have a shock at the amount she was withdrawing and the fact that the money wasn't necessarily hers. But little details . . . Martha fished in her coat pocket for a newspaper cutting. She had saved an article about how much bank robberies cost the banks. The headline read: THIS IS A ROBBERY!. These were, in fact, the very words which had inspired her.

The old man at the counter was nearly finished so Martha began to pull herself up from the sofa, to stand as upright as she possibly could. All her life she had been the sort of honest, dependable person that everyone had relied on – she had even been a prefect at school. Now she was about to become a criminal. But in reality, how else could she survive in her old age? She needed money for a decent place to live for herself – and her friends. She simply couldn't back out now. She and her old choir chums were going to have a bright 'third age'. To put it simply, a bit of fun in the autumn of their lives. She would make sure of it.

The aged gentleman at the counter was taking his time, but finally the buzz sounded and her number appeared above the screen where the cashier stood. Slowly, but with dignity, she approached the counter. She was about to destroy the good reputation that she had built up across an entire lifetime in a single moment. But what else could you do in this modern society which treated its elderly members so badly? You put up with it and succumbed, or you adapted to the situation. She was the sort of person who adapted.

During those last few steps to the counter window she had a good look around the room before coming to a halt. Then, giving a friendly nod to the female cashier, she handed over the newspaper cutting:

THIS IS A ROBBERY!

The cashier read the headline and looked up with a smile.

'And how can I help you?'

'Three million – and quick!' cried Martha.

The cashier widened her smile. 'Would you like to withdraw some money?'

'No, *you* are going to withdraw money for me, *now!*'

'I see. But the pension money hasn't come in yet. It doesn't arrive until the middle of the month, you see, my dear.'

Martha had rather lost her momentum. This wasn't going the way she had imagined. Best to act quickly. She lifted up her walking stick and poked it through the gap under the window, brandishing it as best she could.

'Hurry up! My three million now!'

'But the pensions aren't—'

'Do as I say! Three million! In the basket – now!'

By this time the girl had had enough. It was closing time and she wanted to go home. Martha watched as she got up and fetched two male colleagues. Both men looked equally handsome and smiled politely. The one closest to her looked like Gregory Peck – or was it Cary Grant? He said:

'We'll sort out your pension, don't you worry. And my colleague here will be happy to phone for a taxi to take you home.'

Martha peered through the glass. She could see the girl in the back office, already picking up the phone.

'Oh well, I suppose I will have to rob you another time,' Martha conceded. She quickly withdrew her walking stick and closed her fist around the newspaper cutting. They all smiled sweetly and helped her out the door and into the taxi. They even folded the Zimmer frame up for her.

'Diamond House retirement home – OAP rate,' Martha told the driver as she waved goodbye to the bank staff. She carefully put the cutting back into her pocket. Things hadn't gone quite according to plan. But, nevertheless, a little old lady could do a great deal of things that people of other ages couldn't. She put her hand in her pocket for another fruit pastille and hummed contentedly to herself. Martha realized now that in order for her grand plan to work, she needed the support of her friends from the choir group. These were her nearest and dearest friends; the people who she had socialized and sung with for more than twenty years. Of course, she couldn't ask them straight out if they wanted to become criminals. She would have to persuade them with more subtle means. But afterwards – and she was quite certain of this – they would thank her for having changed their lives for the better.

Martha was awakened by a distant humming sound, followed by a sharp ping. She woke up, opened her eyes and tried to work out where she was. Yes, of course, she was at the retirement home. And it would, of course, be Rake – which was what everybody called her friend Bertil Engström. He always got up in the middle

5

of the night for a snack. He had a habit of putting food in the microwave only to forget all about it. Martha got out of bed and made her way to the kitchen with the help of her Zimmer frame. Muttering to herself, she opened the microwave and took out one plastic-covered dish of pasta and meatballs in tomato sauce. She stared dreamily at the buildings across the road. A few lamps glowed in the night. On the other side of the street, the houses would surely have proper kitchens, she thought. Here, at the retirement home, they used to have their own fully equipped kitchen but, to save on staff and money, the new owners had axed the catering department. Before Diamond House had taken over the retirement home, the meals had been the highlight of the day and the aroma of good food wafted through to the communal lounge. But now? Martha yawned and leaned against the sink. Almost *everything* had got worse and things were now so bad that she often found herself escaping into dreams. And what a lovely dream she had just woken up from . . . it had felt exactly as if she had been there at the bank for real, as if her subconscious had taken charge and tried to tell her something. At school she had always protested against things that she believed were unjust. Even during her years as a teacher, she had battled against unreasonable regulations and daft innovations. Strangely enough, here at the retirement home, she had just *put up with it all*. How could she have become so docile and lethargic? People who didn't like the rulers of their country started a revolution. They could jolly well do that here, too, if only she could get the support of her friends. But a bank robbery . . . that would be going a bit far, wouldn't it? She gave a nervous little laugh. Because that was what was a bit frightening – her dreams nearly always came true.

1

The next day, while the guests, or the 'clients', as they were now called, at Diamond House were drinking their morning coffee in the lounge, Martha thought about what she should do. In her childhood home in Österlen, down in the south of Sweden, people didn't just sit and wait for somebody else to take action. If the hay must be put in the barn, or a mare was going to foal, then you simply pitched in and did what was necessary. Martha looked at her hands. She was proud of them – they were reliable hands, and showed that she had done her fair share of hard work. The murmur of voices rose and fell all around her as she surveyed the rather shabby lounge. The smell was decidedly reminiscent of the Salvation Army and the furniture seemed to have come straight from the recycling depot. The old grey 1940s building, with its asbestos fibre cement cladding, was like a combination of an old school and a dentist's waiting room. Surely this wasn't where she was meant to end her days, with a mug of weak instant coffee to go with a plastic meal? No, damn it, it certainly was not! Martha breathed deeply, pushed her coffee mug aside and leaned forward to speak to her group of friends.

'You lot. Come with me,' she said and gave a sign to her

friends to follow her into her room. 'I have something to talk to you about.'

Everybody knew that Martha had a stash of cloudberry liqueur hidden away, so they all nodded and got up straight away. The stylish Rake went first, followed by Brains, the inventor, and Martha's two lady friends – Christina, who loved Belgian chocolate, and Anna-Greta, the old lady who looked so old that all the other old ladies paled in comparison. They looked at each other. Martha usually had something special on the cards when she invited you in for a glass of liqueur. It hadn't happened for quite a while, but now it was evidently time.

Once they were in her room, Martha retrieved the bottle, tidied away her half-finished knitting from the sofa and invited her friends to sit down. She threw a glance at the mahogany table with the freshly ironed floral-patterned cloth. She had wanted to replace the old table for a long while but it was big and solid and there was room for everybody around it so it would have to do for now. As she put the bottle on the table she caught sight of her old family photos on the chest of drawers. Framed behind glass, her parents and sister smiled out at her in front of her childhood home in Brantevik, a small fishing village in Österlen. If only they could see her now . . . they would not approve. They were teetotallers. Defiantly, she set out the liqueur glasses and filled them to the brim.

'Cheers!' she said and raised her glass.

'Cheers!' her friends responded joyfully.

'And now for the drinking song,' Martha insisted, after which they all mimed a silent version of 'Helan går'. Here at the retirement home, it was necessary to keep your voice down during sessions like this, so as not to be discovered with hidden alcohol.

Martha silently mouthed the refrain once more and they all laughed. So far nobody had ever discovered them, and this was all part of the fun. Martha put her glass down and looked at the others out of the corner of her eye. Should she tell them about her dream? No, first she must get them on the same wavelength as herself, then she might be able to persuade them all to go along with her plan. They were a close-knit group of friends and in their late fifties they had decided they would live together in their old age. So now, surely, they could make a new decision together. After all, they had so much in common. When they had become pensioners, the five of them had performed at hospitals and parish halls with their choir, The Vocal Chord, and they had all moved into the same retirement home. For a long time Martha had tried to get them to pool their funds and buy an old country mansion down in the south instead. She thought this option sounded much more exciting than a retirement home. She had read in the paper how old mansions were extremely cheap to buy and several of them even had moats.

'If you get some unpleasant visitor from the authorities or your children want to get at their inheritance in advance, then all you have to do is raise the drawbridge,' she had said in an attempt to convince the others. But when they realized that a mansion was expensive in upkeep and required staff, the choice fell on the Lily of the Valley Retirement Home. But their lovely retirement home had been renamed by the ghastly new owners and was now called Diamond House.

'Did your evening snack taste good?' Martha asked after Rake had drained the last drops of liqueur from his glass. He looked sleepy but had, of course, had time to put a rose in his lapel and tie a newly ironed cravat round his neck. He was somewhat grey by now but he still retained his charm and was so elegantly dressed that even younger women stopped to look at him twice.

'Evening snack? Just something to keep hunger at bay. Not that it worked. The food here is worse than on a ship,' he said and put down his glass. In his youth he had been at sea, but after going ashore for good he had trained as a gardener. Now he made do with a few flowers and herbs on the balcony. His greatest annoyance in life was that everyone called him Rake. True, he loved gardening and had once tripped over a rake and done himself an injury, but in his opinion that wasn't a reason for the nickname to stick for the rest of his life. He had tried suggesting other nicknames but nobody had listened.

'Why don't you make yourself a cheese sandwich instead? Quiet food that doesn't go "ping"?' came a muttering from Anna-Greta who had also been woken by the microwave and had found it hard to get back to sleep. She was an assertive woman who knew her own mind and she was so tall and slim that Rake used to say that she must have been born in a drain-pipe.

'Yes, but you can always smell the delicious food and spices that the staff are cooking from up on the first floor. So that makes me hungry for more than just a sandwich,' was Rake's excuse.

'You're right; the staff should cook similar meals for us to eat. The food that we have delivered and served under cellophane wrapping isn't very filling,' said Christina Åkerblom as she discreetly filed her nails. The former milliner, who in her youth had dreamed of becoming a librarian, was the youngest of them all – only seventy-seven. She wanted to live a calm and pleasant life, eating good food and doing her watercolour painting. She did not want to be served junk food. After a long life in Stockholm's poshest district, Östermalm, she was used to a certain standard.

'The staff don't get the same food as us,' Martha agreed. 'The food that we can smell is just for the new owners of Diamond House, who have their office and kitchen on the upper floor.'

'Then we ought to install a lift which can transport their food down to us,' remarked Oscar 'Brains' Krupp who was the solution-finder of the group and was one year older than Christina. Brains was an inventor and used to have his own workshop in Sundbyberg. He also loved good food, which was shown in his plump and cuddly figure. He considered exercise to be a recreation for people with nothing better to do.

'Do you remember the brochure we got when we first came here?' asked Martha. 'Good food from the restaurant, it said. And they also boasted of daily walks, visits from artistes, chiropody and somebody to do our hair. With the new owners, nothing works any more. It is about time we made a stand.'

'Rebellion at the retirement home!' said Christina in her most melodramatic voice, waving her hand vigorously so that the nail file ended up on the floor.

'Yes, that's right, a little mutiny,' Martha agreed.

'A mutiny? We'd have to be at sea first,' snorted Rake in a disbelieving manner.

'But perhaps the new owners have some financial difficulties? It'll get better eventually, wait and see,' said Anna-Greta, straightening her spectacles which dated from the early fifties. She had worked in a bank all her life and understood that entrepreneurs must make a profit.

11

'Get better? Like hell it will,' muttered Rake. 'Those bastards have already raised the charges several times and we haven't seen any improvements.'

'Don't be so negative,' said Anna-Greta and she straightened her spectacles again. They were old and worn out and were always slipping down her nose. She never changed spectacles and instead just updated her lenses because she thought her frames were timeless.

'What do you mean, negative? We must demand improvements. Across the board, but starting with the food!' Martha said. 'Now listen, the owners must have something nice to eat in the kitchen upstairs. So when the rest of the staff have gone home, I thought we could . . .'

Enthusiasm spread round the table as Martha talked on. Before long, five pairs of eyes were glowing just as brightly as the water on a lake-shore on a sunny summer's day. They all glanced up, looked at each other and made a thumbs-up sign.

When her friends had left her room, Martha put the cloudberry liqueur back into the depths of her wardrobe and hummed happily to herself. Her dream about the bank robbery seemed to have given her new energy. *Nothing is impossible*, she thought. *But in order to succeed with a change, you must put forward alternatives*. And that was what she was going to do now. Then her friends would think that they had made their decisions all by themselves.

2

After everyone had stepped out of the lift and stood outside the Diamond House office, Martha held up her hand and hushed the others. She had inspected the contents of the key cupboard and had chosen one with a triangular bow, the sort that locksmiths can't copy. She put the key in the lock, gave it a turn and the door opened.

'Just as I thought. The master key. Excellent, in we go, but remember to be quiet.'

'Look who's talking,' muttered Rake, who thought that Martha always talked too much.

'But what if someone discovers us?' Christina worried.

'They won't, we'll be as quiet as mice,' Anna-Greta said loudly. Like all those who are hard of hearing she spoke in a resounding voice without realizing it herself.

The Zimmer frames squeaked out of time as the five of them slowly and cautiously entered the room. It smelt of office and furniture polish, and there were folders arranged in a meticulous order on the desk.

'Hmm, the kitchen must be through that set of doors,' Martha said, pointing across to the other side of the room.

As they entered the next room, Martha took the lead and closed the curtains.

'Now we can turn the lights on!'

The lights flickered into action and before them appeared a sizeable room with a fridge, freezer and large fitted cupboards on the wall. In the middle was an island on wheels, and beside the window a dining table with six chairs.

'A proper kitchen,' declared Brains as he stroked the fridge door.

'There will certainly be some good food in here,' Martha declared as she opened the fridge door. The shelves were filled with chicken and fillet steak, a leg of lamb and several different types of cheese. The drawers below contained lettuces, tomatoes, beetroot and fruit.

The door to the freezer took some effort to open. 'Elk steaks and lobster. Goodness me!' Martha exclaimed, holding the door open for everyone to see. 'Everything except a Christmas cake! They must have lots of parties up here.'

For a long while they all stared at the contents without uttering a word. Brains rubbed a hand over his cropped hair, Rake put his hand over his heart and sighed, Christina gasped and Anna-Greta grumbled: 'This must have cost a pretty penny!'

'Nobody will notice if we help ourselves to a little bit,' said Martha.

'But surely we can't steal their food?' Christina queried.

'We're not stealing. Whose money do you think bought this food? We are simply taking what we have paid for. Here you are, take this.'

Martha held out a leftover piece of cooked chicken and Rake – who always felt peckish in the evenings – was first to bite.

'And we need rice, spices and flour so that we can make a sauce,' said Brains who had now woken up. He wasn't just an inventor but a good cook too. Since his ex-wife had only made food that was inedible, he had been forced to learn to cook. Then, in time, he had realized that not only was she incompetent in the kitchen but she also saw life itself as one great problem, and so he had divorced her. Still to this day, he had nightmares about her standing beside his bed brandishing a rolling pin in her hand whilst complaining. But she had given him a son, and for that he was grateful.

'We must have good wine for the sauce too.' Brains looked around and caught sight of a wine rack on the wall. 'Well, I never, look at those bottles . . .'

'We can't take those. We'd be found out if we did,' said Martha. 'If nobody notices that we have been here, we can come back a few more times.'

'Pah. Food without wine is like a car without wheels,' announced Brains. He went up to the wine rack and pulled out two bottles of the finest wine. Seeing Martha's face he put a reassuring hand on her shoulder. 'We'll open the wine bottles, drink up the wine and pour beetroot juice into the bottles instead,' he said.

Martha gave Brains an admiring glance. He always had a solution for everything. He was an eternal optimist who thought that problems were there to be solved. He reminded her of her parents. When she and her sister had dressed up in their parents' clothes and made a dreadful mess everywhere, her father and mother had, of course, told them that they had been naughty, but then had laughed at the whole thing. Better to have a messy home and happy children then a perfect yard and unhappy children, they thought. Their guiding motto in life was: 'Everything will sort itself out.' And Martha agreed. It always did.

The chopping boards, frying pans and saucepans were soon in place and they all got involved in cooking the meal. Martha put a fresh chicken in the oven, Brains made a delicious sauce, Rake prepared a tasty salad and Christina tried her best to be of use. She had gone to a domestic science school when she was young, but since then she had had help in the kitchen all her life, and so she had forgotten everything she had ever learned. The only task she really felt safe doing was slicing a cucumber.

Anna-Greta took charge of setting the table and saw to the rice.

'She's good at doing what you tell her,' Martha whispered, nodding towards Anna-Greta. 'But she is so slow and always has to count everything.'

'As long as she doesn't start counting the grains of rice, that's OK,' said Brains.

Soon a delicious aroma spread through the kitchen. Rake went around serving wine and very much looked the part in his blue blazer with a crisp cravat around his neck. He had combed his hair and smelled of a nice aftershave. Christina noticed that he had dressed smartly and she in turn discreetly pulled out her powder and lipstick. When nobody was looking, she added some colour to her lips and powdered her nose lightly.

Talk and laughter mingled with the clatter of plates and pans. Admittedly, it did take rather a long time before the food was ready, but what did that matter when everyone was drinking good wine and having a lovely time? Finally, they settled around the table as happy and enthusiastic as youngsters.

'Another glass?'

Rake poured out more wine and it was just like the old days when he had been a waiter on cruise ships in the Mediterranean. He was a bit slower now, but he held himself with the same dignity. Between mouthfuls they toasted one another and sang aloud from their choir repertoire, and when Brains found an old bottle of champagne, that did the rounds too. Christina raised her glass and knocked back her wine.

'Wicked,' she said – an expression she had picked up from her grandchildren. She liked to try and keep up with the times.

Christina put her glass down and looked about her: 'Now, dear friends, we must dance!'

'You can do that,' said Brains, putting his hands on his stomach.

'Dance, yes, absolutely,' said Rake, getting up, but he was so unsteady on his legs that Christina had to dance on her own.

'"It is better to dare to cast the dice, than to fade away with a withering flame,"' she recited, with her arms out wide. Although Christina had never achieved her dream of becoming a librarian, she had always maintained her interest in literature. And what she didn't know of the Swedish classics wasn't worth knowing.

'Here she goes reciting the old favourites again. As long as she doesn't recite the *Odyssey* too,' muttered Martha.

'Or goes on and on about *Gösta Berling's Saga* . . .' Brains added.

'"It is more beautiful to hear a string that snaps, than never to draw a bow,"' Christina continued.

'We could have that as our motto!' Martha suggested.

'What, a string that snaps?' Rake interrupted her. 'No, the

17

motto should be "It's better to be in the bed that broke than always to sleep alone.'"

Christina, blushing, came to a halt mid-step.

'Rake! Must you always be so coarse? Behave yourself!' said Anna-Greta, pouting.

'Well, we've drawn our bow now, haven't we?' said Christina. 'From now on, we must come up here at least once a week.' She fetched her glass and raised it.

'Cheers! Here's to the next time!'

They all toasted each other and they kept going until their eyelids got heavier and heavier and they started slurring their words. Martha reverted to her old southern dialect, something she only did when she was really tired. It was a warning sign, and she saw the danger.

'Now, dear friends, we must wash the dishes and tidy the kitchen before we go downstairs,' she said.

'You're welcome to start on the dishes,' Rake replied, as he filled up Martha's glass.

'No, we must tidy up and put everything back in the cupboards so that nobody will see that we've been here,' she insisted, and pushed the glass away.

'If you're tired, you can rest on my arm,' said Brains as he gave her a friendly pat on the cheek.

And so it came about that Martha leaned her head against his arm and fell asleep.

The next morning, when Ingmar Mattson, the director of Diamond House, came to work, he heard strange sounds from inside his private rooms. The heavy humming noise sounded like a group of bears had just escaped from the zoo park. He looked around the office room and saw nothing untoward, but he noticed that the kitchen door was open.

'What in heaven's name . . .' he muttered, before bumping into a Zimmer frame and falling onto the floor. Swearing, he got back on his feet and looked with amazement at the scene before him. The extractor fan was on, and five of the old people from the retirement home were seated around the table, fast asleep. There were dirty dishes on the table, emptied wine glasses, and the fridge door was wide open. Director Mattson looked at the mess. The clients in the retirement home evidently had more freedom than he had been aware of. He must ask Nurse Barbara to deal with the matter.

3

A car alarm was going off down the street, and somewhere far away a fan was whirring. Martha blinked and then opened her eyes properly. A ray of sunshine seeped in through the window and her eyes slowly grew accustomed to the faint light. The windows were dirty and needed to be cleaned and the same could be said about the floral-patterned curtains that she had hung up herself to brighten up the room. Evidently, nobody cared about keeping things clean nowadays, and she certainly couldn't manage such chores herself any more. Martha yawned widely, but her thoughts were all confused and she couldn't really think straight. Oh dear, oh dear, how slow and tired she was feeling. Ever since the party it had felt as if she had small clouds of chewing gum clogging up the inside of her head. Of course, the wine and all the pills she took every day didn't mix very well. But what fun they had had! If only they had had time to tidy up and return to their rooms . . . Yes, if only they hadn't fallen asleep . . .

Martha sat on the edge of her bed and manoeuvred her feet into her slippers. Oh, it had been so embarrassing and Director Mattson had shouted at them in such an irascible manner. She glanced at the bedside table. There lay the corkscrew that

Brains had given her 'for future parties', as he had put it. But, sadly, there'd be no more. After the party, Nurse Barbara had locked them all in their rooms and now they could only leave the residents' floor if a member of staff accompanied them. And on top of that, they had been given small red pills 'to calm them down'. How boring life had become!

And talking of pills – why did old people always have to have so many pills? They almost seemed to receive more pills than food. Perhaps that's what had made them so dull? They always used to play cards and had gone into each other's rooms after 8 p.m. But since Diamond House had taken over, things like that didn't happen any more. Nowadays they hardly did anything at all, and if they got the chance to play a hand of cards, they either fell asleep or forgot what they were doing. Christina, who loved her literary classics, didn't even have the energy to thumb through magazines, and Anna-Greta, who had liked to listen to horn concertos and some of the Swedish popular folk singers, now just stared at her record player and couldn't muster the energy to get any of her records down from the shelf. Brains hadn't made any inventions for ages, and Rake didn't look after his plants properly. Most of the time they just watched TV and nobody did anything special. Something was wrong, really horribly wrong.

Martha got up, supported herself on her Zimmer frame and went into the bathroom. While she washed her face, brushed her teeth and went about her morning routine, she mulled everything over. Hadn't she been the one who had intended to protest and make a revolution? But now here she was, doing nothing again. She stared into the mirror and noticed how worn out she looked. Her face was pale and her white hair stood on end. Sighing loudly, she stretched out, reaching for her hairbrush, but in so doing happened to knock the bottle of red pills onto the floor. They scattered across the bathroom floor and lay there like angry red dots by her feet. She didn't feel like picking them up. Martha snorted and just swept them all down the floor drain with her foot.

She got rid of some of the other pills too, and after a few days, already felt much chirpier. She started knitting again and, having always loved crime thrillers, went back to working her way through the stack of ghastly murders on her bedside table. And her revolutionary zeal had returned.

When Brains heard the knocks, he knew it must be Martha. Three distinct knocks on the door right next to the handle and then silence. That was definitely her. He dragged himself up from the sofa and pulled his sweater down over his round belly. He hadn't had a visit from Martha for quite some time, and he had wondered if she was OK. Every day he had intended to go and see her in the evening, but instead he had always fallen asleep in front of the telly. He looked around for an empty cardboard box and quickly tidied away the pile of drawings, chisels and screws from the coffee table into the box, before hastily pushing it under his bed. Two blue shirts and some socks with holes in he hid behind the sofa cushions, and he brushed the breadcrumbs scattered across his side table onto the floor. Having done that, he turned off the TV and went to open the door.

'Ah, it is you, come in!'

'Brains, we must have a talk,' Martha said, striding into his room purposefully.

He nodded and put the kettle on. In the cupboard he found two printed circuit cards, a hammer and some cables before he reached the instant coffee. There were two coffee cups behind the coffee jar. When the water had boiled, he filled the cups and added some coffee granules.

'I haven't got any biscuits, I'm afraid, but—'

'That will do just fine,' said Martha, accepting the cup of coffee and sitting down on the sofa. 'You know something, this might sound crazy, but I think they are drugging us. We get too many pills. That is why we have been so lethargic.'

'Really? Do you mean—' He discreetly pushed aside a gutted Grundig radio under the armchair and hoped she hadn't noticed it.

'Well, we can't allow it to go on!'

'Exactly! We should have acted when we said we were going to protest.'

He took her hand and patted it lightly.

'But, my dear, it still isn't too late.'

Martha's eyes sparkled and her face lit up.

'You know what, I've been thinking of something. In prison you are allowed out in the fresh air at least once a day, but here we are hardly ever let out at all.'

'I wonder how fresh the air is around a prison, but yes, I get your point.'

'Prisoners get out for at least an hour every day, and they are given nourishing food and can take classes in a workshop. In fact, they have it better than we do.'

'A workshop?' That got Brains' attention.

'You see? I want to live for as long as possible – but I want to live an exciting life for as long as I can too.' She leaned over and

23

whispered something in his ear. Brains raised his eyebrows and shook his head. But Martha didn't give up.

'Brains, I have thought this over very carefully . . .'

'OK, why not, why not . . .' he said. He leaned back in his armchair and burst out laughing.

4

The sound of her heels echoed harshly in the corridor as Nurse Barbara hurried along. She opened the storeroom door, wheeled out her trolley and put the medicines on the tray. Each and every one of the twenty-two clients had an assortment of pills that it was her job to keep track of. Director Mattson was fussy about medication, and each of the elderly clients had their personal prescriptions. But some of the pills, like the red ones, were given to all the residents. As were the light blue pills that he had recently introduced. They helped the old folk to lose their appetite.

'They will eat less and then we won't have to buy so much food,' he had said.

Nurse Barbara wondered if this was ethical, but she hadn't dared make an issue of it with the director since she wanted to keep in his good books. She wanted to make something of her life. Her mother had been a single mum and had worked as a maid in the posh district of Djursholm. She had never earned very much and they had been quite poor. When Barbara had accompanied her mother to work one day, she had seen fancy paintings, shining silver and patterned parquet floors. She had seen the 'fancy folk' her mother worked for dressed in furs and beautiful clothes. That glimpse of a different sort of life was something she had never forgotten. Director Mattson was one of those successful people too. He was twenty years older than her, energetic, quick-witted, and had many years' experience of doing business. Above all, he had a lot of influence and power, and she realized he could help her along in life. She hung on to his every word and she admired him. He might be carrying a few extra pounds, and perhaps he worked too much as well, but he was rich, and with his brown eyes, dark hair and charming manner he reminded her of an Italian. It wasn't long before she fell in love with him. He was married, but she hoped for more and they soon embarked upon a relationship. And they were going to go on holiday together.

She hurried down the corridor and distributed the pills to the old people. Then she parked the trolley in the storeroom again, and returned to her office. Now all she had to do was tidy up the paperwork on her desk, so that Katia, her replacement while she was on holiday, had a clean desk when she arrived. Nurse Barbara sat in front of her computer with a dreamy look in her eyes. Tomorrow, she thought, tomorrow. At last, she and Ingmar would be able to get away from it all and just be together.

The next day, Martha observed that Director Mattson picked up Nurse Barbara in his car. Aha! She had suspected that there was something going on between them. The director was going to a conference and was taking her with him. Good. That suited her perfectly. The car was barely out of sight before Martha was gathering all her friends to tell them about the pills, which were promptly discarded.

★

A few days later, laughter was heard in the lounge again. Brains and Rake played backgammon, Christina was painting her watercolours, and Anna-Greta listened to music or played patience.

'Patience is good for keeping your brain in good shape,' Anna-Greta chirped as she placed the cards out on the table. She was careful not to cheat, and never forgot to tell everyone whenever she solved her card solitaire. Her long, thin face and the bun on her neck made her look like an old school mistress rather than an ex-bank clerk. Some smart investments had made her rich, and she was proud of her ability to do sums in her head so quickly. When, once, the staff at the retirement home had offered to help her with her bank accounts, she had looked daggers at them and nobody had dared ask a second time. She had grown up in Djursholm and had learned the value of money. At school she had always been top of the class in mathematics. Martha looked at her out of the corner of her eye and wondered if it would be possible to get such a correct and proper person to join her on an adventure. She and Brains had concocted a plan and were just waiting for the right opportunity to put it into action.

The days without Nurse Barbara were the calm before the storm. On the surface, everything seemed as normal, but inside each of them, something had changed. The five friends sang 'Happy as a bird' and the first movement from Lars-Erik Larsson's *God in Disguise*, just as they had done before Diamond House took over, and the staff applauded and smiled for the first time in ages. Nineteen-year-old Katia Erikson from Farsta, Nurse Barbara's temporary replacement, baked some cakes for afternoon coffee, found some tools for Brains, and let everyone get on with their own thing. The guests at Diamond House became all the more self-confident and when the day came for Katia to cycle home for good, and Nurse Barbara returned, a defiant rebellious seed had started to sprout.

'Oh well, I suppose we must prepare ourselves for the worst,' Brains sighed when he saw Nurse Barbara on her way in through the glass doors.

'She's probably all set to make even more cuts for Director Mattson,' said Martha. 'On the other hand, it might help our cause,' she added with a barely discernible wink.

'Yes, you can say that again,' said Brains and he winked back.

Nurse Barbara had barely been back at the retirement home for a few hours before doors could be heard slamming and her high heels echoed down the corridor. In the afternoon, she asked everybody to come to the lounge. Once she had them there, she cleared her throat and placed a pile of papers on the table.

'Regrettably, we must make some cuts,' she started off. Her hair was nicely done up and there was a new gold bracelet visible on her wrist. 'In bad times we must all do our bit as much as we can. Unfortunately, we must cut down on staff costs, so starting from next week there will be only two members of staff. Besides me, that is. This will mean that you can only go out once a week for a walk.'

'Prison inmates can get exercise every day, you know. You can't do that,' Martha protested loudly. Barbara pretended not to hear.

'And we must cut costs for food, too,' she went on. 'From now on, there will only be one main meal a day. At other times you will be served with sandwiches.'

'Over my dead body! We must have proper food and you should buy more fruit and veg too,' Rake roared.

'I wonder if the upstairs kitchen is locked,' whispered Martha.

'Not that kitchen again,' said Christina, dropping her nail file.

Later that evening, when the staff had gone home for the day, Martha went up to the kitchen anyway. Rake would be so pleased if she could get him a salad. He was rather down-hearted because his son hadn't been in touch, and he needed cheering up. Martha often wished that she had a family too, but the great love of her life had left her when her son was two years old. Her little boy had had dimples and curly blond hair, and for five years he was the joy of her life. The last summer in the countryside they had visited the horses in the stable, picked blueberries in the woods and gone fishing down at the lake. But one Sunday morning, while she was still asleep, he had taken the fishing rod and disappeared off to the jetty. And it was there, next to one of the jetty posts, that she found him. Her life had come to a tragic halt and if it hadn't been for her parents she probably wouldn't have found the strength to carry on. She had relationships with several men after the death of her beloved son, but when she had tried to get pregnant again she had mis-carried. In the end she grew too old, and gave up on the idea of having a family. Childlessness was her great sorrow, even though she didn't show it. Instead, she hid her pain, and a laugh can disguise so much. She found people were easy to fool.

Martha shook herself from her thoughts, tip-toed into Nurse Barbara's office and opened the key cabinet. She remembered the smell of food and expectantly pulled out the master key. But when she got to the first floor her plans came to an abrupt halt. Instead of the keyhole, there was one of those strange protuberances for plastic cards. Diamond House had transformed the kitchen into an impregnable fortress! Disappointment washed over her and it was a good few minutes before she was able to gather her wits together and leave. But she didn't give up; instead, she pressed the lift button to go down. Perhaps there was a larder or storage area in the cellar.

When the doors of the lift opened, she hesitated for a moment, not sure where she was. At the far end of the corridor she could make out a weak light from an old-fashioned door with a pane of glass at the top. This door was also locked, but the master key worked. Cautiously, she pushed open the door and a cold, invigorating winter air blew in. Lovely, here was a way out! The chill helped to clear her mind and all of a sudden she remembered the old key from her parents' home. It was very similar to the master key with a triangular bow. If she switched keys, she was sure nobody would notice the difference. Martha closed the door to the outside, turned on the light and entered another corridor. On one of the doors was a sign which read: GYM – FOR STAFF ONLY. Martha unlocked the door and looked inside.

There were no windows and it took a while before she could find the light switch. The fluorescent lights blinked to life and she could see skipping ropes, small weights and exercise cycles. There were benches beside the walls, a treadmill, and weird contraptions she didn't know the names of. So Diamond House had cut back on prophylactic exercise for the residents, but at the same time had a gym just for the staff! They had repeatedly asked to get back their own exercise room, but the new owners had said no. Martha felt like kicking in the door, which would be rather difficult at her age, but instead blurted out all the swear words she could think of, arched her back like a cat, and made a threatening gesture with her fist.

'You'll pay for this, just wait!'

Back upstairs she put the old family key under her door and pulled it as hard as she could to bend it out of shape. Then she hung the crooked key in the key cabinet, so that nobody would be suspicious if the key didn't fit. She hid the master key in her bra, went to bed, and pulled the covers up to her chin. The first step in a revolution was to be able to move about freely. And now they could do just that. Shutting her eyes, and with a smile on her lips, she fell asleep and dreamed of a gang of oldies who robbed a bank and were hailed as heroes when they got to prison.

5

The plans for the future that Martha and Brains had concocted grew increasingly bolder. Their vision had given them a new energy and they were becoming all the more daring. Meanwhile, the retirement home was still cutting costs. The management stopped providing buns with the afternoon coffee, and coffee was limited to three cups per day. When the old folk came to decorate the Christmas tree, they got another shock. The management would no longer supply the decorations.

'I bet they have Christmas trees with decorations in prisons!' Martha seethed.

'And not only that. They even let the inmates go out on trips to see the shop windows in the Christmas season,' said Brains, as he got up and did his best to storm out of the room. After a while, he returned with a Bethlehem star he had made from silver tape.

'This star is as good as any,' he said, reinforcing it with some pipe cleaners and then taping it onto the top of the tree. Everyone applauded, and Martha smiled. Brains may have turned eighty but there was still a little boy inside him.

'Surely a star for the tree can't cost much, can it?' said Anna-Greta.

'They are just stingy people who begrudge everything for others. I can't see things getting any better here; in fact, it's the opposite. Brains and I met some other members of the new management yesterday and proposed some improvements, but they wouldn't listen. If we want our life to change, we must do something ourselves,' said Martha, getting up so quickly that her chair fell over. 'Brains and I are determined to make a better life for ourselves. Are you going to join us?'

'Indeed!' cried Brains and he got up too.

'Yes, let's meet in your room and enjoy a glass of cloudberry liqueur?' Christina suggested. She felt a cold coming on and wanted something tasty.

'Cloudberry liqueur again? Well, I suppose it will have to do,' muttered Rake.

A few moments later, the five of them entered Martha's room in single file and squeezed onto the sofa – all except Rake, who chose the armchair instead. The previous day he had happened to sit down on Martha's knitting-in-progress and he didn't want to risk a repeat of that experience. When Martha had got out the liqueur and poured it into glasses, the discussion got started. Their voices grew louder and in the end she had to bang her stick on the coffee table.

'Now listen to me! We're not going to get anything for nothing; no, we will have to work for it,' she said. 'And to do that, we must get into better physical condition. Here is the key to the staff gym. In the evenings we can sneak down there and do some exercises.' She triumphantly held up the master key.

'But that's not on, surely?' objected Christina, who preferred dieting to exercising in a gym. 'We'd be found out.'

'If we tidy up after us, then nobody will notice we have been there,' said Martha.

'You said that about the kitchen upstairs too. And my nails will break straight away,' Christina complained.

'And I thought I'd be able to take it easy in my retirement,' moaned Rake.

Martha pretended not to hear, but exchanged a few meaningful glances with Brains.

'After a few weeks' exercise in the gym, we'll be fit for anything and we will all be in a better mood too,' she enthused, with a half-truth. Because at the moment she couldn't share what she *really* meant: that if you were a criminal, you had to be fit enough to commit crimes. The previous day she had nodded off in front of the telly, and when she opened her eyes again they were screening a documentary from a prison. This had immediately woken her up. She had snatched up the remote and eagerly pressed record. With growing amazement, she had followed the reporter in the workshop and laundry, and seen the prisoners showing their rooms. When the inmates had gathered together in the dining hall, they could choose from fish, meat or vegetarian and even have chips to go with it. And there was salad and fruit too. Martha had then hurried off to see Brains. They watched the recorded programme together and, despite it being late, they talked on until midnight.

Martha raised her voice enough to emphasize her point, but not enough to attract the attention of the three members of staff at Diamond House.

'We *are* going to improve our conditions, aren't we? In that case, we must get fit. And we must do it now! Time is precious for us all.'

Martha knew how important it was to keep trim. In the 1950s, when her family had moved to Stockholm, she had joined the Idla girls. For many years she had exercised regularly to improve her general condition, coordination, speed and strength. Despite the fact that she never managed to look seductively feminine she still felt healthy. But then she had become careless, had put on too many pounds, and, even though she had tried to diet, she had always been a little bit overweight. Now she had the chance to do something about it.

'Exercises in a gym! Talk about slave-driver!' Rake exclaimed and downed his cloudberry liqueur as if it had been a shot of neat vodka. He started coughing and looked angrily at Martha. But that plumply little lady just smiled at him and looked so friendly and sweet that he felt embarrassed. No, she wasn't a slave-driver, she just wanted what was best for them.

'Now listen! I think we should give Martha a chance,' Brains chipped in, because although he didn't care much for physical exercise, he did know that he wouldn't get very far from Diamond House if he didn't improve his physical condition. Martha gave him an encouraging glance.

'OK, but what are we going to do?' wondered Christina and Rake, with one voice.

'Become the most troublesome oldies in the world,' Martha answered. The word *revolution* would still have to bide its time.

6

Rake took the cigarette out of his mouth and did another session with the dumb-bells. It was getting easier now, but then they had been exercising every evening for more than a month, even at weekends. Christina was next to him on the exercise bicycle, and a bit further away Anna-Greta and Brains were busy with those weird contraptions which help you to build up your chest muscles.

'How are you doing, Rake?'

Martha showed her warm smile and gave him a friendly pat on his shoulder.

'Fine,' he panted, red in the face. He put the dumb-bells aside and gave her a tired look. At seventy-nine, there she was going from one piece of apparatus to another without a care, and she hardly seemed to be out of breath. When the day came for her final moment, she would walk to the grave, crawl into the coffin and put the lid on herself, he was certain of that.

'Just one more session, you can manage that?' she went on. 'Then we'll put everything away and tidy up.'

Rake pulled a face.

'But we mustn't leave any trace of our being here, Rake, you

36

do understand that? And please, please, cut out the smoking. The smell will give us away.'

Rake thought that Martha reminded him of his aunty in Gothenburg. The old gal was dead now, but she had been a school teacher and had weighed in at 150 kg. When her pupils misbehaved she'd threaten: 'If you don't keep quiet, I'm going to sit on you.' She and Martha could have been related. But Martha had another side to her: she cared about other people. She would sneak out to the corner shop as much as possible to buy fruit and veg for all of them. And she wouldn't let them pay for it either.

'Everything green is good for you,' she claimed, and flashed one of her winning smiles while her eyes glowed. Sneaking out of the retirement home when nobody was watching had turned into a game for Martha, and she was always in a buoyant mood when she returned. Sometimes she would even give them an encouraging little pat on the cheek. If he'd been a little boy and had fallen off his bike, he probably would have let her give him a hug to make it feel better.

'We'll soon have something to show for all this hard training,' Martha went on. 'A few vitamins and some carbohydrates on top, and then, my friends, we can conquer the world.'

'You can go conquer it,' Rake muttered as his pessimism took over once more. There was something a little bit fishy about all this. Martha sounded so very *purposeful*. His gut feeling told him that she was planning something, something bigger than he could even imagine.

'Right, that's enough for today,' she called out. 'And don't forget to wipe the floor and dry off all the apparatus. Let's meet in my room in half an hour.'

★

A little later, when they had showered and freshened up a bit, they gathered together in Martha's room. She had put out a basket with particularly nourishing bread and some fruit, while Brains had got out some bottles of energy drink. She had a new tablecloth, one with red and white flowers.

'One more month of training, and we ought to be in good enough condition,' he said.

'Yes, and by early March the snow will have melted. Then we can set sail!' Martha filled in.

'You what? Set sail!' Rake wondered. 'We're not out at sea, are we? Anyway, where would we go? For God's sake, tell us what you're cooking up!'

'I want to make you all happier and livelier, and when the day comes that you are in good condition, then . . .'

'Then what . . . ?'

'Then, and not before, you'll be told the Big Secret,' Martha answered. It was important that, for now, the plans were only known by herself and Brains. She didn't want things getting out of control, and as her mother always said, too many cooks spoiled the broth. Besides, she quite liked having a secret that only she and Brains were privy to. It was nice for them both to have a reason to spend time together without the others. Brains wasn't exactly the most conventionally attractive man she had ever met, but Martha had started to admit to herself that sometimes brains really were worth more than beauty.

Nurse Barbara put the dumb-bells aside and adjusted her sweatband. It was strange how the gym had a faint smell of smoke. She went over to the treadmill and pressed the button to start it up. In fact, it was just here and in the cupboard with the weights that the smell was strongest. She stepped up onto the treadmill and started to jog. There were no windows in the gym, so the smell could hardly come from outside, unless the ventilation system was the guilty party.

She didn't really care for all this gym stuff, but she wanted to make an impression on Director Mattson of Diamond House. He had said that she had a beautiful body, and she wanted to live up to that. If she was going to reel him in, then she must look pretty and have firm thighs. Everything had gone all right so far, although there had been rather a lot of secret meetings lately. Most of the time they had to meet at work, because he had his family. But sooner or later he would leave his wife, Barbara was certain of that. After all, he had told her that his marriage was finished and that he and his wife were married in name only. 'Since I met you, my darling, I am happy for the first time in my life,' he had said to her. Nurse Barbara smiled. Director Mattson, or Ingmar, as she called him in their more intimate moments, had told her that they belonged together. She could just imagine what it would be like if they could go off on holiday again, or, even better, if she could live with him. She might even become a partner in his business. For the time being, she would have to make do with those stolen moments at work and the conference trips that they went on together. But if she could make Diamond House even more profitable than it already was, he might see her worth, and get divorced quicker. She stretched out on the mat and wished that he was lying there beside her. She and Ingmar. An official couple. She must make sure it happened soon.

When she got up from the floor, she caught sight of something. A white hair? Weird. None of the staff had white hair, and nor did any of the cleaners. And nobody else used the gym, did they? Barbara almost puzzled over the matter, but instead went back to her dreams of life with Director Mattson.

7

The next day the friends went across to Martha's to have one of their assigned daily coffees. It was easier for them to sneak around now that Diamond House only had three members of staff. On arrival, they found that the TV was turned on. When they had got their cups of coffee and had sat down on the sofa, Brains turned up the TV.

'You simply must see this programme,' he said. 'It's a documentary about Swedish prisons.' He drew the curtains.

'Usch, no,' complained Anna-Greta. This really wasn't her sort of programme.

The five friends drank their coffee with the usual dash of cloudberry liqueur, and had seen little more than the introduction when the atmosphere in the room became charged with anger.

'It's incredible that such things can go on,' exclaimed Christina, waving her nail file. 'Just look – the criminals are better off than us!'

'And besides, it's our taxes that pay for them,' Anna-Greta snorted.

'Now, now, some of the tax money pays for the care of the elderly too,' Brains pointed out.

41

'Oh no, not much. Local councils would much rather build sports halls than retirement homes,' Anna-Greta countered.

'Politicians ought to end up in prison,' said Martha as she dropped a stitch. She found it hard to knit and to watch telly at the same time.

'Prison? But that's where we're going,' exclaimed Brains, and then Martha had to give him a quick kick on his shin. They had agreed not to proceed with too much haste. If they did, they would never get the others to go along with them. But during the entire programme, acrid comments could be heard and finally Anna-Greta couldn't keep silent. She rearranged the bun on her neck, put her hands on her knees and looked around her with a stern expression.

'But if prisoners are better off than us, why on earth are we sitting here?'

A deathly silence ensued. Martha looked at her in amazement, but soon adapted to the situation.

'Exactly. Why don't we do a little burglary tour and end up in prison?'

'No, you are joking, aren't you?' Anna-Greta answered, and giggled strangely. It didn't sound like her usual horse-like neigh.

'Burglary tour? Over my dead body!' exclaimed Christina, her Free Church upbringing having left its mark. 'Thou shalt not steal, amen, and that's that!'

'But just think. Why not?' said Martha, getting up and turning the TV off. 'What have we actually got to lose?'

'You're crazy. First you want to make us all do physical exercises, and now to become criminals. Is there no end to this folly?' said Rake.

'I just wanted to see your reaction,' Martha lied.

A collective sigh of relief could be heard all round, and soon the conversation moved in other directions. But when everyone had left, Brains stayed behind a few moments with Martha.

'I think that gave them something to ponder on,' he said. 'Now they've seen another world outside the retirement home.'

'Yes, this was the first step. Now we leave the dough to rise,' Martha replied.

'You know what, we'll soon be on the run from here.'

'Yes, we will,' said Martha.

A week went by without anybody mentioning the TV programme. It was as if the subject frightened them, and nobody really dared bring it up again. But while Martha read her new crime novel, *Murder in the Retirement Home*, Brains was busy with preparations. He had made reflector arms to attach to their Zimmer frames so that they wouldn't get run over in town – and he was also adding the final touches to his invention of the week.

'Have a look at this, Martha,' he said, and handed her a red cap with five small holes at the front. 'Press the peak and then you'll see.'

Martha took the cap and pressed, and the next second you could see a bright ray of light crossing the room.

'Better than a headlamp. Caps with LED lights are just what you need for robberies.'

Martha burst out laughing.

'You are clever,' she said, not without some tenderness in her voice.

'But now we need some more LED lights.'

'Well, if I can buy fruit and veg in the corner shop, then I'm sure I can sneak round to the hardware store too. But, really, it is crazy that we have to do our shopping in secret,' she said. 'Do you remember the advertisement for the retirement home? *A gilt-edged life after seventy* was what it said.'

'If everything goes according to plan, then we'll do better than that,' said Brains as he put his cap back on again. 'And in prison they'll certainly be nice to us because we are so old!'

'It does sound exciting to become a thief, doesn't it? First you have to plan and carry out the crime which is a thrill in itself, and then there will be all the new experiences in prison.'

'Exactly. We aren't fit enough to do parachute jumps or to travel around the world, but with this we will make things happen anyway.' Brains looked out of the window with a dreamy look on his face.

'But we must find an innocent crime that doesn't hurt anybody,' Martha went on.

'Economic crime is serious enough to render a prison sentence, and then we'd probably get the others to go along with it,' said Brains. 'Ideally, we ought to steal from people who are *extremely* wealthy.'

'That will increase our personal funds,' Martha mused. 'We won't touch nice rich people, the kind who donate money to research and charity. But we'll target those who don't pay tax and always want more. We can steal from them.'

'The capitalist predators, the extortionists and . . . ?'

'Yes, those greedy money-grabbing types. Have you thought about how wealthy people always compare themselves with somebody who is even richer? And then they want more. If they don't understand how to share, then we can help them along. Quite simply, we'd be doing them a service.'

'They might not see it like that,' Brains answered, 'but you are right, of course.' He had had very little money when he was young, a fate he shared with many of his childhood friends in Sundbyberg. His father had worked at the Marabou factory, and Brains had earned some extra money as an errand boy. The factory had, in fact, had a good management and they had built a park where the workers and their families could relax. Brains thought that was great, and he had felt considerable respect for the old men in their bowler hats. They had understood how to share with others. In fact, he had liked it so much in Sundbyberg that he had stayed there despite offers of jobs and a place to live in Stockholm after he had graduated as an engineer. At first he had worked for a firm of electricians, but after his parents had died he had opened his own workshop on the ground floor of the building where the family lived. His first major move in life was to Diamond House.

'Everything we steal will go into the Robbery Fund,' Martha went on. She picked up the knitting that was in her lap, untangled the ball of wool on the sofa and started knitting the back panel of a cardigan.

'Robbery Fund?' Brains wondered.

'We can collect the money and dole it out to culture, care of the elderly and everything else that the state neglects. That will work well, don't you think?'

Brains agreed and as the evening wore on they aired many different ideas between them. When finally it was time to go to bed, they had decided to target the place in the country where the very richest people were to be found. They had planned a real robbery – of the type that they had only ever seen at the cinema before.

8

A light snowfall had just begun when Martha and her friends from Diamond House stepped out of their taxis outside the Grand Hotel in the very centre of Stockholm. As they did so, Martha realized that perhaps they didn't really blend into the crowd. Brains was wearing his red cap and, thanks to him, they all had bright reflector arms sticking out from their Zimmer frames. 'I don't want you to get hurt while we are in such a big city,' Brains had said. His Zimmer frame looked rather chunky. The steel tubing on the sides looked wider than Martha's. She must remember to ask him what he had done.

'People who go to the Grand Hotel usually give a tip,' one of the taxi drivers informed them.

'My good man,' Martha interrupted him, 'we're not going to the Grand Hotel; we're going to the island ferries from the quay here.'

'Why are you lying?' Anna-Greta whispered.

'You must realize that every proper criminal leaves a false trail,' Martha whispered back.

'Soon you'll get the biggest tip imaginable,' Rake chipped in, and was immediately poked in the ribs by Brains.

'Shush! Be a bit more discreet.'

'Listen to you in that cap! You could at least turn the lights off.'

Brains quickly pressed the peak and the LED lights went out. Martha folded the reflector arm back into the Zimmer frame and made a sign to Brains to do the same. Better to be on the safe side. Witnesses always noticed odd details.

'And now the great adventure starts,' said Martha when the taxi drivers had got their tips and driven off. She looked up at the Grand Hotel and nodded at Brains. What they had at first just talked about as a joke was in the process of becoming reality, even though it had been quite an effort to get there. It had taken them several weeks to persuade the others, and deep down Martha was afraid that one of them might bail out of the adventure. She so very much wanted to enjoy life *before* they ended up behind bars. She had had nightmares about one of the others dropping out at the last minute, or, even worse, giving them away before they had even managed to stage the first raid by The League of Pensioners.

It had been Christina's idea to have a group name and they all thought that *The League of Pensioners* fitted their purpose perfectly. It sounded like an important and mysterious code name too. *Outlaw Oldies*, which Martha had proposed, had been voted out because the others thought it sounded far too criminal.

Thanks to Nurse Barbara, the step from helpless geriatric to prospective criminal had been quicker than expected. Martha had gone to the hardware store to buy some parts for Brains, but his handwriting was so bad that neither she nor the shop assistant could read what he had written.

'We'll have to phone your good friend,' said the assistant, and, without thinking, Martha gave him the number for Brains.

It was too late when she realized that all private conversations went through the Diamond House main line.

'There is an elderly lady here with a Zimmer frame who wants to buy something, but I don't know what it is,' the assistant explained to the woman on the other end of the line. In vain Martha had tried to call a stop to the conversation but Nurse Barbara had already understood that somebody from the home had sneaked out without her permission. A week later, the locks on the front door of Diamond House were changed and Martha cried against Brains' shoulder and said that now everything was lost.

'But Martha dear, don't be sad. Our new life as criminals is about to start at last. We must get out of here before they put a new lock on the outer door.'

And then he sat down in front of his computer.

'We were going to find where the rich people are. Well, this is where!' He smiled as he opened the home page of the Grand Hotel in Stockholm. 'Now we'll book some rooms for ourselves.'

'The Grand Hotel?' Martha swallowed. From a little country farmhouse outside Brantevik, via a two-room flat in the southern part of Stockholm to . . . the swankiest of swanky hotels? Her parents had always said that you should be satisfied with what you have. But this was to be her next stage in life, so ignoring her nervousness, she took the plunge. 'Yes, of course. The Grand Hotel, the obvious choice.'

'We can book the celebration special with flowers, champagne and fruit for all so that everybody will be in a good mood.'

'And fresh strawberries?'

'But of course,' Brains went on enthusiastically but suddenly came to a halt. 'What if Christina and Anna-Greta have too good a time at the hotel? They might not want to go to prison afterwards . . .'

'That's something we must risk,' said Martha. 'But in the long run it can become boring to live amidst too much luxury, or so I've heard.'

Brains scrolled down the screen and after a while he had booked the most expensive hotel suites for them and ordered five celebration specials. Martha felt a pleasant thrill run through her body.

'We've got exactly forty-eight hours to do this,' said Brains as he turned off the computer. 'On Monday the locksmith will be coming, and by then we must be out of here.'

On the Sunday evening, the five of them sneaked out of the retirement home with their walking sticks and Zimmer frames. It was early March and there were still grey skies and snow in the air, but that didn't bother them. Now a new phase in their lives awaited them. *The adventure era*. Martha closed the cellar door and locked it after them. Then she pinched her lips together and brandished her clenched fist at Diamond House.

'Rogues! That's what you are! You went too far when you took away our Christmas tree decorations! Do you hear me!'

'What did you say?' Anna-Greta wondered, being rather hard of hearing.

'What scrimping makes, the devil takes.'

'Oh, I see, him,' said Anna-Greta.

'Now we must make sure we get taxis,' said Martha, wrapping her winter coat tighter and leading the way towards the taxi station. Half an hour later they were at the Grand Hotel. When they had paid their taxi drivers and were approaching the hotel entrance, Martha stopped. Devoutly she looked up at the traditional old hotel.

'What an exquisite building,' she exclaimed. 'Pity they don't build them like this any more.'

'You'd have to blame the architecture schools,' said Rake. 'I can't understand why they have to study for years if they're only going to design square blocks. I could manage that when I was four years old. And mine looked nicer too.'

'Perhaps you ought to have been an architect then?'

'Welcome to the Grand Hotel!' a handsome porter interrupted them and bowed.

'Thank you very much,' Martha answered and tried to look as if she was a woman of the world. But however much she smiled, her voice gave away a certain lack of confidence. Being on the run *and* turning criminal at the same time was rather stressful at her age.

9

The Zimmer frames rolled nicely and smoothly on the wall-to-wall carpet all the way to the reception desk. Martha looked with delight at the deep blue edging with the beautiful gold crowns. She thought of all the royalty that must have stayed here. A glance at the edge of the carpet and they would have seen their own crowns several times over.

It took a while to check in because the staff discreetly did a check on their bank card. Luckily, Anna-Greta was well-off and there was enough in her savings account to cover them all, but, nevertheless, they all felt nervous. The others had little more than their pension and none of them had experience of being in such grand surroundings. Finally, the reception staff confirmed their bookings and they were welcomed with smiles to the hotel.

'We have to take the second door to the left after the stairs,' said Brains, taking the lead. 'You girls can have the Princess Lilian suite where the big stars usually get to stay, and me and Rake can take two of the luxury suites.'

'Heavens above, that will be far too expensive,' said Anna-Greta, always the careful bookkeeper.

'But, my dear, have you completely forgotten? We are not intending to pay,' Martha whispered.

In good cheer they walked along the corridor leaning on their Zimmer frames. After all that training in the gym they had good balance and didn't really need them, but they knew that their walking aids could come in very useful all the same. Martha smiled. Who would suspect an old lady with a Zimmer frame of any criminal activity? And the basket at the front was good for keeping loot in too.

They slowly continued down the corridor until they saw a door on the left.

'Here it is,' said Brains self-confidently. He opened the door and entered, with the others close behind him. His eyes were like saucers. 'Not much here that reminds me of Sundbyberg, that I'll say.'

'Heavens above, what a sight! The whole room is shining as if it was gold,' said Christina.

'And what lovely red upholstered chairs. Is this how rich people really live?' wondered Brains.

'But . . .' muttered Rake. 'Doesn't it smell rather too much of perfume?'

'I hardly dare go in. Have you seen the mirrors and the beautiful washbasins? Is this the Princess Lilian suite?' Anna-Greta asked.

'I don't know,' muttered Brains. 'Perhaps rather too many mirrors for that . . .'

'Eight mirrors in the same room,' said Martha. 'And just look at those fancy chandeliers in the ceiling, and all the marble and lamps over the washbasins.'

'But where are the beds?' wondered Christina, who was feeling tired and wanted to rest a while.

'The beds?' Brains looked around him. At that very same moment they all heard a very familiar sound.

'Well, I'll be damned . . . the toilets?' Rake smirked. 'I was wondering why there were eight washbasins.'

Amidst a great deal of laughter they left the ladies' room and made their way to the lifts. Brains put his plastic card into the reader and pressed the button for the eighth floor.

'My apologies. I didn't have my wits about me. The Princess Lilian suite is on the top floor.'

While they were going up in the lift, Martha was deep in thought. Muddling up a luxury suite and a ladies' room was not a good omen. And if they were going to get all confused while they were sober, what would happen after a drink or two at the bar?

10

'So what do we do now?' wondered Christina after she had done several laps of the luxury suite and been overwhelmed by the choice presented to her. She had mostly been fascinated by the televisions everywhere – all of which she had turned on. 'It's hard to know which TV to look at and then there are so many other things to do here too.'

She looked about her, taking in the opulent rooms. Should they make themselves at home in the library, play the grand piano, watch a movie in the private cinema or just sink into the closest enormous armchair? That big bathtub with the lovely mosaic and the sauna were also very tempting. The house-keeper had told them that they could have green lighting and jungle music in there, or blue lights, if they preferred. Or per-haps she should just lie down and have a rest in the large double bed, which came complete with an amazing view of the royal palace across the water.

'You can look at the stars, if you like. There's a telescope in the suite,' said Brains. 'Or why not point the telescope at the palace? I'm sure the King will be doing something exciting.'

'But he doesn't even live there!' Martha pointed out.

'Never mind telescopes and TVs, is there a loo in here some-where?' Rake wondered, looking about him.

'One on your right, one in the bathroom and two more a bit further away,' Christina informed him.

'Stop, one john is sufficient, I can hardly use four at once!'

'There are four showers too. You could use all four of those,' joked Martha.

After they had all unpacked, everyone settled in the arm-chairs with a glass of champagne for a first run-through of their plans.

'Planning is important,' said Brains. 'We must map the entire hotel. We'll visit the spa, have a drink in the bar, spend time in the library, eat in the restaurants and mingle with the other guests. When we discover where the richest ones hang out, then we pounce.'

'I've worked it out already. There are forty-two luxury suites and many of the guests use the spa facilities and the pool,' said Anna-Greta. 'They are bound to put their watches and bracelets in the lockers there.'

'Brilliant! We shall steal their valuables. Simple. And then we shall hide the loot so that we can use the money when we get out of prison,' said Martha.

'Sounds like you've been reading too many crime novels,' Rake muttered.

'Oh no. All major criminals sit out their prison term and then use the money when they get out. Like the British train robbers, for example.'

'Then we'll follow their example,' Anna-Greta decided. Her eyes shone with excitement.

'Now listen, let's go down to the spa and have a look around.

At the same time, we can do some water gymnastics in the pool,' Martha suggested.

'No, no, we didn't come here for exercise –' Rake exclaimed, but managed to stop himself just before adding, '. . . you fitness fiend.'

'But if we do steal lots of stuff, where shall we hide it all?' Christina wanted to know.

'We'll think of something,' said Martha, blushing violently because she hadn't thought of that.

'Now listen to me. We must commit the robbery before the authorities find us. Why not do it tomorrow or the day after?' suggested Brains. 'And then we can stay on here a while.'

'Stay on at the scene of the crime, God help us!' said Martha, who had never read of such a thing in any detective story. 'The scene of the crime is where you return to, not where you take up residence!'

'That is precisely why the police won't look for us here in the first instance,' said Brains with a flourish. 'Come on, let's get changed and meet at the spa later.'

When the men had gone, Christina browsed the hotel's leaflets while she filed her nails slowly and with considerable care.

'I think we ought to get a beauty treatment down in the spa,' she said, pointing with her nail file.

'Spa and beauty treatment?' Martha gave her friend a weary look. Christina was always reading about ways to keep yourself looking young. When she was fifty-five she had had a facelift, but that was something she forbade the others to refer to. She wanted everybody to think that she was naturally attractive and that her beauty shone from within. She hadn't even mentioned the fact that she had had her teeth whitened. Perhaps it was her upbringing. Her parents had forbidden her to use make-up, and throughout her childhood she had been told it was sinful. You should accept your natural appearance because that which God had created was a gift. So as a teenager she had been forced to do her make-up clandestinely. Now she was equally secretive about her cosmetic operations.

'Now listen to this,' her friend went on. 'There are spa treatments that can dissolve emotional and physical blocks, and give your body a pleasant sense of calmness. And in addition we can have an eye mask which reduces all signs of tiredness and age.'

'I don't think I'd look any younger even if I wore a mask over my whole face,' said Martha.

'It is beneficial to massage the important marma points in your eye area. This signals to the nervous system that the musculature should retain its vigour,' Christina went on, completely fascinated by the hotel's advertising.

'Marma? What is that?' asked Martha.

'No, this is better,' said Anna-Greta, who had now found the hotel's spa and fitness brochure. 'We can have a sixty-minute facial acupuncture treatment. The needles stimulate production of collagen and strengthen your body's connective tissues.'

'Just what I've longed for,' said Martha, rolling her eyes.

'The treatment leaves your skin firm and soft,' Anna-Greta went on.

'Firm and soft. That was how men used to describe my breasts,' said Christina in a different tone of voice. 'Unfortunately, the same can't really be said about them now.'

'Listen to me. We are on a stealing spree, nothing else,'

Martha said authoritatively and picked up all the brochures. '*Never* forget the reason we are here.'

The ladies nodded, changed into their bathing costumes and put on the hotel's white bathrobes. On her way to the door, Martha paused.

'When we get down there, have a good look around for safes where guests can store valuables such as watches, money, rings and the like.'

'Are we really going to commit a proper crime?' Christina suddenly exclaimed.

'Shush! No, no, just a little adventure,' said Martha, entering the lift and giving her a calming pat on the shoulder. Then she felt a gnawing worry deep inside. Would Christina ruin the whole thing?

11

At the spa reception desk a heavily made-up woman gave them a welcoming smile. She was just about to say something when Brains and Rake arrived too. Their 1950s polka-dot swimming trunks could be glimpsed under their bathrobes.

'Would you like some towels?' the receptionist enquired.

'Yes, please,' Martha said, smiling.

'This reminds me of when I was in Turkey,' said Rake. 'Lovely baths, mosaic, women and—'

'Music?' Anna-Greta pursed her lips. 'Don't get carried away, Rake. Those days are well and truly over!'

The men got their towels and disappeared to take a shower, while Martha and the others went into the ladies' changing rooms. There they found a whole wall of numbered safes.

'Jackpot, look at that!' Martha whispered, delighted, and gave Anna-Greta a tap on her shoulder.

'It's almost as if they have been waiting for us,' said Anna-Greta as she started counting the security boxes.

They entered a room with a cold-water pool where one of the walls depicted a Scandinavian coastal landscape.

'Oh, how beautiful.' Christina beamed. 'This is the exotic Scandinavia the tourists pay for.'

'Except in reality it is free,' Anna-Greta pointed out.

'But exclusive is expensive,' said Martha. 'Especially at the Grand Hotel; only businessmen, heads of state and film stars stay here.'

'And us, of course,' Christina piped in.

'The leaders of the world stay here in this hotel,' Martha continued, with a tremor in her voice.

'Lucky them. Do they even realize how ordinary people live?' wondered Christina.

'That's the point. They don't,' said Martha.

'But if you yourself were a movie star or an empress, why would you stay in a hostel? You'd stay in the best place possible,' Anna-Greta said logically. 'It's like the fancy Djursholm district – if you live there, you have one of the best addresses in Stockholm, and that's what counts.'

Moving nearer to the pool, they saw that Brains and Rake had already got in. They were swimming at a civilized pace round the pool. The water glimmered in various shades of blue and there was a fresh scent of lavender and rose-leaf in the air. The bottom of the pool was lined with large black stone slabs and the four steps leading up from the water were framed by high Roman arches. At the end of the narrow corridor to the right they glimpsed the steam room.

'Over there we can get the steam treatment, with hot birch-leaf wrapping for our feet and an organic peat body pack,' said Anna-Greta.

'The peat stimulates one's breathing and digestion, and makes you calm and harmonious,' Christina cut in.

'Like I said earlier, that's not the reason we are here,' said Martha crossly.

Brains and Rake were climbing up the steps out of the water, looking happy and revived.

'That was nice. Steam room next,' said Brains.

They went down the corridor, opened the doors into a wet room and sat down. Inside the steam room hung a heavy damp mist which made it hard to see anything. A youngish man, a woman and a group of middle-aged men were already seated there. It was quite a large room with the benches arranged like a half-moon around a sort of black pillar, which reached up to eye level and was equipped with nozzles that emitted steam. The air was dripping with humidity and full of the smell of birch leaves. It was hot and invisible drops of water hung in the air.

'This is going to warp my walking stick,' Anna-Greta complained.

'For goodness' sake, you ought to have left that in the changing room,' Rake groaned.

'Good thing you didn't bring your Zimmer frame along. That would have rusted,' said Martha.

Brains stared at the pillar, fascinated.

'Hmm. A hole here that sprays steam. That'll do perfectly,' he muttered.

The five of them sat there a while, and then went out and showered. After passing the security boxes one more time, they took the lift back up to the suites.

'Did you notice, the security boxes don't have any keys. You open and lock them with plastic cards,' said Martha when they had settled down on the sofa.

'The same in the gents' changing rooms too,' Rake sighed.

'They don't even have a magnetic stripe. Every card has a

61

password which opens the box, and there must be at least three hundred boxes down there. Even if we break the code for one of the cards, we'd still have two hundred and ninety-nine more to go.'

A depressing silence descended in the room, because they all knew what this meant. The champagne would have to wait.

But Brains was already fidgeting. 'I reckon on coming up with something by the morning,' he said.

'In that case, I think we should meet tomorrow morning at ten o'clock and go through what we should do,' said Anna-Greta, who was used to morning meetings at the bank.

'Before we pounce?' Christina asked solemnly.

'Exactly!' said Brains and Martha at the same time.

'Problems which seem very difficult often have simple solutions,' said Martha. 'Now we'll go down and eat. Food usually helps.'

'And charge it to the room,' said Anna-Greta.

Dressed in their best clothes, the five friends took their seats in the hotel's restaurant, Veranda. The narrow restaurant, which reminded them of one of the decks of the *Titanic*, had tables laid alongside the big panoramic glass windows.

'Maybe it isn't such a good idea to sit next to the windows,' Martha voiced. 'What if someone sees us and locks us up in Diamond House again?'

'Nobody notices who's dining up here,' said Rake, but all the same he threw a worried glance out towards the street. He had started to like the idea of being on the run and didn't want to be found out straight away.

They ordered *turbot à la meuniere* with *haricots verts* wrapped in bacon and mashed Swedish Mandel potatoes. When the food was brought in, they looked at it in such astonishment that the waiter asked if there was something amiss.

'No, no, not at all. We've simply forgotten what real food looks like. Food without plastic,' said Martha. They all tucked in and a contented silence washed over the group for a while. Then came the sighs of appreciation.

'It melts on your tongue like warm butter,' said Rake as he patted the fish with his fork. 'On the MS *Kungsholmen* the food in first class used to taste like this.'

'Amazing. This is real fish,' said Christina, staring at her plate.

'And have you noticed how the seasoning is just right? I'd forgotten that food could taste this good. It's almost enough to make you religious,' said Brains.

They ate on in happy silence, as one does when eating with relish, and were further amazed by the dessert – *crêpes Suzette flambées*.

Anna-Greta wiped her mouth with the linen serviette for a long time and then finally cleared her throat.

'This is wonderful, but there is just one thing that I am a bit worried about. We are going to be able to get into those safes, aren't we? If the hotel charges my credit card – well, I don't really want to foot the bill for all of this . . .'

An embarrassed silence ensued.

'Don't worry, Anna-Greta,' Martha attempted. 'There's enough in those safes to cover the bill *and* the Robbery Fund.'

'But is it right to steal like this?' Christina wondered. '*Thou shalt not steal*, it says in —'

'It depends entirely on *who* is doing the stealing. If you are the state or a bank, it seems to be completely accepted,' said

Martha. 'So all you have to do is pretend you are managing our pension funds. Then you can do exactly as you wish.'

They all nodded heartily in agreement.

On their way up in the lift after the meal, Brains asked Martha to come along with him to his room.

'I've got something to show you,' Brains added.

At first she felt a tremor of expectation, but then she realized it was something serious he wanted to talk about. They went into his Gustavian suite, fitted out soberly but stylishly in the elegant late eighteenth-century style favoured by King Gustav III. Although his majesty would surely not have tolerated such a mess. Martha couldn't understand how Brains had managed to make such a mess in such a short time. Clothes were flung carelessly over chairs, a toothbrush and a tube of toothpaste lay on the desk, and there was an opened carton of milk in the hall. Torn-out pages from a writing pad were scattered throughout the room, and one of his slippers stuck out from under the long heavy curtain by the window.

'Excuse the mess, but I've been busy. Just look at this.' He went up to the bed and extracted his writing pad from under the mattress.

'Sit down.' He gestured to a chair. 'You read detective stories, take a look at this . . .'

Martha sat down and watched him leaf through his drawings. There was an aura of calm and warmth about him and she always felt safe in his company. They had known each other a long time and Martha had always liked him. But they had become a lot closer now that they were partners in crime. She gave a chuckle to herself. Life was funny. You never knew how it would turn out.

'Here we are. This won't be as simple as I had first thought. It isn't like in the old films when you stole the keys from the security guard and then just helped yourself to everything.'

'So even thieves had it easier in the old days?'

'It would seem so.' Brains pointed at the opened page of his notebook where he had drawn the locks and hinges of the safes. 'These safes have electronic locks which are opened and closed with coded cards. Of course, a fancy hotel doesn't buy its safes from a high-street store. These safes are an expensive and sophisticated model. That system down in the spa would have cost a fortune to install. They may as well have a sticker on them saying "burglar-proof". I didn't dare say that to the others. To be honest, I really haven't a clue as to how we can pull this off.'

'Don't worry, Brains. We'll arrange a power cut.'

'That won't help. Those boxes have a battery back-up and all that will happen is that they will all automatically lock themselves.'

'Well, then! I know what you can do,' Martha called out in delight. 'You can go down early tomorrow morning and arrange a short circuit so that all the boxes become locked. When the spa guests can't put their valuables in the usual safes, the receptionist will have to offer them somewhere else to keep their jewels and expensive items. Did you see that storage cupboard, the metal one in reception? It looks like one of those old-fashioned cabinets with an ordinary lock. I bet you the receptionist would have to put the jewels in there.'

Brains looked at Martha, astounded.

'My dear, I've been mulling over that problem all evening without finding a solution. You should have the nickname "brains"!' he said as he looked at her in a rather wistful and admiring way.

Martha couldn't help but smile at his praise but she tried to recover herself as quickly as possible. She stuttered a response, 'You men mainly think about the technical stuff. There is the human factor to consider too.'

'There is one other thing that we need to do, though. We need to create a diversion and also distract the other guests somehow. And I think I have got just the thing!'

Brains smiled, got up and came back with two white plastic bags.

'Here are some herbs. I got the henbane from Rake, thinking that this could be useful. He has given us a small, safe dose. If we put this into the nozzle on the pillar in the steam room then the powder ought to spread across the entire spa. This should make everyone a bit dozy. That's when we can open up the cupboard in reception – and steal all the valuables!'

'And what about the contents of the other pouch?'

'We'll put that down the nozzle too. Rake has a bit of cannabis left from his experiments on the balcony, or was it from his days at sea? I can't remember. Whatever, it makes you happy and gives you the giggles. Just think of all those unfortunate people we'll be stealing from. At least if they have a few cannabis fumes in their lungs they won't be sad when they see that all their valuables have gone.'

'You are a kind man, Brains, always thinking of other people's feelings,' Martha said, delighted. 'We will end up with happy victims of crime. These people will be laughing their heads off as they are searching in vain for their jewellery.' She started giggling, and Brains joined in her merriment.

'If you can take responsibility for spreading the contents of the pouches in the steam room, then I'll deal with the locked cupboard behind the reception desk,' Brains proposed.

'But what about the others, aren't they going to do anything?'

'I think that for this first time we should do most of it ourselves. Then we can't blame anybody else if it doesn't succeed. And we will gain some experience too.'

'Not many people start a new career at our age,' said Martha.

'Age equals wisdom!' Brains answered, and then they laughed again and it was quite a while before Martha left to go back to her own room.

12

Just as Rake had started to get undressed he heard a knocking at his door. He pulled up his trousers again, put on his jacket and took a few hesitant steps in the direction of the door.

'It's me, Christina,' a small voice said from outside.

Rake quickly combed his hair, tied a cravat round his neck and opened the door.

'Come in, come in!'

When she entered the room, he immediately noticed that she looked worried.

'A little champagne?'

She shook her head and sank down onto the sofa.

'Your suite certainly does look masculine,' Christina said. Rake watched as she rubbed her hand across her forehead, as though she had a headache.

'I thought it suited me. It has a pure style and it reminds me of my time at sea.' His cheeks acquired a little colour.

'To think that people live in such luxury. I heard that guests who return to the hotel always want to have the same room as before. That's totally understandable. I don't want to end up in prison. I want to stay here.'

'But Christina, that's the whole point. We've got to commit

crimes in order to live in this sort of luxury,' he said and sat down beside her.

'Well, I don't want to steal!' Christina's voice was shrill. 'We can't. It's not right. It is *wrong* to take things from other people.'

'But, my dear Christina, you can't abandon ship now. You'll be ruining things for the rest of us.'

'But what about my children? What are they going to say? Emma and Anders will be ashamed of me and what if they turn their backs on me for ever?'

'Oh no. They are going to be proud of you. Think of Robin Hood, who stole from the rich. The English love him.'

'So my children will come to respect me because I steal like Robin Hood? But Robin Hood and safes at the Grand Hotel are not exactly the same thing.'

'Oh yes they are. We are stealing from the wealthy and people always make allowances if you steal from those who have a lot of money. Anders and Emma will do that as well. Do you remember the Great Train Robbery in England? Most people think that they were really clever and the man who masterminded it is admired by some.'

'But that was a gigantic robbery. We are only stealing on a small scale in comparison.'

'Well, enough to get us into prison.'

'Yes, rather that than electronic tagging, I suppose. That would be awful. Just imagine going around with one of those ugly ankle tags!' Christina looked at Rake with tears in her eyes. He put a comforting arm around her.

'You can't imagine how brave everybody is going to think you. It will be a famous robbery coup and you will be a part of it. You will become a legend.'

'Me?'

'Yes, you. People are going to talk about you with respect. I am proud of you and I am so glad to have you on board.'

'Do you really mean that?' Christina lowered her eyes and Rake saw that he was gaining the upper hand. He knew that he was good at handling women and continued, confident of victory.

'You are very pretty, you know that?' He cupped her face in his hands and looked deep into her eyes. 'I have faith in you; I know that you can do this.' Then he stroked her softly on her cheek, leaned forward and held her for a long while before finally getting up and pulling her up from the sofa too.

'I'm going to be with you the whole time. You can trust me,' he said, and kissed her on the cheek. Then he led her amicably all the way to the door.

When Christina got back to her room she lay awake a long time with her hands on her chest. With a smile she thought about how sweet Rake had been, and how lovely it had felt when he had embraced her. But when it came to stealing . . . her parents had been Pentecostalists, always preaching the importance of righteousness. Should she just abandon that now? Every single Sunday they had made her go to church. It had been boring, and if it hadn't been for the music it would have been unbearable. In her home town so much of life seemed to be about going to church and doing everything right. When the huge Lake Vättern shone like silver without a ripple on the surface, she had believed that God was in a good mood and was stopping the waves. But when there was a storm and waves sputtered against the shore, she was afraid that He was angry and would come and punish her. Her mother and father had said that God would punish her if she did something stupid – and she often did. At the thought of these memories, Christina couldn't help but smile to herself there in the dark.

Her parents had kept a fabric shop and had hoped that she would take over. And perhaps that might have come about if she hadn't fallen in love with Ollie, the tenor in the church choir. He was always wanting them to go to the old Brahehus Castle and look at the view across Lake Vättern. The ruins were fascinating with their thick walls and those empty black eyes for windows. It frightened her and tempted her – as did he. After just a few visits, he had pulled her down behind some bushes and she lost her virginity. Just like now, she had been unable to resist doing something new and exciting. But when she became pregnant, her parents had forced her to marry him. Things had admittedly gone well for Ollie and they had had a lot of money during all their married years. But the marriage was never a happy one, and after years spent as a housewife it was a relief when the children had grown up and they finally got a divorce. After that, she had opened a milliner's shop, with the money from the divorce, and her new life proved much more rewarding. She had studied literature and there had been the choir and her friends. It had been such fun. Christina closed her eyes and thought about Rake. If he became a criminal, she would too. It was like those outings to the old Brahehus Castle. Something forbidden and exciting . . .

71

13

The League of Pensioners had finished their morning meeting, at which Martha and Brains had revealed the new plan to the others. Everyone was supportive of the idea so now it was time for Martha and Brains to get going. Brains got out his cutting pliers, a length of electrical wire, some silver tape and a tube of quick-drying glue. He put them all into a white translucent plastic bag, which then fitted easily into the spacious pocket of his bathrobe and couldn't be seen from outside. He looked at his watch. In five minutes he had a rendezvous with Martha down in the spa.

In the lift, Martha yet again went over the robbery plans. The various phases were carefully thought through, and the only thing that worried her was that Brains might get electrocuted and drop down dead when he short-circuited the wires. The receptionist looked up when Martha walked into the spa's reception area.

'One towel, please,' Martha asked.

'Right. I see you already have a bathrobe,' the girl said as she turned towards the shelves where the towels lay. That very same moment, Brains slipped past and disappeared into the men's changing room with his bag. The receptionist handed over a large white towel.

'So delightfully soft,' said Martha and pressed it against her cheek. The girl behind the counter handed over a plastic card for the safe.

'When you've put your valuables in the safe, you engage the lock by holding the card against it. And when you want to get your things out again, you just hold the card against the lock, and the box will open.'

'How clever.' Martha smiled. She hoped that her behaviour was exactly the same as normal and that the receptionist couldn't detect the nervous beating of her heart.

The changing room was brightly lit and a gentle, sweet aroma hung in the air. A dark-haired woman was getting changed, and a bit further away, Martha saw another woman come out of the shower. Otherwise it was empty. This early in the morning, only a few of the safes were occupied. Martha showered, put on her bathing suit and went into the pool. But she didn't have time to swim more than a few strokes before the lights started flashing. She stopped, went up the steps out of the pool and back to the changing room. There, the lamps were all off and it took a while before the light came back on again. She tried her plastic card. You couldn't open the box with it. She smiled to herself, put on her bathrobe and went out to reception again. The lights were on there.

'My safe won't open,' said Martha.

'We'll fix it,' the receptionist answered.

'But where shall I put my valuables?'

'You can leave them here,' said the receptionist, and she pointed to the storage cupboard right behind her, a robust white-painted metal cupboard. 'But surely your things are already locked away in your safe?'

'Oh, yes, I'd forgotten,' said Martha.

'Well, how was it?' Anna-Greta wondered a few moments later when Martha had returned to the suite. She and Christina had not yet finished breakfast and were still sitting wearing their dressing gowns. Christina held up Martha's knitting.

'This was on the sofa. For once could you just finish your knitting so that we could dare to sit down without getting pierced?'

'Sorry, I always forget. It's going to be a cardigan,' said Martha and she tidied away the yarn and knitting needles. She poured a cup of coffee for herself. There were no limitations here, so she could drink as many cups as she liked.

'When the safes didn't work, the receptionist put the valuables in the storage cupboard behind her, just as we thought,' said Martha.

'Good. How many valuables will fit in there?' Anna-Greta wanted to know.

'Quite a lot,' said Martha vaguely.

Christina looked sceptical, took a chocolate wafer and waved it in her hand.

'You seem satisfied, but we have made a big mistake,' she said. 'We came here to steal from the rich, but have ourselves occupied the most expensive suites.'

There was silence for a few moments as Christina's words sank in.

'It isn't easy being a crook for the first time,' Martha said defensively, and she, too, helped herself to a chocolate wafer. Times like this justified some chocolate.

'We ought to have booked another room and waited until a really big star came along, a rich, famous artiste, a king or a president,' Christina maintained.

'It's a lot to think about at our age – being on the run *as well as* robbery. We have to take one step a time,' said Martha.

'But on the upside, the price of gold is high at the moment. Three thick gold bracelets would be a hundred thousand kronor straight away,' said Anna-Greta, proud to show off her speedy mental arithmetic.

'Don't forget that the robbery needs to be enough to get us into prison,' Christina pointed out. After realizing that Rake thought prison really was a good idea, Christina was now much keener on the idea.

'We'll go down to the spa at lunchtime when it's crowded. The storage cupboard in reception will be bulging with gold by then,' said Martha.

The others agreed. When they were dressed, Martha went down to see Brains for a final run-through. He showed her his drawings.

'This is where I have short-circuited it,' he said, putting his finger on the paper. 'It'll be a while before anybody finds the break in the circuit of the safes,' he went on and pointed at some strange-looking lines. 'And the wiring to the pool and the steam room is only temporarily repaired. Two seconds flat, and I can cut off the lot. Duct tape is fantastic!' He looked so delighted that Martha was reminded of a boy in front of a computer game.

'And what if things don't go according to plan?'

'Something could go wrong but if it does, then we simply need to make a new plan. And I've got some spare tools as well,' he answered, and put his hand on the sports bag.

There was a knock on the door and Rake came in. He looked sleepy and smelt of garlic. He caught sight of the two small plastic bags that lay on the table.

'Be careful with the herbs,' he said, but didn't get any further before there was more knocking on the door. It was Christina and Anna-Greta.

'All set, then,' Martha said, trying to make her voice steady. 'Now all we have to do is wait for lunchtime.'

They all nodded and looked very serious.

14

A few hours later they all took the lift and went down to the spa together. Martha kept patting the pockets of the white bathrobe, where she was keeping the bags of powder. She looked at Brains out of the corner of her eye. He had put one of the hotel towels on top of everything else in his bag so that the tools were hidden. He looked so exhilarated. Like a little child who was about to do some mischief. And truth be told, that's exactly how Martha felt too.

For the sake of appearances, they showered and spent some time in the swimming pool. They splashed around while they waited for the number of people using the pool to increase. Anna-Greta kept on encouraging the others to be patient.

'It could mean another piece of jewellery,' she insisted as soon as anyone suggested they should get going. In the end, Brains said he couldn't cope with waiting another minute, and then he leaned against Martha and whispered: 'Have you got the bags?'

She nodded.

'When the lights blink, get the powder out and pour it into the steam nozzle. Do it quickly so that nobody notices.'

'I have seen the films, you know!' Martha replied.

Brains went off towards the corridor by reception, leading to the fuse box, while Martha went along with the others to the steam room. The henbane would make the spa guests lethargic, and before they got too drowsy Martha would also pour the cannabis into the nozzle. Then Christina and Anna-Greta would stagger out of the sauna and pretend to faint, while Martha would hurry to fetch the receptionist for help. As soon as the receptionist had left the counter, Brains would black out the lighting for the entire spa and then he and Rake would break the lock on the cupboard behind reception and empty it of the valuables. Brains had fitted a row of LED lights into his slippers so that he and Rake could see. Martha was a bit worried because she feared that this might give them away, but he assured her it would be all right. The slipper lights would only be used in case of an emergency and he was sure that, in the general confusion, nobody would notice where the light was coming from. But Martha still thought that she was right and that Brains hadn't recognized the danger of the lights because he was a man and had little imagination. But with age she had learned that sometimes it was simpler just to give in.

When they entered the steam room they were immediately enveloped by a warm cloud, which meant that they could hardly see anything. Christina and Anna-Greta sat down on the benches while Martha looked around as best she could in the mist. It seemed as if at least twenty people were in the steam room. She counted a few elderly gentlemen, several ladies and a middle-aged couple, all seated on the two half-moon-shaped benches that faced each other. Martha knew that she had to be careful of those who were sitting closest to her. She could feel the plastic bags chafing inside her swimsuit and began to wish that she wasn't doing this. It would have been better if Rake had taken care of this part of the plan, but he had said that nowadays he only occupied himself with *living* plants. Dried leaves weren't his concern. She straightened her back. Christina would just have to do the job – and show him how it was done. Martha sat down at the end of one of the benches, as close to the door as possible – so that she would be near to the fresh air outside – and put the birch twigs down next to her. Her hand felt its way to her swimsuit neckline. With the plastic bags next to her bosom, she looked like she had in her prime. She sighed; it was so dark inside the room that nobody would be able to admire her figure anyway.

'How long are we going to sit here for?' Christina whispered.

'Not long at all,' Martha reassured her. 'I'll tell you when it's time.'

'One certainly wouldn't want to stay in here for too long,' Anna-Greta added, and put her hand over her mouth. 'There's far too much steam.'

The mist hid the facial expressions of the people sitting there, and Martha grew worried. It would be difficult to judge their reactions. She had hardly had the chance to brood on this, before the lights flickered. Brains had cut the power off. This was it! Martha's hand felt for the bags inside her bathing costume. Where were they? At the same moment, she realized that she didn't have her glasses with her. She, who had preached about how important the little details were. Oh well, the cannabis bag had the most contents and that was all she really needed to know. The man sitting opposite her was beginning to take an interest in her cleavage search.

'I thought I had three with me, when I left home,' she joked.

The man gaped at her.

'Well, two perhaps?' she attempted.

Martha could hear an embarrassed clearing of somebody's throat and somebody else coughing nervously in the mist. Old ladies shouldn't joke about such things, is that what they were thinking? This made Martha angry; the elderly could have a bit of fun too.

The steam became even more intense and several of the guests covered their faces with their hands. It was now really hot and sticky, and two people got up and left. Martha couldn't delay any longer. She located the bags and carefully pulled out the henbane powder and opened it. Now she only had to take a few steps to the black pillar and pour it all into the nozzle. But her thumb and index finger couldn't find anything inside the bag. Martha withdrew them. She had put the powder there herself. Confused, she dug her fingers back into the bag and found a soggy mess right at the bottom. Oh, heavens above! The pouch had leaked! In her mind's eye she imagined how all those who had been swimming in the pool would have inhaled the henbane and fallen asleep. But then a moment later she recognized a man she had almost collided with in the pool and she calmed down. Most of the henbane was probably still in the bag, and had just got wet. Did that mean it had lost its effectiveness, or would she start hallucinating herself from the henbane that had leaked? Martha didn't know. The best thing to do now would be to act quickly and then rush out to the shower. But what if there was so little henbane left that nobody reacted? She dipped into her cleavage again and took out the bag with the cannabis. Thank God that hadn't leaked. Rake had told her just to put a small amount of the powered cannabis in, but you had to adapt to the circumstances and Martha decided to use the whole lot. She tottered over to the pillar, and after the nozzle had puffed out a hot cloud of steam she threw in the henbane and the cannabis and covered it all with the birch twigs. Then she sat at the very end of the bench, as close to the door as she could, and waited.

15

Nurse Barbara stood smoking in her newly renovated flat in Sollentuna. She inhaled deeply and blew out the last of the smoke before stubbing out the cigarette in her wine glass and closing the window. Ever since the day Director Mattson had taken over the retirement home, she had dreamed of how they could work together. Her and him. The two of them would be successful. He had the money and could invest; she could run the business. But as time passed, she started to become impatient. She wanted to talk with him about the future. At the same time, she realized that she must tread carefully so that she didn't scare him off.

'Hurry up, darling,' he said and held out his hands. Director Mattson lay on his back and was stark naked. She didn't need to be Einstein to see what he wanted. As she took the few steps across to the bed, she was thinking that she must make him dependent upon these moments together. Then when she had managed that, she would be able to achieve her goal. Times like these, when she had his full attention, were when she should try and persuade him to her line of thinking.

'Darling, we do have a good time together, don't we?'

He pulled her down towards him and kissed her in response. She pulled away and gave him a serious look.

'If only we could see each other more often. I miss you when we aren't together.'

'And I miss you too, my darling.' He tried to embrace her again.

'Have you thought about your wife? I mean, about the divorce?'

He stopped her, and held her tightly to him.

'Silly billy, a love like we have doesn't need to be confirmed by marriage. What we have is enough.' Just then, his mobile started ringing on the bedside table. On the second ring he hesitated, and on the third ring he stretched out his hand.

'Hello, oh, it's you. Right, yes, OK. Are you having a nice time? Oh, is that right . . . ?'

Barbara could discern the high-pitched voice on the other end of the line; she got up and went into the kitchen. She didn't like listening to his conversations with his wife; it reminded her that there was another woman in his life. A woman who looked as if she was going to be sticking around for a while longer.

'So you're going to stay another week, darling? Right, I understand. Dear me, what a pity. And I was going to take you and the children out for dinner.'

His wife and children had travelled to London. Now it seemed as though their return would be delayed. Perhaps this meant that she and Mattson could be together a little longer? At last the conversation came to an end. Barbara went back into the bedroom.

'Darling, my family is stuck in London. So I think I'll take a few more days off work and we can spend some more time together.'

'How wonderful! But what about the residents?'

'We'll get a temp to cover for you.'

'Can we afford it?'

'My dear, Diamond House is a veritable profit-making machine. What was the name of the girl who replaced you last time? Katia, wasn't it? Ring her!'

He stretched out his hands towards her again, and this time she didn't need any more encouragement. Pleased with how things were developing, she crept in under the covers and put her arms around him.

When the stand-in nurse, Katia, went into the retirement home the next day, she found it unusually quiet. The old people ate their breakfast and gathered in the lounge as usual, but there was no sign of the choir gang. When they didn't turn up for lunch either, she went up to their rooms and found that everything was neat and tidy, but their coats were all missing. They must be out singing somewhere. She had heard them talking about performances in Strängnäs and Eskilstuna before. Nurse Barbara must simply have forgotten to inform her. Katia smiled to herself. Perhaps they would perform *God in Disguise* which they had been rehearsing for such a long time. They loved singing and she didn't begrudge them that joy. She immediately felt calm. They would turn up soon enough.

16

Inside the steam room, water was dripping from the ceiling and the noise of the spray was very audible. With the herbs inside the nozzle, a distinct smell started to spread. Martha felt sleepy and found it hard to gather her thoughts. She stole a glance through the door. Then came the first giggle. The man opposite her stretched his feet out towards the stone in front of him, slipped, missed again and started laughing. The others next to him joined in with the laughter and the mood was suddenly all the merrier. There was an oddly sweet smell in the room now and Martha thought that probably she hadn't used enough birch twigs. She turned around to pick up some more but then the thought slid away from her. There was something she was supposed to do . . . but what was it? She should have written it down on a piece of paper, but it would have looked dreadfully suspicious if she had started thumbing through a wad of to-do notes in a steam room!

Suddenly she heard Anna-Greta's neighing laugh, followed by another hysterical laugh. Christina followed suit with an uncontrolled fit of giggling and Martha, too, found herself smiling. Then the lights blinked and went out. After a moment they started flickering again. It wasn't particularly funny, but the men were grinning in a bemused fashion. Martha could hear her own giggling and she realized that she couldn't sit in the steam room for very much longer. There was something she was meant to do . . . what was it? She couldn't for the life of her remember what it was. It didn't dawn on her until the man opposite her put his hand over his mouth and started yawning. Anna-Greta and Christina were meant to faint and she was then meant to rush off to fetch the receptionist. She prodded her friends in the ribs and whispered.

'It's time now. Lie down on the bench. Hurry!'

'Not here, surely,' Anna-Greta squeaked. Then she pulled down one shoulder strap of her bathing costume and winked at the man sitting opposite her before emitting another piercing horse-like neigh.

'Lie down, faint, be quick!' Martha demanded as quietly as she could.

'Not for him there, oh no, he is too old,' said Anna-Greta who had regretted her boldness and was pulling her shoulder strap up again. Then she laughed so loudly that nobody could have fainted in the vicinity of her noise.

'Please lie down so that I can go and fetch help,' hissed Martha, who was starting to feel a bit dizzy. Christina, who was used to following orders, stretched out on the bench. Anna-Greta, now finally aware of what was happening, lay down next but was unable to stem her laughter. The lights then all gave a final flicker and went out. Martha hurried to the reception area, where the lights were still working.

'Two people have just fainted in the steam room. Come quickly!' she cried.

The receptionist went pale and hurried after Martha. As

soon as the girl opened the door to the steam room, Martha went back into reception. Brains was already standing in front of the metal cupboard. He was wearing his gym clothes and was busy working with a picklock in his hand.

'Nice to have a large, old-fashioned metal cupboard with a proper lock,' he whispered and asked her to hold his sports bag open. The lock was surprisingly easy to open, but just as they were about to start taking out the valuables, the lights in the reception went out.

What happened? Brains wondered, but then he remembered his slippers and bent down to turn the LED lights on. Then he froze. Rake had told him to put on his gym shoes and now he was standing there in his trainers. In the dark. He was well aware that time was of the essence, so quickly he reached inside the cupboard and simply swept the entire contents into the bag. The lights flickered into action again, and Brains closed the cupboard door hastily.

'See you later,' he said to Martha, grabbing the gym bag as he went. Brains took the bag upstairs to the gym, where he put it down and went to one of the exercise bicycles. The next moment, Rake entered the gym. The two friends exchanged knowing glances. Rake then picked up the closest dumb-bells and started exercising.

Meanwhile, Martha returned to the steam room where she found the receptionist in the process of trying to get Christina and Anna-Greta out into the corridor. They had both come round very quickly and were now giggling wildly. Gales of laughter could be heard in all directions and two elderly gentlemen were snorting and slapping their knees in amusement.

The receptionist looked very confused as Martha caught her eye.

'They seem to have had a little too much champagne at breakfast. I don't know what the world is coming to,' the receptionist said. 'The worst ones are your age.'

'They are young at heart,' Martha mumbled as she caught up with Christina and Anna-Greta on their way out into reception.

'Now, girls, let's have a shower,' Martha said, but it took quite a while before she could get her woozy friends into the changing room area.

'This was the most fun I've ever had,' Christina wheezed merrily when they were back in the ladies' changing room again.

'Can't we do this at the retirement home too?' Anna-Greta wondered.

'Shush!' Martha urged, but this only triggered a new attack of laughter from her friends. It required quite an effort to get them both up to the relaxation room. They were going to pretend to be taking it easy by enjoying fresh juice and leafing through the day's newspapers – so as to appear innocent. Martha thought it was risky to remain at the scene of the crime, but Brains had reassured her that they wouldn't attract the slightest attention. However, they hadn't been relaxing for very long in the loungers before they heard loud voices coming from downstairs. They couldn't resist going down to have a look. The closer they got, the louder the noise became and they were met with a great commotion. The door to the metal cupboard was wide open and a group of unsteady guests stood next to it, pointing.

'The cupboard is empty. Everything's gone – necklaces, jewels and passports,' one middle-aged lady chuckled, almost incapacitated by laughter. 'Disappeared into thin air!'

The receptionist looked extremely unhappy.

'And my gold bracelet has vanished too. Without a trace!' her grey-haired friend chirped in.

'And that ghastly watch I got from my mother-in-law, that's gone too,' one of the old guys guffawed. 'Got rid of it at last! Hahaha!'

'But what about our money? I told you that we shouldn't bring any valuables down with us,' his wife grumbled.

'Don't be upset, darling, you were right. But things like this don't happen every day. Just enjoy the drama!' And with that he dissolved into fits of laughter.

Amidst the chaos, Martha took her friends by the hand and herded them towards the lift.

'We'd better go,' she said. And their silly giggles lasted all the way up to their luxury suite. Martha even sang a traditional Swedish drinking song, in her old childhood dialect.

Martha thought it was probably for the best that Rake had not been in charge of the herbs, because she knew that he would not have been so generous with the amount used. She, however, had poured out every last grain of powder. She had had to think on her feet and had succeeded in doing so!

17

The League of Pensioners had drained the last drops of champagne from their glasses, and calmed themselves as much as possible. Now the moment to open up the sports bag and reveal the loot had arrived. Brains lifted up the bag with a solemn gesture, tipped it upside down and let the contents pour out onto the table. The five newly fledged villains sat like expectant children, watching as the pile of goodies grew. With a gleam in their eyes they started to sort through the items. Then a silence descended over them.

'What's all this?' said Martha while she rummaged in the pile. 'Make-up and hairbrushes?'

'No lipstick for me, thank you,' Rake muttered. 'Who's idea was it to raid the safes at the swimming pool? You've only got yourselves to blame. What did you expect – the crown jewels?'

'The men do at least seem to have deposited their mobile phones. Perhaps we can cash these in?' Anna-Greta suggested and poked around in the heap of stolen property. 'And look here; there are some bracelets and watches.'

'But we won't end up in prison for stealing this,' Martha sighed.

'And it isn't much to share either,' Christina added.

'This thick bracelet must be eighteen carat and the watch should fetch a hundred thousand,' Anna-Greta pointed out.

'And here is a gold compact,' said Martha as she picked out an engraved, showy case. It was opened with a buckle, but it was so small that Martha couldn't release it.

'I'd like that compact, unless somebody else . . . ?' said Anna-Greta and quickly snatched it away before anyone had time to react. Christina gave her a withering look.

They became silent again and each of them tried to find something to be pleased about, but however thoroughly they rummaged in the pile they found little of value. The robbery had been successful, but the loot was just knick-knacks.

'This is our first attempt. I don't suppose Robin Hood was successful the first time either,' Christina mumbled and looked dismally at the nail she had broken while rummaging in the pile.

'I hardly think he stole hairbrushes, though,' Rake answered.

'Here we are risking our freedom for a load of junk. We must raise our game next time. A kidnapping or some such,' said Anna-Greta, waving her walking stick around – which, as she had predicted, had become totally warped from the steam room.

'A kidnapping?!' A unison gasp of horror could be heard.

'Yes, you take a hostage and demand ransom money!'

'I have read about kidnapping in lots of novels,' said Martha, 'but the victims are usually overpowered and I'm not sure we'd manage that. What if we got beaten up in the process?'

'But can't we knock somebody over just *a little*?' questioned Christina.

'You mean, just trip them up?' Rake grinned.

Nobody managed to laugh and despite the champagne the mood of the group was low.

'We can ask down in reception whether any famous guests are arriving soon?' Brains suggested after a moment.

'And then we kidnap them? People like Clinton or Putin, for example? I'd like to see that!' Rake shook his head in disbelief.

'I know what we can do. We'll arrange a poker night up in one of our rooms. The suite is so fancy that nobody would suspect anything. Robbery and card-sharping ought to render a prison sentence,' Martha suggested.

'Good God, soon you'll be opening a brothel too. We must be more realistic,' chided Anna-Greta.

'Card-sharping could be interesting,' Brains mused, 'but it wouldn't lead to more than a conditional sentence.'

'Quite right. We must fit the robbery to the amount of time we want to spend behind bars – and don't forget that we want to get to the best prison too,' said Martha, who had developed a taste for high standards.

'So much to think about, as if it wasn't hard enough to commit a crime.' Christina pulled out her nail file. She was clearly agitated.

'Time is not on our side, though. And we must decide our next move before somebody nails us for the robbery down in the spa,' said Martha.

'Or Nurse Barbara reports us as missing persons.'

The long discussion tired them all out, and it was a gloomy gang of pensioners that went off to bed a little later.

'Don't give up. By tomorrow morning we'll certainly have thought something up,' Martha encouraged.

*

In the middle of the night Martha woke with a start. Her heart was thumping and she had to wait quite a while before the palpitations stopped. With some effort, she sat up in bed and reached out for her glass of water. Then she remembered, and a broad smile spread across her wrinkled face. No wonder her heart had been thumping so hard. As usual, her old brain had been busy while she was asleep, and had calmly and quietly found a solution to their delicate problem. Now she knew. They would indeed carry out a kidnapping – but in a very modern way. Martha could hardly restrain her enthusiasm, and couldn't sleep a wink for the rest of the night.

18

When the five old friends went down for a morning swim, they discovered that the entire area had been cordoned off. Police officers were examining the area and talking quietly to each other.

'I think we should use the bathtub in the suite instead,' said Christina and she did an about-turn.

'Hmm, I believe I left my flip-flops up in the room,' Anna-Greta filled in, and followed her. So the two women and Rake retreated to the lift, while Martha and Brains hung about for a bit and watched the proceedings. Martha studied how the police officers worked and she noticed that they all had gloves on. She had read about DNA and fingerprints. That was very important, and even a little thumbprint could give away major villains. She must bear that in mind in future.

After yet another continental breakfast up in the Princess Lilian suite, the League of Pensioners gathered for the day's meeting. As they all settled themselves onto the sofas, Martha took the last bite of the fourth chocolate wafer she had eaten that day. She considered taking yet another but she didn't want to be a bad example for the others, and restrained herself. To her horror, in just a couple of days she had become used to the high standard at the hotel – not to mention the Danish pastries on the breakfast table – and felt worried about how she and her friends would acclimatize to life in prison. But she didn't utter a word about this to the others. It could destroy their criminal careers before they had even begun.

Brains was the first to speak.

'Did anybody listen to the radio this morning?' he asked. 'Did they mention missing old people or anything like that?'

'Nobody misses old people! Just think of those descriptions in the old Icelandic sagas where people over a certain age were simply pushed over cliffs!' said Christina, who was rather gloomy the day after their first robbery.

'Now we mustn't get all depressed about the meagre loot yesterday. Instead we should be pleased that we were successful. We got away! See it as a trial run,' said Martha.

'Perhaps they aren't even on to us yet, and – who knows – maybe the hotel will want to pretend that there hasn't been a robbery here at all. They'll want to protect their *image* – isn't that what they call it?' said Brains.

'But it's weird that Nurse Barbara hasn't sounded the alarm,' said Christina, almost a bit offended by the fact that nobody had missed them.

'I bet she's gone off with Director Mattson. They'll be cavorting in bed and won't have noticed that we've gone,' was Rake's opinion.

'Now, now, must you always—' Anna-Greta started, frowning at him.

'Stop it,' Martha interrupted them. 'We are here to discuss our next move – which won't hurt anybody but will give us a lot of money for the Robbery Fund. I have a suggestion. A kid-napping somewhere close to here.'

They all gasped, and Rake looked really aghast. He had been staring out the window and immediately said, 'The palace? Have you gone completely bonkers?'

'No, no, don't be silly! That would get us into far too much trouble. No, just an innocent little kidnapping which would give us one or two years in one of the plushest prisons. That will give us the chance to see what it is really like in the prisons. Perhaps they aren't quite what they are made out to be, like our retirement home was? If it isn't as nice as we expect, then we can always return to Diamond House.'

'Never!' they exclaimed with one voice.

'We'd choose a better retirement home, of course. We'd be able to afford it.'

'That would have to be a major robbery,' said Anna-Greta, who suddenly remembered the bill she used to pay every month for Diamond House. 'If we are going to get something really good for our money, that is.'

This resulted in a discussion about various types of retire-ment accommodation and what you actually got for your pen-sion. Some of them wanted politicians to experience living in the retirement homes which were run on a budget but that was seen as too severe a punishment. Besides, the elected represen-tatives would then have to be locked in their rooms after eight in the evening and then they wouldn't be able to take part in the discussion programmes on TV.

'We must concentrate!' Martha declared in an attempt to bring them to order. 'I believe I have come up with the perfect crime.'

An expectant silence ensued and even Rake paid attention.

'Only about fifty metres from here is the National Museum. They've got more than ten thousand paintings there, including many old masterpieces, and you know what I think?' She looked around triumphantly. 'It stands to reason that they can't *all* be wired up with alarms. If we steal a painting to the value of three or four million, that ought to earn us two or three years in prison.'

Nobody applauded, but she could see the interest in their eyes.

'And how do you intend for us to go about doing this?' Brains wondered.

'Nothing complicated. We just have to create a distraction, then one of us takes down a painting or two and we hurry out. Much the same as we have practised at the spa reception,' explained Martha.

'We can't exactly run,' Anna-Greta reminded them.

'That's precisely why we must distract the guards.'

'We can streak and run naked through the exhibition halls,' Rake suggested.

'You need to be younger for that, you dirty old man,' Anna-Greta snorted.

'Don't say that. At our age we would arouse *even more* attention,' Christina remarked. 'But I certainly have no intention whatsoever of running naked through the museum.'

'Martha was getting annoyed with such ridiculous suggestions and tried to move the conversation on: 'I was thinking of a different sort of distraction . . .'

'Now hold on. This isn't as simple as you think. What do we do about the surveillance cameras, for example?' Brains queried.

'We cover them over. Then we take the paintings down and

walk out, calm and cool. We just pretend that we are not the thieves,' said Martha. She opened her purse belt and took out a bag of fruit pastilles. She shouldn't eat sweets, but this was another one of those times when she needed a serious sugar boost. 'Anybody like one?' she offered and then put the bag on the table. They all shook their heads.

'*Pretend that we are not the thieves*? Now you must explain what you mean,' said Rake, who was beginning to get impatient.

'We put the paintings in the basket of my Zimmer frame and then I simply put my coat over them.'

'Your coat over a huge old masterpiece while the alarm is sounding off?' Rake rolled his eyes.

'Don't be so negative,' Martha hissed.

'But if somebody asks what we are doing, what do we say?' Christina asked.

'You don't have to answer everything,' was Martha's retort.

'How do we know which paintings are connected to an alarm?' Brains asked, and immediately started to think about various possibilities to short-circuit the alarm system.

'I should think Rembrandt and Van Gogh are,' Martha explained, 'and probably Paul Gauguin. But perhaps Carl Larsson won't be and he sells for high prices at Bukowskis.'

'Ahah, the auctioneers,' said Anna-Greta knowingly. 'So first we are going to steal expensive paintings and then try to sell them at Bukowskis? I don't think that will work. People will recognize them as stolen artwork.'

'That's why I have thought of something else,' said Martha. 'We are not going to just steal paintings like your average simple thief. *We are going to kidnap them.* Nothing will be destroyed, nobody is going to be robbed in person, and nobody will be sorry. The owner – in this case the museum – only needs to pay a few million to us and then they'll get the paintings back.'

A little 'Ooooh' went round the table and even Rake had to admit that Martha had thought this through properly.

'A few million – but Martha, dear, you make it all sound so simple,' said Anna-Greta. 'The National Museum does not have much money.'

'Of course it does! There are the donations, for a start. They can take the money from the Friends of the National Museum. They will cough up. These paintings at the museum are national treasures.'

'Well, I like the idea,' Christina piped up, 'but how would we actually go about the kidnapping?'

Christina looked expectantly at the others. She had started to acquire a taste for adventure, and she had had so much fun robbing the spa that she was keen to commit new crimes.

'I propose that we draw a diagram of where the best paintings are, where the alarms and the security cameras are, and then we decide how to arrange the robbery,' Martha went on. 'We really should check out the getaway routes too. Brains, have you got a notepad?'

Rake swallowed a few times as if to protest, but couldn't think of anything to say. He realized that they couldn't stay at the hotel indefinitely, and he, too, wanted to swap the retirement home for a good prison. He stretched out to reach the bag of sweets and helped himself to some fruit pastilles.

'You lot, I think we should watch a film this evening and have a nice time. Then we will be in good shape tomorrow.'

At first Martha intended to protest, but she realized that it was important that everybody was in a good mood. A bit of relaxation wouldn't do any harm. So she fetched some nuts and dark chocolate and ordered two films: *Murder on the Orient Express* and *The Ladykillers*.

'We need some inspiration,' she said, but then Christina looked so terrified that Martha felt obliged to explain.

'Christina, dear,' she consoled her, 'it isn't the murders but the planning which is going to inspire us.'

The next day, Martha and Brains strolled around amongst the public in the exhibition halls at the National Museum. The building was almost next door to the hotel. They tried to give the impression of being very interested in art, but while they examined the paintings Brains was diligently writing away in his notepad.

'I've got a feeling that the guards are watching us,' Martha said after a while, glancing over her shoulder.

'Do you think so? If they ask anything, just say we are artists.'

'As if that would explain everything.'

'It explains a lot.' Brains smiled.

Martha was concerned. This looked as if it was going to be more difficult than she had expected. They had discovered cameras and alarms everywhere and in every room there was a flashing red lamp. Not only that, but security guards seemed to materialize when you least expected it. The new crime would demand meticulous planning.

While she wandered around in the exhibition halls, she found herself trying to plan the 'perfect coup' – but at the same time, they must, sooner or later, make sure they were caught. How else would they end up in prison? It was, however, so pleasant at the Grand Hotel that none of them had any desire to leave yet. At any rate, not *just now*. She recalled the old proverbial phrases about wealth making you blind, and that the more you had the more you wanted. Had their transformation come about so quickly?

Brains wrote down his observations in his notepad and they moved on to the next exhibition hall. The ceilings were very high and Martha wondered why this was, since you could hardly hang paintings up there. Indeed, she had pondered so many things and walked around so much that in the end she needed to sit down on a bench and rest. She hadn't just studied the paintings from the front, but had also checked the alarm connections at the sides. As she sat there, she became more and more dejected. There were alarms everywhere, and then there were all those guards with their mobile phones and walkie-talkies. If they saw anything suspicious, they would call the police immediately. But there was what they called the 'human factor', of course. The security guards patrolled here day after day. Sooner or later they must surely lose concentration? And they must have coffee breaks just like everybody else?

'I think we can pull this off,' Brains said quietly. 'We can deal with the guards too.'

'You think so?' Martha said hopefully. 'That's what's so wonderful about you, you are always so positive.'

Brains squeezed her hand gently and her heart fluttered.

'But you are the one who inspires me, Martha dear, I promise you. We'll fix this together. I've got an idea. Come and have a look.'

He stood up, helped Martha to her feet, and together they steered towards the hall with the temporary exhibitions. Perhaps the security wasn't as good in there?

19

Katia clicked the telephone off and stared at the display as if that could help her. She had lost count of how many times she had rung, without Nurse Barbara answering. The manageress had spoken somewhat vaguely about the length of her holiday plans. Katia hadn't given it too much thought; the last time she had worked at Diamond House she had been able to phone and ask for advice. But now, when she really needed it, she couldn't get through. Katia sighed and looked out over the lounge. A woman was sitting there sewing a blanket, and two elderly men were playing chess. The choir gang had still not returned, and that frightened her. They were a group of friends who made the best of life and they had livened up the others at the home. Now it was quiet, boring even. Katia thought about Brains who used to do his woodwork when he believed nobody could hear him, and about Rake who sang his navy songs. Even a little neigh from Anna-Greta would have cheered things up. She would never have believed that she could miss them so much. She thought about Rake who cultivated his plants on the balcony even though he wasn't allowed to, and Christina who helped him to water them. Katia had noticed how she looked at him on the sly and guessed that the old gal fancied him. She was, at any rate, always careful to look nice when she knocked on his door. Unlike Anna-Greta, who only seemed to wear clothes for warmth. If more people had been like her, models would have nothing to do and Europe's fashion houses would have long since gone bankrupt.

Where were the choir gang? She went into the staff room and looked through the papers to see if there were any clues there. Perhaps Nurse Barbara had written a note for her? She had previously helped Katia with good advice, but now there was nothing to be found. If the oldies were doing a concert in Strängnäs or Eskilstuna, they should have been back by now. She couldn't stall any longer; she must act on her own, and do something that unfortunately might well cast a long, black shadow upon the reputation of Diamond House.

Katia sat down in front of the telephone but couldn't bring herself to ring the police straight away. Instead, she called the various parishes in the district and asked if the five pensioners had visited them. Perhaps the welfare officer knew of a choir concert that was going to be given by a group of elderly singers? She didn't? Oh, what a pity.

Two hours later, Katia gave up. Nobody knew anything. Had Martha and the others merely invented their concerts? Now Katia was getting really anxious, and realized that she should have sounded the alarm sooner. Her hand shook as she lifted the receiver of the phone. She tried to calm herself and while she listened to the ringing tone reflected that five was better than one. After all, they could help each other, couldn't they, if something was wrong?

'Police. Can we help you?'

Katia inhaled deeply and tried to say in as roundabout a way as possible that five elderly people had disappeared from the retirement home.

When Martha and Brains had returned from their museum visit, they rested for quite a long time. Towards the end of the evening they ordered champagne and gathered everyone together for dinner. They had been inspired and now that they had slept a little they were in a really good mood. They might even be considered rather giggly. Whilst they were ordering food, Brains had ticked the wedding special menu, with three courses including wedding cake, by mistake. Martha had caught sight of the order in time and changed it to an ordinary luxury menu. Then she blushed bright red and thought about Freud. Perhaps Brains had subconsciously done what he longed for deep inside? She glanced in his direction and saw that he was looking at her.

'I've been downstairs and have read the newspapers in the library,' Brains said after having poured out a glass of champagne for each of them. He put the bottle down. 'There was no mention of us, but I caught sight of some policemen. They weren't in uniform but it was obvious who they were – they all looked as if they trained at the same gym and had the same crew cut hairstyle. They were questioning the staff.'

The police? The theft that had for the most part been an unreal game now immediately seemed serious. A certain unease spread through the room, because, regardless of the circumstances, they still had some respect for the authorities. Their loot lay hidden in shoes and socks in the wardrobe, which was perhaps not the best of hiding places. They had had so much else to think about and were, of course, busy planning the next crime.

'Brains and I explored the museum today and we found some weak points,' said Martha after they had been served the dessert. Brains flashed her an encouraging look.

'Tell us more!' said Rake, putting down his dessert spoon. Christina wiped away a lick of chocolate mousse from the corner of her mouth, and Anna-Greta leaned forward.

'This is how it is. The museum is going to open a new exhibition called Sins and Desires,' Martha went on. 'We peeped in and saw that it was extremely sinful and erotic with several indecent paintings.'

'I can keep watch there,' Rake volunteered.

'Early in the morning there usually aren't very many visitors in the exhibition rooms, so most of the security guards will probably be in that room,' said Martha.

The others nodded in agreement.

'I propose that we seize the opportunity then. We can fool them all if we work as a team.'

This time, too, the others agreed and Martha got the feeling that they had gained some experience from their earlier crime.

'You, Anna-Greta, have a crucial role. I want you to go into the room with the old Dutch masterpieces. You must have your walking stick with you, and you will go and stand in front of one of the Rembrandt paintings, lean forward and point at the painting so that you break the seal to the alarm.'

'But my stick is all warped. You remember – from the steam room.'

'Exactly, and it should be too.'

'But then the alarm will go off.'

'And that's what it should do too. But listen, I'm not going into all the details at this stage. For now, we are only going through the basic outline.'

'That's good, otherwise the meeting would never end,' Christina murmured, having realized that she had forgotten to paint her nails. She must do that before going to bed.

'There are a lot of fancy alarms at the museum,' Martha went on, 'and they have surveillance cameras in every room. But I noticed that there was a large humidifier on the floor under the camera that covers the room with the Impressionists. You only have to step up onto that and spray the lens with black paint. Christina, you are little and nimble and can manage that.'

'What, me?'

'Yes, or would you rather faint?'

'Go for the fainting, that's more comfortable,' Rake said as he took hold of her hand under the table. 'I can spray the lens. Or maybe we only need to put a lens cover over it?'

'I'll take care of it,' said Christina. 'You are needed for greater and more important tasks.'

'OK, we're agreed on that then.' Martha settled the issue. 'So if you, Anna-Greta, activate the alarm in the Rembrandt room, then you, Christina, can spray the camera when I give the word. And you, Brains, cut the cable to the paintings while I stand in front of you. Will that work?'

Now they all started talking at once, and a long discussion ensued before they could settle on who would do what. When finally they agreed on a plan, some important problems still remained unresolved.

'How shall we get the paintings out?' Brains questioned. 'We can't run down the stairs.'

'We'll take the lift. And because it is rather compact, we will have to target small paintings.'

'Small paintings without an alarm,' said Christina, who had started to think like a real villain. 'Small enough so that we can put them in the basket of a Zimmer frame.'

'Exactly. We are not out after a Liljefors or a Rembrandt,' said Martha.

'And not something like *The Coronation of Gustav III* by Pilo,' said Anna-Greta, and she gave a loud neigh. Her father, a well-known lawyer, had had many valuable paintings at home in Djursholm, and from her childhood she knew quite a lot about art. Ever since her student days, she had gone to gallery openings and art exhibitions, and after becoming a pensioner she had improved her knowledge and studied art history at university. Pilo's painting of Gustav III . . . that painting must be all of five metres wide and two metres high.

'I've had a look at what sort of paintings they have,' Martha continued. 'There are some small works by August Strindberg and Anders Zorn, but they are meticulously wired up with alarms and firmly attached to the wall. Some of the other smaller paintings are only protected by a surveillance camera or a movement sensor, and one or two presumably don't have any alarm at all.'

'Really? How brilliant!' Christina exclaimed in delight and already started to plan what she would buy with the money. She had a tendency to spread her lipsticks and nail files all over the place, and was in need of a beauty box, for example a Titan beauty box in a pretty colour.

Their dinner turned into a sing-song beside the grand piano. Later on the playing cards came out. Rake sat with a beer and thought they ought to play bridge with real money. Anna-Greta pointed out that he didn't have any, and even if they – in the course of time – were to be swamped in money, what mattered was the here and now. With that, his proposal lost the vote. This made Rake a bit grumpy, and he whispered something into Christina's ear. He and Christina had spent some summers in Finland in their youth and both of them knew a little Finnish. So while the bridge game went on, Rake sang a Finnish folk song and then, with a verse he had made up himself, he told Christina which cards he held in his hand.

'I've learned five languages, and you insist on singing in Finnish. Can't you sing in Turkish, Greek or some other language I know?' Brains grumbled.

But Christina and Rake explained that Finnish folk songs simply couldn't be replaced with any others, and during the entire card session they continued to sing, including hints in the verses which meant that they won most of the card hands. It wasn't until Rake saw the prize – a bag of pistachio nuts that Anna-Greta had found in the bar cupboard – that he suggested they should go to see a film instead. With that, they marched off to the hotel cinema and enjoyed the skilfully made English film *The Great Bank Robbery* – where all the villains got away with their heist. Martha and Brains made copious notes, but Anna-Greta fell asleep and started snoring. When her snores started to match the volume of her neighs of laughter, she was quickly woken up and they agreed to call it a night.

By then, Brains had filled his notepad and had drawn lines back and forth between various squares, and seasoned the whole lot with a sudoku puzzle and parts of a crossword.

'Should the police happen to catch sight of this, they won't understand anything,' he said, pleased as punch, and he winked at Martha. 'I have learned a thing or two about false trails.'

Martha had such a nice, cosy feeling inside, that she simply had to smile.

A few hours later, Brains woke up. The first light of morning was filtering through the curtains, and he felt cold. Brains heard Rake's voice. Yes, his friend was standing outside the door and bawling for all he was worth. Brains went and opened the door.

'I'm freezing to death,' Rake complained and asked for a warm blanket and a glass of the hard stuff. When Brains had filled a glass for him, Rake sat up. He had slept with the window open, he said. And when it got colder he had retreated deeper and deeper under the covers. In doing so, he hadn't noticed that the temperature in the room had gone below zero. As a result, the radiator had frozen and then started to leak. When he woke there was water on the floor.

'"We're sinking, we're sinking, man the lifeboats!" I shouted out in panic and rushed to the door,' said Rake and emptied his glass.

'Really?'

'It's true! I phoned reception, but the staff down there didn't believe me – just like you. You should have seen their faces when they saw the water.'

'Rake, stop telling stories!' Brains replied, knowing all too well Rake's night-time excursions, which usually involved a quest for food or drink of some sort.

'Please, can you fill the glass and lend me some warm socks too.'

'That's enough for now. We must get some sleep.'

Rake was always wanting to tell lots of tall tales.

'You do know that truth beats fiction, don't you?' Rake ventured, and indicated the empty glass. 'Just a little more?'

Brains shook his head.

'Rake, I'll see you in the morning. Make sure you are in good shape then. We've got our second crime to commit.'

'I'm well aware of that. That's why I couldn't sleep. But the story about the radiator wasn't so bad, was it? Worth a glass of the hard stuff, don't you think?'

'Rake, go back to bed!'

'Sorry I disturbed you. I thought you'd be awake too.'

'Well, I certainly am now!'

'Yes, well, sorry. But the story is true. It must have happened to someone, somewhere, at some point.'

After his friend had left, Brains stared at the door for a long time. It wasn't easy being a member of a gang. Even if you did everything right yourself, others could mess things up. He was already worried about Christina. Now he would have to keep an eye on Rake too.

20

What a magnificent building! The National Museum exuded power and influence. Martha looked up at the monumental hall and the enormous staircase and felt very little. All those huge, famous paintings – and here was her small, humble self standing before them. The mural-like paintings with the scenes from Swedish history towered above her. The thought of what she was about to do – commit the art theft of the century – did nothing to soothe her nerves. After all, she had been a PE teacher during her working life, not a thief. They had discussed their plans time after time, putting the finishing touches to every part, but just one little mishap could derail the whole thing. Martha felt some consolation in the fact that they had rehearsed the theft of the paintings in the Princess Lilian suite. Now all they had to do was stay calm and not forget anything. She went up to the ticket office and paid for their tickets. The museum had only just opened for the day and they had unanimously chosen the earliest time to go so that they could be as undisturbed as possible. They assumed that the security guards would not be 'on their toes' at this time of the morning.

'Welcome to the museum, madam. Are you cold?' the

cashier enquired when she saw that Martha had not taken her gloves off.

'My rheumatism,' Martha answered with a smile, and returned to the others.

She looked up at the staircase. The steps were as high as tombstones. Why did the paintings have to hang so *very* high up on the walls? Wouldn't it suffice if they were hung fairly high up? Surely half that height would have been more than enough. She handed the tickets out to her friends, and they all swiped them through one of those little scanners and proceeded to the lift.

'I wonder whether we can all fit in at once,' said Brains.

'It's probably best if we go in with our Zimmer frames facing forward,' Martha advised. She was eager to have time to check the layout of the room upstairs.

The lift went up very slowly and it seemed to take an eternity before it reached the second floor. Martha felt the tension increase, and she hoped that Rake would remember to put up the OUT OF ORDER sign on the lift. It was a very simple trick, but they were sure it would work. Brains had printed out the sign on his computer, glued it onto a piece of cardboard, and then made two holes for a piece of string so that they could hang it up. Martha was proud of how they had thought of so many details. Rake was also keeping watch down by the lift doors. He hadn't liked being given that task. Not until Martha had explained that the success of the robbery depended on him had he given in and agreed.

Having arrived on the second floor, the four of them started to walk towards the exhibitions. The following day would be the opening for the sensational Sins and Desires display in the temporary exhibition hall. Or was it Desires and Sins that the exhibition was called? Martha couldn't really remember. But it was indecent, nevertheless. Martha had assumed that most of the security guards would congregate there today. They would certainly be taking the opportunity to have a close look before the exhibition opened to the public.

They walked in the direction of the great halls. As expected, nobody was there yet, but it wouldn't be long before visitors started arriving on the second floor, so they had to act immediately. Supported by her warped walking stick, Anna-Greta turned to the left towards the Dutch masterpieces, while the others went off to the French nineteenth-century paintings. They all tried to walk nice and slowly, and Brains had greased the wheels of the Zimmer frames with his special rapeseed oil mixture. After a while, Christina suddenly stopped.

'I've forgotten my medicines,' she said.

'But surely you don't need them just now.' Martha looked at her with a worried expression.

'They are for raising my blood pressure,' said Christina, ashamed of her carelessness.

'Then you don't need to worry. This won't take long, and we will soon be back at the hotel,' Brains consoled her. 'Besides, you are actually *meant* to faint.'

Martha walked slightly behind Brains, now and then glancing at his Zimmer frame. She recalled that she had wondered about the sturdy construction, and had asked him why the tubes on the sides of the frame were so wide. 'For my tools, of course,' he had answered with a big smile across his face. The wire cutters fitted nicely inside. After a while they reached the Impressionists and other nineteenth-century French artists. For a brief moment Martha forgot why she was there, and her interest in art took over. She was particularly fond of Cézanne, Monet and Degas, and would gladly have laid her hands on Degas' lovely bronze sculpture of a ballet dancer as a present for Brains. But regrettably it was far too heavy. They moved on and went past the doors to the erotic exhibition, Desires and Sins – or was it Desire and Beauty? Oh dear, now she had got it muddled again. From inside the exhibition room one could hear shouts and laughter, and Martha marvelled that looking at nudity could inspire such hilarity. At least the attention of the security guards had been diverted.

Martha and Brains exchanged furtive looks and confidently approached two small paintings signed Monet and Renoir. They pretended to study the French Impressionists but their eyes were directed discreetly up towards the cables. These weren't reinforced with steel tubes but they were pretty thick. Martha laid her winter coat across the Zimmer frame basket and stood to the right of Brains, while Christina discreetly positioned herself to the left. Brains quickly unscrewed the top of his Zimmer frame bar and lifted out the cable cutters.

'Christina, give me a bit more cover, please,' he whispered.

'Wait, I have to do the camera lens first,' she said, and hurried across to the surveillance camera. But when she got there, she saw that the humidifier had been removed and now there was nothing to stand on. Luckily she discovered the electrical wire to the camera. She quickly pulled it out, and went back to her post. Then she stood on her toes next to Brains and made herself as broad as possible.

'Now we just need to wait for Anna-Greta to trigger the alarm in the Dutch room,' Martha whispered. Christina and

Brains were ready for action, but found it hard to stand still. Brains was licking his lips and Christina was picking at her cuticles. Waiting. At last the alarm went off, and Brains lifted the cutters up to the cable. At that moment, Christina fainted, sending her handbag flying.

'Oh my God, she wasn't meant to faint now,' said Martha, horrified. 'She was going to cover you.'

'Lift her legs up, that usually helps,' Brains answered, while cutting the first cable.

'But I've got to stand in the way of the other surveillance camera,' Martha answered. To be on the safe side she gave Christina's feet a bit of a pull. A few more snips could be heard and then Renoir's *Conversation: An Impression From Paris* fell forward and almost hit the floor. At the last second, they managed to catch it and push it in under Martha's coat. The alarm was screaming madly in the other room and Martha was glad of the relative calm here among the Impressionists. In this room, there was a silent alarm where the signal went directly to the police, a feature that Martha had noticed during her exploration of the museum. The diversion Anna-Greta had created had given them the few extra minutes they needed. Brains hurriedly nailed up a sign where the painting had hung, a sign that had also been printed out on the hotel's printer, and then glued onto cardboard: INVENTORY BEING UNDERTAKEN, it said.

That was the Renoir out of the way. Next was the beautiful Monet painting *From the Mouth of the Scheldt*. They moved to the right and Martha saw how Brains was struggling with the two cables before finally managing to cut them. He rapidly pulled out the third sign and hung it up in place of the painting. He was stressed, and Martha could tell that he just wanted to be off. She felt the same way but knew that they must restrain themselves. She had already seen the doors opening at the far end of the hall and noticed that the security guards were on their way. She just managed to stash the second painting under her winter coat before one of the guards caught sight of them. Martha hurried to bend down over Christina – now was the time she really should have fainted, and only as a pretence, not for real!

'Wake up!' Martha hollered, raising her friend's legs up in the air. The security guard hurried to her side.

'Help us! A man tried to steal her handbag – he ran that way!' said Martha, pointing towards the Dutch room. The guard looked confused, but when Martha tried to lift up her unconscious friend, he helped her. Together, they got Christina back onto her feet and leaned her against the Zimmer frame. The guard picked up her handbag and handed it over. Then Christina came to her senses.

'Is it finished now?' she asked.

'Catch him, catch the thief, he ran that way,' Martha shouted shrilly, trying to drown out Christina's voice. 'He had a beard, long brown hair and smelt horrid.' Martha pointed again. The Zimmer frame was overloaded and she expected it to collapse at any minute. Brains had worked out how heavy a weight her Zimmer frame could cope with for the paintings – but that had not included Christina's sixty kilos. Martha sneaked a look at Brains, and caught his eye.

'I'll look after her,' Brains said to the guard. 'She's my wife. I shouldn't have turned my back. She must be very shocked.'

The security guard nodded, somewhat perplexed, and hurried towards the alarm which was still sounding. When he had disappeared, Martha cast a final glance at the place where the Monet had hung. She looked, closed her eyes and opened them again. Instead of INVENTORY BEING UNDERTAKEN, there was a handwritten sign. Martha had to adjust her specs: BACK SOON, she read.

'Oh my God! It's the sign that Christina hung up when she went down to buy something in the shop,' Martha exclaimed, and was just about to rush forward and take it down when a group of tourists entered the room.

'We've no choice, we must leave,' Brains hissed.

'But the sign—'

'Nobody knows who has put it there. Come on!'

Martha swallowed, took a deep breath and pretended to be unperturbed. Slowly and majestically, she and Brains took their Zimmer frames towards the lift, closely followed by Christina. Martha had given Christina a fruit pastille, and when they had reached the lift her cheeks had reacquired quite a nice colour. Martha patted her encouragingly on her cheek, opened the lift door and pushed both Christina and the Zimmer frame with the paintings in. Then she pressed the DOWN button. Now they just had to wait for Anna-Greta.

In the entrance lobby, Rake heard the lift descending. He removed the OUT OF ORDER sign and opened the lift doors.

Christina stepped out of the lift and then Rake stepped in, taking her place. Once inside, he quickly switched his Zimmer frame with Martha's. After he had done that, he covered the two stolen paintings in her basket with his own coat, and put her winter coat on the Zimmer frame which would now go back up with the lift again. He carefully opened the lift doors.

When Christina gave the sign that the coast was clear he quickly left the lift together with the loot.

'Righto,' he mumbled and put the OUT OF ORDER sign back onto the doors. Then he smiled encouragingly at Christina, took out his comb and combed his hair into a neat parting.

'Right, off we go,' he said and walked calmly out of the museum with Christina supported on Martha's Zimmer frame, which was somewhat more wobbly than his own and now weighed down with valuable art.

That maddening shrieking noise! The alarm was absolutely unbearable and Anna-Greta wished she could have rushed straight out of the room. Never in her wildest dreams had she imagined that an alarm could be so loud. And she had only leaned forwards and poked at Rembrandt's *The Kitchen Maid*. Then all hell had broken loose. When the alarm's howl filled the exhibition hall, she got such a fright that she almost forgot to lie down on the floor as planned. She flopped onto the floor a bit too quickly and exclaimed, 'Ouch, ouch!', and it didn't get any better when a horde of security guards rushed towards her to overpower the thief. Just as they were about to throw themselves over her, they noticed what kind of person was lying there.

'Stop, look, it's an old lady!' The first security guard yelled – in time to stop the others pouncing on her.

'Oh, I'm sorry, I don't know what happened. I must have lashed out with my stick when I tripped,' Anna-Greta shouted in an effort to be heard above the alarm. At the same time she attempted to get back onto her feet. One of the guards helped her up and handed over her walking stick.

'But it's completely crooked,' he said.

'That's probably why I fell,' Anna-Greta shouted in answer. 'I really do apologize profusely.'

The guards looked perplexed.

'The alarm!' said Anna-Greta with her hands over her ears. One of the guards rushed away to turn it off, while the others remained with her. She brushed the dust off her clothes.

'Did you see a bearded man with long brown hair running through here?' one of the guards asked her.

'Oh, yes, indeed. There was a young bearded man here a little while ago. He seemed very nice. Unfortunately, I don't know where he's gone. I just fell down.'

The guard's smile vanished.

'Young and kind?'

'Oh yes, I wish he were my son.'

'Usch, we'll go back,' the other guards mumbled.

'Was there a thief?' Anna-Greta wondered.

'Nothing's been stolen, as far as we know,' said the guard.

'Well, that's good.' Anna-Greta smiled and leaned some of her weight on her walking stick. It misbehaved again and she would have fallen over once more if a guard hadn't got hold of her. 'I really ought to buy a new walking stick, don't you think? This one is rather dangerous.'

'Indeed, madam, and now you really must take care,' said the guard, holding her under her arm. 'Are you all right?'

Anna-Greta nodded.

'Right then, we must report back that it was a false alarm, but if you see the bearded man again, please contact us. We are sitting over there,' he said and pointed to the room with the temporary exhibition.

'Ah, I see, that's where you are – well, enjoy yourselves,' Anna-Greta said before she could stop herself. Then she thanked them for their help and limped off towards the lift. She hurried as much as she dared without arousing attention, and sincerely hoped that she wasn't walking suspiciously fast. To her relief, Martha and Brains were waiting for her at the lift. Martha had come up in the lift with Rake's Zimmer frame and her winter coat, and so far everything was going well.

'Hurry now!' Martha urged, and when all three had entered the lift she quickly pressed the DOWN button. Once back in the entrance lobby, they looked cautiously around, waited while a visitor walked past and then discreetly nipped out the lift. Brains immediately removed the OUT OF ORDER sign, but then he had second thoughts and hung it up again. After which they went towards the main entrance doors at a leisurely pace. Reaching the door, Martha put her coat on just as the first police officers were rushing into the museum. Martha, Brains and Anna-Greta politely stepped aside and let them pass before continuing through the door and down the outer steps. Out on the street they headed straight towards the Grand Hotel.

The police officers arriving in the second police car also happened to catch a glimpse of the group of old people before jumping out of the car and rushing into the museum. But inside the lobby they came to a halt: the lift was out of order and they would have to use those long stairs.

21

The champagne was almost finished and the bowls of straw-berries and jelly babies had been emptied. But the five old friends still danced around the suite, as best they could, waving champagne flutes in celebration. Each of them kept going up to the paintings to admire them – they couldn't believe that they had really done it!

'Just imagine, we've got hold of a genuine Renoir,' Anna-Greta sighed devoutly and carefully patted a corner of the painting. 'I could never have dreamed of this.'

For a large part of the day, they had discussed which painting was best – without coming to any agreement. Martha was especially fond of the Monet and remembered that there were more paintings by him at the museum. For a moment she wondered whether they should go and steal them too. But then she recalled what she had read in several novels: it was foolish to repeat one's crimes. It increased the risk of getting caught. First they must get some ransom money for the paintings they had already stolen. She calmed down and went out onto the balcony where her fellow criminals were standing with champagne glasses in their hands. With smug expressions, they watched the chaos down on the street below.

'To think that we are the ones who have caused this,' laughed Christina as she pointed. A large area outside the National Museum was cordoned off, journalists were running around, police cars drove back and forth, and several TV teams were filming. Lots of people were standing outside the barriers, gawking.

'There couldn't possibly have been a robbery at the National Museum, could there?' said Anna-Greta before releasing such a horsey neigh that the others couldn't help but join in. They toasted one another and even took a few dance steps up there on the balcony. When the police cars had disappeared they tired of the spectacle and withdrew to the suite. Rake and Brains wanted to have a swim before dinner, and, while the men were doing this, the women sat on the sofa and looked out across Stockholm through the enormous panorama window. Christina was busying herself with a watercolour of the Royal Palace, and Anna-Greta unwound with a sudoku puzzle. Martha observed them and was envious of their calmness. She was unable to take it easy at all because she had suddenly thought of something: *Where could they store the paintings while they waited for the ransom money?* When she was young, she had planned many consecutive things, and was proud of her planning skills, always having been able to keep several things in her head at the same time. Now she had completely overlooked this essential detail.

She got up and went into the bedroom where the paintings were leaning against the foot of the bed. If she looked at them long enough, perhaps she might think of something? But while she stood there, she became all the more worried. She was the one who had planned the theft and urged the others to join her, so she must be the one to complete the assignment in a smart manner. *But where in the name of heaven could they put the paintings?* All day long they had watched the police going in and out of the museum and surely soon they would be coming to the hotel to seek out witnesses. What if they searched the premises? Martha wasn't too sure if they could do this. The English crime novels were only fiction after all. And as she stood there she thought of something else. The staff down in reception had taken the number of their credit card when they checked in. So the hotel would not only know who was staying in the Princess Lilian suite but they would also have done a credit check. If the account with the monthly pension deposits were to suddenly increase by several million, undoubtedly it would attract attention. Martha let out a little sigh. Being a criminal was more difficult than she had thought. She would simply have to discuss this with the others.

'Has anyone thought about which bank account we can use for the ransom money?' she asked.

'Haven't you?' Anna-Greta wondered, and looked up with surprise from her sudoku puzzle. 'You were the one who was organizing everything – you made a particular point of emphasizing that.'

Martha tried to keep calm.

'They took the number of the credit card when we checked in. So where can the museum deposit the ransom money?'

'It will have to be like in the good old days, a suitcase full of banknotes,' said Anna-Greta.

'First and foremost, we must hide the paintings,' Christina interrupted them, being of the opinion that one should deal with things in the right order. 'I saw a good place under the bed.'

'That's too risky. What if they vacuum there?' said Martha.

'They never do that at hotels.'

'Oh yes, they certainly will here at the Grand Hotel,' Martha answered and she started to pace the room. 'No, we must think of something else. The simplest things are always the hardest to think of.'

That sounded too abstract for Anna-Greta, who shook her head. Christina chewed on the end of her paintbrush.

'"Hear a prayer from devout lips",' she mumbled.

'You what?'

'A quote from Carl Jonas Love Almqvist,' Christina answered.

Martha sighed; Christina was quoting from her Swedish classics again. She wandered round the suite once more. She peered in at the kitchen, walked slowly through the library, visited the bedroom, and finally ended up in the lounge again. Not a single good idea had occurred to her. For a long time she stood there and stared at the palace and the Riksdag building before she turned round.

'Have you thought about how different we are? We belong to a very rare group of thieves who aren't afraid of ending up in prison; we just want to delay that a little while. So we can take bigger risks. I suggest that we hide the paintings right under the nose of the police. Where they won't think of looking, and won't start searching until we have got the ransom money.'

'I know where – the museum!' Anna-Greta called out.

'No, I'm serious,' said Martha.

'Well, we have the paintings here, so why not enjoy the fine art in the meanwhile,' Christina said, putting down her paintbrush. Her watercolour of the palace was not finished but mainly resembled one of those paintings you can buy at the Salvation Army charity shop. With a sigh, she put her brush and paints back into her big bag.

'Enjoy some fine art?' The others looked at her, puzzled.

'Yes, I know a safe place where nobody will look. Give me a few minutes and I'll arrange it.'

Martha and Anna-Greta watched as she walked out of the room with her bag over her shoulder.

'Leave her to it,' said Martha. 'You never know what she might come up with.'

22

Rake sat with Brains in the luxury bathroom of their suite and listened to exotic drum music from the loudspeakers. The green light pulsated and steam rose up from the stones. He stretched out to reach the water ladle and gave Brains a questioning look.

'A little more steam, don't you think?'

Brains grunted and Rake took that as a 'yes'. He poured a ladle of water onto the stones and then leaned back with a satisfied sigh. He was so pleased about all the praise he had received. After that night visit to Brains he had finally fallen asleep but had subsequently woken with a persistent headache. At that point, he had doubted whether he should take part in the robbery at all, but after an ice-cold shower he had managed to pull himself together. Now Martha had said that it was thanks to him that the robbery had succeeded. And that was of course true. He had undoubtedly had the greatest responsibility, and if it hadn't been for him they would never have got the paintings out of the museum. The music streamed out into the sauna room, and he hummed along with it.

'Shall we throw some more water onto the stones?' He stretched out to pick up the ladle.

'No, take it easy, it'll get too hot. This isn't an international competition for sauna bathers,' said Brains.

'Don't worry. We aren't in Finland, we just want to get clean.' Rake laughed and threw on a little more water, which resulted in clouds of steam. 'Incidentally, this reminds me of the steam room,' he went on, and held his hands in front of his face when the steam reached him. 'And the safes.'

'The security boxes? I've already forgotten about that robbery. Stealing a Renoir and a Monet – that beats everything,' said Brains as he raised his beer bottle. 'And without machine guns and diversionary fires, too. Cheers to you, you old crook!'

The men clinked their beer bottles and Rake thought that this was one of the best moments of his life. They had been gone from the retirement home for only four days and he had already experienced more during that time than during the whole of the previous year.

A heavy knocking on the door gave him a start.

'Listen, you two, hurry up. You must come out and look at something,' Martha called out. Rake threw up his hands, spilling the beer.

'I don't know how you can tolerate the way she bosses everyone around.'

'That's just what is so good about her, Rake. She keeps track of us all. Without her, we wouldn't be here at all.'

Rake went quiet for a moment; he hadn't thought of that. 'But I prefer Christina. She is quieter and doesn't make such a song and dance of things. And she is pretty, too – indeed, I would say elegant.'

'She's a lovely woman, but all sorts of women make the world go round, don't you agree?'

'Oh, yes, you should have seen when I was a sailor on the boats to the Philippines, the women there! One of them had such enormous—' Rake exclaimed but was cut short by more knocking on the door.

'Rake, we can talk about that later,' said Brains and got up. 'We'd better find out what she wants.'

The men wrapped their towels around them, took their bottles of beer and opened the door. For a brief moment Brains felt a flutter of butterflies in his tummy. Surely the police hadn't already tracked them down? Then he saw Martha's determined look.

'Have you thought about where we will keep the paintings while we're waiting for the ransom money?' she barked.

Brains and Rake looked at each other in confusion.

'No, not exactly.'

'And nor had we. But now Christina has hidden them. I want you to try to find them!'

'Oh God, how childish!' said Rake.

'This will be fun,' Brains chuckled.

And with that they started to hunt around, wrapped in their wet towels, in the Princess Lilian suite for two stolen paintings worth about thirty million kronor. But try as they might, they couldn't find either of them.

23

Inspector Arne Lönnberg had received a telephone call from an overwrought young woman at the Diamond House retirement home. Five people had disappeared, even though the home had been closely guarded. He looked through his papers. Could it really be true? Five people didn't usually disappear at the same time, especially since the people concerned were not exactly young – they were at least seventy-five years old or more. The woman who phoned him had sounded rather anxious and had asked him to be discreet. If it became known that people had disappeared, the retirement home risked losing their clients, she had said. Clients? He snorted. Being a client was surely something you chose yourself. Nowadays it was mainly children and grandchildren who put you away in a home. You could hardly be considered a client then, could you? He was lucky that he was single, and would not have to put up with well-meaning children who involved themselves in his living arrangements when he got old.

He thumbed the piece of paper on his desk and wondered what he should do. Old people could walk out from retirement homes as the mood took them, at least in theory, and the police had neither the will, the resources, nor the authority to go out looking for them. One could, of course, put them on the observation list in various registers, that was true, and then they would be noticed only if they tried to leave the country. But otherwise, no. As long as no next of kin reported them missing, and they hadn't committed a crime, it was not the business of the police. Inspector Lönnberg leaned back in his chair. He did not begrudge the old people having a good time. He hoped that they had gone on a ferry cruise in secret or were keeping out of the way of some greedy relatives. There were, in fact, some cases where old people didn't get a moment's peace because their children were so intent on getting their inheritance.

He took the piece of paper with his notes and wrote down the name and telephone number of the girl who had phoned, in case she got in touch again. But then he changed his mind, screwed up the paper and threw it into the waste-paper basket. If they phoned from the retirement home again, he could note the oldies' names in the register. But they should at least be able to enjoy a few days at liberty before being forced back into the fold.

The men had become impatient after having to walk around the suite with their wet towels looking for the paintings. The Princess Lilian suite was as large as a big city flat with its five rooms, and full of potential hiding places. So they quite simply failed to find the paintings. In the end, they returned to their room, had a shower and got dressed. They had hardly finished when they heard Christina's joyful voice.

'You are not allowed to give up, try again!' Her eye glowed, and she quoted yet another of the classic Swedish poets, but playfully added in a few words about towels – which indicated that she was in a particularly good mood. She was otherwise always very careful to treat the classics with due respect.

Since nobody had found the paintings, she organized everything like a game and the person who found them was promised a large bowl of chocolate creams. Anna-Greta pursed her lips, Brains raised his eyebrows and Rake smiled to himself. Martha, for her part, was pleased that her friend had brightened up and was so full of ideas. She thought it was because they had left Diamond House and that she enjoyed Rake's company. Perhaps Christina had even gone and fallen in love?

'It was such a lot of trouble to steal the paintings that I really hope you haven't hidden them so well that we can't find them again,' said Rake.

'Oh no, But as you have travelled so much in the world you ought to have enough imagination to find them,' Christina teased.

Rake straightened his back and looked around him with the air of somebody who knew what he was about. He so very much wanted to please Christina, so it must be he who found the paintings. Granted, he was not a connoisseur of fine art, but during his years as a seaman he had now and then visited various museums when in port. He started looking at the paintings on the walls in the various rooms, went up to them, lifted them up in the air and checked if there was anything written on the back. Then he came to an abrupt halt. Above the grand piano hung some paintings that he recognized. One showed a man and a woman sitting and talking at a café; the other was a river scene with old sailing boats. But in the painting that he likened to the Renoir the man had acquired a strange hat, long hair and spectacles. And in Monet's painting from Scheldt there

131

was a modern little yacht that hadn't been there before. Now he understood. Christina had hidden the paintings in her own very special way. A wave of tenderness flooded over him. The clever woman had quite simply altered them with the help of some watercolour paint – not very much, but just enough to confuse the observer. The signatures had been altered too. He examined the bottom-right corner. Instead of Renoir's signature he could now read Rene Ihre and Monet had been given the name Mona Ed.

24

The day after the great Zimmer frame robbery, the five of them sat down in the library at the Grand Hotel and read the daily papers. Now and then the rustle of paper, mutterings and titters could be heard, but it was otherwise quiet. None of them wanted to be disturbed in this delightful reading and they savoured every word. In the end, Martha couldn't restrain herself.

'Have you seen this? It says that it was one of the most skilful art robberies ever carried out!' Her eyes sparkled. 'Much smarter than when the museum was robbed the last time. Then the robbers had machine guns, set fire to cars and went off with the paintings in a stolen boat. Completely wrong. You shouldn't attract so much attention.'

'No, indeed,' said Rake with a disapproving glance at Martha's Zimmer frame. Brains had reattached the orange reflector arm to it.

'They think it's a bearded man with long brown hair who carried out the robbery,' Martha continued.

From Christina came a low, chuckling laugh and Anna-Greta was close to exploding with joy.

'And he – the bearded man – had a kind look,' Martha read on.

'Yes, I said that because it sounded so genuine. A real criminal would never express themselves like that,' said Anna-Greta, releasing such a joyful neigh that Rake was forced to put his hands over his ears. Anna-Greta had never married, and that didn't surprise him one bit. Perhaps there may have been suitors in her youth, but she would have laughed them to death – if they hadn't already been blown away.

'Well, I never! Have you heard this?' exclaimed Martha as she looked up from her newspaper. 'It's in the *Express* on page seven. The reporter is speculating about the BACK SOON sign. He thinks it is about a religious sect which believes in the return of Jesus to earth. His alternative suggestion being that it is from a terrorist league planning new deeds. The police have increased their resources regardless of the speculation.'

'Increased their resources on account of some oldies on the run,' Brains said, smiling.

'And a sign saying BACK SOON,' Christina giggled and pulled out her nail file. Now they were all laughing so much that they could be heard out in reception. Martha noticed this and hushed the others.

'Mind you, perhaps it was rather unfortunate that the sign was handwritten. That is a clue that might be our downfall,' she said.

'But Martha, you surely haven't forgotten why we are doing this?' Brains pointed out.

'No, but prison can wait a while.'

A murmur of agreement was heard from the others. Some other hotel guests walked past on their way to the Veranda restaurant, but they remained undisturbed in the library. Martha leaned forward.

'Even if they suspect other villains, we mustn't relax,' she started. 'We never know when they might start to look for us, and what if Nurse Barbara—'

'The most important thing is that we get our money,' Anna-Greta cut her off. 'Why don't we send our ransom demand to the press today?'

'Yes, we can send a fax, that's quick,' Christina suggested.

'That's old fashioned now there are computers,' Brains objected.

'But they can trace those,' said Christina, who had borrowed one of Martha's crime novels, *Silent Traces in Cyber Space*, now that she didn't have access to her beloved classics.

'Pah, then we'll do it in the traditional way, like at school,' said Rake after a moment's thought. 'We'll cut out the words and letters we need from a newspaper. Then we can glue them onto a piece of paper, put the message in an envelope and put that in a postbox.'

There was silence for a few moments while they all pondered the idea.

'But the post is so slow nowadays,' Anna-Greta pointed out, 'and it doesn't feel really safe.'

'Then I've got a better idea,' said Rake. 'We'll phone. I am good at disguising my voice.'

'No, let me phone,' Anna-Greta chipped in, but then they all protested. Nobody wanted to risk that she would start laughing by mistake. After much discussion they finally agreed to put together a message with letters cut out from the papers. And they would all wear gloves so as not to leave any fingerprints.

'But one problem still remains,' said Martha. 'How are we going to receive the ransom money?'

135

'We shall ask them to put the money in a suitcase on one of the big cruise ferries to Finland. Then we will get to go on a round-trip cruise to Helsinki too,' Brains suggested.

'What a brilliant idea,' said Martha, who was keen to go on a cruise with him. Those big ferries were like floating hotels with dance bands and the works, and she might be able to get Brains onto the dance floor.

'A cruise, yes, why not, it would be fun to go to sea again,' Rake said. 'When I sailed to Australia the waves were so high that you couldn't even imagine it. In fact, they were—'

'Wouldn't it be smarter to ask them to leave the suitcase at Arlanda airport?' Anna-Greta interrupted him. 'Then they might think that we are major international-league criminals.'

'But what if they confuse us with terrorists and start shooting at us?' said Christina, who was by nature a rather anxious type. The others didn't think this likely, but to satisfy everybody they settled for the cruise. It did after all feel like the safer option.

'We'll post the letter today and give them a week to get hold of the money,' Martha proposed. 'But first we must buy newspapers and write the letter indicating the ransom required.'

'Right you are. How much shall we ask for, do you think?' asked Brains.

'Ten million,' Rake suggested.

'But' – Anna-Greta looked suddenly concerned – 'that would be an awful lot of banknotes. Let's see . . . one thousand thousand-kronor notes makes a million, and ten thousand thousand-kronor notes would be ten million. And all of it in a suitcase? No, I don't think that would work. An honourable bank transfer would be preferable.'

A somewhat pained silence ensued as nobody had considered that detail.

'Thousand-kronor notes would attract attention. Perhaps it would be better with five-hundred-kronor notes,' Brains said.

'Or why not twenty-kronor notes with the nice portrait of Selma Lagerlöf? They look so distinguished. And then it would be a bit cultural too.'

'Can't you count? How many banknotes do you think that would be? No, let me think. A five-hundred-kronor note weighs about half a gram. All in all it would be about seven kilos of notes,' said Anna-Greta after some quick mental arithmetic. 'But the notes will take up a lot of room. Let me see now, if we pack twenty thousand five-hundred-kronor notes they would make a pile four metres high,' she went on.

'Then perhaps it would be best with shopping trolleys,' said Martha. 'Let me see. Four metres of notes ought to fit into two decent-sized canvas trolleys. Urbanista has one of those shopping bags on wheels. There is one brand which they call Pink Panther. That will hold fifty-five litres.'

'A pink shopping cart? Let's keep a bit of order here,' muttered Rake.

'They have ones in black or a more masculine brown too, and with an extendable handle,' Martha continued. 'And they are rather flat and high so the museum ought to be able to stack the notes in them really neatly.'

'Keep talking. I'll go and buy the newspapers in the hotel shop in the meantime,' said Rake, who had tired of the discussion and wanted to do something constructive.

'I need some things from the shop too. I've been wearing the same outfit for three days,' Christina mumbled. She put away her nail file and got up too.

'But Christina, why go to the shop when you could do an Internet order?' Anna-Greta asked.

'Because I like my clothes close fitting.'

'Mark my words, that is not an advantage at our age,' said Anna-Greta, but by then Christina had already gone off with Rake.

Half an hour later, they were back in the suite. Now Christina was wearing a red jumper in the same shade as her newly purchased nail polish and a new scarf around her neck. On her wrist she had a shiny new silver bracelet.

'Ahah, close fitting, I see . . .' said Martha.

'We are staying at the Grand Hotel,' Christina explained. 'And it will go on the hotel bill.'

Anna-Greta glared at Christina. Not only was the silly woman spending her money, but she was also fawning over Rake! She herself wouldn't have anything against a bit of courtly behaviour from him, and she couldn't understand why he was interested in Christina of all people. Anna-Greta was much more intelligent, well educated and had lived in a large house on Strandvägen in Djursholm, one of the most desirable suburbs in Stockholm. But evidently it didn't make any difference. Men's tastes were very strange. She would have been only too happy to marry a suitable beau, but the problem was that she had never been courted by the right person. Her great love from her student days had come from the working classes, and, at the time, her father had intervened and forbidden the romance. She was going to marry someone who was well educated or at least wealthy, he had said. So in the end she didn't marry at all. For some years she had considered putting an advert in the paper, but although she had come close to doing so several times she hadn't dared. She sighed and felt sorry for herself, but then found herself thinking about the cruise to Finland. Perhaps she might meet a nice widower on the ship . . .

'Don't just sit there dreaming, Anna-Greta, we must put our ransom letter together,' said Martha.

The five of them sat around the table. The champagne bottle came out, the nuts and strawberries too, and they started to compose the most hard-hitting message they could think of. Although they only had to put together a few sentences, it took a long time, and it took until the champagne bottle was empty for them to produce a note that they were all satisfied with. While Anna-Greta hummed the tune of a popular hit from the sixties, which happened to be about money, they carefully cut out the words and letters and glued them onto a sheet of A4 paper.

Renoir's Conversation and Monet's From the Mouth of the Schelde are in our custody. The paintings will be returned in exchange for a ransom of only 10 million kronor. The money should be put into two black Urbanista shopping trolleys and placed on the Silja Serenade cruise ship bound for Finland and leaving Stockholm on 27 March, before 16.00 hours. Further instructions will be sent later. As soon as we have received the money, the paintings will be returned to the museum.

P.S. If you contact the police, we shall destroy the paintings.

Christina nearly signed the note with her own name, but the others stopped her at the last moment. They read through the

139

message, singing a song while they did so. Anna-Greta was pleased that she had got them to write 'only 10 million'. The museum people would understand that they were being offered a good deal – other villains would certainly ask for more. Martha, however, was not completely satisfied.

'Doesn't it sound a bit too kind to be written by real criminals?' she wondered. 'Do art thieves give the paintings back personally? Oughtn't they to be fetched from somewhere? What I mean is, shouldn't we spice it up a little so that they don't think we are amateurs?'

'But if we are nice, they might be more likely to pay,' said Christina.

They all thought this was probably correct, and in the end they agreed to post the ransom note without making any amendments. Since they didn't dare use the hotel's notepaper and envelopes, they simply folded the paper in half and taped it, wrote the address of the National Museum and put a stamp on. Wearing gloves all the time.

'In fact, we could just have gone across with the letter and then we'd have saved a stamp,' Anna-Greta pointed out, but then she was spontaneously booed by the others.

A little while later, Martha took the note to the postbox next to the underground station just round the corner. She looked at the flap on the postbox for a long time before dropping the note in. Then she patted the postbox a few times and realized just how nervous she actually was. Now it wasn't a question of an inconsequential minor robbery. They had chosen the path of crime, and now there was no return. They had become *criminals*. On her way back to the hotel she pondered the word. Criminal . . . it sounded so exciting! She wanted to do a little dance step despite her age, and immediately felt years younger. Her life had acquired a new purpose and she was pleased at the thought of getting so much money in two shopping trolleys. It would have been much more boring if they had been simply sent to a bank account via an abstract financial transaction. Now they could go on the cruise ship to Finland and enjoy themselves, as well as experience the excitement of trying to get the ransom money home without anyone discovering them. How many people her age got to take part in such adventures?

25

Chief Inspector Petterson found it incomprehensible. Two valuable paintings had been stolen from the National Museum, and although the police had set up road blocks, checked all the passengers on trains and planes, and contacted various car-hire firms, they had no leads. There were no witnesses at the museum either. Of course that couldn't be right. The thieves couldn't simply have gone up in smoke. They had obviously escaped in a car before the museum staff had realized that the paintings had been stolen. He had heard that museum staff don't always realize the value of what they have in their collections. Chief Inspector Petterson was a middle-aged man in his prime but with a melancholy frame of mind. The case seemed hopeless. He had no idea at all as to how the art theft could be solved. He knew everything about weapons, ammunition, car chases and blackmail attempts, but this? The police hadn't even got in any tips from the underworld. The informants they had contacted had not heard a thing.

'There must be several years' planning behind this,' said his colleague Rolf Strömbeck, a bearded man of upper middle age, as he sorted the papers on his desk. 'Imagine getting away without leaving any tracks or other leads. We don't have fingerprints and we can't see anyone suspicious on the pictures from the surveillance cameras either. I just don't understand this.'

'The camera that covered the room with the French Impressionists was not on – the thieves had pulled out the plug.' Petterson sighed. 'Pah, let's go and get a cup of coffee.'

The two men got up and then remained standing beside the refreshment table where the coffee machine stood along with a selection of fruit and biscuits. This was Chief Inspector Petterson's sixth cup of coffee that day. The coffee was hot and smelt of old plastic, but at least it provided him with some much-needed caffeine. There must be other clues; it was just a question of discovering them. That set him to thinking about the museum visitors.

'It's time to map out who was at the museum that day, and bring them in for questioning. There must surely have been other people there besides those confused old folks that the security guards mentioned.'

'The old people talked of a man with brown hair that one of the old girls thought was terribly kind. She had even wished that he was her own son,' sighed his colleague.

'But one of the other old girls accused him of being a thief. He is said to have tried to snatch her handbag. Those poor OAPs must have been shocked by the alarm.'

Petterson went quiet, and started ruminating about old age. To think that you could become so confused. Would he himself end up like that? From now on he ought to eat more fruit and veg; he had heard that such a diet was good for your brain. He grabbed an apple from the fruit bowl and nodded to his colleague.

'Shall we take a look at the signs? They are all that the thieves left behind.'

'As if we're going to be any the wiser for those . . .'

They returned to the investigation room and sat down at the desk. There lay the three signs that had been found at the museum: OUT OF ORDER, INVENTORY BEING UNDERTAKEN and BACK SOON.

Chief Inspector Petterson tried to remember what had happened. The signs had delayed the police, and several hours passed before they realized that the lift actually worked. Then there were the other two signs. The police officer in charge at the scene of the crime had thought that everything was as it should be in the room for nineteenth-century French paintings, and had directed their efforts to searching for stolen paintings in the other exhibition rooms. They had concentrated on the temporary exhibition, Sins and Desires, where every painting was scrutinized closely. It was only when one of the curators established that there were no paintings missing from the new exhibition that they enlarged the scene-of-crime investigation to include the other areas. After that, they had started studying the two signs in the Impressionist exhibition with renewed interest. INVENTORY BEING UNDERTAKEN . . . Petterson had sent a group of colleagues down to the storerooms to see if the paintings were there, while his technical staff checked through ledgers and computer files. The police devoted a great deal of time and effort to this, but when no Renoirs or Monets were found, they realized that those were indeed the paintings that had been stolen. They weren't just any old paintings. Claude Monet's Schelde scene and the work by Renoir had been stolen once before. It was incredible that it could happen again!

'Smart thieves,' said Petterson, pointing at the sign INVENTORY BEING UNDERTAKEN. 'What a red herring!'

His colleague Rolf Strömbeck looked at the sign for a long time, put a portion of tobacco under his gum, and nodded. 'And we fell for it – so simple yet so damned cunning.'

'The sign saying BACK SOON, what about that? Do you know what that's about?'

'I've never seen anything like it in all my years in the police force,' his comrade answered. 'Who can have put up such a sign, and why?'

'It is at any rate handwritten, while the other signs have been printed on an ordinary printer. That is somebody's handwriting.'

'But has the BACK SOON sign been written by somebody who discovered the theft and then ran off to sound the alarm? In which case, we ought to get in touch with the person concerned as soon as possible.' He chewed the tip of his pen while he pondered. 'We ought to ask that person to step forward, but the question is, how do we go about doing that?

Chief Inspector Petterson thought over various alternatives, but couldn't think up a good one.

'If we say we're looking for a person who has written a sign with the words BACK SOON, then we'll get replies from all over Sweden – and you can guarantee that none of those will be the thieves. No professional criminal leaves such an obvious trail. The printed signs have been handled with gloved hands, but this one has distinct fingerprints in the actual ink. Can you see the thumbs in the corner? The black ink must have been sticky.' Petterson pushed the sign across to his colleague.

'You know what? This sign doesn't lead anywhere. I can only see one use for it.' Strömbeck got up, opened the door, and hung up the BACK SOON sign on the handle outside. 'Now we'll take a walk and eat lunch in town. Then at least we'll have a bit of peace for a while.'

26

The day before the big ransom was to be paid, the five friends took a taxi to the Viking Line ferry terminal where they bought their tickets. Anna-Greta paid in cash, of course. The League of Pensioners sat waiting to go on board. They didn't have their own Zimmer frames with them as they had left these in the Princess Lilian suite in the Grand Hotel. Brains had pocketed all of his tools and they were now using frames supplied by the shipping line. They went on board the Viking Line ferry and once there put their Zimmer frames and some small items in their cabins. Then they discreetly went down the corridor, took the stairs to the car deck, and walked out via the car ramp, off the ferry and onto the quay. If anybody was after them, then they would have been fooled. These five passengers were actually going on a totally different ferry.

When they were back in the Viking terminal, they fetched the Urbanista shopping trolleys they had stored there, ordered a taxi to the Silja Line terminal at Värta docks on the other side of Stockholm, and managed to arrive just before the *Silja Serenade* ship departed. Martha was very proud of this little out-flanking movement. The League of Pensioners' feint, as she called it. Now the police and other authorities could search for them all they liked on the Viking *Mariella* ferry, while in actual fact they were comfortably ensconced on the Silja Line's flagship *Silja Serenade*. Rake had asked her what the point with this bothersome extra outing was, but Martha had explained that she had read about leading pursuers off the trail in many crime novels. If you led them down a sidetrack, you would gain time. And hadn't they agreed to have a bit of fun before they ended up in prison?

The five of them joked merrily about robberies and thefts while they queued for their cabins on *Silja Serenade*. The passengers standing closest to them cast an amused glance at the happy-go-lucky group of pensioners, and couldn't help but smile. Perhaps growing old wasn't so bad after all? When Martha and the others had got their plastic key cards they didn't go directly to the cabins, but wheeled their black shopping trolleys to the lift and pressed the button to go down to the car deck. Once they were down there, amidst the lorries and cars, nobody paid them any attention and they could walk unhindered along the side of the ship towards the ramp. En route they examined every partition and recess, searching for a good place to hide things. It was damp, there were pools of water here and there, and it smelt of diesel, but that didn't bother them. They were all concentrating deeply on their purpose. Close to the ramp they caught sight of the partition meant for boots and rain clothes. A wooden box and two large duffel bags could be seen on the floor.

'Here!' said Martha triumphantly, and they carefully pushed their black shopping trolleys in among the rain clothes. To be on the safe side, they looked over their shoulders to ensure that nobody had seen them, and then quickly went on their way.

Admittedly, they were not going to get the ransom until the return journey to Stockholm, but this way they could test whether the shopping trolleys would be left in peace or whether the police had set up a trap, and this would give them a little bit of distance from the stolen goods.

The morning sun shone into the Princess Lilian suite, causing the grand piano and the grey carpet to sparkle. The young hotel cleaner, Petra Strand, puffed the cushions on the sofa and out the window. She had vacuumed the carpets and cleaned the bathroom, as well as dusting all the furniture. She straightened her back and fluffed up her red, newly washed hair with her fingers. Now she had finished cleaning the room, the fun part was next. She was going to make an inventory of the decorations in the various rooms and see what could be improved. She was admittedly only a cleaner, but when the hotel management found out that she studied art, surely they would want to hear her opinion about colour schemes and fittings and decorations. Even though mainly older people were guests at the Grand Hotel, the Internet revolution had, nevertheless, meant that many younger millionaires had also started to stay there. She was exactly the right person to help the management of the hotel adjust to the times and see to it that their new clients felt at home.

Petra threw a glance at the sunlit palace across the water in front of the hotel, put her duster into the cleaning trolley and then walked all round the suite. While she studied the decorations, carpets and textiles, she thought about what could be improved. The dominant colours in the suite were white, grey and black, and she liked the deep-pile wall-to-wall carpet which had a slightly silverish tone. The turquoise floral bedspreads matched the magnificent view, and even the rooms with the somewhat lighter shades were stylish. But . . . something was lacking: the decoration in the 330 square metres of the suite did, without doubt, need something doing. Perhaps some new paintings?

Her first impression was that the works of art were a little 'tame' and she would rather have seen more dashing colours adorning the walls. A large painting depicting a sailing ship had been hung up above the bed in one of the bedrooms, there was an etching in the corridor next to the kitchen, and two small still lifes hanging on the walls in the library. She came to a halt in front of two small oil paintings above the grand piano. They looked fairly decent, but no more than that. One of them portrayed some small cargo vessels and fishing boats in an estuary, and the other was some sort of Paris exterior with a man and a woman at a café. The painting with the river motif was dominated by brown, dirty-grey colours and had far too many vessels and boats in relation to the area of water. The Paris exterior wasn't much better. The woman at the café was shown from behind and the man looked strange with his long hair, enormous moustache and a hat which didn't fit with the period. There was too much of everything, and it would have been enough to have just the woman's hat in the painting. Nevertheless, the motif seemed familiar. She had a closer look. It did actually remind her of a work by Renoir. The great masters were often copied but the results were usually poor. This was by one of the many artists who had clearly failed. Regardless, the two paintings didn't look good above the grand piano. She would rather see a large modern painting there. Why not an

Ola Billgren, a Cecilia Edefalk or a Picasso? Quickly she lifted down the two paintings, put them on her cleaning trolley, and took the lift down to the annex.

The rooms in the annex were being renovated and the paintings from these rooms had been taken down and leaned against the wall in some of the rooms which were going to be repainted. Petra looked through them and studied each painting carefully. One of them reminded her of a genuine Chagall, and the largest, a Matisse-like watercolour, would look perfect above the grand piano.

She left the paintings from the Princess Lilian suite on the trolley, put the other two under her arm and went up with them. With great enthusiasm, she hung first one and then the other above the piano. Then she took a few expectant steps back into the centre of the room. Her eyes lit up. It looked so very much better this way! The management would be really pleased!

27

After the League of Pensioners had installed themselves in their cabins and rested a while, they changed and went up to the dining room. Martha kept a sharp lookout to make sure that they were not being observed. After all, it was a bit scary to be demanding a ransom, but it was very exciting at the same time.

'Á la carte or smorgasbord?' Martha asked when they went into the dining room.

'Smorgasbord, of course,' they all chimed and headed off to queue for the buffet delicacies. Rake and Christina stood next to each other and chatted, while Martha kept company with Brains and Anna-Greta. In the cabin, before they had gone up for dinner, Anna-Greta had asked a strange question. It was a surprising one for her to ask, especially when they had so many more important things to think about.

'What is it that causes men to be interested in certain women but not in others?' Anna-Greta wondered out loud.

Martha had tried to make light of such a question, but then she saw that Anna-Greta was serious.

'You must be well dressed, joyful and an extrovert,' she said with a glance at Anna-Greta's outfit. Her skirt in a greyish-brown and black with a dirty-green pattern was more like camouflage than design. The only advantage was that it was not very visible.

'Well dressed? I don't understand that,' said Anna-Greta with a glance at Martha's purse belt.

'Yes, you must wear beautiful clothes, have some make-up on, and flirt a little,' Martha attempted to explain.

'And you think that is what you do?'

'Not me, no, but in general that's it,' said Martha vaguely and thought that it would be a good idea if Anna-Greta met somebody because she evidently felt herself excluded. Christina and Rake seemed to have something going and she mainly socialized with Brains.

'But you know what is so delightful about life?' Martha tried again. 'You never know what is going to happen – and it is never too late to hope.'

'Any more clichés?' Anna-Greta snorted, and Martha immediately stopped speaking. She had only wanted to encourage her. What she really wanted to say was that Anna-Greta was too formal and correct, dressed in a very dull way and laughed like a horse – but no, she couldn't do that.

They finished their meal with a helping of cream trifle in the dining room. By this point, Anna-Greta was in a better mood and by the second glass of wine, she was talking and laughing as usual. Martha was relieved to see this but thought that they ought to take more care of her. To outsiders, Anna-Greta always gave the impression of being so prickly but, like everyone else, she wanted to experience love and friendship too.

After dinner they continued the evening in the karaoke bar. The wine had them in high spirits and, experienced choir singers as they were, they felt the urge to sing. Martha stepped up onto the podium and started with 'Yesterday', while Rake, as usual, sang the Jussi Björling classic 'Towards the Sea'. Even Anna-Greta plucked up courage and stood up and sang 'My Way' in an extremely personal interpretation which she reinforced with even more original gestures. Afterwards, everybody gave a friendly applause, but when Anna-Greta thought of following it up with the Swedish national anthem, Martha suggested that it was time for them to go somewhere else. Anna-Greta protested heartily and it wasn't until Martha informed her that there were sure to be many widowers in the bar that she agreed to go along. They took the lift to the deck above.

Nurse Barbara's cheeks were burning and she was completely exhausted after spending several hours in the cabin with Director Mattson. She had thought that he was going to take her on a holiday to Europe where they would stay in a luxury hotel, but instead they were on an ordinary cruise trip, aboard the *Silja Serenade* to Helsinki. It was a little bit of a disappointment, but when she heard his explanation she calmed down.

'You see, my little sweetie, on European flights there is a greater risk of me meeting my colleagues. On a cruise ship I know we'll be undisturbed and can devote ourselves completely to each other.'

With those words she had allowed herself to be appeased. It made her happy that she was so important to him. It could only mean that he was planning to marry her in the future. Soon, very soon, she ought to have achieved her goal. Yes, indeed, he seemed to be totally engrossed. After they had boarded at half past four, they had gone directly to their cabin. Now it was past eight o'clock and she hadn't even noticed when the ship left the harbour.

'What do you think, shall we have a drink in the bar and get a bite to eat?' she asked when hunger made itself felt.

'Of course, but we must eat quickly, mind you!' he said, and pulled her towards him. 'My little, little treasure!'

She felt the words echoing inside her head, begging to be spoken out loud: *Get divorced and marry me!* She wanted to shout this out, but controlled herself. She must try to find the right occasion. Perhaps after a drink or two in the bar, she thought.

The five fugitive pensioners stood with their drinks at the bar and looked out across the dance floor. Several couples were already dancing and Martha wondered if she would dare dance herself. After all their gym exercising she was feeling more agile than ever. She heard her friends' laughter and reflected upon the transformation that had taken place. Just a few months earlier they had been tired and lacking in energy. Now they were a happy gang and even Anna-Greta seemed to be in good spirits. Now and then, her voice cut through the murmur around them and drowned out everything, but she sounded happy and that was the most important thing. Martha thought about what she had dared to suggest earlier that evening.

'Anna-Greta, don't take this the wrong way, but what you asked earlier about men . . .'

'Yes?'

'Don't talk so loudly, and try to restrain your peals of laughter. Men like themselves to be the ones who are seen and heard.'

Martha was amazed that she had dared to be so direct, but she only meant well. Then she had taken Anna-Greta with her to the ladies'. There she had lent her a lipstick and helped Anna-Greta to comb her hair into a more becoming style. She had persuaded her to loosen the bun on her neck, and with her hair falling diagonally across her brow she looked more attractive. Martha had also lent her a skirt and blouse that suited her well. But then Anna-Greta had turned into her old self. She had started to chat with an elderly gentleman and, in her eagerness, her voice had become just as piercing as usual. Then it got all the louder. Martha shook her head. Soon he was bound to be put off. However, the evening wore on and the man made no attempt to leave. Instead, the two of them stood very close to one another and talked away, and when Anna-Greta let off one of her classic neighs, he didn't even react. Had Anna-Greta finally met a soulmate? Indeed, anything could happen once you had escaped the isolation of the retirement home. Martha thought about how much they had actually achieved during their days of freedom, and wished that more people in retirement homes could have such adventures. Although something was seriously wrong when you had to become a criminal to have a bit of fun in your old age!

Anna-Greta's neighing laugh could be heard again, but now the man had put a hand on her shoulder. Lord above, he seemed to want to ask her to dance – yes, now he turned round, put his hand under her arm, and started to move towards the dance floor. Martha saw that Anna-Greta really had met Mr Right. The man had a hearing aid. He had probably turned it off.

The music started up again and just as Martha was wondering whether she would dare to have a slow dance, Brains came up to her. Since she was only too willing to hold him, she hoped he would ask her to dance so that they would have a few moments together. Unfortunately, her romantic notions were spoilt because as soon as they got onto the dance floor, Brains leaned forward and whispered in her ear:

'Nurse Barbara is here. What shall we do now?'

28

The choir gang became the main topic of conversation at the retirement home in the days following their disappearance. Where had they gone? Nobody had seen the five of them and Katia had tried and tried to get hold of Nurse Barbara but without success. She had no more luck when she phoned the police. Inspector Lönnberg told her yet again how impossible it was for them to help.

'The police don't have the authority, you see,' he had said. 'If the old people want to go off on their own, then let them do so. It is nothing we can interfere in. And remember that they do have each other. I am sure there is no need to worry.'

'But I *am* worried,' she exclaimed.

'The law is as it is, you see,' he went on, and finally Katia put the receiver down. It was a waste of time talking to him, but what else could she do? She didn't even dare think what Nurse Barbara would say when she found out what had happened. Katia put her coffee cup down and went out into the lounge. As usual, calm and quiet reigned. A television was on in the corner, but the sound was turned off, and the two men who usually played chess had dozed off. An elderly lady was reading, and her friend sat and looked out through the window. It wasn't just quiet, it was boring. She was just about to get ready to go home when the door opened and one of the clients called out:

'You've got a visitor.'

'A visitor?' Katia hadn't booked any visit.

'It's somebody asking for Nurse Barbara and you are her replacement, aren't you?'

Katia nodded, smoothed her skirt and went to the visiting room. There sat a middle-aged man with a crew cut and beard. He had a ring in his ear and a leather jacket and tattoos on his wrists. He stood up when she came in.

'I am Nils Engström, I'm here to visit Dad.'

'Dad?'

'Yes, Bertil Engström, Rake, you know.'

'Oh yes, Rake. Can I give him a message?'

'No, I want to see him.'

'His room is over there, but—'

'I have promised to visit him every time we dock in Stockholm, and that's a promise I intend to keep.'

Before she could stop him, he was on the way to his father's room. She hurried after him but couldn't stop him from opening the door.

'Well? Where *is* he?'

'I don't know, but—'

'So you don't know where he is? What the hell do you do at this place?'

Katia blushed.

'Rake and the others in the choir are probably out singing.'

'Oh, I see, that explains it,' said the man somewhat calmer, and he sank into a chair. 'It's a pity to miss him. I'm here so rarely, we don't always get the chance to leave the ship.'

'So you are a seaman?'

'Yeah, like my dad. We lived fairly near the docks in Gothenburg. You could see the river from the hill and all the ships by the quays. Dad used to talk about when he had been at sea, and he took me to the Maritime Museum.'

Katia sat down on the chair next to him. Rake's son looked rather wild, but, nevertheless, seemed quite a decent man.

'And your mother?'

'Usch, they weren't married long. Dad had an eye for the ladies. It was tough for her, she deserved better. She never remarried. I think she loved Dad all her life.'

'Rake is liked here too,' said Katia.

'Dad can be rather curt, but he's a nice guy. We used to go fishing in the moat. He put out lines and we would sit there and talk about the sea. I ended up going to sea.'

Katia smiled.

'We caught pike and eels, and even hooked the odd salmon. But then the water got dirty and that was the end of that. Bloody shame.'

He got up.

'Anyway, best be on my way. We leave port tomorrow. But say hello from me.'

Katia got up and accompanied him to the door. There stood Henrik, ninety-three, leaning on his stick.

'It's really quiet here, you know,' he said. 'None of the choir gang has been seen since Sunday.'

'What the hell are you saying?' Nils turned to Katia. 'Not since Sunday? You didn't tell me that!'

'I have tried speaking to the police but they won't listen. I'm sorry. It'd probably be better if a relative phones them,' said Katia.

'Then that's what I'll bloody well do, and I'll report him missing.'

Rake's son Nils pulled out his mobile and keyed in 112 to the police.

29

'Is Nurse Barbara here on the ship? It can't be true! Oh, Lord above!' Martha exclaimed in such a loud voice that she almost drowned out the dance music. Instinctively, she took hold of Rake's hand as she passed him, and pulled him back towards the bar counter. They had to warn the others.

'Let's get out of here,' suggested Rake, but then he saw that Nurse Barbara was not alone. She was in the company of Director Mattson. 'No, wait, take it easy. Those two only have eyes for each other.'

The five bided their time and tried to make themselves as invisible as possible.

'Perhaps she hasn't noticed us,' said Christina after the couple had disappeared down to the cabin decks.

'They didn't see anything. They didn't even stop to get a drink,' said Brains.

'That isn't why they are here,' Rake pointed out.

'She is probably just as afraid of being seen as we are. Now we know for sure that they're having an affair,' said Martha.

'They'll be between the sheets as usual,' commented Rake.

'Must you always—' Anna-Greta started to say, but she was cut off by Martha.

'Barbara mustn't see us. What if she messes up everything?'

'Then we shall simply ask her what she is doing on the ship with Mattson,' said Rake with a wink.

They all consoled themselves with that, but the jovial mood had disappeared. The only one who didn't seem to care was Anna-Greta. Out of the corner of her eye, Martha could see that the elderly gentleman had steered her out onto the dance floor again. Martha was pleased for her, but at the same time hoped that the whole thing wouldn't end in disaster. Anna-Greta's hip was not what it ought to be after her faked fall at the National Museum. Luckily for them, she at least hadn't fallen for real.

'Righto, we might as well call it a night. I, for one, am ex-hausted. See you at breakfast,' said Martha, who was worried about the day to come and wanted to get some sleep. The others nodded and headed for their cabins, all except Anna-Greta, who remained on the dance floor. What if Nurse Barbara were to come back? On the other hand, her friend seemed to be having such a good time with her new beau that Martha didn't want to spoil things. Anna-Greta could probably take care of herself.

Early next morning, Martha found it difficult to wake Anna-Greta up and Martha wondered what time she had actually got to bed.

'As if I was thinking about the time,' Anna-Greta answered with glowing eyes, and Martha couldn't get her to say any more. It wasn't until after the morning meeting in the cabin that she provided an explanation.

'We're going to meet again – his name is Gunnar,' she said,

bright red in the face, just as the captain's voice was heard over the loudspeakers. Anna-Greta went quiet and they all looked at each other. Martha clapped her hands.

'Right you are, my friends, we have arrived in Helsinki. It is time to go down to the car deck.'

They all nodded as if in silent agreement; they got up and left the cabin. They followed the flow of people waiting to use the lifts down to the car deck. When they reached the partition beside the ramp, they heard the engines racing during the docking manoeuvre. Martha and Brains exchanged quick looks. The empty black shopping trolleys were still there. The five of them stood there for a while until the ship had come to a stop and the deck crew signalled to the car drivers that it was time for them to drive out. After that, Martha and Brains took hold of their Zimmer frames and started to walk towards the exit while the others pulled the shopping trolleys with them. Then the little group calmly walked out from the ship and down the external car ramp. Nobody stopped them and nobody called after them. But if they had been stopped, Martha had prepared for that too. She would have demanded to speak to the management. Then she would have complained about how badly they were treated because they were old – and no company would be prepared to risk being accused of 'age-fascism'– or ageism, as it was called nowadays.

Once out on the quayside, the tension in the group lessened because they all felt certain that it wouldn't be difficult to collect the ransom. In the old Market Hall they bought some smoked salami sausage, slices of ham and Swiss cheese and then took the jolting tram into the city centre. At the fancy old Fazer coffee house they enjoyed the coffee, had a sandwich and bought some cream cakes, after which they ended their Helsinki outing by buying liquorice, Kinuski fudge and a large stock of cloudberry liqueur.

'Do we have to collect the ransom now? Can't we wait until later?' Christina wondered, as she had begun to get nervous. They were going to collect the ransom money on the return journey and then they would irrevocably become major criminals.

'Like I always say, at our age there is no "later". It has already past,' Martha cut her off. She felt that she must put her foot down. They must all stand united now. 'Incidentally, I saw that they had Belgian chocolate in the shop on board. Let's go and do a bit of shopping.'

You didn't need to say any more to distract Christina.

They went back on board the ship. Martha led her friend by the arm and they went towards the shop. Martha bought five boxes of Belgian chocolates for Christina, and while she stood in the queue to pay, she ran through the whole plan in her head. When the ferry got back to Stockholm they would find two identical shopping trolleys like theirs in the partition. Two which they would swap for their own . . . the only thing that distinguished the trolleys was the tiny hole that Brains had drilled for the reflector arm to stick out – a hole that was so small no one but themselves would notice it.

'Here, take this chocolate and go and rest a while. Then we'll meet in an hour in my cabin and have a drink before eating,' said Martha, handing the carrier bag to Christina. Her friend clutched the present against her chest and did as Martha had said.

*

Shortly afterwards, down on the car deck, when Martha and Brains crept along the side of the ship towards the partition, she wanted to slip her hand into his for support, but she restrained herself. They did, after all, have shopping trolleys as well as umbrellas to keep track of, and they did not have enough hands. They proceeded slowly and cautiously to the hiding place close to the ramp, and when they were almost there they put up their umbrellas. This was because Brains had said that the surveillance cameras would certainly be on. Once at the partition, they stopped and inhaled deeply. Martha hardly dared look. There were the rain clothes, boots and – yes, right there in the far corner stood two new black Urbanista shopping trolleys, just like their own. Now it all depended on whether the museum had put the ten million in them too – quite a hefty addition to their pension, as Martha had called it.

Martha really wanted to take the shopping trolleys right away, but the minute she took them up to the cabin she and her friends could be discovered. It must all be taken care of much more discreetly. The trolleys would have to stay where they were until it was time to disembark when they were back in Stockholm again the next morning. But, still. She ought to open them to check that she and her friends hadn't been conned. Perhaps she could lift the cloth lid a little? First she just touched the trolley quickly, then she pushed it hard. But when she heard the rustle and thought she could feel the bundles of banknotes inside, she was so pleased that she took several dance steps. Brains quickly stopped her, but she saw the warmth in his eyes. She wanted to hug him, but that, too, would have to wait. Not until they had put their own shopping trolleys next to the others, turned round and were going into the lift again, did they close their umbrellas and give each other a big hug.

Up in the cabin again, Martha and Brains told their friends what had happened. After a short discussion they all went into their own cabins for a short and well-needed rest. Martha pulled out her knitting and sat on the bed with some soft, comfy cushions behind her back. Now the museum would get two shopping trolleys with old newspapers, and they themselves would get their ten million. Not a bad exchange. But would it work? She racked her brains, it seemed to be far too easy. But she didn't get any further in her thoughts before she fell asleep with her knitting on her tummy, and she only woke up again when Brains knocked on the cabin door. It was time for dinner.

When they gathered together in the dining room they were still looking very pleased with themselves, but to be on the safe side they kept an eye out for Nurse Barbara. They looked keenly around them in every direction, but she was nowhere to be seen.

'She and Mattson will be lying there and—' Rake started, but was broken off by Anna-Greta.

'Not again,' she retorted haughtily, and gave him a severe look.

'But she'll be on her back in the cabin,' Rake persisted. He smelled of garlic again and held a large beer glass in his hand. Anna-Greta gave him a disapproving look and Christina quickly stretched out her hand to quieten him. But then Anna-Greta suddenly thawed, and the wrinkles between her eyes vanished.

'You know what, Brains, if Nurse Barbara is in love with Mattson, then let her be.'

30

It had already got dark and Chief Inspector Petterson observed the lights of the city glowing in the rain outside. Once again he was working overtime, because the painting theft was haunting him and giving him no peace. He tried to find leads from the surveillance cameras at the National Museum, and even though the camera in the room with the Impressionists hadn't worked there were, of course, other cameras. The recordings ought to show all those who were at the museum that confounding day, and he ought to be able to find the thief – or thieves – among the visitors. He had gone through the material thoroughly but had not discovered anything suspicious. On Floor 1, where they had Modern Design, you could see three elderly gentlemen and a family with two children who were wandering around aimlessly. In one corner of the exhibition, two women in their thirties looked at coloured glass in a display cabinet and an elderly woman studied objects from Gustavsberg. None of them looked like thieves. The visitors walked slowly and looked at the displays with interest.

On the way up the large majestic staircase to Floor 2, you could see two girls with high-heeled shoes and he zoomed in on them. No, no paintings there, but goodness they were wearing extremely short skirts. A bit further away, three middle-aged couples were on their way into the room with the Renaissance paintings, and beside the door to the French Impressionists he saw an elderly woman with a Zimmer frame, an old man and a slender little woman. Nothing remarkable there either, except they looked as if they were cold, since they were wearing gloves. It was troublesome when you got older, poor circulation could really make itself felt.

What about the section for paintings from Holland and Flanders? This is where the valuable Rembrandt painting hung, but in this room it was empty except for an old lady with a stick. He couldn't see any security guards on any of the images, which he thought was strange. The collections in the museum were worth many millions, and probably more besides. Also, he didn't find a single image of the bearded youth that the pensioners had spoken of. According to the interrogation with the security guards, two elderly ladies at the museum had seen the bearded man. But why hadn't he been caught on a single camera?

Chief Inspector Petterson got up and opened the window. He must examine the material in more detail, not just fast-wind the tape, he admonished himself. He should look through all of the material once more in peace and quiet. He inhaled air in deep breaths, fetched a cup of cappuccino from the coffee machine, then sat down in front of his computer and started afresh.

The images that flickered past were not particularly exciting, and Chief Inspector Petterson found it hard to concentrate. When he came to the cameras in the Rembrandt room, he was rather bewildered. In the images, you could see an elderly woman walking up to one of the Rembrandt paintings. She went far too close and waved back and forth with a crooked walking stick. He had an elderly mother and knew that old people could do all sorts of daft things, but this did look a bit too bizarre. Now that he studied the footage again carefully, he discovered yet another odd occurrence. When the old woman had waved her stick, she then looked thoroughly around her before cautiously lying down on the floor. When he had wound through the tape it had looked as though she had tripped, but now it looked as if she had lain down on the floor deliberately! Surely that couldn't be the case? Shortly afterwards, she supported herself on her elbows and shuffled closer to the painting. She must have been trying to get up. But then she put her stick next to her so that it looked as if it had landed there when she fell. A few images later, the security guards came running and helped her up. They were the same guards who claimed this woman had seen a bearded youth go past.

Why hadn't any of the security guards been in the exhibition rooms? There was certainly something suspicious about that. Another point to consider was that none of the surveillance cameras showed a thief carrying any paintings out from the museum. Equally, none of the visitors had a rucksack or bag in which they could hide the paintings. All you could see were the two Zimmer frames that an elderly lady and a hunch-backed man leaned on. But the man could later be seen calmly walking out of the museum together with another old-looking woman, and the other little old lady couldn't possibly be involved in the theft. She took her coat off and put it on her Zimmer frame when she entered the museum, and put her coat back on again when she went out. And there was nothing in the Zimmer frame basket – not even a book or a pair of spectacles. No, the theft must have been an insider job! It could only have been carried out by the museum staff or the security guards. Mind you, the old lady with the warped stick seemed a bit mysterious, but, on the other hand, she was so thin and weak-looking that he doubted she would be able to carry two paintings. The chief inspector leaned back and ran his fingers through his hair. The reason the security guards were not in the exhibition halls must be because they were preparing for the theft. He made a whistling sound, and immediately felt most satisfied with himself. Funny that he hadn't thought of that straight away. It was high time to bring the security guards in to interrogate them.

31

Soon after the ship had left Helsinki for the return journey to Stockholm and passed the little island of Sveaborg, Martha felt how the wind caught the hull, but she wasn't worried. These big modern ferries had stabilizers. None of the others seemed to care, they just carried on helping themselves at the enormous smorgasbord buffet, chatting and laughing.

'The restaurants here are not bad at all, but the cabins can't compare with the Princess Lilian suite,' Martha commented.

'Soon we will be back at the hotel, thank God,' said Christina. 'The standard is much higher there, and there we are on firm ground.'

'It's crazy how quickly you get used to things. We booked luxury cabins, after all, but they feel like tiny wardrobes compared to the suite,' Martha admitted.

'Well, soon we can put the art coup of the century behind us, and plan new deeds,' said Rake, and he put his arm round Christina. 'Why don't we stay on at the hotel a little longer? We can pay our way.'

'But we weren't going to pay for the hotel,' Anna-Greta protested. 'And you haven't forgotten that we are meant to be going to prison, have you?'

'No, certainly not, but I don't think we will determine when that happens; it will be the police,' Brains pointed out.

'We'll see if the museum has involved them, but I don't think they dare. Remember that P.S. we put at the end of the ransom note? *If you contact the police, we shall destroy the paintings,*' said Martha. 'Granted, we're not going to do it, but that is what we wrote.'

'Regardless, we must be careful,' Anna-Greta reminded them. The money is ours now. But we must think of future plans, Martha. Where are we going to put all this money? It won't fit in a bank deposit box.'

An embarrassing silence followed, because nobody had thought about that. That was one of the drawbacks with planning in several stages. Now they had missed something again. Martha sighed. It wasn't like in her childhood home at Brantevik, where you just threw things into the shed. Loot in the big city was quite another matter.

'This is not a problem as long as we have mattresses,' she said to distract them.

'Mattresses? That won't work,' the others protested, and a lively discussion immediately got under way about where the money should be stashed. The five of them couldn't agree. As time wore on, the waves got higher and became more noticeable so they withdrew to their respective cabins. The League of Pensioners would have to be in good shape the following morning when they fetched the shopping trolleys. Just before Martha fell asleep, she went through all the details in her head to ensure that they hadn't forgotten anything. She thought about the second letter that they had posted the day after the first one:

The two Urbanista shopping trolleys are to be filled with
10 million kronor and placed on the Silja Serenade *car deck*
in the partition for rain clothes right next to the car ramp.
Don't try any tricks. No police. Just do as we say and nothing
will happen to the paintings.

Martha remembered how pleased she had been with the twist at the end, but the others had been uncertain.

'It sounds threatening,' Christina had said.

'Pah, it will do nicely. You mustn't be too soft,' Anna-Greta stated.

'Can't we just remove the last two sentences and sign it Bandidos?' wondered Brains. 'That sort of says it all.'

They had discussed the wording for a long time before finally agreeing on a compromise where they took away Bandidos – even though all of them admitted it was an interesting suggestion. But the ominous sentence at the end had been kept. Now that she thought about the wording again, Martha didn't like it. It sounded so irresponsible. She had gone to the postbox and posted the letter, so it was done now.

The ship rolled and a large wave hit the bow. Now it wasn't just Martha's thoughts that kept her awake, but the rough sea too. She went through the letter in her head again, and wondered if the museum had managed to get hold of ten million kronor in such a short time. Perhaps they had simply put make-believe money in the shopping trolleys – museums didn't usually even manage to get funds for lockable cupboards and decent equipment for the toilets when they asked for it. She pulled the covers up over her chin and decided to stop worrying. Renoir and

Monet were priceless. Ten million ought to count as small change.

During the night the wind blew all the stronger and by the early hours there was a moderate gale. When they could sail near the islands they were comparatively sheltered from the weather and wind, but between Åland and Stockholm the ship rolled alarmingly. Soon they were in a full storm. The five of them lay in their cabins and held on tight, and twice during the night Martha came close to vomiting. She sincerely hoped that the others weren't feeling quite as miserable. Luckily, when the ship reached the shelter of the outer islands of the Stockholm archipelago, the sea was much calmer, and when the wake-up call came on the loudspeaker Martha had, against all odds, managed to get dressed and make her way up to the cafeteria. The others, too, looked somewhat the worse for wear and none of them had more than a cup of tea and some toast for breakfast. An hour later, the five of them were already standing by the lift when the captain came over the loudspeaker again and asked all drivers to go down to their cars. They quickly pushed the button to go down to the car deck.

At first, none of them really noticed anything different; everything just seemed a bit messier than usual. However, when they came close to the ramp, Martha saw that things were not as they should be. Instead of four shopping trolleys, there was now only *one*! She looked around, but couldn't see any of the others. She felt a knot in her chest and was finding it hard to breathe.

'Brains, have you seen this?' she whispered and was so upset that she forgot to put up her umbrella. Brains still retained his cool; he opened his umbrella and Martha's too, and moved forward with caution. He stopped and had a good look all around.

'If we start searching for the other shopping trolleys it will look suspicious. One filled shopping trolley will give us about five million. I think we should be satisfied with that.'

'You're right. In crime novels, the thieves always get caught when they try to get that last bit of the loot. If we just take the trolley and leave the ship as if nothing has happened, the guards will think we are the innocent pensioners that we are pretending to be.'

'The only thing is that they might claim the disappeared millions back the day we get caught,' said Brains.

'Pah, we shall simply let Anna-Greta sort that out later.'

They smiled at each other and when they reached the shopping trolley Brains quickly looked for the tiny hole he had drilled for the reflector arm to stick out. He couldn't see one. Therefore this must be the museum's shopping trolley. They took it without looking around, raised and lowered their umbrellas twice as a signal to the others, and then slowly walked down the car ramp. Despite what had happened, Martha was not worried about going through customs. The customs officials never used to check anybody from a neighbouring country, and they certainly wouldn't care about five poor pensioners. But when the five of them got close to the control point, two customs officials suddenly stepped forward and stopped them.

'We haven't got any spirits,' Rake quickly informed them.

'No drugs either,' said Christina and sneezed. She had caught a cold again.

'So what have you got in your shopping trolley, then?' one

175

of the customs officials asked, and gave Brains a sign that he should open it.

'It is full of banknotes. It's the ransom money we got for the painting robbery at the National Museum,' said Martha and smiled courteously. She was certain that if she said how it was, not a soul would believe her.

'No, it's the money I won at roulette,' Anna-Greta interjected. 'Now I'm going to put it in the bank.'

Martha shot an irritated glance at her. You should never say too much; that would only make the customs men interested. And so it did.

'Gambling? Oh, right. Can you please be so kind as to open it?' said the customs man, and he started to pull at the zip.

Then Christina fainted. This wasn't anything they had planned, but when Christina had been seasick she had thrown up all the pills that raised her blood pressure, and now she was felled by the fact that her blood pressure was so low. Martha rushed forward and lifted up her legs as she usually did, while the others tried to shake her back to consciousness.

'Please can you give me a sweet?' Martha asked the customs official and when he wasn't quick enough, Anna-Greta poked him in his tummy with her stick.

'You will help the poor woman right now! Otherwise she could die!' She roared with her razor-sharp voice, and the customs officials obeyed her immediately. While the men were trying to revive Christina, a long queue of passengers formed behind them – and it just grew and grew. Finally, when Christina – pale and confused – managed to get back onto her feet, the customs officials' patience was exhausted.

'Be on your way!' they ordered her and the League of

Pensioners moved along as quickly as they could. After this, the officials didn't wave any more passengers in for control, but returned to their office for a cup of coffee to get their strength back. So it came about that on this particular day more goods were smuggled into Stockholm than in the rest of the week.

32

Nurse Barbara sat with her hands by her sides and stared at Katia with her mouth open. What was the girl saying? Five of the guests had gone AWOL from the retirement home? And this had taken place just when she had relaxed from work for a week? It couldn't be true! What would Ingmar say? Barbara was so shocked that her tongue seemed to get tangled inside her mouth and she could only manage a bleating noise. If somebody hadn't rung the bell in one of the rooms that very minute, she probably would have grasped the girl by the neck and given her a good shaking. Nurse Barbara swore out loud. If only she had been there herself, this would never have happened. Could one never hand over responsibility to somebody else? And what if the pensioners had sneaked out anyway? Well, she would certainly have ensured that those singing corpses would have come back long ago. Yes, Nurse Barbara was in a really rotten mood. Ingmar hadn't proposed to her yet and if he found out what had happened at Diamond House he would be absolutely furious. Then she could stop hoping. But no, she mustn't give up. If she had got this far, she wasn't going to give up until he had involved her in his business projects. She didn't want to continue as a low-paid nurse, she wanted to be rich and to be able to afford a decent life! She took a deep breath, let her shoulders sink and took a grip of herself. She would solve this.

'The police are thinking of registering them as missing, and then as soon as they use their bank cards or travel in or out of the country, we should be alerted,' Katia attempted to console her.

'My dear, don't you worry. This is the sort of thing that can happen now and then. It will sort itself out,' said Nurse Barbara. But inside she felt really queasy. She *must* find the missing choir singers at once before anybody squealed to the management. But where on earth should she look? She put her head in her hands and started sobbing.

When all the passengers had left the ship, crewman Janson and his comrade Allanson went over the car deck with a hose to clean it before the ferry departed again in the evening. The two of them had worked for Silja shipping line for ten years and were used to the job, but that didn't make it any more fun. After the rough crossing from Finland the previous night, there was quite a mess on the car deck and more than usual to sort out. Janson went towards the starboard side and sighed at the sight of all the debris and rubbish that lay everywhere. He started the boring job of picking up old packages, glass and other junk. A wooden crate on the port side had got loose, the lid had broken off and nails and tools lay spread out across the deck ahead of him. Lifebelts, rain clothes and a sack of floats had also been thrown about. He directed the hose at the rain clothes and sent them across to a corner where there was already a pile of other stuff. Right next to that lay a roof box from a car. It was amazing that the driver hadn't noticed that it was gone! On these trips

179

between Finland and Sweden, lots of passengers got confused and after storms it was always worse. Next to the roof box there were several lifebelts, shopping trolleys and some broken bottles of spirits. The black shopping trolleys were damp after having been thrown around on the deck, but were otherwise undamaged. He tried to open one of them, but discovered it had a little padlock. He tried the other one, but that too was locked. Then he pulled his knife out to cut open the cloth, but was stopped by his comrade.

'Have a look at this. Several crates of Finnish vodka. Can't believe someone has left these.'

'The owner will be stone drunk, of course.'

'What about this, then? Urbanista shopping trolleys and a roof box.'

'I suppose it should go to Lost Property as usual.'

The men finished the cleaning, hitched the trailer to their car, and loaded everything onto it. Janson had already turned the ignition key when he stopped.

'You know what? If there was Finnish vodka in those wooden crates, perhaps there is something exciting in the roof box and the shopping trolleys?'

'OK then, we'll take them to the shed.'

Janson climbed into the car again and they drove off down the ramp. They always used an open trailer so that nobody would suspect anything untoward, and they waved to the customs officials as they drove past. It worked. Nobody had ever stopped them so far. Today they were in a hurry. They didn't have much time before new passengers would start to come on board.

33

When the five old friends returned to the Grand Hotel, the staff asked them in a friendly tone how long they intended staying for. The girl in reception looked through what had been charged to the rooms. Champagne and anniversary specials alternated with luxury meals, chocolate and innumerable purchases in the hotel shop.

'The rest of the week,' Martha answered politely. 'Or are you expecting somebody? Perhaps you would like to replace us with the president of the United States?'

But then Anna-Greta burst out in such an enormous neigh that the receptionist quickly flashed her widest smile and wished them a nice day. Once they were back up in the suite, they immediately opened the shopping trolley, gasped at the sight of the banknotes and oohed and aahed a long while. They merrily thumbed through all the five-hundred-kronor notes and that was such a pleasant occupation that a long, long time passed before they tired of it. In the end, they shut the trolley, put it into the wardrobe and took out the champagne. Martha looked at the others and saw what joy they radiated. Their adventure had brought them closer together, and they had had lots of fun. At the retirement home, the occasional visiting artiste would sing for them, they drank coffee and now and then there was a religious service. But they were *passive* occupations; the secret was to do something *yourself*, and you didn't necessarily have to become a thief for that. She felt at least ten years younger since they had left Diamond House. Nevertheless, they had worked hard almost every day. Two robberies in a single week was probably more than most professional robbery leagues could manage. Then, after only a few days of rest, there had been the exciting journey to Helsinki. Even Anna-Greta had blossomed.

Martha thought about what it had been like in bygone times in rural Sweden, when old people moved to a cottage next to the family farm but continued to take part in the farm work. They felt that they were still needed. But now? Who wanted to live when nobody needed you? Society had become so crazy. By committing crimes, they had at least shown how much energy old people could have. *Old people can do things too*, Martha thought, and she believed that they had provided a good example of that. Contented, she went into the kitchen, took out the champagne flutes and put them on the dining-room table. Humming to herself, she filled the glasses.

'We must have something to go with it,' Christina proposed, and Martha returned to the kitchen. On the way back, she went through the lounge, but just as she passed the grand piano, she had the feeling that something was different. She stopped, stared, shook her head and stared again.

Nurse Barbara lit yet another cigarette and inhaled deeply. These godforsaken unruly pensioners! The police had managed to trace them to the Viking Line *Mariella* ferry to Helsinki, but when the ship returned to Stockholm they were not on board. In her mind's eye she could see how they were wandering about lost in Finland somewhere, or perhaps even further to the East. The friendly Inspector Lönnberg at the Norrmalm police station had tried to reassure her and had said that they would turn up sooner or later, but now more than a week had passed.

'Don't forget that they are five adults who can take care of each other. This will certainly work out all right, young lady. As soon as they turn up, I shall get in touch with you.'

But she didn't want to sit there idly and wait for the scandal. She must do something. Rake's son had already started making inquiries, and at Diamond House the residents didn't talk about anything else. She had asked around among the remaining pensioners, but she wasn't able to get any indication of where the choir gang had gone.

'Nobody runs away without cause,' said an old lady wiggling her false teeth.

'The Christmas-tree decorations, that was the last straw,' grumbled another. 'You should never be niggardly. Then people will turn against you. By the way, when will we get back buns with the coffee?'

'If we don't get Danish pastries or buns, then we might disappear too,' ninety-year-old Elsa chipped in with a cunning grin. 'And why don't you serve traditional Lent buns? I like them with lots of cream and almond paste.'

Nurse Barbara couldn't understand what had happened. It had always been so calm and pleasant at Diamond House. Everyone had sat in their armchairs all day and watched TV. Now they were all grumbling. Barbara was very worried about

Martha, Rake and the others. She couldn't fathom how they had managed to get out of the retirement home. They must have had outside help, perhaps from their children. Their kids, yes. Rake's son had phoned from his ship and sworn and bawled her out, so she couldn't count on him. But perhaps Christina's children might help her? Nurse Barbara decided to phone them. She couldn't manage this on her own any longer.

34

It simply couldn't be true! Martha leaned over the piano, stared wide-eyed, shook her head and looked up again. No, she must simply be tired and confused after the journey. As soon as she got some food in her, she would feel better. Some nice roast lamb and a glass of wine, and everything would all be all right. It would be lovely to eat a meal without the whole table rocking as it had a tendency to do on the cruise ship. Martha tried to convince herself, but deep inside she knew that something was very seriously wrong, that somebody, quite simply . . . no, she couldn't believe it. She shook her head and went in to the others without saying a word.

After lunch, Martha sat in silence while the others discussed whether they should mourn the loss of half of the ransom money. In the end, they thought they should settle for what they had got, because despite everything they now had more money than they could ever have dreamed of in their old life. The only one who complained was Anna-Greta.

'How are we going to find that money?' she asked. 'It is ours after all.'

'Not so loud,' said Rake and he held his finger in front of his lips. 'And I don't know about it being "ours" . . .'

'But if we're not going to go looking for it, what are we doing here? Weren't we meant to be going to prison?'

Rake kicked her under the table.

'Things don't always go exactly according to plan,' Martha answered, thinking about the missing paintings. She still hadn't dared say anything.

'I agree with Anna-Greta. It is time for us to move on,' said Rake. 'Here it's the same old luxury food every day with strange sauces and jellies. An ordinary hamburger would taste really good.'

'Yes, good, plain, everyday food. I saw what they served in prison – all properly nutritious too – meatballs, fish and salad,' Christina added.

Martha ate the last of the strawberry sorbet, pushed her plate aside and carefully wiped her mouth with the linen serviette. Before she could say anything, Anna-Greta started speaking again.

'I don't know what we are doing. We were only going to be here a few days, a week at the most. Now it is already the first of April and before we know it, two weeks will have passed. The idea was that we should leave Diamond House to have it better in pris—'

'Quiet!' hissed Rake.

'I mean, have a better permanent residence.'

They became silent again. Martha looked at Anna-Greta out of the corner of her eye. She was right, of course. However much fun it was to steal, they couldn't live in the hotel for ever. Besides, they had also acquired the money that would gild their

186

life *after* the stretch in prison. It was just that the police had not done their bit. Imagine how silly everything could become. The police did not even suspect them, and nor had anybody contacted them from the retirement home. Added to that was the problem of the missing paintings. Martha cleared her throat.

'Now listen, everybody, we have a little problem.'

'Martha is going to give us another speech again,' Rake commented.

'We should have this talk up in one of our rooms,' said Martha.

When she said this, you could clearly hear her regional dialect, and Brains knew this was a sign that she was very tired. On their way up in the lift, he took her hand and gave it a slight squeeze. Martha wanted to rest her head against his chest and be consoled, but she restrained herself.

'Is there anything in here that looks different, do you think?' she asked when they had all settled on the sofa with a cup of coffee and a cake. Well, all of them except Rake, who had sat on an armchair after having yet again sat on Martha's knitting.

'No,' said Rake quickly.

'You can at least look first,' muttered Martha.

'It does perhaps look a little different, that's true. They have cleaned the room, after all,' he said, getting up and going to the piano.

'Shall we sing something? "Towards the Sea"?' he wondered, but was cut off by a shrill cry.

'My paintings are gone!' Christina roared.

'I don't know about *yours*,' said Brains.

'By God,' Anna-Greta called out, and put her hands in front of her face. 'Now we're going to owe them thirty million.'

'Yes, you can see for yourself,' said Martha. 'Not only do we have to find a hiding place for the money we have, but we must also find the paintings.'

'What are my children going to say? They won't be proud of me at all. Robin Hood never lost any of his loot,' snuffled Christina, and she had to blow her nose.

'You do know that we have spirited away some of the most valuable paintings in Sweden? Our negligence has led to the loss of two national treasures!' said Anna-Greta, giving Martha a severe look. 'This is *really* not according to the plan!'

'That's enough! This isn't Martha's fault, we were all agreed about this,' said Brains. 'Perhaps we can find the paintings again?'

'But how? We can hardly go around asking for a Monet and a Renoir,' said Christina.

'Quite simply, I think we ought to own up to what we have done,' Martha said. 'The time is ripe. The police don't seem to be on our trail. If we give ourselves up, we might get a lighter sentence.'

'And help to find the paintings,' said Brains. 'You are very clever!'

There was silence for a moment. Martha fetched the champagne to lighten the mood, but they all shook their heads.

'Next stop, prison. Couldn't you fetch some water instead, so that we can gradually acclimatize?' said Rake.

'Have you noticed that they don't have pea soup here? Just think, a really good thick pea soup with lots of pork in it,' said Brains, licking his lips.

'You talk about food, but just think of that mosaic bathtub.

It is far too low for my hip. I'm sure they won't have that sort of tub in prison,' said Anna-Greta.

'And the cinema here is much smaller than an ordinary cinema. And besides, we have already seen all the best films. In prison they will probably have rather different films for real men,' said Rake and he grinned.

Christina looked at him with suspicion.

'What do you mean?'

But before he had time to answer, Martha butted in.

'OK, we can vote on it. How many of us vote for prison?'

A long murmuring followed, but nobody wanted to put up a hand.

'Has anyone got a different idea?'

They discussed the matter back and forth and finally arrived at the conclusion that it would be good form to give themselves up. Nobody wanted the police to come rushing into the suite and put handcuffs on them. It would be much better for them to take their baggage and their Zimmer frames and knock on the door of the police station. Although they couldn't take the shopping trolley with them.

'Where shall we hide the money until we get out?' Rake wondered. Martha looked around and waited for suggestions from the others. Nobody had any ideas.

'Brains, you always have good ideas . . .'

He stroked his chin a few times.

'Yes, I do have an idea, but it's so crazy that I don't know if you will accept it.'

'What is it?' Martha asked.

Brains fetched the shopping trolley and started to demonstrate. This relieved the atmosphere somewhat because the problem of where to put the money had been worrying them all. The crazy idea Brains had was completely feasible. In theory, at least. Everybody except Anna-Greta put up their hand to support him, but as she didn't have any better ideas, Brains got to do as he wished. Finally, they also voted about whether they should go to the police or not, but there were still differences of opinion so they adjourned on that one. Just a few days more, then they could probably give themselves up, Martha thought. But first they must hide the money. Brains looked at the clock.

'We'll have time to do this today,' he said, 'but take as much money as you need first.'

The others agreed with him, and Martha, Christina, Anna-Greta and Rake gathered around the shopping trolley and helped themselves to their share. For a few moments, Christina wondered whether she should give some of the money to Emma and Anders, but the children were adults, after all, and ought to be able to manage for themselves. When they were all finished, Brains asked Martha if she could help him choose some pictures on the Internet. He opened home pages for various parachuting clubs and selected the most joyful and colourful parachutes he could find. Martha realized what Brains was intending to do. She then searched on the Internet for texts about golden handshakes and bonuses. As the sheets of paper came out of the printer, Martha picked them up, cut out what she wanted, and put them in the shopping trolley on top of the banknotes.

When it was almost four o'clock, they left the hotel and set off for their next destination – the Modern Museum.

'Has it occurred to you that people might think that this is a joke and not a serious installation?' said Brains, who was starting to have doubts. 'It is the first of April today!'

190

'No, I'm mostly thinking about how we have lost two paintings and half of the money so far. It would be great if we don't lose the last banknotes too.'

'But it has been fun, hasn't it?'

'Oh yes, it has indeed,' said Martha, blushing.

They went out of the hotel, walked past the National Museum, and then over the bridge to the little island, Skeppsholmen. After managing the steep hill, they reached the main entrance to the Modern Museum. When they entered the museum, the guard wanted to stop them, but Martha said that her Zimmer frame had broken and she must use the shopping trolley to lean against as she walked. Then they were let in and, after hanging up their coats, they went into the exhibition halls. They wandered around for quite a while and finally caught sight of a podium on which there was a sculpture of a man stretching out his hand.

'Brains, are you thinking the same as me?'

'Yes, it's perfect!' he chuckled, and when the exhibition hall was empty for a few moments they lifted the shopping trolley up and put it on the podium in front of the outstretched hand. It looked so ridiculous that Martha could hardly keep from laughing, but she pulled herself together and lifted up the lid of the trolley so that the parachute pictures and the banknotes could be seen. Then, next to it, she taped an article about the finance sharks and their bonuses and, to finish it off, Brains put up a home-made sign: 'The Miser by the Countess Christina Nobleheap,' it said in fancy gold lettering. The installation was now complete. To name the artist Christina had been obvious to both Brains and Martha since their friend had been so sad about the paintings having disappeared and they wanted to

191

cheer her up. They took two steps back and looked at their handiwork.

'Do you really think this will be left in peace?' Martha wondered.

'Nobody dares move a work of art. Especially if it has been made by a countess.'

'No, that's true, of course,' Martha mumbled, without being entirely convinced.

They walked around in the exhibition hall and observed their installation from different angles, and thought it looked really professional. With that, they felt that they were done for the day. They fetched their coats and were just leaving when somebody called out after them.

'You there! Come back here!' They turned round and saw one of the guards running towards them. Behind him you could see the shopping trolley. 'What do you think you're doing?'

Martha felt a somersault in her tummy and Brains swallowed and put his cap on.

'Forgive an old person who wanted a bit of fun,' he said. 'We thought it looked better like that.'

'Are you completely mad? You can't destroy a work of art!'

'But it did look good, didn't it?' Martha insisted.

'April Fool! We were just—' Brains gave a forced laugh and for the first time in her life, Martha would have liked to have heard Anna-Greta's neigh.

'An April Fool's joke? But for goodness' sake, they are usually funny,' the guard grunted, and gave the shopping trolley back to them. 'Now get out of here before I call the management.'

Martha became sulky.

'If you think that it is only young people who can have fun, you've got another thing coming! Us old people have our fun and games too, you can be sure of that!' Having said this, she snatched back the shopping trolley, pulled the lid down and held out her hand. 'We want the sign back too.'

Not until he had fetched it did they leave the museum and return crestfallen to the hotel. When the others saw they still had the shopping trolley, a dark cloud seemed to cross their faces.

'Oh well, let's have a drink and we'll be sure to think of something else,' said Rake, trying to console them. He could identify himself as a failure and immediately this thought emboldened him. Just think how often he had done things wrong and how many times everything had gone to pot, but in the end things usually sorted themselves out. He fetched glasses and something to pour into them, and proposed going out onto the balcony. The sun was still shining, and when they put their overcoats on it was really nice to sit outside. While the sun slowly descended over the water, they sipped their drinks, totally occupied with their own thoughts. Rake knocked his drink back, and put his arm round Christina.

'We'll sort this out, my dear, don't you worry,' he said.

'I'm getting cold, I must go inside and change into warmer tights,' she answered, but then suddenly stopped. 'Rake, look!' she shouted in delight, and pointed at the downpipe going down from outside the balcony. Rake followed her gaze and could only see the roof and the black, wide drainpipes. Not until she lifted her skirt and showed her legs, did he understand what she had in mind.

'Now listen, don't be disappointed. We've solved this,

Christina and I,' Rake said. 'We can hide the banknotes in the drainpipe. Ladies, who has some tights that I can borrow?'

'I've got some ordinary ones,' said Martha.

'I've got some modern, patterned ones,' said Christina.

'Mine aren't exactly modern, but they do have a reinforced heel,' said Anna-Greta.

'Well, then,' Rake summed up. 'We've got about nine thousand five-hundred-kronor notes, if I've counted right. We'll stuff them into the tights. Then we need some plastic wrapping and some rope.'

They immediately cheered up, and the champagne was brought out again. They ordered yet another anniversary special to be sent up to the suite; they were going to have a three-course dinner after all. They ended the evening by singing 'God in Disguise', accompanied by Rake on the grand piano. *Everything will turn out for the best*, Martha thought. *It always does*.

The next morning, Martha hurried out to buy some black refuse sacks and Rake went to the ship store and bought some tarred rope – or marline, as he called it in sailor-speak. Christina, in turn, bought three pairs of tights in the hotel shop. Anna-Greta quickly put on one of the new pairs which looked really smart, and claimed that her old tights would do perfectly well for the banknotes. Then they locked the door to the suite very thoroughly and started stuffing the legs of the tights with bundles of notes. Since Anna-Greta had the longest legs, they took her tights first and it turned out that they only needed two pairs for all the notes. Rake knotted the nylon tights with professional seaman's knots, after which Brains wrapped them in two black plastic bags rolled into tubes. Finally, Rake wound the marline round and round the black tubes, with a long piece of line left to hang them up with.

'Right, that's everything,' said Brains with that bright, boyish look in his eyes. 'And you guarantee that the rope will be strong enough?' he went on, turning to Rake.

'I have never failed before, and this time I have secured everything with two ropes, double knots and bowlines,' he answered.

This sounded safe, and the next morning when the gentlemen woke as usual at about five o'clock to empty their bladders, they got dressed and knocked on the door of the ladies' room. Then they got down to work. While Rake held the rope, they lowered the black sausage-like tube into the downpipe from the balcony. Since they had bundled the notes tightly before putting them inside the tights, the almost two-metre-long banknote sausage didn't take up much room in the pipe. The water would run a little slower just there, but not *suspiciously* slower, Brains had worked out. Finally, they fastened the ropes to the top of the pipe with Rake's special knots. Since the marline was just as dark as the drainpipe, you couldn't see anything from above, and not even a fortune-teller could work out that there was almost five million in notes hidden there.

Almost an hour had passed before the two men finished and traffic was gradually starting to increase down on the road between the hotel and the water. So while the sun continued to rise all the higher, the five of them ate their breakfast, satisfied with what they had achieved. This time they didn't make do with the usual continental breakfast, but ordered a really super spread including their favourite ingredient – champagne. Their mission was complete and the only thing that reminded them of the art coup was the empty, black Urbanista shopping trolley.

35

The day that they had so long delayed had arrived: the day they would report their crimes to the police. Martha had intended that they should go to a little, cosy police station where she could talk to a nice police constable in peace and quiet. But the old police station in the Old Town – the one that had a charming red lantern over the entrance – had been closed. They would have to go to Kronoberg, the huge complex on Kungsholmen, the one with the remand cells and all. She threw a glance at the huge red-brick building and shuddered. The place made her feel like a real villain, and that irritated her until she realized that that was what she was. With her companions and the shopping trolley in tow, she stopped at reception, gave the receptionist a piercing look, and said:

'I wish to report a crime.'

'Yes, right, have you been robbed?'

'No, it is about a kidnapping.'

'Kidnapping?' The girl behind the counter went pale and quickly contacted somebody on the internal telephone. Martha couldn't hear what she said, but soon afterwards a large, muscular policeman made his appearance. He didn't seem nearly as nice as she had anticipated, and when she curtsied he just looked surprised.

'This way,' he said.

'But my friends?' Martha protested.

'You're surely not all going to report the same crime?'

'Yes, the same crime,' said Martha and she noticed how silly it sounded.

'One of you is enough to start with,' the policeman made clear, and then showed her the way to the interview room. He sat down in front of the computer.

'Well?'

'Yes, I want to report a robbery,' she said and blushed a little.

'Oh, I see, nothing else?'

'Well, in fact, it was a kidnapping.'

'Excuse me, but you will have to explain what you mean.'

'You know the robbery at the National Museum? Well, we are the ones who did it. Me and my friends.'

'So, you are saying that you stole two of the most famous paintings in the history of art?' he said with an acid ring to his voice. 'And did so without leaving any trace?'

'Yes, actually; nobody discovered us.'

'Well, I understand,' said the policeman and looked at the clock. 'But you also mentioned something about kidnapping. Who has been kidnapped?'

'Nobody. We kidnapped the paintings at the National Museum.'

'Oh, did you indeed? And how did you manage that?'

'We took them down from the wall and put them in the basket of my Zimmer frame.'

'I see. And if I've understood you correctly, then you

wheeled them out. Do you have any more crimes to confess to?'

Martha thought it over. Should she mention what they did to the safes too? Despite everything, they hadn't raked in very much from that, and it would hardly make any difference to the sentence. But deep inside she was proud of it. How many people committed crimes wearing white bathrobes at the Grand Hotel?

'Well, this wasn't really our first crime,' she said. 'Before we stole the paintings, we plundered the safes at the Grand Hotel.'

'Oh, I see, that too. You have been busy, haven't you? So how did you manage that?'

'We short-circuited the cables to the boxes and then we anaesthetized everybody with henbane and cannabis.'

'Ah, yes, I understand,' said the policeman who as yet had not written anything on his computer. 'And what did you do after that?'

'We shared out the loot.'

'Yes, of course you did, and you did that at home, I suppose?'

'No, we actually live at the Diamond House retirement home, but we have absconded. Now we have moved into the Grand Hotel.'

'Well, what a tale! So you have run away?'

'Yes, they had such poor food at the retirement home and they locked us in. So we took a couple of taxis and left.'

'Taxis, yes, right,' said the constable and wiped his brow. 'When they locked you in, you took a couple of taxis . . .'

'Yes, to the Grand Hotel. That was where we planned the painting theft. Regrettably, it didn't work out as we had antici-pated,' Martha went on, and felt embarrassed about admitting how comical it had all been. 'When we were going to fetch the ransom money for the paintings, the sea grew very rough and all the money disappeared. On the car deck, that is.'

'You don't say. Goodness me!' said the policeman and he tried to be serious. 'The money disappeared on the car deck. Was that down in reception?'

Martha wasn't listening; she was completely absorbed in her own thoughts.

'But really, perhaps it was fate, you know. You can't control these things. However, it was one thing to lose the ransom money, but what concerns me is what happened to the paintings. They've disappeared.'

'Which paintings?'

'The ones we stole. We hung them on the wall when we went to fetch the ransom money, and when we came back, they had disappeared.' Martha looked miserable. The policeman sighed.

'And what were these paintings?'

'Monet and Renoir. Don't you read the newspapers?'

'Yes, indeed, I just wanted to be sure that we were talking about the same paintings,' the constable explained.

'But what worries me more than anything else,' Martha went on, 'is that nobody might realize just how precious the paintings are.'

'But there isn't a soul who doesn't know that Renoir and Monet are precious.'

'The problem is that we painted sailing boats onto the Monet painting.'

'Oh, did you really? Painted sailing boats?'

'Yes, indeed, and also we added a hat and a larger moustache to the Renoir painting.'

'Oh, yes, very funny. My word, there is so much one can do!' said the constable, turning off the computer.

'But I haven't finished yet,' Martha protested. 'Now who is going to know that the paintings are valuable? We were going to give them back to the museum when we'd received the ransom money. You must help us to look for them. They are a part of our cultural heritage.'

'So the paintings you kidnapped have disappeared, just like the ransom money? You haven't exactly been blessed with luck, I'll say that,' the policeman commented. 'You know what? If you like, I'll make sure somebody can take you and your friends back to the retirement home.'

'But we are *criminals*,' said Martha, offended.

'Yes, I realize that, but you don't always end up in prison anyway. I shall phone for a car.'

Martha understood that he didn't believe her. Not one word. And the only proof they had of their involvement in the robbery was the money in the drainpipe – but they wanted to hang on to that for when they got out of prison. She hesitated a few moments, then got angry, opened her purse and pulled out a banknote.

'Study this five-hundred-kronor note. You must have the serial numbers of all the banknotes in the ransom. Check them. Then you will also understand that we are the ones who are guilty.' She threw the banknote down onto the table. 'The fact that the money blew away on the car deck wasn't our fault. It was the rough sea. The money was in this shopping trolley, and all we could save was a few banknotes. Now it's empty. Look for yourself.'

She got up, pulled the shopping trolley forward and opened

the lid so that the policeman could look in. Her indignation came in waves. She had seen herself as a skilled thief who had committed an almost perfect crime, and then she wasn't even believed.

'If you don't take my confession seriously, I shall report you for dereliction of duty,' she went on in a sharp voice. 'In fact, I shall wait here until you have checked the serial number. Until then, my friends and I refuse to leave the building.' She brandished her fist and at this stage the constable picked up the phone and made some calls. When he had contacted several departments and double-checked the number, he put the phone down and looked at her in amazement.

'You are right. But how on earth have you got hold of that five-hundred-kronor note? We never thought we could solve this theft. I mean, it was the perfect crime.'

'Do you think so?' said Martha, delighted. 'The perfect crime?' All at once she felt a marvellous sense of joy.

36

'Your mother has been remanded in custody, and is at the Kronoborg police station. That's how it is. I have spoken to the police.'

Nurse Barbara had received a visit from Christina's two adult children at the retirement home, and judging by their expressions, they had been deeply shocked.

'Mother must have become senile,' said Emma, forty-two, with a sigh. Like her mother, she was blonde and dainty, but instead of round, clear blue eyes, hers were light green and as oval as mussels.

'Pah, nonsense, she must have tagged along with the others as usual,' said Anders, who was seven years older. He had curly hair which was far too long and shrugged his shoulders as if to say that his old mum could do as she liked.

'Or she must have had a blackout,' said Emma.

'Your mother was in excellent shape when last I saw her. Otherwise I know no more than what we can read here.' Nurse Barbara pushed across the two evening papers. The theft at the National Museum filled the front page of *Aftonbladet*.

'"Big art theft – paintings disappeared",' Anders read, and shook his head. 'I can't believe Mum is involved in this.'

'Oh yes, look, there are photos of them too,' said Emma, holding up *Expressen*.

Nurse Barbara studied the old black-and-white passport photographs in which Martha, Christina, Anna-Greta, Rake and Brains were smiling. In some weird way, Barbara felt they were sneering at her. She had read the headline over and over again.

ACCUSED OF THE GREAT ART THEFT, the newsprint shouted out. But worst of all was that their proper names stood under the photos, along with the fact that they lived in a retirement home. Thank God they hadn't named Diamond House, but if that became known, Nurse Barbara realized the consequences. Ingmar would think she was completely incompetent and would never, ever marry her, let alone transfer part of the business into her name. He might even give her the sack. She went into the office to fetch a packet of cigarettes.

'And I had thought mother was a wimp,' Emma giggled when she had read the article. 'She evidently has more guts than I thought.'

'Women are capable,' said her brother, echoing the old rallying call of the women's libbers and turning the pages of the paper. 'And listen to this, they haven't found the paintings or the money.' He immediately perked up and looked happier.

'Mother seems to be something of a goer. Just imagine, they got a ransom too. What a robbery!' Emma's voice immediately sounded really cheery.

'The League of Pensioners.' Anders smiled. 'Mum claims that the ransom was lost on one of the Finland ferries. That the money was washed overboard. I don't believe that for a moment.'

'No, they must have hidden the dough somewhere. Mum will have her share of the loot somewhere, believe me.'

'You haven't started thinking about our future inheritance, have you?'

'Yes, actually. She ought to share this. Several million is missing – if you believe the newspapers.'

'Mum is likely to get at least a two-year prison sentence,' Anders went on, and he pointed to an analysis in *Aftonbladet*. 'You know what, Emma, we'll visit her in jail and ask where the money is. Try to get an advance on our inheritance.'

'But Anders, there is something fishy about all this. Why did they give themselves up? Nobody suspected them. First they carry out the perfect crime, and then they go to the police station and confess. It's as if they *wanted* to end up behind bars.'

'Don't you treat your pensioners well here at Diamond House?' Anders asked when Barbara returned. 'Nobody goes voluntarily to prison, do they?'

'Old people can be a little special,' she said deviously. 'You never know with them. Would you like some coffee? We have a coffee machine here.'

'Yes, please,' Emma answered.

'Do you have a five-kronor coin?' Nurse Barbara held out her hand.

Emma and Anders each gave her one. While Barbara fetched the coffee, they continued to read the morning papers. They, too, had written a lot about the theft.

'I've got an uneasy conscience; we ought to have visited Mother more often,' said Emma after a while, putting down *Dagens Nyheter*.

'Yes, then all this wouldn't have happened,' Anders admitted, but he stopped what he was saying when Barbara came back with the coffee. 'Do you have any buns? We haven't had time to eat lunch.'

'I'm sorry—'

'Cakes or biscuits perhaps?'

'Unfortunately—'

Emma looked at the pile of newspapers on the sofa. Next to them lay two copies of yesterday's *Expressen*. She put down her cup and held up one of the newspapers.

'We didn't have the opportunity to buy this yesterday. Can we take it?'

'No, I'm afraid it belongs to the retirement home,' Nurse Barbara answered.

Then Anders let out a laugh.

'Come along, Emma, let's be off.' He got up and went towards the door.

'And the room, we should decide about that,' said Nurse Barbara.

'We'll keep it for the time being. Mum hasn't been convicted yet, and as long as they aren't here, you won't have to fork out for coffee.'

Nurse Barbara gave a start. She had gone to the trouble of contacting Christina's children, only to be treated like this. Perhaps she should have given them coffee on the house after all.

'Right, we'll leave it for now, but there was something else . . .' Barbara wrung her hands and didn't know how she should formulate this. 'Yes, well, about our conversation here. I would appreciate it if you could keep it to yourselves. I would rather not have the name of Diamond House associated with crime.'

'You don't want it to come out that our mother has lived here?'
Nurse Barbara nodded and got up.

'You know what I think,' said Anders. 'If she and the others had liked it here, then this wouldn't have happened. You should take a look at how you run this place.'

They went towards the door and on the threshold Emma stopped.

'Incidentally, if I were you, I would look after the guests who are still here so that they don't run away too,' she said. Then the brother and sister trooped out.

They stood for a while down in the lobby. Anders had to go to his job at the Employment Centre; Emma was going to do some shopping before going home. Now that she was pregnant, she only worked part-time.

'Mother can't have had it easy here; she lived in a large flat in Östermalm almost all her life. It was plucky of her to make a break for it,' said Emma.

'Yeah, it's quite something. When she lived with Dad, she never dared say what she felt. He was so dominant. Her role was simply to arrange fancy dinners and to be a good hostess. She can't have had much fun. It was good that they divorced, and now – *now she has gone on the run!*'

'At last she has dared do something. In the past she always wanted to please everybody. She is of the generation of women who were taught to believe in God, trained in domestic science and were expected to take care of a husband and children. Why didn't Dad see that she was miserable?'

'He only thought of himself. But now she is making up for all that. You know what? I'm beginning to like this.' Anders shoved his hands into his trouser pockets.

'Mother reminds me of a metal spring in an old mattress. One that has been pushed down for a long time but which suddenly pops up and is then impossible to push back again.' Emma gave a giggle.

'But criminal – I would never, ever have dreamed of that. On the other hand, did you see what it said in the paper? "One of the biggest art thefts in Sweden!" Hell, I'm beginning to admire Mum. She has done something to change her life, while I've just been rolling along on the same old tracks. However much I work, it only gets worse.'

'That's the same for all of us,' Emma chipped in.

'Yes, but my salary isn't enough any longer. Since they renovated the plumbing and drains in our block of flats, the rent has tripled and now the wife and I will have to move. I don't bloody well want to live in a suburb.'

'Well, then, you'll have to become a criminal too, or ask Mum for an advance on the inheritance,' said Emma.

'There might not be any inheritance, Mum might live another twenty years.'

'You're right. Besides, we must do something so that we *deserve* an inheritance.' Emma looked at the grey building with its asbestos fibre cladding where her mother had lived for the past few years. She inhaled deeply. 'If she ends up in prison, we'll have to make sure we visit her a bit more often. Take care of her. Or else we'll have to fix the dough some other way.'

'You bloody well sound like a criminal yourself.'

'Now, now, I've not gone that far,' said Emma, 'but, it is rather inspiring . . .'

*

When the temporary cleaner, Petra, went to fetch the cleaning trolley in the annex, she got a surprise. Her rubber gloves were gone and the paintings that she had taken down from the Princess Lilian suite were no longer on the trolley. Her Ajax window cleaner had disappeared, and the cleaning fluid for the floors was almost empty. She was angry with herself. She had intended putting the cleaning trolley back in the storeroom and had only stopped in the annex to put the paintings from the Lilian suite there. But at that moment her boyfriend had phoned. He had seen her with a stranger in the bar, and demanded an explanation. It had taken a long time to convince him that the guy was one of her workmates. The conversation had irritated her to such a degree that she had completely forgotten the cleaning trolley, and it wasn't until she was in the underground on her way home that she remembered that it was still in the annex. Now it was too late. Somebody had used the trolley and the paintings had disappeared into thin air. She looked for them among the other paintings, but couldn't find them. For a while she wondered whether she should tell the management, but she was afraid that she might have done something she shouldn't have. After all, she didn't want to risk her job. If nobody else had discovered it, she didn't need to say anything. The paintings would turn up eventually.

She put a new bottle of window cleaner and an unopened container of cleaning fluid on the trolley, fetched a pair of plastic gloves and went up in the lift. As usual, she had lots to do.

37

Crewman Janson drove in among the sheds in the Värta docks area. He stopped the car in front of the gate and opened it with his remote control. The quay was deserted and, besides a solitary dockworker who was snoozing on a pallet, he didn't see a soul. He drove on and braked at Hall 4b. Allanson stepped out of the car, unlocked the shed and with deft hand signals directed his mate who reversed in with the trailer. Janson turned off the engine and jumped out.

Although they had only rented the shed for the last nine months, it was already getting full. Down one long side stood pallets, a compressor and car tyres, and along the other you could see rows of shelving filled with things. There were car parts, contraband alcohol, copper piping and all manner of junk. But most of the space was taken up with bicycles. They would have been sold directly to Estonia, but the police had been tipped off and they had been forced to lie low for a while.

'Let's see what we have this time,' said Janson with a glance at the trailer.

'A crate of Finnish vodka isn't bad at all!'

'What about the roof box?'

They tried the lock. Allanson picked up a screwdriver and

poked with it a moment until there was a click and the lock opened.

'Do you remember that time when the roof box was full of dirty laundry?'

Janson grinned and opened the lid. Inside lay a cat cage, cat food, some blankets and tins of food. Two pairs of skis with ski sticks could be just seen underneath that.

'Fuck!'

'We can take it to Lost Property,' said Allanson.

'Pah, throw the rubbish away!'

'What about these, the shopping trolleys?' Allanson cut off the lock and pulled the zip aside. 'What the hell! Paper . . . who on earth fills a whole shopping trolley full of old newspapers?'

'There must be some Chinese porcelain or something like that underneath.' Janson eagerly started to pull out the paper but the floor got covered with paper without him finding anything. Allanson raised his eyebrows and had a closer look at the trolley.

'Perhaps there are drugs in the handle. It's best we take it easy. Have you seen that little hole up at the top? Perhaps they've put some shit in it. I don't want to get involved in anything.'

'Nor me. We'll dump it. But what about the other shopping trolley?'

'It's bound to be the same crap,' said Janson but, nevertheless, he opened the lid and looked inside. He groaned. 'Newspaper in this too.'

'Has it got a hole in the handle?'

Janson felt with his fingers.

'Oh yes, there's a hole in this too.'

'And this one?' Janson kicked the third shopping trolley.

'Mmm, no hole here, but what the fuck, feel how it rustles. I don't get it, three trolleys with newspaper. Let's just dump the lot.' Allanson threw the shopping trolleys back onto the trailer and looked around in the shed.

'You know, we'll soon have to try to sell this stuff.' He nodded towards the innermost part of the shed where the bikes were stacked along the short side. Three weeks previously, they had raided cycle stalls in the city and got several trailer loads of bikes.

'Next week perhaps. The weekend journey should be good, and I've asked the Estonians to pay in euros,' said Janson.

'Good, but we must push off now.'

Janson sat behind the wheel and drove out. When Allanson pushed the door shut and locked the shed, he jumped into the car. He pulled out a cigarette, lit it and wound down the window. A few raindrops landed on his face.

'It's going to rain. Get moving!' he said.

'You know what? Those shopping trolleys are water resistant. We can save them,' Janson said.

'That rubbish? Why bother?'

'One, at least?' Janson insisted, having completely forgotten about the hole in the handle.

'Are you going to drag the shopping trolley around like an old lady?' his mate sneered.

Janson didn't listen, but got out of the car and grabbed one of the trolleys off the trailer. Then he opened the shed door and put the trolley on a pallet right next to the entrance. When he had done this and had locked the door again it was raining heavily.

'A shopping trolley like that is great. It is useful if we want to move something and keep it dry. We'll have a use for it sooner or later.'

'All right, but if you turn up with a hat with a veil too, then I'm going to look around for some new friends!'

The men drove to the skip further along the quay, and threw in the rubbish bags and the two other shopping trolleys. They took the roof box and a few of the smaller items to the Lost Property office. This routine had gained them a reputation as reliable and trustworthy employees.

The sun shone into the room and made Chief Inspector Petterson sweat. He got up and opened the window, but closed it just as quickly when a gust of wind blew his papers onto the floor. Swearing to himself, he picked them up again and instead took off his jacket. Then he sat down, dried his face with a handkerchief and picked up the case file on the top of the pile. What a huge investigation it had become! Now six men were involved – six highly trained police officers who were trying to find the missing paintings and the ransom money. He sighed. It was a very peculiar case: they had five confessions but both the masterpieces and the money had vanished. He had never been involved in anything remotely similar. Although that officious old lady had brandished one of the missing banknotes, that wasn't enough to secure a conviction in court. Old people did, after all, have a tendency to mix dream and reality, and they could have got that banknote from anywhere at all. But, regardless, the prosecutor had wanted to keep them on remand so that the police would have time to collect evidence. So far, however, they hadn't got very far, but they had sent fingerprints and DNA samples to the forensic laboratory in Linköping for analysis. That might lead to results. Petterson phoned his colleague.

'Hello, Strömbeck. We must search the hotel today.'

'Yes, I know, I've phoned them. You know what? The pensioners evidently stayed in the Princess Lilian suite. Like film stars! This is just crazy!'

'Hmm, sounds lovely to me. Then that part of their story is true at least. But the bit about hanging up paintings worth thirty million in the room, I don't believe that,' said Petterson.

'The paintings that disappeared when they were in Finland,' Strömbeck added. 'They could have made all that up and how can we get any evidence for something that has disappeared?'

'That's just the point and the old lady claims that they went on the *Silja Serenade* to Helsinki,' said Petterson. 'But they are registered as having boarded Viking Line's *Mariella* and some of their belongings were found on that ship.'

'Perhaps they just *call* the ship *Silja Serenade*,' Strömbeck hazarded a guess. He had been involved in many complicated investigations and knew that you had to relieve the atmosphere when you got bogged down with the details.

'Jesus, not even the ship is right,' Petterson sighed.

'Searching their rooms at the retirement home might lead to something,' their colleague Lönnberg, who had been temporarily assigned to them from Norrmalm, went on in his leisurely manner. He had spoken to the staff at Diamond House earlier, and might be able to see things from a new angle. 'The thefts are thoroughly planned. There must be notes in a drawer somewhere . . . bits of paper they've forgotten.'

'You are right. Take two men with you to Diamond House,' Petterson said.

The inspector nodded, got up and fetched his coat. Admittedly it was sunny outside, but there was quite a cold wind.

'A search in a retirement home,' Lönnberg sighed, standing in the doorway. 'This job never ceases to amaze me.'

'Don't forget to look in the cake tin too,' Strömberg teased him. 'Or why not under the mattress?'

'We must actually take this seriously,' said Petterson in a biting tone. 'We can't ignore the case just because five elderly people confess to the same crime.'

'But could five pensioners have carried out an art theft that no professional criminal has previously managed? To be honest, I think they are taking the mickey,' said Lönnberg.

'Yes, that's a very likely explanation, because despite the fact that both the paintings and the ransom money are missing, the old pensioners are raving on and on about it being the perfect crime,' sighed Petterson.

The men couldn't help but exchange smiles.

'They said that they were going to receive the money in two shopping trolleys which they then intended to switch with two identical trolleys which they had filled with newspaper. But then, and listen carefully –' Petterson went on – 'then they say that *all the money must have blown overboard.*'

'Ten million doesn't blow overboard – nor do shopping trolleys,' Strömbeck protested. 'What do the surveillance cameras show?'

'Not much. The seamen who work there, Janson and Allanson, usually hose down the deck and evidently dirt and salt have splashed onto the lens. I don't understand why they even bother to have those cameras there. As soon as you need them, nothing can be seen on the film. I've gone through them. It's like studying porridge. In a few sequences you can see what look like dark shadows with umbrellas. As if car drivers would go around with an umbrella on the car deck! No way! But otherwise Janson and Allanson haven't noticed anything special either and they certainly haven't seen a group of elderly people or the shopping trolleys.'

'My bet is that the money is in that cake tin at the retirement home,' said Strömbeck with a wide grin.

'No, now we're going to the hotel,' said Petterson and got up. 'But don't forget that we are looking for a *changed* Renoir, one with a newly painted hat and moustache.'

'Right you are! Newly painted it is!' said Strömbeck, getting up too. The men put on their coats and took the lift down to the garage. The Volvo started at the third attempt, and after getting stuck in a traffic jam in the centre of the town they finally reached the Grand Hotel. The detectives discreetly showed their badges and asked to see where the quintet of pensioners had stayed.

'Are you looking for those lovely pensioners? The ladies who were staying in the Princess Lilian suite?' asked the girl in reception. She smiled courteously. 'Why?'

'We can't say . . .'

'Oh, they were just so nice. But unfortunately they have checked out. A pop star is staying in the Princess Lilian suite now.'

'We would like to look through the suite.'

'That's not possible. It's against our policy.'

Petterson and Strömbeck waved their warrant cards demonstratively. The receptionist seemed to be considering something, made a telephone call and after a while the Grand Hotel's housekeeper turned up. When Petterson explained the situation, she nodded and took them up to the suite. She knocked, but when nobody answered she opened the door with her master key.

'Oh, Lord, what a mess!' the housekeeper exclaimed before the police officers trooped past. Bottles and full ashtrays stood on the coffee table, a T-shirt had been thrown onto the sofa and up on the grand piano were a pair of red knickers. On the dining table were four empty champagne bottles and on one of the chairs you could see the remains of food and some crumpled serviettes. 'Yes, well we haven't cleaned in here yet . . .' she explained.

Chief Inspector Petterson noted the guitar leaning against the sofa, but what were the red knickers doing on the piano? Above the unmade beds two paintings were hanging at an angle, clothes had been thrown all over the place, and on the way out Strömbeck almost got tangled in a bra on the floor. The bathroom smelt of aftershave, and there was a pile of dirty laundry on the floor. Several kiss marks decorated the lower-left corner of the mirror, and on the shelf next to the electric razor you could see a hairbrush full of blond hairs.

'Rod Stewart?' Strömbeck asked.

'We protect the confidentiality of all our guests,' answered the housekeeper.

They stopped beside the grand piano and Chief Inspector Petterson was reminded of what Martha had said in the interrogation. Renoir and Monet had hung there. Now in their place you could see two colourful paintings reminiscent of Matisse and Chagall.

'How long have these paintings been here?' Strömbeck wondered.

'We bought those in 1952, but the suite hasn't been here that long. Let's see, it was opened a few years ago . . .'

'And the paintings have hung here since then?'

'I assume so.'

'You haven't seen a Monet or a Renoir?'

'Chief Inspector, great art should be enjoyed by everybody. That is why we have museums. If you go to the National Museum next door then you can see them and many other fine paintings.'

Strömbeck gave his colleagues a helpless look, and whispered: 'What are we doing here?'

'Looking for a Renoir and a Monet and ten million kronor. That's all,' muttered Petterson.

They had a good look round for a while, but finally gave up. In the lift on the way down they were joined by an elderly cleaning lady. At the front of her cleaning trolley was a feather duster and a rubbish bag and on the shelf above a bottle of cleaning fluid, Ajax window cleaner and some rags. There were some paintings on the trolley too.

'And what are these?' Chief Inspector Petterson wondered, and pointed.

'Paintings to go to the Salvation Army.'

'The Salvation Army?'

'Yes, they are poor reproductions. We should have original works of art here at the Grand Hotel, not this sort of junk,' answered the cleaner haughtily and poked at the paintings with the feather duster.

'I see,' said Petterson. 'So where does the hotel store its original paintings then?'

'In a storeroom. There are some sculptures there too. And
we have moved some paintings into the annex while they are
renovating.'

A little while later, Petterson and Strömbeck had one of the
hotel doormen take them to the storeroom. Together they
looked carefully through all the works of art and paintings that
were there and in the annex, but couldn't find a Renoir or a
Monet. Not even a reconstruction with a painted-on moustache. Tired, they returned to the police station.

Nor had the search at the retirement home led to anything.
Inspector Lönnberg had had a difficult time. A Nurse Barbara
had been pestering him all day and had constantly nagged
about discretion, while at the same time upsetting all the other
residents in the home. In the midst of it all, a religious service
was being held, and he hadn't even had a bite to eat. Not even
a proper cup of coffee and a slice of cake. Four of the rooms
belonging to the missing pensioners had been well cleaned, and
were therefore easy to search. Besides old-fashioned clothes,
sensible shoes, photo albums and jars of pills, there wasn't
much there. One of the rooms, however, had looked more like
a sort of storeroom and had been full of tools, screws, motors
and LED lights, but none of this could be connected to the theft
of the paintings. Lönnberg had searched everywhere but not
found anything of value for the investigation. If only one person had confessed to the art coup of the century, the whole
thing could have been dismissed as a hoax, but because there

were five of them they had to investigate. The inspector sighed and, due to the lack of other 'evidence', he did at least take their hairbrushes with him. You could always check DNA, even though you had to pay through the nose for the laboratory tests in Linköping.

When the three police officers gathered at the station to go through what they had seen, they were exhausted and very dejected. Chief Inspector Petterson folded his hands on the table in front of him.

'As you all know, the paintings and the money have disappeared, and five people have confessed to the crime. Even though we haven't found anything incriminating, the prosecutor will want to have the five suspects remanded in custody. After all, we are talking about paintings to a value of thirty million, and we don't have any other leads.'

Strömbeck put his feet up on the desk, and stared right in front of him.

'Can you see the headline before you: "Five pensioners remanded in custody. The police have no other leads".'

They all sighed, said they would call it a day and that it was high time to go home. Not only did they have a perplexing art robbery to solve but now they were also landed with five troublesome oldies!

38

The Volvo drove past the underground station and stopped at the Sollentuna remand prison. The driver Kalle Ström and two prison service officials helped Martha out of the car and made sure she had her purse belt, walking stick and Zimmer frame.

'Weird thingamy that,' said Kalle and pointed at Martha's reflector arm.

'I don't want people crashing into me, do I?' she explained. 'Rather a Zimmer frame with a reflector than a damaged hip.'

Kalle smiled to himself. He had driven many criminals in his time, and most of them were highly unpleasant, but he particularly liked this unusual lady. She seemed fascinated by prisons, and had hummed 'God in Disguise' all the way from the Kronoberg station.

Martha thanked him for the ride, leaned on her Zimmer frame and looked around her. She shook her head when she saw the huge grey buildings of the Sollentuna Centre.

'Now, boys, look at those, they are like horizontal skyscrapers. Ugly as sin. The people responsible ought to be in prison – not me!'

'But this building isn't so bad, is it?' Kalle objected, and pointed at the Sollentuna remand prison. Martha leaned her head to one side and looked up at the façade. The tall construction stood out from the grey buildings surrounding it, and shone when the light touched the glass. Here were interesting reflections to look at from outside – it seemed so silly that from now on she would be stuck inside.

'This way,' said one of the officials, showing the entrance. It was now that she would have to hand over all her belongings and would be admitted as a remand prisoner. Suddenly the seriousness of it all struck her, and she remembered the shock when the constable at Kronoberg had leaned forward, looked them in the eye and said:

'We don't put men and women in the same prison.'

At that moment, Martha had thought she would faint. How could she possibly have missed something like that? She was ashamed, and realized that if they were convicted both she and Christina would be parted from their old-fashioned suitors for an entire year. If she had known that, they might have preferred to stay in the retirement home – but then, on the other hand, they wouldn't have experienced any of their adventures. As usual, everything in life was a trade-off. Regrettably, she wouldn't have the company of Christina or Anna-Greta either.

'You won't be able to be together,' the constable had said.

'Why not?' Christina had asked.

'When several people are involved in the same crime, we must keep them apart.'

'But you can't do that,' Martha protested. 'We are like one big family, we must stick together.'

'But that's exactly what we want to prevent. The paintings and the money are still missing, and you mustn't have a chance to agree on a story.'

The five looked helplessly at the constable and couldn't even feel any pride about the indirect praise. A heavy silence descended upon them and they all looked at Martha.

'You went on so about how much better it would be in prison,' said Anna-Greta, indignantly. 'This is nothing like you said it would be.'

'I'm sorry, I didn't dream of –' Martha swallowed and felt the tears swelling. Brains must have noticed, because he put his arms around her.

'My dear, we all make mistakes. Don't cry. We'll soon be out again.'

But then Martha lost all self-control, leaned her head against his chest and started sobbing.

'What if Rake can't visit?' said Christina and she too started to sniffle. Rake put his arm around her shoulders.

'Don't forget, as a seaman I was often away at sea for long periods,' he said. 'Prisons are at least on land, and they are generous with pre-release outings. You'll see, we are sure to meet again soon.' He stroked her hair off her face and kissed her on the cheek.

Rake cleared his throat and Brains scratched under his nose a few times. They all looked very unhappy, and Martha got a pain in her stomach when she realized that she was the cause of all this. Almost nothing had ended up as she had expected. Since they had confessed at the police station, Christina and Rake had regretted doing so. Suddenly they wanted to stay on at the hotel. The same had happened with Anna-Greta who had started dreaming about Gunnar from the Finland ferries. From one day to the next, they all changed their minds about wanting to go to prison.

'You could have researched this a bit better,' said Christina, who was mourning the fact that she would be parted from Rake. She was also worried about the children, and what her old friends in Stockholm would say, the ones in the church choir.

'And you? Couldn't you have done something?' Martha defended herself. 'I was fully occupied planning the thefts.'

'You silly woman!' was Rake's comment, and Martha, who had just stopped crying, started over again.

'I'm so dreadfully sorry,' she sniffled. 'Next time I won't make any mistakes.'

'Next time?' the constable looked askance. 'Is it as bad as that? You haven't even got to prison yet, and you are already planning new crimes.'

'No, no, I mean in life,' Martha tried to distract him. 'From now on, I am going to think first, and act later.'

'Well, I wish you the best of luck with that,' said Rake.

They hugged each other for a long time before they were taken to their cells and promised they would soon meet again. Martha tried to end by saying something encouraging.

'Time passes quickly. Soon we will be sent to an open prison or be allowed out with an electronic tag. Before you know it, we'll be free again,' she said, and lowered her voice so that nobody else could hear. 'Listen now. Don't forget to demand a visit from the clergyman. It is not only God who talks to him,' she went on cryptically and winked. Then she quickly squeezed their hands three times and with that signalled to her friends that she had thought of a new plan.

39

The Sollentuna remand prison smelt new and fresh, and it did actually feel better than the older Kronoberg prison where they had been remanded in custody. However, it was all a bit much to take in at once. Martha walked through the premises with her head held high and tried to look as if she was calm and collected, but she was actually very irritated. Above all, she couldn't understand why the policemen at Kronoberg had been so rude. The five of them had, after all, gone there to confess their crimes. Instead of the pensioners being met with gratitude, those uniformed types had been almost scornful. There was no respect for old people, that much was clear. When Anna-Greta had cried over the missing paintings, and Christina had told of how she had embellished them, the police officer had had enough. He'd phoned his senior and had asked to have them all put under arrest. Then they were all interrogated a little bit more, and soon they were all remanded in custody on the grounds of there being reasonable suspicion of their committing a crime – a crime they had already confessed to!

'Come along now!'

Martha felt a poke in her side and the official from the prison services took her to the admission unit. She went into a room that was rather sterile and smelt of newly sawn timber and plastic. She was shown an armchair in a small, cold area in front of a wide glass wall, and asked to wait. After a while, she saw some people in dark blue sweaters inside the glass and waved politely. They must be the screws. She found herself mumbling the word *screw* several times, because she had heard that it was what the guards were called by the inmates. She didn't want to make a fool of herself now that she had ended up in a prison, and wanted to try her best to fit in. At Kronoberg she had heard talk of bullying and other dreadful things, so she would need to be alert. A hatch opened and one of the guards looked in.

'Welcome,' said the guard, and Martha thought this sounded strange. As if the guards thought you were here on a holiday visit. A conversation followed, where the guard asked how she was feeling, whether she took any medicines, if she needed a special diet, and how she looked upon her coming prison stay. She also had to hand over her watch, purse, rings, bracelet and other personal possessions, after which she had to change and put on prison clothes. The guards would want to be able to see who was a villain and who wasn't – and she had to admit that it would be difficult to tell in her case. So she conceded that the prison clothes were a good idea. You couldn't exactly see from looking at her that she was a crook, especially when she used the Zimmer frame.

When the admission procedure was over, she was led to her cell. It was one of many in a row, one after the other, in a long grey-painted corridor with flickering fluorescent lights. Martha came to a halt, and took a deep breath. It looked just like in the movies.

'This is it,' said the guard and opened the door to cell number

12. The room was very similar to her cabin on the Finland ferry, except with the big difference that here she had unfortunately ended up in second class. The room couldn't have been more than ten square metres, perhaps as little as six or seven. There was a shower and a toilet, but there wasn't space for more than a bunk, an unmovable table, a shelf and some weak-looking plastic hooks to hang clothes on. As soon as Martha went in, she was overtaken by a creeping feeling of being cooped up. Previously, she had thought of herself as being on an exciting holiday, but suddenly she started to feel as if she was being punished.

The guard closed the door and she felt a growing sense of uneasiness. She looked around and discovered that the top of the shelves and wardrobe sloped. There was nothing loose in the room, and nor was there a lid for the toilet or any clothes hangers. That was so that nobody could injure themselves or hang themselves. Martha started to panic. If this was what it looked like in the most modern remand prison in the country, then the other prisons wouldn't be much better . . . she looked at the crooked surfaces of the shelf and wardrobe. On the Finland ferry the furniture was straight and rectangular, but the ship heaved. Here, everything was crooked and out of alignment, but the floor kept still. You had to put up with so much in life; nothing was ever perfect.

She consoled herself with the thought that she would only be here until she was convicted in court, and then she would be moved on. Only not to the same place as Brains. She flopped down onto the bunk and felt very sorry for herself. She missed Brains and hardly dared think about how Christina was getting on. It wouldn't be easy for Anna-Greta either, she had had high hopes for Gunnar from the ship. Martha breathed heavily. This wasn't any better than the retirement home and for the first time since they had left Diamond House she wanted to go back there. Prisoners were allowed out on outings – temporary release she believed it was called. They would only have to retrieve the money from the drainpipe and then be off. She imagined how she and the rest of the choir gang would fly off to Florida or somewhere else nice and hot. There, they would stay in a luxury hotel, gamble at the casino, and gorge on good food. Of course it could be arranged, but she must start working on a strategy straight away. *If I start planning now*, she thought, *then I'll have a perfect plan ready for the first time they let me out on temporary release.*

The next morning she called to one of the guards. She said she had been awake all night because she had something important to confess. To get peace in her soul, she would have to talk to a clergyman. Otherwise, she said, there was a risk that a woman as old as she was would not survive the remand period. The guard phoned through to the prison's spiritual adviser right away.

40

The famous pop star in the Princess Lilian suite tottered over to the bar and got out yet another bottle of whisky. His medium-long blond hair was not brushed, and his jeans hung down on one side. He burped, looked at the label and got out another bottle instead. A Macallan from 1952. Down in the bar it cost 1,199 kronor for one centilitre, so that ought to go down nicely. He unscrewed the cork and took a couple of gulps before returning to the bedroom where he put down the bottle and two glasses. The girl on the bed slept deeply and after a moment's indecision he took a cigarette. On the bedside table he caught sight of the whisky bottle from the previous evening. There was still a bit left. That would go nicely with his Marlboro.

He went out onto the balcony and breathed the mild air into his lungs. Stockholm was just waking up, the sun was rising and the colours of the sky were getting lighter. In the lake between the Grand Hotel and the Riksdag building a man was putting out his net and the pop star was astonished that it was possible to fish right in the middle of a big city. Yes, he liked Stockholm. Here you were in the middle of a city, yet still in the country-side. It was a delight to perform in Sweden too. The Swedes were so well behaved and they applauded, while in countries like Italy and France you could get booed. In Stockholm he nearly always received ovations and, whatever he did, the audience cheered. No wonder he had celebrated the previous evening. He caught sight of the whisky bottles he and the band had thrown over the balcony railing. A handful of empty bottles had collected together on the edge of the metal roof, and two had rolled towards the drainpipe. He shouldn't have kept on partying so late, because he had a concert in Oslo that evening and he must be in good shape for that. But he had fallen for that girl in the Cadier bar, and they had had one drink after the other. Then, she had come up to the suite. He thought she was really special. He balanced the whisky bottle in one hand and got out his lighter with the other. With his heavy hangover he shook the lighter a few times before he managed to get his thumb in the right position to get a flame. It was a lovely lighter in gold with his name engraved on it. He held the cigarette over the flame, lit it and inhaled deeply.

Smoking, he stood still and watched the winding paths of the smoke until they dissolved and disappeared. Then he stubbed out the cigarette, drained the last drops from the bottle and threw that over the balcony rail too. It clinked as it hit the other two. Then he saw that one of those bottles hadn't even been opened. What the hell? He released a rattling laugh. In the old days he had ventured onto rooftops and even had a party on a roof once. Now, he was somewhat older but still as keen to have a drink. *I'll be damned*, he thought. He must save that whisky and then he could push the empty bottles down into the drainpipe. The opening at the top was right next to the end of the balcony, and if he lay down and stretched out his arm, well, then he'd be able to get at it. He reached the empties and was just about to push one of the bottles into the hole when he discovered a black rope which went right down into the pipe. What if somebody had lowered a good bottle of champagne down there to have for their next visit? Or, who knows, a wealthy type might have hidden away some diamonds for a narcotics payment, a car deal or the like. His imagination went into overdrive. Now he became bolder. Without any safety line he crawled outside the balcony rail, and crept forward. The rope smelled of tar, so it couldn't have been there long. He was curious, and pulled it upwards. There was a scraping sound, and then it got stuck. By now he was so curious that he yanked at the rope as hard as he could. Then something loosened and the top part of something which looked like a black rubbish bag could now be seen. He continued to pull but then it jammed again. Angrily, he gave it another yank but then the rope snapped. He heard the black bag slide further down the pipe before getting stuck again. Bloody hell! He swore to himself but then finally gave up. He pushed the two empty bottles down the pipe too. He put the unopened bottle inside his T-shirt and crept backwards towards the right side of the balcony rail again. Reaching the rail, he managed to put the bottle on the balcony and slowly pull himself up too. He got up, brushed the dirt off his T-shirt and examined his booty. It wasn't a whisky for 3,000 kronor a glass, but a Lord Calvert for 120! Accompanied by a torrent of expletives, he threw it at the drainpipe and returned to the suite. That very same moment he heard a sound from the room. The girl had woken up. He immediately remembered how charming she was, and hurried into the bedroom.

41

Brains had ended up on the very top floor of the Sollentuna remand prison among bank robbers, murderers and fraudsters. Brains was used to his calm and well-mannered friends at the retirement home so he found this situation all very new. *But*, he persuaded himself, *you mustn't judge people. Everyone is good in their own way.* It was a matter of thinking positively, even though some of the most fearsome types could easily kill him. The whole thing was a little unpleasant, and it had been a great deal safer at the retirement home. Also, the cell he had been placed in was so small that there was hardly room for him at all, and he hadn't been allowed to take any of his tools with him either. He thought about Martha. The old gal had really got them into a mess. She had wanted them all to have a better life, but now the outlook was grim indeed. Oh well, it would be better in the proper prison where they had a workshop. Then it wouldn't be so boring. He stretched out on his bunk to have a snooze, when somebody knocked on the door. A warder came in.

'A clergyman is waiting for you in the visiting room.'

'A clergyman?' Brains shook his head and was just about to ask what the hell the guy wanted, when he remembered what

Martha had said. Don't forget to demand a visit from the clergyman. It is not only God who talks to him.

'Oh, yes, the clergyman . . .' said Brains, getting up and following the warder to the visiting room. Martha must be behind all this and she must have something very important to say. He smiled to himself and politely greeted the spiritual adviser. The warder withdrew and Brains and the clergyman sat down on the sofa. The clergyman pulled something out of his pocket.

'I have a poem with me. A woman I visited wanted you to have it. She hoped it would help you to find the light.'

'The light?'

'Yes, the inmate, Martha Andersson, was very anxious about this. She writes poems every day, and this is evidently one of her best. She particularly wanted you to have it.' The clergyman handed over a sheet of white paper. Brains recognized Martha's handwriting. He unfolded the paper and started to read.

> *He, the one high above,*
> *Stretches out his hand,*
> *Gives you life –*
> *Like water in a drainpipe,*
> *Riches of freedom;*
> *Together we travel*
> *Far away*
> *Never forget me.*

Perplexed, he fingered the paper.

'I don't really understand this sort of thing,' he said. 'Shouldn't poems rhyme?' He handed the poem back to the clergyman who read it silently and then stroked the paper several times with the back of his hand.

'I think this woman cares for you,' he said after a while. 'Look at this, "Together we travel" and "Never forget me".' He gave the paper back to Brains.

'Does she like me, do you really think so? But couldn't she just say so – instead of my trying to interpret this?' He read the poem again.

'People express themselves in such different ways. This is perhaps her way of formulating her feelings.'

Blushing, Brains refolded the piece of paper and put it in his pocket. With Martha no longer close to him, he had felt himself abandoned, and nothing had seemed fun any more. But now, what a poem! He turned to the clergyman again.

'She's a lovely woman, that's for sure. We thought we would be together in prison, but it hasn't turned out like that. I hope we get let out soon. My good friend, Rake, misses his lady friend too.'

'But doesn't she come visiting?'

'No, his Christina can't visit him either. She has been remanded in custody too.'

'Goodness me. So there are four of you pensioners who have committed a crime?'

'No, five. Anna-Greta, who sings in the same choir, was also in the gang.'

'Five sinful souls – well, that is quite a haul.' The clergyman discreetly pulled out a Bible. 'Perhaps we can read something together?'

'That would be nice, but first I must reciprocate those fine words from my Martha. Can you give her a greeting from me?'

'Like what, for example?'

'I don't really know.'

'A Bible quote, perhaps?'

'That sounds nice, perhaps something about Moses wandering in the desert – or maybe I should try to write a poem myself. Then she will understand that I am making an effort for her sake.'

'That is a very beautiful thought.' The clergyman pulled out a pen and ripped out a page from his diary. 'Here,' he said and handed the page over. Brains thought about what he was going to write for a long time while the clergyman sat still without saying a word so as not to disturb him. Slowly and with deliberation he wrote down his poem:

> *Martha, I stretch out my hand*
> *To those secret places, my dear –*
> *I welcome the Light in this alien land.*
> *When you think of me, have nothing to fear;*
> *Together we can a new spring see –*
> *Together, you and me.*

That was about as cryptic as he could manage, and the clergyman wouldn't fathom anything but Martha would understand. He considered what she had written about the money in the drainpipe. The money that would give them a better life the day they got out of prison. But there had been a hidden agenda, too, in her poem. "Riches of freedom / Together we travel". She was planning something . . .

'Like I said, I'm no good at writing poetry,' Brains confessed, and handed over what he had written. 'But do you think she will like this?' The clergyman had a quick look at the poem and smiled encouragingly.

'They are beautiful words. I am sure she will be touched.'

After the clergyman had left, Brains was in the best of spirits. He and Martha had found a way to communicate, and sooner or later he would get to know what this wonderful woman was planning next.

42

By the day that Martha was to be moved on to Hinseberg Women's Prison, the evenings had grown lighter and the first leaves were appearing on the trees. When she came out through the door she saw that a car was already awaiting her. Before getting in, she looked up at the Sollentuna remand prison where the sky, as usual, was mirrored in the glass façade. The sun's rays had a beautiful glisten to them, but it hadn't been so glowing inside there. Now, thank God, a real prison awaited her, although it was a pity that it was only for women. Naturally, it would be much better than the remand cells, but it would be tough. She had discovered how *confined* it felt to be in a prison cell. In the retirement home they had been locked in too, but Nurse Barbara had nevertheless refrained from putting bars on the windows. Martha could hardly appeal against the conviction. Since she had been the driving force behind the project, it just wasn't on to back out at the last minute – although they came close to not ending up in prison at all. The judge had actively tried to find them not guilty. The five-hundred-kronor banknote and the shopping trolley wasn't much in the way of evidence, even though their DNA samples were a match. On top of this the police had found mobile phones, hairbrushes and one or two gold bracelets stuffed in the back of the wardrobe at the Grand Hotel. Still the police and the judge thought that the old people were probably just confused. Besides, it was still not entirely clear what had actually happened at the National Museum. The warped walking stick confounded many police officers, and in the reconstruction they hadn't been able to fit in how it was actually involved in the theft. The judge said that the court should only convict if there was no doubt at all, and it wasn't fitting to demand a one-year sentence for pensioners without any previous criminal records. The lay magistrates, however, had thought that the five deserved the punishment. For several weeks the newspapers had written about the unscrupulous pensioners who had misappropriated Sweden's cultural heritage and laid their hands on paintings worth thirty million kronor – as well as a record ransom of ten million. In one newspaper editorial after the other, this extremely serious economic crime had been highlighted and compared with the ravages of the financial sharks. The lay magistrates had been influenced by this, even though they claimed that they were totally impartial. Martha had emphasized that they had intended on returning the paintings to the museum, and that the ten million was for charity, but nobody believed her. When the sentence was announced, nobody thought there was any point in lodging an appeal. Such a procedure took a long time and, besides, they had been through enough lately. With a bit of good behaviour, they ought to be out in six months, as all Swedish sentences seemed to be halved in reality, and by then they would have had plenty of opportunity to test what it was like in a real prison. Martha was curious about her new residence, and thought it would be exciting to share everyday life with criminals. She had never been in a proper prison before, and was always keen to try something new. It simply couldn't be worse than the remand cells.

The Sollentuna remand prison had been cramped and depressing, and the daily exercise period wasn't at all as pleasant as she had counted on. The guards had taken her to a sterile exercise yard which was hemmed in by the highest walls she had seen in all her life. No charming, swaying cornfields like in Österlen, only concrete. Not even if four convicts had stood on each other's shoulders with her balanced on top would she have been able to see over the wall! While she trampled around on the dirty grey concrete in the exercise yard, she could just about hear birds, local trains and the sounds of normal life outside – but all she could see was a grey grid of metal in front of a sliver of sky. The contrast between this and the Princess Lilian suite was just too enormous, and she even found herself longing to hear the sound of Rake's pinging night food excursions and Anna-Greta's thunderous laugh. If the clergyman hadn't come to see her now and then, bringing greetings from Brains, she probably wouldn't have been able to stand the isolation. The poems had helped her to regain her courage. She found something to occupy herself with. *The New Plan*.

'Hurry up now. Are you coming or not?' the driver demanded. It seemed as though they wanted to get the transfer done as quickly as possible so as to avoid the worst of the Friday traffic. Martha moved slowly with her hands cuffed, and it took time to fold up the Zimmer frame. The guards did try to help her, but they didn't know how to retract the reflector arm. Finally, she managed to instruct them on how to do this correctly and then she flopped down breathless on the back seat. A guard was seated either side of her. The car started, the gates were opened and off they went. The car journey west to Örebro proceeded at quite a pace and while the car passed through the landscape Martha thought about her friends in the choir. Anna-Greta and Christina would both be sent to Hinseberg too, and she was looking forward to seeing them again. She would also be able to initiate them into her new plan. At this stage, it was perhaps more useful to talk about *ideas*. She had to get them on the right wavelength.

After a few more kilometres, the driver changed to a lower gear and Martha caught sight of a white building surrounded by fencing and barbed wire. When they had driven past the lodge, the car entered the yard and came to a halt. She peeped out; she had heard that Hinseberg was a place that dated back to the Middle Ages and that nobility had once lived here. It wouldn't be too bad being locked up in an old country mansion, she thought, even though some of the historic buildings had been demolished. In the background she could make out the shimmer of the lake. There were no high concrete walls here, and you could see through barbed wire and chain-link fencing. She stepped out of the car, thanked the driver for the lift, and said hello to the new screws. A middle-aged, thin woman with long blond hair took care of her.

'Martha Andersson?' the thin woman asked, looking at her papers.

'The very same,' answered Martha and held out her hand. She wondered if there had been rumours about her arrival, because such things happened, she had heard. None of the eighty inmates here would have imagined that a seventy-nine-year-old criminal would be joining them. But what did your physical age actually say? Ninety-year-olds could be just as sprightly as seventy-year-olds. On the other hand, you got seventy-five-year-olds who seemed more like centenarians. Martha herself was still in pretty good shape. She had been exercising in the gym at the remand prison. She didn't really need to rely on her Zimmer frame any more but would make use of this when she had something criminal to do. Martha realized that most of her fellow inmates would be youngsters of about thirty or forty, but that didn't matter to her. On the contrary, she liked younger people – they often had more go in them than her contemporaries.

When the guard with the blond hair and ponytail had checked through all her papers, she took Martha along for registration. This meant that Martha must take off her clothes to be searched. It was degrading to get undressed and have to stand naked in front of strangers, especially when you didn't look like you used to in your best days, but here you couldn't be fussy. Of course the guards wanted to check that you didn't have anything with you that was forbidden.

'Can you fathom why people get so wrinkled when they are old?' asked Martha, pointing at the floppy bits under her chin and stomach. 'What is this good for?'

The woman with the ponytail looked up but didn't say anything.

'I might have to think about getting a whole body facelift. I wonder what that would look like?' Martha continued, and couldn't help but smile at the thought.

'Hold your arms up.'

'Right, yes. I could have something hidden in my armpits.

You know, dear, a lot more would fit under my sagging breasts.'

The woman with the ponytail didn't react at all.

'Sagging breasts are perfect for stolen diamonds – even though it does chafe a bit,' said Martha chirpily, and pointed at the two sagging reminders of a time long past.

'You see, gold is too heavy and falls out.'

'Sorry?' the ponytailed woman responded.

'And what do you do about breast implants? Have you got a special scanner for those?'

'You can put your clothes back on again,' said the ponytailed young girl hurriedly. Martha couldn't even see the slightest sign of a smile. 'Come along with me to the medical unit.'

'But I'm not ill.'

'We are going to carry out a cavity search.'

Martha realized at once what that meant, took a deep breath and let out an audible sigh.

'Well then, unexpected visits are so nice. It's been such a long time. But seriously, you are wasting your time; I haven't any hidden paintings on me.'

The ponytailed woman shot her a murderous look and Martha immediately shut up. Goodness, this one really was surly. Martha had chosen the wrong time and place to be jocular. After all, this was a prison. At that same moment she had a premonition of what awaited her. Being incarcerated in Hinseberg might not be quite as pleasant as she had anticipated.

43

The remand period was at an end, and now a more permanent posting awaited. Brains sat in the cell and looked through the poems he had received from Martha. Did he dare keep them? They might be confiscated and analysed at the new place. At the same time, he doubted whether he would be able to remember everything she had written. So he would have to take them with him. If the worst came to the worst, he could lie and say he had written them himself.

He read through the poems again. In the first ones, Martha had been preoccupied with the money in the drainpipe; in the later poems she had presented constructive suggestions as to what they should do with the millions. Apart from contributions to geriatric care, culture and the poor, she had become sentimental. She hinted that she felt sorry for museums which had such a difficult financial situation, and suggested that they perhaps ought to give some of the money back to the National Museum – why not as an anonymous donation via the Friends of the National Museum? *Much riches, to art in return*, or whatever it was she had written. Then she had said something totally different in later poems, which he interpreted as meaning that the money should stay in the drainpipe after all, but perhaps that was simply one of her usual tricks to send people down the wrong track.

The clergyman who took a look at every poem became all the more confused, and Brains had immediately explained that Martha obviously wasn't feeling very well in prison. In the two most recent poems, she had really gone to town:

> *In a life without borders,*
> *Riches for all,*
> *The sun of the earth welcomes us –*
> *Joy to all . . .*

So Martha wanted them to give money to others – but also be able to afford to journey to the sun. Then the Robbery Fund should become active and kept alive.

> *The heavenly choir's heartfelt fund –*
> *Fill it and keep it afloat;*
> *God's goodness*
> *Sees us all . . .*

Martha seemed to have great plans but was perhaps rather too optimistic. Even though they had stolen valuables and two famous paintings, they could hardly pull off just any robbery they wanted. It was tough in the criminal world, dangerous even. It had been interesting to take a few steps down the path of crime, but if prisons were like the remand cells he had seen so far, then they had a far better reputation than they deserved. If they were going to do something criminal again, then everything must work perfectly so that they did *not* get caught.

Brains found himself thinking about some very shady characters he had met in the Sollentuna remand prison. Juro, a big and strong Yugoslav, had whispered something about a bank robbery. He had spoken Croatian but Brains knew several languages and had understood it all. Brains' father had been a carpenter in the former Czechoslovakia and his mother came from Italy. When his parents moved to Sweden and ended up in Sundbyberg, they had spoken every imaginable language, and Brains had picked up quite a lot. He became interested in languages, and often listened to foreign radio stations when he was busy in his workshop. That way you learned a language without having to make an effort, he thought. So far it had worked. He had even become quite good at Croatian, thanks to his new friend in prison.

The Yugoslav must have seen when Brains sketched his inventions, because in the exercise yard some days later he had crept up to him and whispered:

'You special technic, yes?'

'Oh, I don't know about that. I used to build with Lego when I was little, that's all.'

'No, no, you inventor man. Me know. You clever – locks and alarms.'

Oh hell, thought Brains, who wanted to keep his head down with regard to any criminal skills.

'I studied Polhem when I was a lad and his locks are three hundred years old.' Brains laughed it off.

'Banks, you know,' the Yugoslav went on. 'Stoopid, much stoopid. They take money from state when bad bissness, yeah, but they not share when good bissness. I fix them, you help—'

'There are other ways,' Brains interrupted him. 'The state

can ask for a *bonus*. People make a lot of money from that.' He tried to sound like a man of the world; he had kept up by reading the newspapers and understood that bonuses made people rich. So he wasn't completely hopeless when it came to money issues. The Yugoslav laughed heartily and put his hand on Brains' shoulder.

'You know, here in Stockholm, Handelsbank at Karlaplan, yes? Close to Valhallavägen and quick to Arlanda Airport. But bank locks much difficult.'

Brains shrugged his shoulders to indicate that it was regrettable. 'I'm not at all familiar with that sort of lock.'

The Yugoslav mafia was not something he wished to be involved with, and after that conversation he kept his distance during exercise periods. He noticed how the Yugoslav sought out other inmates there in the yard, including how he tried to milk a former bank employee for information. The man was to be tried for economic crimes and had emptied accounts for many years until his wife gave him away.

A week later the Yugoslav left the remand prison and Brains gave a sigh of relief. Juro had taken too much of an interest in him and Brains had been forced to pretend he was more stupid than he actually was. *He who is silent gets information; stupid people who talk give themselves away* as he used to say. But one thing he did know – Juro and his mates outside the prison had planned a large robbery.

'Sometimes get caught, not dangerous. Just little rest in prison. Then fetch money,' the Yugoslav had explained.

Brains pondered this and wondered if he could adopt that

same attitude, but develop it a bit more. Skip the crime bit, but get rich *anyway*. That would, after all, be the ultimate solution, but as yet he hadn't worked out how to achieve it. He needed Martha. Together they would think of something.

44

'And why are you at Hinseberg? People like you should be in an old folks' home.'

Martha twirled round. She was in the kitchen and had just poured out a glass of milk when a girl with fuzzy hair, a narrow mouth and a pointed nose came into the room. The girl looked to be in her mid-thirties, was chewing gum with her mouth open and kept her hands demonstratively by her sides. What a welcome, Martha thought. She could at least *try* to be pleasant.

'Old folks' home, not likely. I'm not a dinosaur. If I was, I wouldn't still be standing here, I would have stamped on you already.'

The girl's eyelids flickered.

'Oh right, you are one of those cocky types. Watch yourself. Don't forget that you are a first-timer. I've done bird before.'

Done bird before? Martha thought about that. Presumably it meant that she had been here on earlier occasions.

'You don't have to "bird" me. There is nothing to stop you from being decent to a new inmate,' said Martha. She drank a large gulp of milk and put the glass down on the sink. 'By the way, I'm Martha Andersson.'

The girl continued to chew her gum.

'What got you here?'

'Robbery,' said Martha.

'What, someone like you? Is that why you drink milk – to become stronger for your next burglary? Holy cow!'

Two younger girls who had come into the kitchen guffawed. Martha looked out of the corner of her eye at the guard behind the glass of one of the long walls, and wondered whether he could hear them. The gaze of the chewing-gum girl was hard and vacant. She must be the one who bossed people around here, Martha thought, having already gauged how some things worked at Hinseberg. Some leader types took command, she had heard. Even the guards had said that there were several unspoken rules and it was best to follow them.

'Oh, did you just call me a cow?' exclaimed Martha.

The chewing-gum girl nodded.

'If you call me a cow once more, I'll stuff my walking stick where the sun don't shine! There's your warning.'

It became silent, and then some repressed giggling could be heard from the girls in the background. The chewing-gum girl took a threatening step forward.

'Listen to me, you senile old bat. Watch your step or you might just find that your face comes into contact with my fist next time you're in the showers.'

'Showers?' Martha didn't understand, and it must have shown.

'That's where we settle things. Insulated walls and no windows.'

'Oh right, so that's how it is,' said Martha, who guessed what the girl was getting at. She changed her tactic and tried a more friendly approach. 'Do you want some?' she asked, and held out the milk carton.

'You must be kidding!'

'And why are you locked up here?'

'Murder and robbery.'

Martha almost choked on her milk, coughing several times.

'And who did you rob, then?' the chewing-gum girl wondered.

'Oh, it was an art robbery. It was at the National Museum.' Martha shrugged her shoulders as if it had been just a trifle.

'Oh, the museum robbery. I've read about that. Are the paintings still missing?'

Martha nodded.

'Yes, that's right. They disappeared.'

'Like hell they did – where did you hide the paintings? I won't snitch.'

'Neither we nor the police have found them yet.'

'I won't fall for that. Out with it now! We all stick together here, get it? If you don't share, well . . .' The girl took Martha's glass and emptied it down the sink.

'The robbery was successful, but then . . . it couldn't all be perfect,' said Martha, filling her glass again.

'You're a cocky one, aren't you? There are lots of people here who have robbed pensioners, you know. Girls whose speciality is robbing folk like you. Take my advice: cool it a bit.' The chewing-gum girl emptied Martha's milk down the sink again. 'Oh, and one more thing. Since you are overage, we don't want you in the workshop. You can do general duties. We start working at eight, so you must have breakfast ready by seven o'clock.'

'That's for the guards – I mean screws – to decide,' said Martha.

'It's us and them. Anybody who goes into the screws' cage and complains doesn't belong here. Got it? Otherwise you'll get what's coming to you in the showers.'

'You are awful,' Martha muttered.

'Just because you are nearly a corpse, doesn't mean I wouldn't put my fist into you.'

The chewing-gum girl's eyes were as icy as the Arctic.

Martha cleared her throat.

'Right, then, tomorrow morning at seven is breakfast time. See you then.'

Martha left the kitchen with her head held high and out of the corner of her eye she saw the girl smirking. It immediately became clear to Martha that prison reality was something quite different to what she had seen on TV or read about in crime novels. Here it was a question of balancing on a knife-edge.

45

'This is how it should look. Almost nothing left,' said Allanson as he surveyed the shed. A large anchor and a crate of beer stood on the floor, and on the shelves were a couple of nets, some lifebuoys and fishing rods – otherwise it was empty. The cycles had gone, as had the mopeds and the two snow scooters.

'And to think that we got paid in euros just like we wanted. The kids' bikes and the ten-gear jobs sold like hotcakes. The Estonians were pleased as punch,' said Janson.

'Yeah, and the mopeds sold well too,' Allanson added. 'Now we've got some space again. What about a new venture? Bikes and mopeds, for example?'

'I think you might be on to something there. We could start Saturday?'

'I'm off work at the weekend, and I'm going to visit my mum at the retirement home. It's her birthday. But after that . . .'

'You're not going to bloody well visit her at four in the morning, are you?' Janson smirked.

'No, no.' Allanson looked down at the floor. He usually got teased because he visited his mother so often. But he was fond of her, and she was so pleased when he came to visit – even though she usually forgot that he had been there the minute he walked out the door.

'I'll stay with her a while and drive over to you after. But I should get her a present. I can't keep taking her chocolates and flowers.'

'Flowers? She should get them anyway, but take this. It looks completely new and it's only been getting in the way here.' He kicked the black shopping trolley on the pallet.

'The shopping trolley? But she is too old to go out shopping.'

'Don't you get it? Let her think she can. Things like that let people who are past it feel a bit younger. And you can always fill it with something nice.'

Allanson cast a critical eye over the shopping trolley, but then he brightened up.

'She's got one hell of a lot of blankets that she drags around with her. The staff at her retirement home have complained about it. Now she'll be able to put them in the trolley.'

'Exactly. Just don't forget to take out the old newspapers first.'

'Sure, but I should take her something to go with it,' Allanson mused, still not satisfied.

'You said that they had stopped serving cakes and biscuits at the retirement home. So buy some fancy buns and cream cakes for the place. And then you can get something tasty for us too while you're about it.'

Allanson's face lit up.

'You always have such good ideas.'

Janson laughed, closed the doors and locked up the shed. They got into the car again and did the usual round past the skip and Lost Property.

46

When the alarm clock went off at half past six, Martha gave a start. Many elderly people were in the habit of waking up early in the morning, but not her. In her world, it was an un-Christian time of day that was for birds, villains and uncouth youths who hadn't yet gone to bed. She unwillingly forced herself up, had a shower and got dressed. When the guards let her out at seven, she shuffled along to the kitchen at the end of the corridor. There were no kitchen islands and no fancy equipment either. Perhaps that was just as well; otherwise she would only have got confused. She got out the milk and ham and cheese slices from the fridge, and also found the oats and muesli in the cupboard. Cups and plates were on the shelves above the sink, and cutlery lay in the drawers underneath. Yawning, she boiled eggs, made some porridge – the old-fashioned way, in a saucepan – laid the table and put out bread, butter and marmalade. When she had finished, she flopped down on a chair with a cup of coffee in her hand. But she hadn't laid the table for Liza, that chewing-gum girl. Her place at the short end of the table was empty.

The girls came in one after the other, and Martha introduced herself. They said hello, sat down and began to help themselves.

They were all eating their breakfast in peace and quiet, and when Liza came crashing in, everyone looked up. You could tell at a distance that the girl was in a bad mood and it didn't improve when she discovered that nobody had laid her place at the table.

'Where is my cup?'

'I suppose it is in the cupboard,' Martha answered.

'Then put it on the table,' Liza responded.

'The plates are on the top shelf and on the lowest shelf you'll find the cups. The glasses are on the sink top.'

The girls stopped eating and the whole room fell silent. Martha ate her porridge, and slowly stirred her coffee. Nobody could fail to notice the tension in the room, but Martha was too old to care.

'Fetch the cup and lay my place too!' Liza growled.

'I might lay your place tomorrow, but that depends. I am extremely fussy about how people treat me.'

Liza gave Martha's cup a shove and coffee splashed out onto the table. Martha, who had expected something of the sort, calmly filled the cup again and continued to eat her porridge. Then she turned to the girl next to her.

'Is she always this difficult in the morning?'

No answer. Somebody coughed, a spoon clinked against a plate and the girls exchanged silent looks. The next moment, Martha felt how somebody pulled her chair back, grabbed hold of her blouse and yanked her up.

'My coffee!' Liza roared.

'There is tea too,' said Martha and calmly took the hands away from her collar. The girls all gasped, and then came a half-repressed giggle which spread and soon they were all laughing.

Liza glared at her, but Martha knew that she couldn't intervene. The girl had dominated the others by threatening to sort them out in the showers, but with Martha it was different. If she took an almost eighty-year-old woman there and beat her up, she would be the loser. She realized that, as did all the others in the room.

'Take your breakfast, Liza, and I'll do the washing-up later,' said Martha.

Liza pretended not to hear, but fetched a cup, poured out her coffee and sat at the short end of the table. Without a word, she buttered a cheese sandwich, and when she had drunk her coffee she got up and left the room. Martha watched as she went, and wondered how and when Liza would take her revenge.

47

Petra had been slumbering on the underground when she'd caught sight of the headlines about the great art theft at the National Museum. Not so many years had passed since the last robbery, and she'd wondered if the same thieves had struck again. She'd eagerly bought a paper but had been disappointed by the lack of detail given in the article. The police were keeping quiet, and at first they hadn't even announced which paintings had been stolen.

At the time, Petra hadn't followed the case particularly because she and her boyfriend had had a big row and at the same time she'd been studying intensively for exams. She just hadn't had time to keep up with the news and even her cleaning job at the Grand Hotel had been put on the backburner because she was so busy. It wasn't until after her exams that finally she sorted things out with her boyfriend. They had had a good talk and had decided that, after the stress of her exams, they both needed a well-deserved holiday. So they had gone off on a last-minute charter holiday to Spain. After Petra had arrived back from her holiday, well rested and with an attractive suntan, she went back to the part-time work at the Grand Hotel.

That was when she had found out that the two stolen

paintings were painted by Monet and Renoir. She was sitting in the library at the Grand Hotel leafing through some old evening papers when she saw them. The pictures. She gasped. The pictures that she had seen had had a hat and a moustache on the Renoir and extra sailing boats on the Schelde river scene, but apart from that the paintings were very similar to the pair that she had taken down in the Princess Lilian suite. She had simply assumed that they were poor reproductions – but what if they hadn't been? Yet surely it would be utterly remarkable if the crooks had left the paintings behind in a hotel room just one hundred metres from the National Museum. The works of art would almost certainly have been spirited out of the country ages ago. Nevertheless, she felt a growing worry, because when she thought about it in more detail, she remembered that the paintings did have noticeably fancy frames. At the same time, that was what they did, wasn't it? A beautiful frame could make the worst reproduction look almost professional.

Petra bit her nails and couldn't concentrate. The paintings had disappeared from the cleaning trolley, but perhaps they were still in the annex. She would have liked to have asked around if anyone had seen them, but she hesitated to do so. If they had been the real paintings then she could end up in trouble because she had switched them without orders from above. Paintings worth thirty million . . . She looked around her. There was a murmur of people at the bar and, over in the Veranda restaurant guests were sitting and eating. If she went across to the National Museum and asked to see reproductions of Renoir and Monet, she could compare them with what she remembered of the paintings in the suite. Then she smiled at her own stupidity. All she had to do was to look at the museum's home page on the Internet. She got up and went to the computer room on the ground floor.

She quickly surfed into the National Museum site and clicked her way into the collections. It didn't take long to find the two paintings. The hotel's colour printer was right next to her and she clicked on 'print'. Then she put the copies in her handbag and went back to the computer to delete her surfing history. With the papers in her bag, she hurried down to the annex. She simply must look for the paintings once more. They must be somewhere in the hotel because she couldn't imagine that they had just disappeared. Unless somebody had discovered them and realized that they were not worthless reproductions but paintings worth thirty million kronor . . .

48

When Allanson walked into Diamond House with the shopping trolley, his mother Dolores lay in her room and was sleeping. He waited a while out in the lounge but tired of that and went in to wake her. His mother's thin, white hair lay unbrushed on the pillow and she seemed confused, but when she saw who had entered the room her face lit up.

'Ah, my little boy, how nice to see you!'

'Happy birthday! Congratulations on being one year older!' Allanson gave her a hug.

'Nonsense. To congratulate somebody for getting older, my word, it should be the opposite. Every time I have a birthday you should put the flag at half mast and say you are sorry.'

Allanson held out the bag with the cakes in it.

'We've got something here to go with the coffee, and I brought along a surprise for you too. What do you think of this shopping trolley?'

'To put the cakes in?'

'No, your knitting wool and your blankets; you can keep all that in it.'

'Yes, it'll do nicely for that. Put it in the corner over there, and we'll go and have some coffee.'

'I'll just take out the newspaper first.'

'We haven't time for that. I'll ask Nurse Barbara to do it later. I've got some coffee cups here, but can you please go and fetch the coffee?'

Allanson did as his mother had asked. He always had done, and it was probably for the best. He put out the coffee cups and, to make things simple, he went to the coffee machine in the lounge to get coffee. Then he opened the carton and took out the cream cakes and the buns and biscuits. His mother sat on the sofa and indicated that he should sit in the armchair.

'Do you remember when you were a young lad and had picked lingonberries?'

Allanson nodded. Today his mother seemed to want to talk about that time they had been in the forest and seen bear tracks. It was a long and complicated story and his mother would take a long time telling it. He put the cakes on a plate and poured out the coffee into the cups. Eating sweet cakes made his mother tired, and after a while she would fall asleep. However much he liked her, it was trying to hear the same story over and over again. He leaned back in the armchair. After an hour or so she would be sleeping happily and then he could go off and join Janson.

The construction workers had gone home and the annex was empty. Petra went up to the noticeboard to see who had used the cleaning trolley after she had the day she had taken down the paintings. But a new cleaning list had already been put up. Instead, she started to walk around in the annex in the vague hope of finding the two missing paintings. She searched every-where but it was no good. She started to despair and accused

260

herself of being careless to have left the paintings on the cleaning trolley. From now on she would look at every painting with respect – with the utmost attention. She continued to search in the cellar and the storerooms, and then returned exhausted to the annex. Her hands shook when she got out her lighter for a cigarette. What had she done?

She pulled out a cigarette but then remembered that it was forbidden to smoke inside the hotel. She didn't want to go to the bar. She could simply do what she used to do at school and have a ciggy in the toilet. So she went into the bathroom and while she was smoking she admired the stucco work in the ceiling and the beautiful washbasins. The fittings here were all blue and silver and the artistically designed taps looked as if they came from a country mansion. It was a pity that the building workers had left it all so messy. They had thrown in tins of paint, brushes, protective paper and lots of other rubbish. Even though the annex wasn't being used, they could at least have kept the toilet decent, couldn't they? She finished her cigarette and flushed the butt down the lavatory. Then she gathered together several rubbish sacks and painting gear that was in the way. She could never leave anything untidy, even when she was not working. Behind the ladders there was a box marked 'Salvation Army' with things for the charity shop. Then she stopped. Right at the bottom she caught a glimpse of two paintings.

49

Petra moved the other bits and bobs which were piled on top of the paintings to one side. With trembling hands she lifted out the two paintings. They were indeed the very same ones she had taken down in the Princess Lilian suite. She looked around her for an empty surface to put them on. There, the console table. She put the paintings down and pulled out the colour copies. Yes! The paintings and the photocopies were identical, except for the hat and the rather too bushy moustache on the Renoir and the sailing boats on the Monet painting. She turned the paintings over and looked at the backs of them. There was a registration number and she could see that the paintings were on canvas. They both had gilded frames. When she thought about it, she hadn't seen any such frames in any of the other suites. However, she didn't get any further before she heard steps and voices next to the entrance to the annex. It sounded like the chief barman and the new girl in reception.

Petra hunched up in the shadows so as not to be seen. At the far end of the corridor there was a temporary storeroom for the furniture in the rooms that were being redecorated. Perhaps the two of them were on their way there? She waited until the steps silenced, and then lifted up the Renoir painting. To her surprise, she saw that she had some paint on her thumb. Somebody must have splashed the paintings by mistake. It must have been the building workers, or perhaps that rowdy rock star who had stayed in the suite . . . but no, by then she had already switched the paintings and before that the group of eccentric elderly friends had stayed there. She pulled out her handkerchief, wetted a corner and gently rubbed the surface of the painting. When she got to the man's hat, the handkerchief turned black and with each rub more of the man's hair could be seen. She tried the Monet too. A sailing boat disappeared without her having to rub particularly hard. It must have been those sweet old people in the Princess Lilian suite . . . Petra smiled such a wide smile that you could almost hear it. Police throughout Sweden had been involved in the investigation but nobody had managed to trace the paintings. The pensioners in the Princess Lilian suite had fooled the lot of them. Her first thought was that she should rush to reception and tell them, but that very same moment she heard a cry followed by groans and laughter. It was the chief barman and the girl. She quickly put the paintings back in the box where she had found them. Best to get out of there. She wondered what she should do: as everybody was looking for the paintings, surely sooner or later the police would offer a reward? Her student loan had all been spent and she was tired of the cleaning job. A little reward would solve all her problems. If she took the paintings home and kept them there for a while, she could say that she had acted in good faith. She hadn't actually stolen them, but had found them amidst the rubbish in the toilet room. She had taken care of them for the time being while she tried to find a better place for them in the hotel – that's what she could say, that sounded good. Then when she had realized what fine paintings they were, she had immediately phoned the museum – or the police – or whoever it was that had offered a reward. The state usually gave a reward to people who came across gold and silver antiquities buried in the ground. In that case, she too ought to get a reward for finding valuable works of art, she thought. She could tell the press how pleased she was to have saved the priceless works for posterity. The scenario was perfect – nothing could go wrong.

A door opened and she heard steps further away in the annex. The steps got closer. The chief barman and his girl! The pair of them weren't even trying to be discreet, but were talking loudly and cuddling and kissing as they went. She went back into the toilet cubicle, put the toilet lid down and then sat and thought about what she should say if they discovered her. Then she realized that if people saw somebody on a toilet they usually quickly withdrew. She heard how they went past and then waited for the lift to come up, but she didn't dare move until she heard the lift doors close again. She remained sitting a while longer and was now grateful that the two of them had come along. In the darkness she had had time to think. Now she knew exactly what she should do with the paintings.

50

Hinseberg also turned out not to be the best place to spend your summer! There was no Cadier bar or Veranda restaurant here, oh no. No goose or pyramid cake either, for that matter. Martha tossed and turned in her bed and found it hard to get to sleep. It was hot and unfortunately she couldn't go to the window and open it wide. She was in prison, after all. She pulled the covers off, puffed up her pillow and lay down again. But sleep escaped her, and Liza was at the back of her mind all the time. Perhaps it had been foolhardy to challenge her. Anyway, it had happened now and tomorrow she would lay the table for all of them.

When Liza came into the kitchen the next day she pretended not to notice that the coffee cup and plates were set out for her, but just sat down and helped herself to breakfast. As usual she looked as though she was in a mood and she didn't even acknowledge Martha's presence. She held her hands around the coffee cup and now and then threw a glance out the window. Martha wondered what was wrong with the girl, because you could see that she was extremely unhappy. Her facial features were taut, her skin grey and she had a vacant look in her eyes. If anyone spoke to her, she just muttered or simply didn't bother to answer. A little later in the gym Martha decided to try to talk to her.

'Hello,' said Martha.

'What are you doing in here?'

'Even a dinosaur has to keep in shape.'

Some other girls came in and went directly to the exercise machines. Liza ignored them, put out a mat on the floor and started with sit-ups.

'I hear you're going to get a temporary release,' said Martha after a while when Liza took a break.

She got a grunt in reply.

'Aren't you pleased?'

Liza stretched out full length on the floor and began to do press-ups. Martha shrugged her shoulders and lifted some dumb-bells.

'You know what, when I get my first temporary release I won't have anywhere to go,' Martha said after a while in a new attempt to start up a conversation. 'I left the retirement home, now God knows . . .'

Liza, who was now on her way to the exercise cycle, stopped.

'Welcome to reality. Those of us who end up in prison always lose our flats. In the workshop we earn enough to buy sweets and ciggies, but no more. If we haven't got parents or a guy on the outside who'll pay the rent, then we get kicked out. Then the authorities wonder why we relapse into crime.'

Martha had never thought of that. Then how could you make your way back to a normal life when you were finally released?

'You must have been through quite a lot, I suppose?' Martha went on.

'I don't want to talk about it!'

'But—'

Liza got up and left the gym.

During the next few days, Liza governed her domain as before, and she pretended not to even see Martha. It went so far that Martha was pleased when she heard that the chewing-gum girl had now been granted a temporary release. A few days before she was due to go, they came across each other in the laundry room. Martha gave a start.

'Did I give you a fright?' said Liza when she caught sight of Martha. The girl stood in one corner and waited for a washing machine to finish. She nipped past Martha and stood so that she blocked the door. 'Well, look what we have here! So you dare to go around alone?'

The ceiling light was rather weak and there was a smell of wet wool and washing powder. The floor was wet, and a laundry basket had been tipped over in the corner. Martha pretended to be indifferent, but her heart was beating faster than usual. She had gone to the laundry room to see if she could handle the machines without any help. She hadn't counted on bumping into Liza.

'Is this washing machine OK?' Martha asked, and nodded at the one closest to her. She hoped that her voice sounded natural.

'See for yourself. Stick your head in the drum and I'll turn it on,' Liza answered and lit a cigarette.

Martha pretended she hadn't heard the malicious remark, cleared her throat and coughed because of the smoke.

'Is this your washing?' she asked, and pointed at one of the machines that was in the middle of a washing cycle.

'Yes, and I intend to stay here until it's finished.'

Martha started towards the door, but Liza wouldn't let her get past.

'Hinseberg is an aquarium, have you thought about that? The screws can see you everywhere. But not here. Not here and not in the showers. Sit down.' She pointed at the bench beside the washing machines.

'I thought I'd go out and wait till you've finished.'

'No, sit down.'

Martha hesitated at first, but then went and sat down.

'About the paintings. I've been thinking about them,' said Liza and she took a bit of tobacco off her tongue. 'A Renoir and a Monet; a lot of money, that is.'

'For the person who finds them, yes.'

'Come off it. Where are they?'

'Don't know. We managed to steal some of the most valuable paintings in Sweden, and then they disappeared after we fetched the ransom money. I wonder if there is a link there, that somebody traced us and got into the suite when we were gone.'

Liza took a step forward so that she stood right next to her. Far too close, thought Martha.

'OK, you're a first-timer, but you don't seem to have understood. We stick together in here. Out with it. Where are the paintings?'

'They were in the suite when we left the Grand Hotel and they were gone when we got back. I don't know any more than that.'

'Which suite?'

'As if I'd tell you that,' said Martha. 'Anyway, the paintings aren't there any longer.'

'Oh yeah, then it doesn't matter.'

'That's right, of course.' Martha stopped. 'Yes, I wonder myself what happened. Who got into the suite to steal the paintings? It must have been somebody who knew that we had disguised them.'

'Disguised them?'

'Yes, you should have seen what the paintings looked like,' said Martha and now she had to smile. 'We painted in a hat and sailing boats and a bit more besides so that they wouldn't be recognizable. But nevertheless they disappeared.'

Liza knocked the ash off her cigarette, and took a deep drag.

'Somebody could have recognized the paintings and then sold them.'

'But who? We were only gone two nights.'

'The hotel staff or the other guests, of course. If somebody hasn't simply switched the paintings.'

'Actually, there were two others hanging there when we came back,' Martha remembered.

'There, you see, aren't I right?'

'But the police have been round the entire hotel and searched. They didn't find anything. And we were going to give the paintings back when we got the ransom money.'

'And you got it?'

'The money disappeared.' Here Martha did actually stretch the truth a little, since she didn't want to say that some of the ransom money had been saved and lay there waiting for them in the drainpipe.

'Hang on, this is getting confusing. You carry out a record-breaking coup, but you lose the loot *and* the ransom money?'

'Yes, it was our first crime, you see. It's a pity about the pictures.'

Liza took a step closer and leaned over Martha. For a moment she wondered if Liza was going to stub out the cigarette in her face.

'Have the police questioned the cleaning staff?'

'Don't know. The police must have interrogated everybody.'

'Somebody, one of the staff, could have taken the paintings. A bit of money might get them to talk.'

'But I'm locked up for a year.'

'I get my temporary release in a few days. I can help you, but I want ten per cent of the ransom.'

'The money has disappeared, I said.'

'Listen, sweetie. It can't all have disappeared. I'll go along with perhaps some of the money disappearing, but not all of it. And the paintings are out there somewhere. They have either been sold down the line, in which case it's too late, or somebody has them and is lying low. Anybody at the hotel could have recognized them and now they are simply waiting for the police to offer a reward.'

'You're right. Why didn't I think of that?'

'Being a criminal is a profession. You need assistance. Admittedly, you are as old as the hills, but that doesn't make you any the wiser.' Liza gave Martha a measured look. 'I can do the rounds and ask my contacts. When I've found the paintings, I'll get my ten per cent. We will both be winners then.'

'I don't know, there are several of us involved. I can't decide this on my own,' Martha answered.

'Listen. It doesn't actually make any difference. You've already revealed enough for me to fix this myself.' Martha saw a dark expression pass over Liza's face before she continued. 'Did you really think I would share with you? Lesson one here at Hinseberg is that you shouldn't say too much. Lesson two is that you shouldn't trust anybody.'

'But—'

Liza took her clothes out of the washing machine and walked off without another word.

The night before her temporary release, Liza suddenly succumbed to a severe stomach bug. She lay in bed all the next day and the day after, and she and her probation officer never actually left. Nobody except Martha knew what had caused it. She still had some of Rake's herbs. Nobody had searched the reflector arm of her Zimmer frame.

51

It hadn't been easy, and it had taken quite a while for Petra to decide on what she should do. As she heard the lift descend and she was alone again in the annex, she set to work. The building workers had left some things lying around: insulation material, a roll of protective paper, rubbish bags and other bits and pieces. She quickly wrapped the two paintings in the protective paper and put them inside a brown rubbish bag together with some insulation, old newspapers and other junk. Then she put the filled bag in the toilet room. The rubbish wouldn't be fetched until Friday, and until then she needn't worry. She had twenty-four hours to smuggle the paintings out of the Grand Hotel.

As she left the hotel, she said hello to the two receptionists and exchanged a few jocular words with the doormen. Then she went home on the underground. She was on tenterhooks all the way to the university campus, and couldn't help thinking about everything that could fail, but she managed to persuade herself that it would all work out OK. She thought about her parents who had such great hopes for her. 'My conscientious little girl,' as her mother used to say. And her father who always boasted about her. If they found out! If things went wrong, she would be on her own. Her parents had never gone out of their way for her before, and certainly wouldn't do so now. Her mother meant well, but had poor health, and her father seemed to have had children mainly so that he could boast about something. He had worked in a radio shop, and if he hadn't inherited quite a lot of money, they would never have been able to afford to move to Stockholm. She was the first in the family to study at university. If he found out that she had hidden paintings worth thirty million, he would simply faint. No, he would have a heart attack.

In her lunch break the next day, she hurried to the Royal Palace, paid to go into the Royal Armoury Museum but didn't bother about any of the exhibitions. Instead, she went straight into the museum shop and went through all pictures and posters depicting the King and Queen. After having browsed a while, she settled on a colour print of the King in uniform and one of the royal couple. She bought them, and put them in a protective cardboard tube before returning to the hotel.

During the afternoon Petra made lots of trips to the annex to check that everything was still there. When she had finished cleaning, she waited half an hour more until the construction workers had gone home, and then took the lift to the annex. She carefully opened the door and stood there quietly a few minutes until she was absolutely certain she was alone. The chief barman wasn't due to work until two hours later, so she had plenty of time. When she understood that she was on her own, she fetched the paintings and put the Monet on the carpenter's bench. It was quite a lot of bother to get the painting out of the frame, and she had to use a wedge as well as pliers before she managed it. Then she put the colour print of the King in uniform on top of the *Schelde* painting and stapled the print to the edge of the canvas. Having done that, she put it back in the frame, leaned the picture against the wall and took a few steps back. He looked really handsome, the King, standing there in his grey uniform with lots of medals on his chest. His uniform cap fitted nicely and hid the fact that his hair was thinning. He looked much more stylish than those fat politicians you see on TV nowadays, she thought. Perhaps she ought to stop voting for the Social Democrats, because she was a royalist. How could you be against a royal family? If you got rid of a king, you would have to replace him with another head of state – and that wouldn't be any better, would it?

She then moved on to the Renoir painting. The large gilded frame was perfect for a picture of the King and Queen together. Quickly she removed the heavy frame, put the colour print on top of the canvas and stapled it in place. Then she put the wretched frame back around the canvas again – which took some effort. She flicked her hair away from her face and looked at her handiwork. Now the picture really looked rather fancy, but it did, after all, show the Swedish royal couple. The two of them were what represented the country abroad, and the Social Democrats could say what they wanted! It was only a pity that Queen Silvia had had a face lift. One of the most beautiful women in the world had not thought herself beautiful enough. That was a catastrophe for the women's movement, and a great disappointment for women in general, Petra thought. She examined the two pictures again. The colours were just right, and the frames were pretty good too. Perhaps the gilded frame around the royal couple was a bit too fancy. Petra took some dirt from the floor and rubbed it on the frame until it all looked a bit kitsch. Only if you actually lifted the pictures would you realize how heavy they were – otherwise you might well think they were plastic frames!

Petra put back the tools, put the rubbish bag with the other rubbish, and checked that she hadn't dropped anything on the floor. Then she wrapped the pictures in the protective paper again, put them in two black plastic bags and put these in her suitcase. For a few moments, she stared at the suitcase before locking it, pulling out the handle and wheeling it along to the lift. What she was doing was not theft. She was just *borrowing* the pictures a while, and as soon as she had got the reward, the pictures would be back in the museum.

Nobody paid any attention to her when she left the hotel, and on the underground she was just one of many travellers with a suitcase. When she got home, she closed the door to her room and gave a sigh of relief. Her little picture expedition had been a success, and if she hadn't taken care of the works of art they might have been lost for ever. Indeed, she was actually rather proud of her achievement. The paintings were now safe. She made a cup of tea and ate a sandwich before dealing with them. She looked around and decided that the best place for them would be hanging over the sofa. So she hung up the pictures, took a few steps back, and with a look of satisfaction on her face she observed how the King and Queen smiled at her from their gilded frames. Nobody, absolutely nobody, would ever think of looking for a Renoir and a Monet in a student room.

52

Heavy clouds hung over the country-house park and there was thunder in the air when Christina and Anna-Greta arrived at Hinseberg. When the gates were opened, and Martha caught sight of her friends, she was filled with warmth. At last she would be able to spend time with her old soulmates again, and that would be such a relief because the last few days had been particularly trying.

When Liza got better, it turned out that she wouldn't be able to get a temporary release for several weeks because all the probation officers at the prison were fully booked, and then came the holidays. Yes, it would be quite a while before she got out. Liza glared angrily at Martha as if she suspected something. Martha understood exactly. Someone like her would be certain to take her revenge.

It took quite a long time for Christina and Anna-Greta to go through the strip search, get installed in their cells and then receive their first introduction. Evidently, everything went well because only a few hours later you could hear a horn concerto coming from Anna-Greta's room. According to the rules, you could only bring in five private items, including flowerpots, books, cassette tapes and CDs. Anna-Greta seemed to have managed to convince some poor screw that she couldn't survive without her vinyl records. The screws probably just couldn't take her neighing. It had been different when Martha arrived – she hadn't even been allowed to bring in her knitting and the half-finished cardigan.

After lunch, the weather had cleared up and Martha went into the park. The three would meet for the first time since Kronoberg and she was apprehensive. The other two would surely be angry with her now that they had seen what a real prison was like? When the door opened and her friends came out into the yard, she had to inhale deeply several times before going to meet them. The sun was shining and there was a lovely scent from bird cherries and the lilac bushes. The cherry trees were in full blossom, and the air felt warm and mild.

'I hope you aren't angry at me for getting you involved in this,' said Martha, when she greeted them and they had turned down onto The Street, which was what everybody called the old track through the grounds. The birds were singing and everybody except Anna-Greta could hear the wind in the tree tops.

'Angry? But goodness, not at all! I haven't had so much fun since the parties at the bank,' Anna-Greta exclaimed. She fumbled with her lighter and lit a cigarillo. Christina and Martha looked at each other in astonishment. Their friend took a deep drag, coughed and then went on: 'Yes, just look how lovely it is here. This is quite something in comparison to the boring old lounge at Diamond House.'

Christina agreed. 'Why should we be sorry? This is what we were yearning for. A nice place to live with the chance to be outdoors everyday. Besides, they serve us food made in their own

277

kitchens. Pity about the old boys, of course, but we must console ourselves as best we can.'

'Console ourselves?' Martha wondered.

'Yes, without Brains and Rake we will have to make do with the screws. I saw several of them when I arrived here. Good-looking men; handsome and without a beer belly. The ones I saw had lots of muscles. The one with the sideburns isn't bad at all.'

'But Christina! What would Rake say?' said Martha, while Anna-Greta seemed to be dreaming of something far away.

'You know what? Gunnar came to visit me in remand prison.'

'Gunnar, how on earth?' Christina asked.

'He is shy, of course. When finally he plucked up the courage and sought me out at the Grand Hotel, I was already behind bars. That didn't stop him, though; he actually went and found out where I was.'

'That's amazing! Is he the one who has got you to start smoking cigarillos?' Martha wondered.

'Yes, do you want one? I can ask the screw to hand them out to you too.'

'Thank you, but we can manage nicely without,' said Christina and Martha with one voice, and they backed away from the smoke.

'And Gunnar, well,' Anna-Greta went on with a happy smile on her lips, 'he didn't condemn me at all; rather the contrary. He had read about the art coup and thought it was fantastic that we had fooled the National Museum as well as the police. All the women he had met before had been so boring, he said, and in comparison to them I was a wonderful tornado.'

'Tornado?' Martha savoured the expression. Not just a 'refreshing breeze' but a *tornado*. If he was judging by her voice, then he had hit the nail on the head.

'He promised to visit me here too.'

'No!' said Martha.

'And you know what?' Anna-Greta continued, 'Gunnar has a large record collection and has lent me three crates with vinyl records. Best of all, he likes Swedish gospel and there are several records with Lapp-Lisa. He loves it when she sings "Childhood Faith".'

'Jackpot,' Martha muttered.

'Anyhow, it's really nice here,' said Christina with a glance at the lawns. 'It is like sitting in a huge garden.'

'Yes, isn't it!' said Martha. 'In the old days prisoners lived in old wooden buildings, but—'

'Inmates,' Anna-Greta corrected her, as she thought everything should be called by its proper name.

'But it was extremely primitive and you had to ask when you wanted to go to the toilet. The buildings were demolished some years ago, so now we have this park instead.' Martha was proud to share the knowledge she had acquired about their new residence.

'A country-house setting, and almost as grand as the Grand Hotel,' exclaimed Christina and she gestured with her arms as if she wanted to embrace the whole world.

'The Grand Hotel? That's a bit of an exaggeration,' Anna-Greta snorted. 'This is nothing in comparison with a house in Djursholm, and have you seen the chain-link fencing? So taste-less, and it is four metres high. But we don't have to pay for the rooms, of course. When they charged my card at the Grand

Hotel, that gobbled up three years' worth of savings. And I want that money back, just so you know.'

'Of course!' said Martha and Christina at the same time.

'But the Grand Hotel had a fine spa, and we had fun, didn't we?' said Christina. 'At Diamond House we just sat and stared at the ugly blocks of flats across the street.'

'The grounds here are lovely, and there is a gym too,' Martha added.

'Excellent. I have started to build up my muscles – or whatever it's called,' said Anna-Greta. 'Gunnar likes beauty, he has told me. By the way, is there a spa here?' She took a last drag on the cigarillo, threw it to the ground and pushed it into the earth with her heel.

'No, but there is a sauna of sorts,' Martha answered. 'And a kiosk. And we can receive visits. But only from people who don't have a criminal record. A pity about Brains and Rake. You, Anna-Greta, are the only one who'll get to see her man.'

'Neeeiiigh!' she exclaimed, and it sounded louder and more pleased than usual.

The three ladies had a lot to talk about, and when they saw an empty bench by the path, they sat down. In the calm, they inhaled all the scents of early summer and looked out over the greenery. Some girls were busy weeding borders, and a bit further away another was cutting the grass. Christina smiled absently.

'You know what, Emma and Anders visited me in the remand prison. They praised me for the art theft, and wondered if I had anything else in the pipeline. As if one could steal from a prison! I was so pleased when the children came to see me. I hope they come here too, and that they'll bring Emma's new

280

baby,' Christina babbled on. 'You know, I've got three grand-children now!'

Martha, who was childless, pretended to be interested.

'Did everything go all right?'

'Emma had made up her mind to give birth at home, but then her husband said that it was a stupid idea.'

'Usch, yes, what nonsense,' Anna-Greta agreed.

'Then Emma wanted to give birth in water instead, like in the 1970s.'

'Yes, another fad,' said Martha who had read an article about it one day. 'If it's not one thing, it's the other.'

'So how did it go, then?' Anna-Greta asked, now curious.

'She gave birth before they had had time to fill the pool with water.'

Anna-Greta laughed so loud that if she'd still had the cigarillo in her hand she would have dropped it. Martha and Christina joined in the merriment, and had a good laugh just as Liza was walking by.

'You'll have to be wary of that curly haired girl,' said Martha nodding in Liza's direction. 'She's got quite a bite, that one. She asked me about the art theft. Interrogated me, in fact; it was worse than the questioning by the police.'

'Oh dear!' Anna-Greta exclaimed.

'Unfortunately, I told her that the paintings have disap-peared. Then she wanted to help track them down in exchange for a part of the ransom money.'

'What a cheek!' Christina said.

'Yes, and we mustn't involve more people because then we'll lose control.'

'Looks like we already have,' commented Anna-Greta.

'Pah, it'll sort itself out. But before we commit even one single new illegal act, we must find the paintings and give them back to the museum,' Martha stated forcefully.

'Indeed, but how are we going to do that?' wondered Christina, who had started to be obsessed with crime. Now she wasn't reading Selma Lagerlöf and Verner von Heidenstam, the great Swedish classics, but she preferred whodunits. In the remand prison she had listened with bated breath as soon as anybody talked about robberies.

'Perhaps Gunnar can be of help,' Anna-Greta suggested.

'We weren't going to involve anybody else,' Christina pointed out.

'You know, Liza said something about a reward.' Martha lowered her voice. 'Not a bad idea. If we announce a reward of one million kronor to the person who finds the paintings, perhaps they will come to light. We do have four or five million in the drainpipe.'

'Are we going to give away one million?' Anna-Greta opened her eyes wide. 'No, one hundred thousand should suffice.'

'But the museum must get its paintings. Even villains have their professional honour,' said Martha.

'As long as we don't end up in prison,' Christina squeaked.

'As if we weren't already here,' Anna-Greta pointed out.

'I've got an idea,' Christina announced. Momentarily, she was distracted by some sparrows that had gathered in the bushes just close by but then she refocussed her attention and continued. 'We put out an advertisement about a reward as soon as possible and when we get an answer we ask to get a temporary release and—'

'But then we will have a probation officer with us,' Anna-

282

Greta objected. 'Perhaps it would be better to wait until we are let out with an electronic tag.'

'But can you stay at the Grand Hotel with an electronic tag?' Christina wondered.

'No, the police will be able to track us on some computer and see exactly what we do, and then we'll reveal the money in the drainpipe,' said Martha.

'Can't we take the tag off and put it on one of the horses in the guards' parade instead?' suggested Anna-Greta, who had ridden as a hobby once upon a time. Martha and Christina looked at each other and wondered it they had heard correctly. Anna-Greta rarely used to joke. Gunnar must have achieved miracles.

'We shall have to think this over very thoroughly,' said Martha finally, 'concoct a plan and ask for temporary release.'

The others thought this sounded wise, and they left it at that. But Martha was not at all satisfied, because deep inside she felt a gnawing anxiety about Liza. What if that she-devil found the paintings first?

53

Nothing is hopeless and you should never give up, thought Nurse Barbara while she browsed through the papers on her desk. *Love is like politics. Almost like buying shares on the stock exchange. You never know which way it will go.* She had invested her future in Ingmar, and soon something must happen. She took out her white handkerchief and dried the sweat from her brow. Over in the general lounge two elderly men sat barely awake, and Dolores had dozed off on the sofa. Barbara saw them, but without taking it in. In her head there was only Ingmar. He had got problems with his wife. She had returned with the children but then gone back to England the week after. At first, he hadn't spoken so much about his marriage, but she had noticed that he had become silent and thoughtful. When finally she wondered what was wrong, he had told her that his wife had fallen in love with a British businessman in London. No man likes to be cut out, so she realized she must console him. She stayed the night with him and now she had several pairs of shoes and dresses in his wardrobe. She felt as if she had caught her fish, and was slowly but surely reeling it in.

'Ingmar, darling, what's going to happen now?' she ventured to ask some weeks later.

'My wife and I have some things to sort out, but then, dearest, then!'

Her and him. She quickly realized that he was serious about this when he introduced her to his children.

'This is my colleague, Barbara. I hope you will get on well together,' he had said as he introduced her to them. Ingmar had started grumbling more about everything he had to do. 'A pity I have so much overtime, darling, but we've got the evenings and the entire nights together.'

'I can help you,' she said in a sprightly tone and went on working to make herself indispensable.

Now they shared a home and a weekday life. At the end of each day she couldn't wait to finish at work to get home in time to make dinner. Just as if she and Ingmar were already married. She felt she was approaching the goal. *Soon*, she thought. *Soon!*

It was lucky that things seemed to be working out between her and Ingmar, because at work she had got problems. Since the art theft at the National Museum nothing had been the same.

'Why should we sit here? I want a bit of action,' said Sven, aged eighty-four.

'And I want to go on a boat trip on Lake Mälaren,' his friend Selma, eighty-three, nagged on.

'Can't we all go shopping?' Gertrude, who was eighty-six, interposed as she tugged on Nurse Barbara's sleeve. 'Some new clothes would cheer me up.'

The oldies went on like that, and when things were at their worst, Nurse Barbara searched frantically for the red pills. She searched and searched but she couldn't find them. Things didn't get any better when she went to the chemist's.

'Those pills weren't profitable, so we have stopped making them,' she was informed. The new pills she was offered cost much more. Barbara asked Ingmar what they should do.

'Goodness, we can't afford such expensive pills,' he answered. 'You'll have to entertain the oldies instead,' he laughed and gave her a hug.

In the retirement home, things were beginning to get out of hand. Nobody at Diamond House went to bed at eight o'clock as they were meant to, and they refused to eat the food they were served. And the weirdest of them all was Dolores, who was ninety-three. She went around with a shopping trolley full of blankets and old newspapers and claimed it contained money.

'I've been given several million,' she said every day, pointing at the shopping trolley and looking most satisfied. 'My son is extremely generous, I must say. To think that I am so well off.'

Barbara smiled and agreed because that was the best you could do with old people – smile and agree with them. She had learned that on a course.

Dolores hummed to herself, patted her shopping trolley and beamed. 'My millions,' she said and giggled.

'Congratulations,' everybody said at the home. They clubbed together to give Dolores a fancy cream cake with green marzipan, which was her favourite. A week later, Dolores had painted the trolley handle sky blue because, as she said, the money was a gift from heaven.

Barbara's days became all the more stressful. What she really needed was more staff at Diamond House, but every time she broached the subject Ingmar said he was sorry but they couldn't spend so much money.

'You see, my darling,' he explained, 'if Diamond House becomes even more profitable, then we can open more retirement homes. Then, sweetie, I will be rich.'

We *will be rich*, she thought, but didn't say it out loud. Instead, she proposed several ways to cut costs to make him happy. She was even a bit ashamed of one of her suggestions.

'If we make the present staff redundant and then employ immigrants instead, we can give them lower wages. They won't dare grumble, but will be glad to have a job,' she had ventured, uncertain as to how he would react.

'My darling, you are wonderful,' he had answered and from that day on he had regarded her with new eyes. She could sense his respect and now she felt not only like his woman, but also like his business partner too.

She gathered together the papers on her desk, checked that she hadn't forgotten anything in her in-tray, and got up. Then she put on her coat and went towards the door. Yesterday, Ingmar had mentioned something about how perhaps they could run the business together. She smiled to herself. She was getting close to her goal, and recently everything had happened much faster than she had expected.

54

'We must be granted temporary release soon, don't you think?' Martha said one day when she was washing up after lunch. The rain had stopped, and she and her friends intended to take a walk. It had been the rainiest summer for decades, and now and then Martha found herself worrying about the banknotes in the drainpipe. She prayed that Rake had sealed the rubbish bags as well as he had claimed, and that the tarred ropes would bear the weight. Nobody had been able to check them, since they hadn't yet been granted any temporary release and now more than six months had passed.

'No release this week either, but don't you worry, Martha. The money will be waiting for us when we get out,' said Anna-Greta and she put a dirty serving dish on the sink top. Martha squeezed some more washing-up liquid into the sink, and while she scraped the dish clean she thought about how calm and harmonious Anna-Greta had become. While she herself worried about the future, Anna-Greta played the gramophone or sewed prison clothes together with the others in the sewing workshop.

In no time, Anna-Greta had become popular among the inmates. Particularly when she described the various types of bank accounts and money transfers available.

'I like being here, because the girls have respect for my knowledge,' said Anna-Greta. 'They listen to me in a totally different way than at the bank.'

That I can believe, Martha thought, but didn't say it out loud.

Christina, too, was satisfied. She was often in the workshop where they made screen prints on T-shirts. Every day, she talked about some new slogan that a trendy advertising agency had thought up. Sometimes the rhymed slogans sounded just too silly, and Martha wondered if they really had been printed on the T-shirts. Then Christina admitted that the slogans *could* have been used, but that she had actually made them up herself. Her silly rhyming slogans became quite tiresome, and she didn't stop until the workshop got a large order from a Russian company. She couldn't rhyme those letters at all.

Martha felt quite comfortable in the prison too, although sometimes it was odd to have so many criminals around you. None of the inmates actually admitted that they had committed crimes, but they had obviously done something to end up in jail. The worst part was that the most heinous criminals lorded it over the others. Like Liza, for example. Martha gave a start when the serving dish slipped into the water.

'I won't be calm until we have given the paintings back and fetched the money,' she sighed and scrubbed with her washing-up brush on the dish.

'But Martha, the money in the drainpipe won't run away,' Christina consoled her.

'It might drip away.'

'There is no hurry surely. We're doing nicely here, I think,' Christina went on. 'It's such fun doing screen printing and we don't have to visit the gym in secret.'

'Exactly,' Anna-Greta chirped in. 'I can play my Swedish gospel music as much as I like. Have you thought about that, girls? That if prisoners have it as good as this, then old people in retirement homes ought to have the same?'

'Of course,' said Christina.

'Abroad they have more respect for the elderly. In some places you can be president after you're seventy,' said Martha.

'Here in Sweden you get put aside when you are fifty,' said Anna-Greta. 'We aren't worth anything. On the TV news yesterday, some pensioners complained about how they couldn't cross at traffic lights in time before the lights switched back to red. Then the civil servant responsible said that they certainly could cross in time, because the office had estimated the time needed.'

'Bring the guy here, and I'll push my Zimmer frame right into his crotch,' said Martha. 'No, when I come to think of it, that isn't enough. For that, we need a proper wheelchair.'

'I know what,' said Anna-Greta suddenly. 'We can turn the whole thing upside down. We can turn all the retirement homes into prisons, and all the prisons into retirement homes.'

'That would be a pity for the prisoners,' said Christina.

Silence reigned in the room for a long time while they all reflected upon this. Martha put her washing-up brush aside, and looked at the others.

'Now listen! We managed to change our own situation, didn't we? It's high time we started helping others.'

'But the millions in the drainpipe won't go very far,' said Anna-Greta.

'You know what? Yesterday the clergyman was here with a new poem from Brains. It was some sort of utopian poem about a robbery. The idea was that you didn't commit the crime yourself, but just got hold of the money afterwards.'

'Ready money, I like that.' Anna-Greta smiled.

'No, no more crimes,' Christina protested. 'I'm longing to see Rake.'

'But it's not *us* who are going to commit the crime, Christina. We shall only take care of the money *afterwards*,' said Martha.

'Well, it seems we have a new business idea,' Anna-Greta commented. 'Stealing stolen money . . .'

'Commit a crime, and you'll feel in your prime,' Christina tittered.

'Precisely, we must think big, otherwise the money won't be enough for investments in our country's accommodation for the elderly,' said Martha. 'Brains mentions it in his poems. He's got something in the pipeline.'

'But what do the guards have to say about that?' wondered Anna-Greta.

'Pah, everything he writes is between the lines. It's about a bank robbery, girls. Not the *perfect* crime, but the *ultimate* crime.'

'As long as we don't lose the old guys on the way,' said Christina.

'Or the money,' Anna-Greta added.

Martha pulled the plug out of the sink and hung up the washing-up brush.

'But we have at least learned a little since last time, haven't we?'

The others agreed about that, and when Martha had wiped the kitchen sink they fetched their coats and went out onto The Street. While they walked along the path they had a lively discussion about the future. One of the secrets of a happy life, they concluded, was to have something to look forward to. And the *ultimate crime*, what could be better than that?'

At breakfast the next day, they discovered that Liza's place was empty.

'Isn't Liza coming?' Martha wondered.

'Haven't you heard the latest?' one of the girls answered. 'She got a temporary release yesterday and hasn't come back. She has absconded.'

Martha stopped in her tracks. Her hand shook and without noticing it she spilt hot porridge on the table.

55

'Have you seen a curly haired girl who chews gum?'

The chief barman at the Grand Hotel stopped Petra on her way into the lift with her cleaning trolley. She was busy with the last of the Flag suite and only had the floor to do. She halted. A curly haired girl?

'No.'

'The woman was in her mid-thirties, I should think. She talked about cleaning and wondered if she could get some work experience here. I told her to see the housekeeper.'

'Why didn't she go directly to her?'

'A lot of people ask at the bar first. She wondered what it was like working at the hotel and if I knew who cleaned here.'

'Inquisitive type.'

'She wanted to get in touch with one of the cleaning staff, so I thought that if you—'

'Forget it, I've got another exam coming up soon. She can talk to somebody else.'

'It was perhaps stupid, but I gave her your name. You are always so good with people.'

'Well, tell her to contact somebody else, anyway. Sorry.'

Petra went into the lift and on her way up to the Flag suite wondered who the curly haired girl could be. Then she shrugged her shoulders, wheeled the trolley into the suite and got out the vacuum cleaner. After a while she had forgotten the whole thing.

Liza hurried out from the underground and looked around her. She turned her back on the light blue university buildings and started to walk towards the student residences. During the last few days she had sneaked in and out of the Grand Hotel and mingled with the cleaning staff, but still not found any paintings. She had been about to give up when the chief barman had mentioned a temporary cleaner who studied art history. Then she had asked:

'How can I get in touch with her? Perhaps we can share a full-time job.'

The chief barman had said that he couldn't provide any personal details, but she had already felt his gaze. It was the usual. He looked more at her low-cut top than at her face. Without hesitating, she asked him for a cigarette, took an alluring step forwards and put her hand on her hip.

'Is there a decent hotel somewhere nearby which isn't too expensive?' she asked.

The chief barman polished the same wine glass for the second time.

'You've got af Chapman, the youth hostel on the ship, and there are some cheap places in the suburbs.'

'But the youth hostel is full, and hotels in the suburbs . . . do you really think so?' she said and sat on one of the bar stools. She elaborately crossed one leg over the other, and pulled her skirt up so that it caught on the edge of the seat of the stool.

'Hang on, I'll give you a hand,' said the chief barman. He fiddled a long time with the cloth of her skirt, before managing to free it. 'Incidentally, perhaps I can arrange something cheap for you in the annex. If I do, you must be out of there before the building workers start at seven in the morning.'

'As long as it isn't too expensive.'

'Nothing is free,' he said, and winked.

After he finished work in the evening, he had come to Liza in the annex, and the next morning she knew the names of all the cleaners at the hotel. A few days later she even got hold of the name of the temporary cleaner who lived in the Frescati student residences and studied at the National Library. Liza had a hunch about this girl so she tried to find out as much information about her as she could. Petra Strand was in the habit of sitting in the library until it closed, and she didn't come home until about sixish. Liza looked at her watch: it was half past four so she had plenty of time. After a while she reached the address and found the girl's name on a door down a corridor on the second floor. Liza checked that she was alone in the corridor, then pushed her steel comb in the slit above the lock and twisted it. There was a click and then the door was open.

56

Liza crept into a little room not much bigger than a cell at Hinseberg. There was a chair and an unmade bed, and a table with a pile of books. In front of the sofa on one side of the room was a little tea table and two armchairs. Above the armchairs hung two pictures of the King and the royal couple, and two smaller reproductions of old nymphs and angels. There was a noticeboard on the wall to the right with lots of Post-it stickers and a poster for this year's student carnival. She picked up one of the books and started to browse. *The History of Art.* Just like the chief barman had said, the girl evidently studied art history. Liza opened the wardrobe door. There hung some trousers, blouses and skirts and on the floor below them was a heap of shoes and boots. At the back of the wardrobe she caught a glimpse of some paintings. This got her excited and she pulled them out. They were reproductions, but so modern that she couldn't tell what they represented. She shook her head and put them back in again. No Claude Monet or Auguste Renoir there, that was certain. She closed the wardrobe and started to look through the desk. The top drawer contained letters, pens, rubbers, paper clips and a pair of scissors. In the next drawer were photographs and a packet of postcards. She quickly looked through them. Some views of

Stockholm, the *Vasa* ship, the palace, the Grand Hotel and a bundle with art motifs. She went through them slowly. The last two cards showed the missing paintings. Why had the girl saved those? Liza looked up at the wall again and decided to turn the paintings over to see if there was anything on the back. She went up to the picture with the royal couple and carefully started to turn it round. Then she heard steps out in the corridor. The door to the toilet was open and she just had time to nip in there and close it after her before a gang of rowdy young people stormed into the room. For a moment there was silence, and then somebody tried the door handle.

'Petra, we know you are in there!'

Liza heard laughter and cries and then they all started singing: 'Happy Birthday to you, Happy Birthday . . .'

Liza stood still in front of the mirror.

'. . . Happy Birthday to you. Three cheers for Petra!' There was another cry and whispering and then somebody yanked the door open. Liza cowered.

'What? Who the hell are you?' The girl with the birthday cake leading the group took a step back and the others did too.

'I was going to surprise her on her birthday,' said Liza and put her lipstick back in her handbag. 'I'm her cousin.'

'Are you? That's cool!'

'I've got an idea. Wait here in the room for Petra and I'll go and meet her in the lobby,' she went on, and quickly walked past them before anybody could say a word. On her way down the stairs she saw a young girl with red hair and a rucksack over her shoulder. Perhaps this was her, but Liza didn't dare hang around to find out. It was bad enough that she had been seen.

*

When she had got her breath back and was on her way into the city on the underground, Liza started thinking about the pictures. Perhaps she had been too optimistic, expecting that she could find them. If they weren't at the hotel, and none of the staff had them, then they were probably already out of the country. They might possibly have been hidden away in a cellar, or some attic or other, but she didn't really think so. Surely it would be too risky to hide them there? Pity about that Petra girl. Liza had hoped that she would have understood the value of the paintings and taken care of them but she clearly didn't have any taste. To have such fancy gilded frames around an ordinary portrait of the King and the royal couple seemed ridiculous. The frames were far too large too. No, she was certainly no art connoisseur. Liza huddled up on the seat. As she sat there she started thinking about the picture that she had started turning round. It had been surprisingly heavy and had a remarkably large frame. Perhaps there was something fishy about all of it.

57

Cheated. There was no other word for it. For weeks, Brains had been trying to figure out how he could remove a tag from his ankle and put it back again without being found out. But just as he had solved the problem, he discovered that he wasn't going to have a tag. Early one autumn morning, the door of his cell at the Täby prison was opened.

'It's time now. You're going to be moved on,' said the warder.

Brains, who had been lying down reading, struggled to a sitting position.

'What? Moved on? How?'

'You are done here, and will be going to an open prison. After that it'll be home to the wife.'

Thoughts crashed into each other inside his head. Home? He saw Martha and Nurse Barbara in his mind's eye, because he didn't have a real home any longer. His wife had remarried another man and lived in Gothenburg, while his son had moved abroad after a failed marriage. He worked for the Red Cross in Tanzania, and Brains hadn't seen him for nearly three years. Brains had retained his workshop in Sundbyberg, since he hoped that his son, one happy day, would take it over. But of course he couldn't live there. Brains stroked a finger under his nose and thought it over. If he couldn't go back to Diamond House, then what would happen?

'Rake, is he going to be let out too?' Brains wondered.

'As soon as they have finished reviewing his case.'

Brains rubbed himself under his nose again and tried to imagine his new life. But the only thing he saw before him was Martha and the money in the drainpipe.

'At Asptuna open prison you'll be able to acclimatize to your new freedom, so that it will be easier to adjust to society,' the guard went on.

'I'll be eighty. Better late than never,' said Brains.

'We've informed the transport section. You'll be fetched in a few days.'

Yet again, he felt dizzy. Brains had felt pretty comfortable in prison, and if it hadn't been for Martha and the others he would have had nothing against staying on there. Admittedly, the sound insulation had been rotten, and it had been damp at Täby, but here he had at least got to help make the food, and it had been a delight to be able to work in a proper workshop. Above all, it had been edifying to meet people of all ages. He didn't have to listen to all that talk about aches and pains, and times gone by; here people talked about what was happening *right now*. The inmates had such exciting plans for the future. He often listened to them during breaks. Primarily he tried to analyse how they had gone about things when they had succeeded with their crimes, and what had gone wrong when they had failed. The thought of the ultimate crime had not left him. And that, of course, included *not* getting caught.

Rake, too, had been fairly comfortable, because he had been able to do odd jobs in the garden. He liked flowers and watching how they grew, and he had even sown lettuce, cabbages and radishes. In addition, he had planted roses and perennials. He couldn't deny that he found it hard to bend down, but Brains had constructed a tool holder and a foldable chair that could be adjusted to different positions. It was delightful to see how happy Rake had become, and he gladly sung one seaman's ditty after the other while he tended his plants. However, he didn't like being locked in at eight in the evening, so to console himself he had put a calendar on the wall with lightly clad ladies. Instead of Christina, he said, but Brains wasn't fooled. Rake had always had an eye for the ladies.

A few days passed and then it was Rake's turn to be told that he was going to be moved on. The friends packed their few belongings and early one Monday morning they were driven off to Asptuna. Neither of them was seen as likely to try to escape, and there was no security risk either, so they weren't going to be given electronic tags. Or, as one of the guards said: 'A foot tag and a Zimmer frame don't seem to go together.'

A few days later, they were installed at the new open prison and to their surprise found that they had been given wardrobe-sized rooms without a shower or a toilet, and there was hardly enough space for their few belongings. They would get used to it, Brains thought, that's how it was. People get used to anything. It was only the first day and already he had asked if he could start in the workshop and he intended doing some exercising in the gym too. He had been a bit lazy about that when he hadn't had Martha after him, and he wanted to be in top condition when they met again.

'I'd like to go to the gym,' he said to the guards.

'Right, I'll join you,' said Rake, who also wanted to become fitter. Christina had said something about trim men. He took a portion of tobacco and smiled at the thought that they would soon see each other again. But where? He didn't actually have anywhere to live. 'Brains, have you thought about it?' he went on. 'When we get out. What's going to happen then? I mean, we can't stay at the Grand Hotel.'

'It will have to be Diamond House until we find something else,' said Brains.

'Never!'

'But your son has paid for your room, remember that, and that's where we've got our things and then there're the girls.'

'The girls, yes, of course,' said Rake, immediately feeling a sense of warmth spreading inside him.

They discussed various homes and hotels during the following weeks, but before they had solved the problem they found themselves with something else to think about. Late one afternoon a prison van drove in with two new prisoners. Brains gave a start. In the van sat a man he had seen before. Juro, the Yugoslav.

58

'Hey, you!'

At dinner the next day, just as Brains had sat down at one of the tables, he sensed a shadow behind him.

'Hi, matey!'

Juro gave him a thump on his back and sat down beside him with a more-than-full plate of spaghetti. Brains stared at his powerful shoulders and upper arms. Jesus Christ! Not an ounce of fat, just muscle. The Yugoslav looked like one of those people who could straighten a horseshoe with their bare hands. No, the legs of an oil rig!

'Where have you been?' Brains asked, and hoped his voice sounded relaxed.

'Isolation cell. Should be there but paper wrong.'

'Bombed?' said Brains, trying to sound criminal.

'Bombing? No, not yet, bloody hell.'

'No, I didn't mean that.' Brains turned bright red.

'I stay low now a while.' Juro pulled up a trouser leg and pointed at his tag. 'Look, sock under so no rubbing. But more important, you know how short-circuit?' He took a mouthful of spaghetti and it was like filling a container. Almost all the plate fitted in one gulp.

'Mmm,' Brains hummed. 'Yes, that tag can be—' He stopped himself at the last minute. Better to let Juro do his own thing. Otherwise the Yugoslav might try to enlist him again. Brains hardly had time to think that thought, before Juro lowered his voice.

'You not forget Handelsbank, yes? Now we have time, we plan.'

The Yugoslav seemed to have something big coming up. Brains breathed more heavily. He ought to keep well out of this, but . . .

The next morning, Juro was in the workshop waiting for him. He gave a sign that he wanted to talk to Brains. Brains fastened his piece of wood on the workbench and started the lathe. He was busy making a bowl for Rake. Brains had already made the basic shape, now he just had to make the hole in the middle. Rake needed something to keep his tobacco in. Juro cast a glance at the piece of wood.

'You make?'

'Yes, sometimes . . .'

Juro glanced over his shoulder to make sure nobody heard them.

'You. Most ready now, but, the lock . . .'

'Oh yes,' mumbled Brains. 'To the bank vault?'

He nodded.

Brains didn't know what to say. On the one hand, he wanted to know everything about the planned crime and where they intended taking the loot; on the other hand, he wanted to keep as much distance from the Yugoslavian mafia as he could. A gang of pensioners was one thing, the mafia was something else altogether. At the same time, the ultimate crime did involve somebody else carrying out the deed, while the five friends took care of the loot. To do that, he must find out where they were going to take the booty. He turned the lathe off.

'So it's coming up?' Brains threw a shy look in Juro's direction. The tattoo on his arm was of a burning torch, a knife and a sword. At the top, on his shoulder, a skull grinned at you.

'Just take away tag, is all,' said Juro.

Brains breathed deeply. The electronic tag again. Should he say anything? No, perhaps not.

'Now listen. Bank robberies are too risky. Besides, nowadays banks have so little cash. Hijack a security van instead.'

The Yugoslav's eyes glistened.

'But that means a lot of shooting.'

'No, find out which vans are being used. They must go in for an annual service, right? Then you can have your mechanics there and arrange things.'

Juro raised his eyebrows, lifted his shoulders and waited for what was to follow. But Brains started the lathe up again, he felt that he must think this over.

During the break, he wanted to test a new fishing rod, but he didn't get very far before he noticed that Juro had followed him to the jetty.

'What this, then?' he wondered, and pointed at the extendable fishing rod with hooks attached to the line. Brains had an inkling that he might find a use for it in the future – perhaps to go fishing in a drainpipe.

'Have you thought about how often a fish gets off the hook? Now some will get caught on these,' said Brains and held out a bit of the line with barbs.

'But how . . . hurts, yes?'

'No, no. When you carry the rod around, the hooks are covered with protective tops that dissolve in the water.'

'Oh, right,' said the mafia boss and he looked confounded. He sat down.

'You, that money van. Mechanics fix, what?'

'Then I need to know more about the whole thing.' Brains avoided looking Juro in the eye.

'We stop van. Crow feet and machine guns. Then explode van door and drive direct Djursholm with sacks.'

Brains had considerable difficulty interpreting Juro's rather limited language. Crow feet? What on earth . . . ? But, of course, he meant caltrops. Anyhow, he got the gist of what Juro was saying.

'Forget the machine guns,' said Brains. 'The drivers are not armed. You want to manipulate the locks instead. That's all you need to do.'

'Money vans, not bicycle locks, big locks . . .' Juro indicated the size with his mallet-like hands. Brains opened his fishing-kit box with sinkers, hooks and lines, and pointed at the lock. Then he took his chewing gum out of his mouth, put it between the bolt and the hollow, and closed the lid.

'Now it looks as if the lock has engaged, but it hasn't, not for real.' He took a firm grip of the box and without using a key got the lid open again. 'It's the simple things that are difficult, you see?'

Juro was all eyes.

'When the vans are taken in for servicing, your mechanics will be there. They will hollow out a bit more by the bolt, and then fill the hollow with metal shavings and resin so that it won't be visible. The doors won't shut properly but it will look as if they have. And you'll be able to open them, I promise.'

'Raisins? Everybody laugh me like hell.'

'Not raisins, resin, the sticky stuff from fir trees,' Brains laughed. 'But I said that I'm not an expert, don't forget. The post sacks will be going abroad. Switch the sacks with similar ones filled with false money. Deliver them to Arlanda airport. Watertight. Nobody will discover that the money is false until it gets to London, and then the cops can search all they want, but it'll be too late.'

'You not stupid,' said the Yugoslav.

'Nowadays, lots of different firms have these security vans. There's lots of money on wheels just waiting to be picked,' Brains went on. He then went off on a long ramble about the security-van coups in Hallunda, Gustavsberg and some other places, and how the robberies could have been carried out better. He spiced his tales with details that he had snapped up at the Täby prison, and hoped he would sound sufficiently knowledgeable so that Juro would talk with him about the robbery. Then perhaps he would let slip where he was going to hide the money.

'If you don't like that trick with the lock, then I've got another idea,' Brains continued. 'Why not stage a police check-point? Dress up as police officers. When the van stops and they lower the side window, you throw in something to anaesthetize them. Ether, perhaps, or I don't know what. When the guards have nodded off, then you'll have plenty of time to take out the money.'

'You one of us man,' said Juro.

'No, don't get me involved,' said Brains. 'I can't manage another stint in prison. I'm too old. This is my last time in here. Never again will a guard lock me in, and tell me what time I should eat and sleep. I want peace and quiet the few years I have left. You'll understand better when you get older.'

'But—'

'Then there is my heart,' Brains babbled on, and put his thin, sinewy hand on his chest. He wanted to fool Juro into thinking that he had left the life of crime behind him. In fact, his criminal career had only just begun. 'Yes, it is tough getting old, but after the raid, by the way . . . have you thought where you can store the sacks?' he wondered and tried to look as indifferent as he could.

'At eleven.'

'Eleven?'

'Yes, mother-in-law's wine cellar on Skandiavägen . . . in Djursholm. Jesus, she has big house, big like castle, you know, with long fences. Then car to Dubrovnik and—'

Juro went silent when one of the guards approached, and Brains quickly did a cast with his fishing rod. He stared at the float. Juro had been more forthcoming than he had dared hope. If the Yugoslavs stacked the loot from the raid in that wine cellar, then the five of them would get their chance. Now he must find out the date they were planning to carry out the robbery, and do so without Juro getting suspicious. But that wasn't entirely simple. It wasn't only a case of duping the police. The League of Pensioners would have to delude the mafia too.

In the evening, Brains got out pen and paper, and wrote a poem to Martha. This time he was even more cryptic than usual, and he wasn't certain whether Martha would understand his poem. On the other hand, he didn't dare be too specific. Stealing from the Yugoslav mafia was not something you did lightly.

59

Martha's first temporary release didn't turn out as she had intended. She had planned to put on some sort of discreet disguise, walk into the Princess Lilian suite and then check everything was OK with the drainpipe. Instead of having several hours to herself, she had to drag along two supervising warders with her. One of them was the ponytail screw, the stone face who had searched her when she arrived at Hinseberg. This humourless being didn't let her prisoner out of her sight, and followed her so closely that Martha continuously found herself almost running over her with the Zimmer frame.

'Be careful!' Martha hissed, full of defiance, but she realized that she must control herself. The guard with the ponytail would be happy to nail her if she could. The more months that Martha spent behind bars, the happier the ponytail would be. There were people like that. Martha was really meant to spend her first temporary release in Örebro, but she had specially asked to visit Stockholm. She had mentioned her old age and complained that she got dizzy sometimes and had problems with her balance. Now she wanted to see the royal palace one last time in her life.

'And you can see it best of all from the Grand Hotel,' she said when they reached the city.

'First we must deal with your errands at the social welfare office and visit Diamond House,' said the ponytail guard.

'But please, the palace is sooo beautiful,' Martha appealed and nagged until she got her way. It took a bit of time to walk there, because Martha was making herself look as frail as possible. It was necessary not to reveal just how trim she actually was. While she walked, she worried about the money in the drainpipe. What if Anna-Greta's tights had been too old, or Rake had forgotten an important loop in his knots? The worry gnawed and Martha was keen to get to the Princess Lilian suite straight away. She turned to the ponytailed girl.

'When I stayed at the Grand Hotel, I lost my mother's gold bracelet. I'd like to ask in reception whether they have found it,' she said, and she steered her Zimmer frame towards the entrance to the hotel.

'Now? We haven't time for that,' answered the ponytail woman.

'But the hotel has a lift from the street and it's easy for me to quickly reach reception. It won't take long, I promise.'

Her two supervisors looked at each other and nodded.

'OK, I suppose we can do that.'

Martha was relieved and soon the Zimmer frame was rolling along on the familiar blue carpet with the gold crowns. It was rather embarrassing to return there as a criminal, but she had to put up with that. In reception, she explained her errand.

'It would be wonderful if I could find the bracelet,' she ended her explanation.

'Your name?'

'Martha Andersson.'

Martha blushed; she realized that she must give them her real name to get up into the suite.

'Martha Andersson, yes, you stayed in the suite in March this year, right?'

'At the end of March.'

'Martha Andersson, here is the entry.' The girl clicked on the computer and scrolled down lists on screen. 'There were three of you sharing the Lilian suite, is that right?'

Martha nodded.

'No, we don't have a bracelet, I'm afraid.'

'But I think I know where it is. It won't take long to—'

'Sorry.' The girl shrugged her shoulders. 'The suite is occupied.' Her voice suddenly sounded harsh and deprecatory. 'Also,' said the girl after a deep breath, 'we don't have any other room available either. Not for you.'

Martha became sulky. The receptionist had realized who she was, but there was no reason for her to be impolite on that account. Then she remembered. They had left the suite without paying and the hotel had been forced to take the money from Anna-Greta's bank card. But Martha was not going to give up.

'The bracelet was my mother's and it means a lot to me. It is a family heirloom.'

The ponytail woman looked uncomfortable and indicated that they should leave, but Martha stubbornly stood her ground.

'No, we won't let anyone into the suite,' the receptionist repeated, but then stopped. 'Wait a moment, Martha Andersson you said –' The girl disappeared behind the counter and returned with a letter.

'This has been lying here a while,' she said and handed it over to Martha. 'We were going to forward it, but you got here first.'

It wasn't Brains' handwriting, but it did say Martha Andersson on the envelope. The address was written on one of those labels you can print out from a computer. Martha ripped open the envelope before the ponytail could come up to her. In the envelope lay a little note:

Hide 100,000 SEK in a pram. Put it near the back entrance to the Grand Hotel at 13.00 on 30 October. Keep away and don't involve the police. Come back to the same place after two hours. Under blankets and cushions you will find the paintings . . .

Martha didn't have time to read more before she heard her supervisors behind her. She pretended to get a coughing attack and between coughs she quickly chewed and gobbled down the note. Usch, how horrible it tasted, but that was what they did in the crime novels. She turned around.

'Weird, an envelope without anything in it,' she said. Martha then got another coughing attack because a bit of paper had stuck in her throat.

60

No, it couldn't be true! Nurse Barbara trembled with indignation. The criminal choir gang was on its way back! They had
evidently been model prisoners and after a few months in an
open prison they would be living at Diamond House again. The
problem was that they had paid for their rooms all the time
they'd been away and, according to the social welfare office, she
had no possible grounds to refuse them. On top of it all, Ingmar
hadn't thought it a problem – on the contrary, he had been very
pleased.

'What luck for us,' he had said. 'Now the spotlight will be on
us. The media will be bound to follow the oldies and write art-
icles. Can you imagine better publicity? Diamond House will
be so well known everywhere that we can hike up the charges.
Darling, see the possibilities!'

Nurse Barbara had tried to explain that the five were a decidedly poor example for others, and she had warned of the chaos
they would create. But he seemed unable to grasp what she
meant.

'But Barbara, dear, it is your job to deal with that sort of
thing. That's what you get paid for. Surely you haven't forgotten

your job description: *"to see to the welfare and well-being of the old pensioners"*?'

'But not criminals!'

'They have atoned for their crime and have every right to return to society. Now we shall show how well we take care of the poor old outcasts. We shall give them all the care and support they need.'

'But they did actually run away.'

'Yes, precisely. Take care of them, sweetie, give them tender care. *Care*, you see, is the word the council wants to hear.'

'What?' Nurse Barbara gasped for breath. 'But weren't we meant to cut costs?'

'A warm word, a loving pat of the hand . . . that doesn't cost anything. As long as the press keep an eye on us, we shall be perfect. Our retirement home must be a model of excellence. This will be a perfect model for when I open our new retirement homes. I have two deals coming along and there is a lot to do. We need to rationalize. I thought that you could prepare the transaction and take care of the administration. Meanwhile, Katia can take over Diamond House.'

'Are you suggesting I give up Diamond House?' A thousand thoughts rushed through Barbara's head, had she really heard that correctly?

'No, no, just for the time being. Don't think too much about it, darling. Soon you will have a top management position. Three retirement homes will mean more profit than one, and now that I am going to get divorced I'll need the money. Then, dearest, you'll want to join me in all this, surely? I need more people in management. As partners. You and me.'

He hugged her and she forgot everything else. He had at last spoken of divorce and indicated a future for them together. When he put his arms around her and whispered hot words in her ear, she pressed the palm of her hand against his chest and whispered: 'Soon, Ingmar, soon it'll just be us.'

61

'Now here we are; back again. I can't believe it,' said Anna-Greta, pushing aside the gauze on her hat and looking around her. In the lounge, the old guys were relaxing as usual with a game of chess, Dolores was dozing in her armchair and two older women that she hadn't seen before were knitting socks.

'Don't people say that the elderly should have peace and quiet? We have been moved from prison to prison only to *finally* end up back at square one again!' Christina sighed. 'To think that we've landed here. What an anti-climax.'

'Now, now. Don't forget the Grand Hotel. You wouldn't want to have missed that, would you? And this is just temporary. Very temporary,' said Martha and winked.

'I don't understand why they are letting us come back. We are a bad influence on the others,' neighed Anna-Greta.

'Diamond House has, for some reason, specifically requested to have us back. The alternative was a placement without Brains and Rake, and we don't want that, do we? And how would Gunnar find you then?'

'He will always find me,' Anna-Greta protested and looked insulted.

'Be that as it may, this will be a good base for our activities until we find our own solution,' said Martha winking again.

They all smiled, and they were indeed pleased to see their rooms where they had once made a home for themselves and knew where they had everything.

'So this is to be our general headquarters when we plan. Is that how you envisage it, Martha?' Christina asked.

'Yes, indeed. We can have meetings here and lay out our plans. Who would suspect a criminal HQ in an old people's home?'

They put their suitcases in their rooms, tidied themselves up and then went into the general lounge to have a little chat with the others. They had arrived just in time for afternoon coffee, and discovered to their surprise that some Danish pastries and three sorts of biscuits were served with it. Katia had evidently come back.

'I understand that some things happened here that you didn't like,' said Katia, sitting down next to them. 'But now Barbara has been given other duties.'

'About time too. We were locked in like at a kindergarten,' said Anna-Greta.

'That will be changed. Just tell reception when you want to go out, so that we know where you are.'

'Excellent!' Martha blurted out with decidedly imprudent speed.

'I also understood that you have made some proposals for improvements.'

'Yes, but nobody has paid any attention to them,' said Christina.

'I shall look at them,' said Katia.

Martha and the others looked at each other. This was incredible. Would they suddenly find themselves comfortable in the home just now when they had something else in the offing? If Martha had interpreted Brains' poems correctly, things were getting very hot. The *ultimate crime* of their dreams. He and Rake would arrive any day, and then she would find out more. First of all was the question of the paintings. They must get hold of one hundred thousand by 30 October.

A few days later, they discussed the matter over a cup of tea in Martha's room.

'I do have my savings – even though most of them were spent on the hotel and the cruise trip to Helsinki, of course,' said Anna-Greta. 'We can use them for the time being until things get sorted.'

Martha almost choked on her cake, coughed and stared at her friend.

'Without interest?'

Anna-Greta dismissed that comment with a wave of her hand.

'I'll transfer the money to your accounts so that the withdrawals won't look suspiciously large,' she went on. 'Then we will go to the bank together and withdraw the money. It's as easy as that.' She lit a cigarillo. 'It's so fantastic with the Internet. You only have to click on your mouse and everything is arranged.'

Now Martha really did choke on her cake, and her friends had to thump her on her back quite a while before she could breathe comfortably again. Anna-Greta looked at Martha out of the corner of her eye but didn't seem to comprehend why Martha was so flustered. By this point Rake was shaking with laughter and chortled, 'You do realize that "mouse" is sometimes used to refer to . . .'

Martha knew exactly what Rake was going to say, as in Sweden 'mouse' was a colloquialism for a certain part of the female anatomy. Deciding to spare her friend the embarrassment, Martha quickly returned to the conversation at hand.

'Yes, computers are fantastic inventions Anna-Greta . . .'

'I can understand that you are surprised about the money, but Gunnar has said that one should live in the present. When you are as old as we are, you must do whatever you can to have a good time. Then you'll have a richer life.'

'I see, that's how it is,' said Christina who was just as astonished as Martha. But when the friends had managed to remove the expressions from their faces, they thanked Anna-Greta profusely for saving them in an awkward situation. Then they wondered if she might be so kind as to extinguish her cigarillo.

'Sorry. I wasn't thinking. The Internet really is fantastic, don't you think?' said Anna-Greta as she stubbed out the cigarillo. 'Gunnar has taught me lots of things. Did you know that you can find vinyl records there too?'

'Ah, now I understand,' said Christina and Martha with one voice, because now their friend was always playing her gramophone. When Gunnar came visiting, they sat in her room and listened to horn music all the time. Now and then the horse neighs cut through the brass instruments and the piano, and when a record got stuck and nobody did anything about it, Martha wondered what they were really doing. Worst of all was when the needle got stuck at a place in 'Childhood Faith'. Couldn't they at least have listened to Frank Sinatra or Evert Taube?

When it became clear that Anna-Greta would fork out the hundred thousand for the reward, a pleasant calm settled over them all. They drank their tea with cloudberry liqueur in Martha's room and babbled happily about all that had happened to them so far, until Anna-Greta got up saying she had more important things to do.

'The bank transfers, you know,' she said in a solemn voice and made it clear that she did not wish to be disturbed. Then all evening she sat in front of her computer and arranged all the money transfers on the Internet. Slowly and conscientiously she divided the money between herself, Christina and Martha, and at breakfast the next day she proudly announced that it was now time to take a taxi to the bank.

There were a lot of people at the bank and the friends walked back and forth quite a long time until it was finally Anna-Greta's turn. She waved to them to follow her and they went up to the counter. Martha whispered that it would look suspicious if they all trotted up at once, but Anna-Greta insisted.

'It's my money, and I decide.'

The teller flashed them a sunny smile when they came tottering across with their Zimmer frames, but she paled when she saw their withdrawal slips.

'We don't have that much money here.'

'Oh yes you do. I phoned in advance. You have to when you want to withdraw large sums of money nowadays,' said Anna-Greta.

The teller hesitated, excused herself and disappeared to consult a colleague. A few moments later, she returned and looked with regret at Anna-Greta.

'Unfortunately, there has been a little problem. There isn't enough money in the account.'

'Don't try that. I transferred money from my savings account on the Internet yesterday. That's what you encourage us to do. You don't want us coming into the bank, do you? Please go and look yourself how much money I have in my savings accounts.'

'Something must have gone wrong, unfortunately. There is nothing there.'

'But I took my mouse and clicked,' Anna-Greta protested.

'You did what?'

'MY MOUSE, I said,' Anna-Greta shouted.

The teller gave a start and Martha noticed how she tried to remain serious.

'It can be difficult using the Internet sometimes,' the girl tried to console her.

'You think that I can't use my mouse just because I'm older than you,' Anna-Greta hissed.

From inside the office laughter could be heard and the teller discreetly covered her mouth with her hand.

'We had some computer problems yesterday. The transfers might not have been registered. We'll have to check that,' she said.

'I can tell you that I have worked in a bank, and been a customer here for forty years too,' roared Anna-Greta so that the gauze on her hat fluttered. 'You can't treat me just any old how!'

Martha watched the drama. No neighing today, indeed. Anna-Greta had produced her glass-breaking voice.

'If you find it difficult to use a computer, you might prefer to try our telephone service?' the teller said in an attempt to be friendly.

322

'Telephone service? But, my dear, haven't you wondered why I talk so loudly? I AM HARD OF HEARING,' she roared.

The queue grew behind them, and all the chairs were occupied. The door to the office was opened and a smartly dressed man hurried up to them.

'Come back tomorrow, and by then we shall have sorted this out,' he said politely and handed over a little pen with the bank's logo on it. Then he bowed and followed them pleasantly but determinedly to the exit.

When the three returned to Diamond House, they were all somewhat low-spirited. Anna-Greta locked herself in her room and didn't want to talk to anybody, Martha sat in the general lounge and tried to think, and Christina filed her nails obsessively. Nobody said anything. The coffee didn't taste good and nor did the Danish pastries. By the weekend the pram must be full of money, otherwise they wouldn't get the paintings back. Martha sank back in the armchair and closed her eyes. That usually helped when she had a problem to solve, and now they really were in a pickle. She could hear the distant sound of Katia talking on the telephone and some of the old guys chatting about football. Then she heard Katia's voice again . . . problems with the Internet . . . the connection wasn't working . . . service . . . Martha smiled to herself. Good, now she could console Anna-Greta. Then she nodded off and dreamed that she had raided the bank in Ystad. But just as she was about to board the ferry to Poland with all the money, she woke up. The door to Dolores's room had opened with a crash, and the old lady had started her usual walking around in the lounge with her trolley in tow.

'My son is the best there is,' she hummed with a smile all over her face. 'He has sailed around the world and made me a millionaire.' Then she pointed at the shopping trolley and laughed. A pink blanket and a sock hung halfway out of the opening and a shawl trailed on the floor. In the opening you could just glimpse some crumpled-up newspaper.

'That's nice, Dolores,' everybody in the room said.

'Now he has settled back on land. He wanted to be close to his mother, you see. Yesterday he came home from Helsinki.' Then she sang a little more, and did some additional rounds of the room before sitting at the table and helping herself to a biscuit. Martha liked Dolores who was always jolly and wished everybody well, but just for the moment she couldn't cope with her. Martha sank deeper into her armchair and closed her eyes again. The reward? How could they pay that?

62

Martha woke up with a start. She had had yet another strange dream. It was about Dolores walking around with a shopping trolley on a car deck. She walked round and round in circles and sang about her millions. When she went too far along the car ramp and was close to falling into the water, Martha woke up and sat up in her bed, confused. It was still dark and dawn was many hours away. But her brain had been working. The shopping trolley and the ferries to Helsinki . . .

At breakfast, Martha sat down beside Dolores with a cup of tea. They talked about the weather and the food a while until Martha thought the time was ripe.

'Your son, he has been at sea all his life, did you say?'

'Yes, all the time. He is so clever. He works on the car deck.'

'Oh, that's good. Better than being a captain. Because the captain has such responsibility, and what if the ship runs aground? Then he would be in trouble,' Martha fawned.

'He has never run aground.'

'No, I didn't mean that, Dolores, my dear.'

'I am not your dear. Just because you get older, you shouldn't have to be called my dear, should you?'

Martha became silent. This was not a good start.

'And it's even worse when people say old dear, don't you think?' she tried to appease.

Dolores didn't answer her, but had become grumpy. Martha tried again.

'What a lovely shopping trolley you have, with a blue handle and all.'

'My son gave it to me. He looks after his old mother, he does that!'

Martha moved a little closer and stole a furtive glance at the trolley. An Urbanista. A black one too, just like the ones they had received the ransom money in. But this one was dirty and scratched, and it had a blue handle. Of course it could have been spray-painted later. The bag itself was shiny on top, as if it had been splashed with oil.

'Shall we ask Katia to buy a layered cake?' Martha suggested. 'A lovely cream layered cake with marzipan?'

'Cake? No, I'm tired. Now I'm going to my room.'

'Let me help you . . .' Martha said and reached out along the handle to feel if there was a hole for a reflector arm.

'Don't touch my trolley! That's my money!' Dolores shouted angrily, got up and stormed into her room. Everybody smiled indulgently and went back to what they were doing, while Martha looked at the closed door, deep in thought.

Dolores didn't come out all afternoon, and the next morning Katia said she was ill. Nobody was to disturb her. She had asked Katia to phone for her son, and he had promised to come. Then Martha asked first Anna-Greta and later Christina to knock on Dolores's door to get a closer look at the trolley, but Dolores refused to open it for anyone. Not even Katia was allowed to go in. For the evening meal, a serving trolley with a plate of food was put outside her door, and the next morning everything had been eaten. But Dolores didn't show herself. Martha sighed. It was all starting to get very complicated, and she really had no idea what she should do.

That night, Martha couldn't sleep. She *must* get a look inside that shopping trolley. If Dolores's son arrived the next day, he might even take it away with him. Before then, she must be certain that the trolley really did have their money in it. Martha still had the master key. Of course, it wasn't the done thing to break into somebody else's room, but she could have opened the wrong door by mistake, couldn't she?

Sleepily, she put her dressing gown on, and crept out through the lounge up to Dolores's door. She felt the door handle and discovered that it wasn't locked. She cautiously pushed the door open but then stopped on the threshold. Oh my God, she could hardly see anything; she had forgotten that her night vision wasn't what it used to be. Silently, she went back into her own room and looked for the cap she had been given by Brains. She fumbled with it for a few moments before getting it to fit, and then returned to Dolores. Once inside the room, she closed the door behind her, took a deep breath and pressed the peak of the cap. A weak blueish light spread through the room and ghost-like shadows fluttered on the walls. Martha took a few terrified steps backwards and almost fainted with fright before realizing that it was the LED lights that were the cause.

Dolores was asleep and every breath she took ended with a loud, hissing snore. Martha looked about her to find the trolley. Oh damn, it was by the bedside table right next to Dolores's face. What would they have said at Hinseberg? What is the best way to sneak up on somebody? Martha found it hard to think straight, and decided it was best not to think too much at all, but rather just to get on with it. Without a sound, she approached the bed and stretched her hand out towards the trolley. Dolores was breathing deeply but suddenly she turned over so that her nose almost touched the handle of the trolley. Martha abruptly halted, turned off her cap lights and stood completely still. At any moment Dolores might open her eyes and cry out, but soon she started breathing deeply again. When she started snoring once more, Martha finally dared to get hold of the handle and drag the shopping trolley slowly out of the room.

Once back in her own room, Martha parked the trolley and opened the lid. Rarely had she felt so excited. Dolores's son worked on the Finland ferries and that stain looked like oil. Just think . . . although if he had taken a shopping trolley from the car deck after the storm, well, then he would surely have seen what was in it *before* giving the trolley to his mother. But, of course, there had been several shopping trolleys. He might have looked inside the others and thought they all had the same contents. The blue handle was the only thing that she couldn't explain. Regardless, she simply must look. Otherwise she would never forgive herself. As she put her hand in, there was a rustling of newspaper and some old blankets fell onto the floor. Impatient, Martha stuck her hand in deeper. She felt even more newspaper and even more blankets. Good God, was this Dolores's millions?

Martha pulled the crumpled newspaper out and felt deeper down. Still more newspaper, but there seemed to be something else too. Martha's heart beat faster and now she tipped the rest of the contents onto the floor. Goodness gracious! Five-hundred-kronor banknotes! They poured out, and soon there was money all over the floor. Martha had been right: this *was* the second shopping trolley! But what should she do with the money now? She looked around her. The duvet cover on her bed! She quickly took out the duvet and then started to stuff the cover full with banknotes. Armful upon armful disappeared inside the floral cover, and when that was full she started stuffing the pillows. One or two pillow cases ought to suffice for the reward. She put the rest back into the trolley. Dolores must not be allowed to notice anything.

Martha rapidly mixed in some banknotes with the crumpled newspaper and added some more newspaper from the old papers in her wardrobe. Then on top of it all she put a thick layer of five-hundred-kronor notes, and topped this in turn with blankets and the shawl. When the shopping trolley was full again, she examined it closely from every angle and wasn't satisfied until it looked exactly like it did before. Then she crept back through the lounge and opened Dolores's door a few inches to hear if she was still snoring. And she was. Martha then pressed the peak of her cap again to turn the LED lights on. In the weak light she moved into the room as silently as possible. She carefully rolled the trolley up to the bedside table and left it just as she had found it. Dolores suddenly stopped snoring and Martha gave a start. For quite a time she stood absolutely still while Dolores stretched out an arm and seemed to want to get up; she reached out in front of her, opened her eyes and stared straight ahead. Martha arched back, tried to think of an excuse for being there and was just going to open her mouth and say sorry when Dolores closed her eyes again and rolled over onto her side. Then she snorted, pulled the covers over her shoulders and let off a loud fart. Martha didn't move a muscle, waited and stared nervously at the bed. Not until Dolores started snoring again did Martha dare make a move. She hurried out through the door. Back in her own room, she sank down on her bed, exhausted.

'Goodness, what an adventure!' she exclaimed, but at that very moment she heard a mysterious noise. She winced and was so frightened that she almost fell off the bed. With her hand clenched in front of her chest, she stared at the door. Now it was completely silent. Martha waited. Nothing could be heard, and she became bolder. She put a hand on the bedside table and slowly got up. Then she heard the sound again. It sounded like – yes, of course, she had sat on the banknotes. Before she went to sleep she must make sure she wrapped a blanket around them so that they wouldn't rustle. The theft must not be discovered, under any circumstances. It would mean the end of their criminal career.

63

'I have been longing for this moment,' said Brains the next day when he had hugged Martha and stood there with his arm around her waist. He wanted to say so much, but couldn't find the right words. Instead he hugged her again and they stood there a long while without saying anything. The glazed entrance to Diamond House looked different now to how he remembered it, and not nearly as dreadfully ugly as he had imagined. It had, of course, been built in a boring 1940s style, but, after all, Martha lived there. He felt how she leaned her head against his chest.

'At last!' was all she managed to say, and then came the tears. 'At last,' she said again, and Brains thought of all the tender words he had heard in films and in TV series. That was just what he felt like, but it sounded so silly to say those words. So he just mumbled, and stroked her hair rather clumsily.

'Hello, don't you recognize me?' Rake called out, and came up to them. As usual, he had his cravat around his neck and during his prison stay he had even acquired a beard from ear to ear – a Newgate fringe, Martha thought it was called. He grinned happily with all his face, patted Brains on the back and gave him a big hug.

Martha smiled as she looked at the friends she hadn't seen

for so long. It just felt wonderful to be standing beside them again, and the tiredness after the adventure of the previous night meant that she could hardly stop crying. Rake looked great even though he smelt of tobacco. Brains was the one who held her attention, though; after all, he was the only man she had ever written poems to – although admittedly they had mainly been about various ideas for crimes.

'Martha, dear,' said Rake and he kissed her on both cheeks like a real Frenchman and that was probably because he wanted to make an impression with his new beard.

'Oh, that itches,' she couldn't stop herself from blurting out, but quickly she added something more friendly: 'How nice it is to see you again.' Then he smiled and pinched her lovingly on her cheek before returning to his Christina. They seemed to greet each other a long time, and Rake's cravat became crooked and Christina's eyes had a shiny gleam. Martha had seen how she had stood beside the window all morning and kept a look-out for his arrival, and time after time she had combed her hair even though she had just been to the hairdresser's. Now he was here at last.

While they all hugged each other, Anna-Greta kept herself in the background. She was of course glad to see Brains and Rake, and she had given them a hug as well, but Gunnar was nowhere to be seen. She still hadn't got over the confusion of the Internet transfers. She looked totally dejected. Martha saw that something was amiss and went to console her.

'There have been problems with the broadband connection at Diamond House,' she said.

'Is that right?'

'Yes, the whole building has had computer problems. Not

even a fifteen-year-old hacker could have managed to transfer anything.'

'Oh, you don't say!' replied Anna-Greta and immediately looked almost happy.

'It looks as if the money has sorted itself out anyway,' said Martha with an artful smile. She didn't say any more until she was certain that Dolores hadn't noticed anything.

When they had afternoon coffee, Martha sat with her knitting on her knee, but instead of participating in the conversation she kept looking out of the corner of her eye towards Dolores's room. When the door opened, she dropped her ball of yarn from pure fright, and not until Dolores started to go around the lounge with her trolley as usual and talk about her generous son did Martha relax. Relieved, she turned to the others and said: 'Now then. Come up to my room after dinner.'

After a dreadful stew with overcooked beans and cold mashed potato in a plastic trough, Martha thought that something tasty would be nice. She laid out coffee and wafer biscuits, a bilberry pie and – of course – cloudberry liqueur. Brains was the first to knock on her door.

'Do you need any help?' he wondered, and placed a carton with an ice cream gateau on the table. 'I thought we ought to celebrate.' Then he plucked up courage, leaned forward and gave her a little kiss on her mouth. Martha felt such a warm sensation that she simply had to kiss him back, and they stood there with their arms around each other for such a long time that they completely forgot about the frozen gateau. If there hadn't been a knock on the door just afterwards, it would probably have melted and run onto the floor.

333

'Shouldn't that gateau be in the freezer?' said Rake when he came in and pointed at a pool of pear ice cream already surrounding the carton.

'But ice cream is tastiest like this,' Brains maintained and quickly put out some dishes. When they had all sat down, the cups had been filled, and each and every one of them had enjoyed some soft ice cream, Martha knocked on the table.

'Now please listen. I hope you don't feel conned now that we have landed back at Diamond House again.'

'But Martha, for heaven's sake,' they exclaimed with one voice. 'We aren't going to be here long. Cheers to a fellow villain!'

They all raised their glasses and drank, but this time without having to mime when they sang the traditional drinking songs. They all joined in at full volume. Then they listened patiently while Rake sang 'Towards the Sea', after which Anna-Greta did her interpretation of an old pop song.

When they had finished singing and had told of adventures and ridiculous situations from their time in prison, Martha took charge again.

'I have found the missing shopping trolley.'

'Really? Fantastic!' exclaimed Brains.

'How in heaven's name did you manage that?' wondered Rake.

'Don't say it was full of money too,' said Anna-Greta.

'Impossible, I can hardly believe it,' Christina said in a muffled voice – she had a heavy cold again.

Then Martha described her nocturnal expedition to Dolores's room, after which she let on just how much money she had seen.

'There could have been as much as five million in the trolley.'

Several gasps could be heard, and Rake sat bolt upright.

'Five million!'

'Ssshh,' Martha hushed him, went up to her bed and patted the bedspread. 'Here's the money. But the person who has the paintings is demanding a reward. "Hide 100,000 SEK in a pram. Put it near the back entrance to the Grand Hotel at 13.00 on 30 October. Keep away and don't involve the police," it said on the note.'

'Note? Can I see it?' said Rake.

'Sorry, but I had to eat it. Destroying the evidence, you know.'

'Well, you certainly didn't care about the bureaucracy,' mumbled Rake.

Martha made her apologies, and told them about the warders she had had with her and how she had swallowed the message at the last second.

'Last night I put aside one hundred thousand in a pillow case. Two hundred five-hundred-kronor notes, if I didn't lose count. Are we agreed that we should put two hundred beauties in the pram?'

'Beauties?'

'Yes, money of course,' said Martha.

'Pram' – Christina had blown her nose and could manage 'm' and 'n' again – 'Anders and Emma can certainly help us with that. I'll say I can babysit for them, and then we'll borrow their pram. Malin is six months now. It will be perfect.'

'The baby too? Six months and a criminal,' said Anna-Greta with a joyful pony-like giggle.

'Now, now, it won't be as bad as that.' Martha tried to gloss over any complications, but the plan she had envisaged would mean just that. Six months and a criminal.

64

Thank God it wasn't raining, and there was no snow either. It was perfect weather for shady deals.

'Now, we must conduct ourselves calmly and sensibly,' said Martha, keeping a lookout down the street. Her voice was tense and she noticed that herself. No delivery van yet. Why was it taking so long?

'Don't worry. We'll manage this,' said Brains.

'But what if somebody discovers us?' asked Martha.

'You ought to have thought of that *before* you ordered four cartons of disposable nappies and a pram,' muttered Christina. She was still grumpy because she hadn't been allowed to arrange it all with her children. Anders and Emma had, of course, prams and blankets in plenty, and she hadn't understood why Martha must squander money on unnecessary purchases.

'Motherly love can dazzle strategic thinking,' Martha had answered, and Christina had been in a bad mood since then. Martha must try to appease her friend, but she would have to wait for the right opportunity. Now it was time for The Big Delivery. The delivery firm had informed them that the van was on its way and all five had gone down onto the street. While they waited, Anna-Greta described how she had ordered an umbrella pram, baby blankets and several bumper cartons of Bambo ecological nappies on the Internet – and had at the same time demanded that it should be delivered directly to the retirement home, and be paid for in cash.

'Lucky for us that we've got you,' they all said with one voice, and then she looked so happy that everyone had to smile.

They had held a big purchase meeting two days earlier. The first item on the agenda was 'Suitable nappies'. They had all patiently listened to Christina's talk about little Malin and her nocturnal habits. Christina babbled on about her grandchild and how much pee a certain brand of nappies absorbed – while really all they were concerned about was which nappies would hide the most banknotes. Brains and Rake yawned, Anna-Greta drummed her fingers on her computer, and Martha tried to bring everyone to order.

'The nappies should be able to hide five-hundred-kronor notes, darling,' said Martha. 'They must be big enough to cover the notes completely, and they should have a good leakage barrier so that no banknotes will fall out. I vote for Bambo.'

Brains, Rake and Anna-Greta immediately put up their hands to agree and therefore decided the vote.

'Typical that you all decide, you who haven't a clue as to what you are talking about,' Christina muttered. 'What do you know about nappies?'

'Nothing, but that's how things work in real life, sweetie,' Rake consoled her. 'Those who don't know, decide over those who do.'

When they came to the next item, 'Purchase of pram', the discussion hotted up considerably.

'It would have been lovely to cooperate with your children, Christina,' said Martha, 'but unfortunately Emma's pram could be linked right back to us. We must have a pram that can't be traced and if we get a double pram, we will also have room for both paintings.'

'Quite right,' Anna-Greta chipped in. She sat at her computer and was busy googling different prams on the Internet. 'This one – Akta Gracilia – an umbrella pram, is cheaper than the others. We'll take this.'

'But it has had bad reviews,' Christina objected. 'I've heard that the handles and bolts can loosen and, in the worst case scenario, the entire pram can fold up like a fox trap.

'Not this model. It's "Best in Test",' Anna-Greta went on. 'And it has a rain cover with a zip and a pram lock.'

'But if it is a double pram, isn't it going to look strange if we only have *one* baby in the pram?' Brains asked.

'We'll have to buy an authentic-looking baby doll, then,' Martha suggested. 'I, at any rate, can't manage to squeeze out a baby at my age, that's for sure.'

'Is that meant to be funny? You are crazy,' Christina muttered. 'You've got me and my children to help with this, and then you go and propose that we buy a plastic doll. No, now I've had enough!' She rushed out of the room in tears.

They all looked at each other in horror, and realized that sooner or later they would have to involve Anders and Emma, otherwise Christina would tire of it all and perhaps drop out. Martha fetched a box of Belgian chocolates and passed it to Rake who quickly hurried after Christina to console her. It took quite some time and nobody really felt like saying anything because all you could hear was Christina's sobbing. The three remaining members of the League of Pensioners waited for the other two, but as time wore on the discussion started up again. They went into details such as which baby clothes the doll should have, and whether they should cover its head with a little bonnet, or not. Under the rain cover it ought to look like a real baby, Brains thought, and with little Malin there too, people would think there were two babies in the double pram. However, the conversation didn't have the same spark without Christina there so their chatter soon ebbed away. Finally, they heard steps approaching and the relief was great when Rake came in with Christina again. She had chocolate round her mouth but hadn't forgotten the doll.

'For God's sake, how do you think the villains will react when they find a pram with a plastic baby doll in it?' she exclaimed and threw out her arms.

'They'll realize we care about details and have wanted to make everything as realistic as possible,' Brains responded.

'Your grandchild can have the doll to play with,' Martha suggested, and with those words Christina calmed down. To further appease her, they let her choose freely among the cushions and baby blankets and in the end everybody was satisfied. They had agreed on a good double pram with a rain cover and plenty of room for paintings, nappies, cushions and blankets. Then they toasted each other before going to bed.

Martha was interrupted in her musings by a van driving up the hill. The white delivery van slowed down on the crown of the hill, not far from Diamond House.

'There it is!' said Martha, looking pleased. The vehicle approached and stopped next to them on the pavement. The driver wound down the side window.

'Is this Diamond House?'

'That's right,' Martha answered.

'Right, then.' The youth opened the door, jumped down and asked for a Maya Strand. Martha nodded and signed the digital apparatus he had with him. Her handwriting was not as neat as it used to be, and she wasn't used to signing her alias, Maya Strand. In the end she managed to produce one of those illegible signatures that important men and doctors tend to use.

Anna-Greta counted the cartons and checked the delivery note. Then the driver generously carried it all to the lift, which required a few turns with his trolley, and finally they managed to smuggle the cartons into their rooms unseen. They had only just finished when Martha caught sight of yet another delivery van outside the window, so she hurried down again. The driver looked surprised when she claimed that the pram was for her children, and it took a while before she realized that at her age she should have said grandchildren. But it all worked well, and when she got back to her room again she put out glasses and fetched a bottle of champagne.

'Well, then, dear friends. A toast! To the paintings and to art!' she said.

'To the Impressionists!' Anna-Greta added.

Then, amidst triumphant cries, Anna-Greta produced some long open sandwiches that she had ordered via the Internet. Martha locked the door, and after they had eaten the sandwiches and drunk their champagne, they filled several nappies with five-hundred-kronor banknotes. Anna-Greta was in a brilliant mood since the orders via the Internet had worked without any problem. In high spirits she declared that the next day she would phone her bank to explain the computer complications earlier. But the others advised her not to, being of the opinion that it was best not to give anything away. It would be best if she simply told the bank to restore her accounts to how they were before the transfers – when she, or a virus, had deleted everything.

'What if they ask about the big withdrawals I wanted to make?' Anna-Greta asked.

'Just say that the interest has gone up and you have changed your mind.'

All in all it was a lovely day, and when Gunnar turned up after dinner, Anna-Greta's delight knew no bounds. She disappeared with him into her room and, despite it being so late in the evening, the notes of 'Childhood Faith' were soon heard. When Lapp-Lisa sang 'Childhood faith, you are a golden bridge to Heaven', the two of them sang along as usual, but then the needle got stuck at 'golden bridge, golden bridge'. This repeated itself for quite a long time until finally a scratching sound could be heard when the needle moved across the record. Then there was complete silence and the others looked hopefully at each other. Perhaps Gunnar had quite simply deliberately prodded the gramophone with his foot? But then the record was put on once more, and 'Childhood Faith' was heard again but now with two places at the end where the needle stuck. At this point they all said goodnight, thanked each other for a nice day and went to their rooms.

It wasn't long, however, before two doors opened again and Brains and Rake bumped into each other in the lounge.

'Finding it hard to sleep,' they both said and returned to their rooms. Shortly afterwards they each opened up their doors again, but at different times, and each of them sneaked in to see the woman that they had been missing for so long. Neither of them had planning crimes on their mind, but, considering how things turned out, perhaps they ought to have made better use of their time.

65

'Usch, this makes me nervous,' said Christina to herself when she pushed the newly purchased pram in front of her. It was the end of October and the wind that blew in from Nybro Bay was chilly and heralded winter. Her well-wrapped-up grandchild, Malin, slept in one half of the double pram, and in the other lay the authentic-looking baby doll with its little bonnet. Christina and Martha took turns to push the pram in front of them, because it was much heavier than they had imagined. Earlier that day, they had tucked in the baby doll, the blanket and the nappies stuffed with banknotes, and even added a little baby's bottle, some baby socks and an extra jumper. Then they had taken a taxi to Blasieholm Square together with the little girl. The taxi driver helped them with the pram and everything, and when they had put Malin and the doll in the double pram, they started to walk in the direction of the Grand Hotel.

While they walked, Martha wondered who the painting kidnappers could be. She considered everyone from the Yugoslav mafia to the hotel staff, or a rich businessman. But it didn't really matter. The most important thing was for them to get them back. When they reached Hovslagargatan, they looked carefully around them and then on the corner of Blasie-holmgatan and Teatergatan they left the pram on the pavement as stipulated. Just as Christina had lifted her grandchild out of the pram, she nudged the baby doll. She stopped.

'Martha, we've thought this out wrong. If people see this authentic-looking doll, then they'll think we have abandoned our child and will come rushing after us.'

'Don't worry. We'll pull the rain cover up so nobody will see anything,' said Martha, lifting the plastic and zipping up the cover. 'Because I certainly don't want to carry this around,' she went on, pointing at the doll.

'They are called children,' said Christina with a sharp voice. 'But Martha, if you can't see anything in the pram under the rain cover, what is the point of the doll?'

'Hmm, well, we thought . . .' said Martha, and she couldn't for the life of her remember why they had bought it. Why did Christina always have to be so sensible *afterwards*? When it was too late. 'Well, we—'

'What do you mean, "we"? Don't include me in that deci-sion,' said Christina. 'I wanted us to use Emma's pram. Those villains must think we are crazy. A plastic doll! If I had been in charge of this, well, then—'

'We'd best be moving,' Martha broke in. 'They said we must stay away for two hours. Then we can fetch the paintings.'

'A Monet, a Renoir and a plastic doll in a pram,' Christina churned on.

'Now, now, these are Swedish cultural treasures that are being returned to the nation,' said Martha.

Christina shrugged her shoulders and locked the pram to a railing. The street was deserted; people rarely walked there as they preferred the street alongside the quay. She wrapped Malin in a blanket and put her little bonnet on.

'She's so cute,' said Martha with a gentle voice, trying to lighten the mood.

'Yes, she's REAL, you see!' Christina snapped.

There wasn't a café nearby, so they went to the Veranda at the Grand Hotel. Martha hesitated, because she was worried that they would be recognized and it had been so embarrassing last time when the receptionist had been so rude to her. But it was cold and there wasn't really anywhere else to choose from. They ordered a starter, hardly ate any of it and, two hours later, when they left the table they were rather unsteady on their legs. To give themselves strength, they had each had a drink, and it wasn't until they had finished it that they had they realized that the sweet drink was not a liqueur as they'd thought but a raspberry-flavoured vodka, but what did that matter when their self-confidence had escalated to unimagined heights. Besides, Christina had been given some Belgian chocolate with her coffee, and she was beaming. Indeed, she was having such fun with Malin that Martha had to discreetly ask her to quieten down.

'I hope we are dealing with an honest villain and not one who has taken the money and not bothered to give us the paintings,' said Martha when they got out onto the street. 'Otherwise, I wouldn't like to be in their shoes. I'd give them a really good walloping.'

'Or a karate blow to his crotch,' Christina giggled, and almost danced a step.

Martha stared at her friend. It was amazing how bold she had become. It must be the *Crime Journal* and all those crime novels she read nowadays. Christina held Malin up high.

'A crime a day, keeps the doctor away,' she declaimed. Then Martha realized that Christina was in top condition. They were going to carry this off.

It would soon be getting dark and it had started raining. In her mind's eye, Martha envisaged damp picture frames and paintings, so they hurried along. Indeed, she walked so fast that she found it hard to breathe and in the midst of it all they had to stop so that she could get her breath back. Then she remembered the rain cover and calmed down. When they got round the corner, they could see the pram. Martha's heart beat faster. What if the umbrella pram had stood there for two hours without the villain coming past? Or what if there had been a catch somewhere? They cautiously approached the pram and when they were very close Martha stretched out her walking stick. There might actually be a bomb or some other dreadful thing in the pram, so it was best to be careful. The stick wasn't long enough. She had taken Anna-Greta's walking stick by mistake, and it was still warped. Instead, they walked round the pram a couple of times before, after a lot of deep breaths, they dared to lift up the rain cover. Then they saw: the baby doll had slipped down and somebody had rummaged among the blankets. The cushion and the nappies with the money were gone, and under the blankets you could see a hump, indeed, two humps, like on a camel. Martha felt with her hands and let out a big sigh because there were actually two paintings there. They were well wrapped and her fingers felt two solid frames. One was rectangular like on the Monet painting and the other wavy, wide and with round corners like on the Renoir painting. She tried to lift up the Renoir painting to look at it, but she couldn't manage – the gilded frame was too heavy.

'All right, we'll go straight to the museum, shall we?' she said in a low voice, and Christina nodded. They unlocked the pram and together started to walk towards Hovslagargatan. There they stopped again.

'It is a bit lighter here. First we must check that the paintings aren't damaged. Have you got the gloves, Christina?'

'The white gloves are in the bag. I must hold Malin. Her nappy needs changing too.'

'Typical!'

Martha dug out the gloves, put them on and started to rip off the paper wrapping. It had been wound round the painting several times and was much harder to remove than she had expected. But when she saw the gilded frame shine from one corner, she beamed with joy.

'Look, Christina. Oh, I am so happy. You know, owning something isn't always the greatest joy. To be able to give something back is also a great feeling, perhaps even greater. But to be able to give back something really valuable that you have stolen – that is almost the best feeling of all!'

'Martha, we've no time to philosophize now. I must change her nappy.'

Martha quickly pulled the blanket over the paintings again, and took a few steps back so that Christina had more room. The nappy change was soon accomplished and you could see that Christina had a natural maternal instinct, although this was her third grandchild, after all. An unmistakeable smell spread around the pram.

'Good job that Monet and Renoir don't still have their sense of smell,' Martha commented.

Christina didn't answer, but put the old nappy down at the foot end of the pram. Then she tucked Malin in again as best she could.

'We must hurry. Pull the rain cover up. People are coming.'

Martha looked up. Quite right: a group of pensioners was coming in their direction. She quickly zipped up the rain cover.

'That lot will certainly be going to the National Museum.'

'How can you tell that?'

'Just one or two men and lots of elderly women. They must be on a cultural outing.'

They walked round the corner and down towards the museum, but when they approached the quay in front of the Grand Hotel, a gust of wind caught the pram. It was a strong gust which caught the rain cover so that the pram rolled towards the quay. Martha realized the danger and grabbed one of the handles to hold back the pram. But that came loose, and she found herself holding a handle in her hand. Instinctively, Christina leaned over the pram and grabbed Malin, but then came the next gust of wind. Now that the pram had been relieved of part of its burden, the wind had an easier job of rolling it towards the water.

'Save it, save it,' Christina shrieked and Martha hurried after it. In her mind's eye she could see the pram tipping into the bay, and Monet and Renoir sinking to the depths while she looked on helplessly. An imminent danger can give you unsuspected energy and an unrealistic mindset. Martha tried to run. After only three strides she realized her limitations and shouted for help. Yes, she shouted and gesticulated, even though they had planned to approach the museum quietly and discreetly. A skipper from one of the island ferries beside the quay had seen what was happening. He ran after the pram, managed to get hold of it, and steered it back towards the pavement again.

'It might be best to take off the rain cover, so that the wind doesn't catch it again,' he said amicably.

'No, no, that's not necessary,' Martha answered, not wanting him to discover what lay in the pram. 'Thank you so very much.'

Then she grasped hold of the pram, put the handle back in its place and started to walk briskly towards the museum.

'But, my dear, is that where you are going? I can give you a hand,' the man insisted.

'No, we can manage,' Martha attempted, but the skipper pushed forward and took command. When they reached the steps he said in a friendly tone:

'Don't think I'm not going to help you up the steps. You need a man for that.'

Then he lifted the pram up all the steps and put it down beside the entrance with an audible crash.

'There we are, now you'll have to manage on your own.' The man smiled, raised his hand to his cap like skippers do, and Martha and Christina mumbled even more thanks.

'It's not good that he saw us,' said Martha.

'But surely the police won't be angry with us for bringing the paintings back? Calm down, Martha. Anyway, he seemed kind. We would never have managed up those steps without him.' Christina had been exhausted by all the drama. She leaned against the pram to rest a little, but immediately discovered that it had become weirdly crooked. A bolt fell to the floor.

'Just look at this, and the pram was so expensive too. I had been hoping to be able to give it to Emma,' she grumbled.

'Emma will probably be relieved she doesn't get it,' said Martha and she tried to push the damaged pram through the door. The wheels had received quite a blow, and since it wouldn't roll so well, the pram had become heavier to manoeuvre. Panting, she leaned against the wall.

'If we push it into the lift, we'll get rid of it,' said Christina, looking around her for somewhere to put Malin down.

'Good idea,' said Martha. The lift was to the right of the entrance, and next to it was a bench. Christina carefully laid her grandchild down on the bench, and with a joint effort they steered the pram towards the lift doors. Some people gave them funny looks, but Christina and Martha pretended not to notice. Thank God the lift was already on the ground floor, and when they pressed the button the doors immediately opened. Two youths offered to help and together they pushed the pram into the lift. However, the visitors were young and strong and unfortunately pushed a bit too hard so that the pram hit the side of the lift.

'Oh, sorry!' they apologized.

'Thank you, my dears. That doesn't matter, it was so kind of you,' Martha panted. 'We can manage now.'

That wasn't quite true, though, as when she got hold of the handles to put the pram into the corner of the lift, a screw loosened and several bolts followed it.

'Best to close the lift doors,' she said to Christina, pressing the button from outside. More chaos was to follow as, when the doors closed, they must have bumped into one of the handles because a sudden crash could be heard from within.

'What happened?' Christina wondered, and Martha quickly pressed OPEN again. The lift doors opened, and there lay the pram.

'Oh dearie me, what a mess!' said Martha.

'You should never buy something online without it being recommended,' said Christina.

They gaped at the tangle of the rain cover, wheels, nappies and blankets that was in there, topped by a baby doll and two hump-like raised parts which must have been the painting frames. The pram – just like the net blogs had warned – had collapsed like a fox trap. Martha acted instinctively and pressed CLOSE. While the lift doors shut again, she signalled to Christina that it was high time they departed. On top of everything else, Malin had started screaming, and with forced smiles they took the baby and moved towards the exit. They left the museum in the slowest and most dignified manner they were capable of. Not until they were behind the Grand Hotel and a taxi drove up beside them did Martha pull out the mobile phone. She had borrowed a pay-as-you-go card and she immediately dialled 118 118 to get a number.

'Can you connect me to the National Museum, please,' she said while Christina got into the taxi with Malin under her arm. A telephonist answered and Martha asked to be put through to the director of the museum.

'Hello, how can I help you?' the operator answered.

Martha took a deep breath and disguised her voice: 'There is a pram with Monet and Renoir in the lift in the museum's entrance lobby,' she said and then quickly turned the phone off. Then she, too, climbed into the taxi and asked the driver to drive them to Bromma airport. Domestic as well as foreign flights flew from there, and Martha thought it was an excellent false trail.

'The mission has been accomplished,' she said.

'Accomplished? Are you quite sure about that?' said Christina. 'We forgot the baby doll.'

'Oh dear,' said Martha and, despite it being a serious mistake, she started laughing. 'Paintings worth thirty million – and then we forgot a doll with a bonnet on. You can't say that life isn't full of surprises.'

When they arrived at Bromma, they went for a walk inside the terminal and the departure hall and made sure people noticed them before they took the bus back into the city. Once there, they gave Malin back to Emma, after which they returned to Diamond House. Brains and Rake helped them off with their overcoats, and Anna-Greta was in such high spirits that she didn't even bother with her record player. Instead, she laid the table in her room with tea and biscuits for them to have a celebration.

There they each helped themselves to a cup of tea and sat down on the sofa. Before he sat down, Brains remembered to remove Martha's discarded knitting.

'Well?' Anna-Greta wondered, polishing her spectacles and holding them up against the light. She had bought new, modern frames which suited her perfectly and didn't slide down her nose. She had given the old 1950s frames to a jumble sale.

After a few gulps of tea, Martha and Christina started to retell what had happened. When they came to the part where the pram collapsed Anna-Greta wrinkled her face in delight and chuckled in a completely new manner which made the others look nervously at each other. But when Martha mentioned the baby doll they had left behind, Anna-Greta let out her usual neigh of laughter and they were all most relieved. Anna-Greta had just been tired, so the horsey neigh had taken a bit longer to materialize.

'That "Best in Test" is evidently not very reliable,' she said at the end, when she had more or less pulled herself together.

'In the old days, you had shops with knowledgeable staff who could answer questions,' said Martha. 'Now everything is sold on the Internet and anybody at all who doesn't know a thing can give their opinion. "Best in Test"? Of two prams which collapsed, this one collapsed the least, perhaps?'

'But society develops. The Internet is here to stay,' declared Rake.

'Just because society develops, it doesn't mean it gets better,' said Martha. 'Not always.'

'You and your philosophizing,' he muttered.

Silence reigned a while, and they all occupied themselves with their teacups. Christina made a bit of extra clatter with hers, and finally put the cup down.

'You know what? I think we have missed something again,' she said.

They all listened carefully – when Christina used that special tone, she usually had something important to say.

'Missed what?' Brains wondered.

'Why all this sneaking around with the paintings? Martha, you said in the police interrogation that we only wanted to kidnap the paintings and then give them back again as soon as we got the ransom money.'

'Yes, indeed,' Martha replied.

'Well, then. There was no need at all for us to complicate things. We could have taken the paintings under our arms and walked in with them – and avoided all the hassle with the baby doll and everything. It is not a crime to give something back. The false trail out at Bromma airport was completely unnecessary.' Christina gave a light snort which developed into several sneezes. She had sat in a draught, and was catching a cold again. 'It was totally pointless to do all that,' she concluded, pulling out her hanky and blowing her nose.

Martha looked down at the table and her face had turned bright red. Brains held his hands on his stomach and Rake hummed to himself. It was Anna-Greta who broke the silence.

'But for goodness' sake! When you are old, you make mistakes sometimes. It doesn't matter, does it?'

'For future crimes we need young and strong people who can think straight,' said Christina. 'Like Anders and Emma, for example. If you can't manage everything yourself, you need help, and we're not getting any younger.'

'Pah, they wouldn't be able to keep up with our pace,' said Anna-Greta. 'And haven't we had fun? Surely that's the most important thing? Nobody and nothing came to harm – except that wretched pram, of course.'

At the word 'pram' she couldn't control herself any longer, and now came a happier and louder laugh than ever before. At that moment, Martha wanted to give her a big hug, because on the way out to the airport she herself had realized that she had been wrong again. She needn't have sneaked around with the paintings at all. She hadn't dared say anything then, and had hoped nobody else would realize. Now she consoled herself with the fact that the visit to Bromma airport had been useful as regards research. She had got a good look at the check-in counter as well as the security control. That was something that would certainly be of use for future crimes.

66

The shrill ring of the telephone cut through the room and Chief Inspector Petterson glared at the apparatus. He had been talking on the phone all day long, and didn't want to accept yet another call. Besides, he hated the ringing tone. It sounded like the Norwegian national anthem and he had become fed up with that after the last skiing world championship. Petterson lifted the receiver.

'What! Paintings found in the lift? A large gilded frame, two paintings, you think they are Renoir and Mon— no, no, don't touch anything . . . no, ABSOLUTELY NOTHING, I forbid it! We'll come at once!'

Chief Inspector Petterson gasped. Could it really be true? He had been convinced that the paintings had been sold on the international market long ago. The lady on the phone sounded quite certain. Best to hurry. Inspector Strömbeck understood how important this was. He grabbed his coat and together they drove at high speed to the National Museum. They parked on the quay beside the Cadier bar outside the Grand Hotel, and just as Petterson closed the car door, he thought he saw a banknote on the pavement. He bent down and picked up a five-hundred-kronor note, but when he looked around he couldn't see anyone nearby.

'Who the hell scatters five-hundred-kronor notes around?' he muttered, and put it into his jacket pocket.

In the museum lobby they were met by a uniformed guard. He showed them to the lift, the same lift that had been out of order the last time they had been there. Now it didn't say OUT OF ORDER but simply CLOSED on the door instead. A group of pensioners who had booked a guided tour of the Sins and Desires exhibition on the first floor were standing in a ring outside the lift doors.

'We demand that you start the lift immediately. How are we going to get upstairs otherwise? Do you expect us to fly?' an elderly lady bawled as soon as she caught sight of the guard.

'Or do you intend to carry us up the stairs?' a grumpy-looking man joined in.

'Take it easy, take it easy,' Chief Inspector Petterson urged them and pushed his way through to the lift. 'We are police. I'm afraid you must wait a little.'

'The police?'

A distinguished middle-aged lady held out her hand. She had glasses and lipstick and was wearing an elegant suit.

'I am Tham, the director of the museum,' she said.

'Chief Inspector Petterson.'

'The paintings are in here.' She pressed the button to open the lift doors. An unpleasant smell spread through the lobby.

'Is this some sort of joke? The remains of a pram – and what is that? Good God, a baby doll with a little pink bonnet.'

'No, can't you see the paintings? You said that I was absolutely forbidden to touch anything so I haven't taken the paper off, but I recognize the frames,' the director said and pointed.

'Oh well, in that case.' Chief Inspector Petterson bent down and with feverish eagerness put his hands into the pram.

'Be careful, the pram can trap your fingers,' Strömbeck warned him.

Petterson stopped, but only for a moment. He had worked so long on this case that he couldn't restrain himself.

'It would be fantastic if the art robbery could finally be solved,' he said and dug deeper in the innards of the pram. 'What the hell?!' Swearing, he took a step back, pulled out the dirty nappy and threw it onto the floor.

'I am so terribly sorry, chief inspector, but the p-p-paintings –' the director stuttered.

With fast, jerky movements, Petterson wiped his hands and continued somewhat more cautiously. Only the gilded frame stuck up, and he pulled out his penknife.

'Are you certain these are the missing paintings?' he demanded acidly and started to carefully cut the paper loose.

'As I said, we were forbidden to touch anything. I understood that you wanted to secure DNA, so we haven't poked or prodded anything. We know you have a problem with international art smugglers,' said the director.

'Yes, indeed,' mumbled Petterson, cutting carefully so as not to damage the painting. He ripped off a large piece of the paper and threw it on the floor. At that moment he heard a gasp, and saw how the director covered her face with her hands.

'Oh my God!'

Chief Inspector Petterson pulled off the rest of the paper and took a step back. He recognized the painting and had seen it many a time. Inside the fancy gilded frame was the well-known motif with the little girl in tears, the painting that almost every Swede had a copy of hanging out in the privy at their summer cottage. Without a word, Chief Inspector Petterson put the painting down on the floor and went on with the other one. This time he wasn't so careful. He made some quick slits in the paper and then ripped it off.

'I might have known!'

The painting depicted a skipper with a sou'wester and a pipe.

'Kitsch,' the director gasped.

'So you don't think the police have more important things to do?' said Petterson with his voice rising to falsetto. 'Not to mention this.' He held up the baby doll and sat it astride the frame – but so roughly that the little pink bonnet fell off.

'If only I'd known, I really am sorry,' said the director and her cheeks had turned bright red. Then a guffawing laugh was heard. Inspector Strömbeck had been standing on one side and had filmed the whole time. Now he couldn't restrain himself any longer.

'For the investigation,' he said, and grinned. 'I'll put this on the net.'

'Like hell you will! Just think, if that got into the papers . . .'

'Yeah, right. "Police tricked. The League of Pensioners has struck again." Strömbeck burst out laughing.

'Stop it!' said Petterson, and stood there in silence for a few moments. 'Do you remember? Martha Andersson said that she had wanted to give the paintings back to the museum, but they had been stolen from the suite at the Grand Hotel. So how do we explain this? Now we've got the frames but not the paintings.'

'We will have to look to see who came here with the pram. We do have the film from the surveillance cameras, after all.'

'What? CCTV images? No, not again!' Petterson groaned.

'Now listen, I know what we can do,' said Strömbeck, now in a serious voice. 'We'll send out a press release saying that we have found the paintings. Then the real villains will be uncertain. We'll lure them out into the open, quite simply. That can give us some leads.'

'That sounds too far-fetched. What if the press want to look at the paintings?'

'Then we'll say that they can, but they will have to wait since the paintings are being examined.'

Hmm, thought Petterson, and the museum director was so shocked she couldn't say a word. Petterson caught her eye.

'What shall we do with these, then?' he wondered and pointed at the painting of the girl in tears. Strömbeck managed a wide smile.

'Jumble sale?'

'No, there could be some valuable DNA here,' said Petterson.

'That's just what I said,' the museum director pointed out. 'In that case, we can store the paintings in the museum warehouse for the time being.'

'Don't forget the pram,' said Strömbeck. 'What an installation! *A Frozen Moment* by . . . yes, whoever the artist can be.'

'This isn't the Modern Museum. At the National Museum we only have proper paintings,' the director's sharp voice could be heard saying.

'Yes, we understand,' said Chief Inspector Petterson. 'Regardless, we have made no progress in the investigation. The paintings are still missing and—'

'Yes, exactly, the paintings are still missing and a lot can happen yet,' Strömbeck noted.

67

Liza scratched her itchy scalp and shook out her hair. She stared at herself in the mirror and swore. Why should she bother combing her hair? She was back at Hinseberg again. No wonder she was in a lousy mood. She didn't enjoy many days of freedom before the police nicked her again. Just because she had tried to snatch that old guy's wallet. OK, she had faked that signature at the jeweller's and got away with some jewels too – but not very many. It was when she took that guy's wallet she was caught out. Jeeesus, so embarrassing. To get nicked for a few hundred kronor, when she had set her sights on millions – it was a disaster! If only she had had time to look for the paintings a little longer, she probably would have found them. That heavy kitschy gilded frame around one of the royal pictures wasn't just any old frame, and sooner or later she would have got Petra to squeal. That girl must be involved – who else could it be? Liza was dead certain that it was an inside job.

She had intended to visit the student residences at Frescati again, but the police arrested her first. Clumsy of her to mess things up like that. Oh well, she would have to wait for her next temporary release or quite simply abscond in some way. If she couldn't find anything at Petra's, then she would put the pressure on Martha. The old cow was back at the retirement home so it would be easy to find her. Martha certainly knew more about the paintings than she had let on and that ten million in ransom money that the museum had forked out was hardly something you mislaid! Liza went into the communal room to fix a cup of coffee when she saw one of the guards wave to her from behind the glass. He opened the door and came up to her.

'Well, now, there's something I wanted to ask,' said the guard.

'Oh yeah?'

'Do you remember Martha Andersson?'

'Who could forget that old gal?'

'Did you ever talk to her about the painting theft?'

Liza didn't answer. The guard tried again.

'She admitted to committing the robbery but then claimed that the paintings had been stolen. Do you know if she suspected anybody in particular?'

Liza pretended not to have heard the question.

'Anyhow, now the paintings are back at the museum. But nobody knows where they have been and why they have been returned just now.'

'Then you'll have to find out, won't you?' said Liza.

'I just thought that you might know something about it.'

'I don't give a toss about all that,' said Liza and she went off. Then she started swearing and clenched her fists tightly. So the paintings were back! Her idea of getting her hands on them and blackmailing Martha for a million or so was ruined. For the rest of the day, Liza worked in the screen-printing workshop, but everything went wrong there too. She hadn't been paying attention to what she was doing and by mistake she had printed all the slogans on the inside of the T-shirts.

Petra turned the TV off, opened the fridge and poured out a glass of wine. Her exams were over for the time being and she wondered what she would do during the weekend. She had broken up with her boyfriend again, and this time it was for good. Strangely, she didn't feel sorry, but rather was relieved. At last they had drawn a line under things. She didn't feel lonely either and several other boys had already expressed an interest in her. She just couldn't make up her mind which one to go out with. On her way to the sofa she cast a glance at the posters of Stockholm. They hung in the same place she had hung the museum paintings, and now, looking back, it was hard to believe that she had works of art worth thirty million hanging there – paintings that she had very nearly destroyed. It could all have ended up a real mess that evening when she spilt her bilberry juice over the pictures. She had been on her way from the kitchen to the sofa when she had tripped and the contents of her glass had splashed onto the wall. A lot of it had ended up on the paintings. The King's fancy grey uniform had turned all blue-spotty, and Queen Silvia had acquired a sticky covering of lilacish blue just where she had had a facelift. Thank God that the posters had absorbed most of the bilberry liquid and not damaged the works of art behind them, but the royal portraits had got all buckled and were likely to fall out of the frames. Not only had she had a mysterious visit from someone claiming to be her cousin, but she had also almost destroyed some art treasures too. It was high time she got rid of the paintings before something serious happened.

That same evening she sat down and wrote her note to the League of Pensioners. She assumed that they still had money left from the art theft and that one hundred thousand as a 'reward' was a fair amount to demand. Not too little, and not too much, but perfectly feasible. To demand more would have felt dishonest. Admittedly, she did consider asking for half a million, but that would have made her a proper criminal, she reasoned. This felt more like compensation for her work, and surely she deserved something for having rescued the paintings from the annex? Now she could live and eat for the rest of term without thinking about money, and she could even afford some new clothes and holidays too. She didn't ask for much from life.

She couldn't leave the masterpieces covered by the royal posters which were now damaged with the bilberry stains. The solution was to be found in the antique and bric-a-brac fair that was held in Kista and which she visited just two days later. There she had caught sight of a painting of the girl in tears and the skipper with his sou'wester and pipe – and that was that. Once she was home again, all she had to do was to trim the edges of the newly purchased paintings so that they would cover the real paintings and fit inside the frames. What a commotion the kitsch art must have created at the National Museum, she thought, and even wished that she could have been there.

Petra sat on the sofa with a glass of wine, picked up the newspaper and once again read the article about the paintings. It said that the missing paintings by Renoir and Monet had been found in a pram together with a doll. She smiled at that memory and wondered why the pensioners had done that. A baby doll! It all seemed to have been cleared up, though, except that surprisingly little had been written about the case. The most important thing of all was that Petra had got her hundred thousand – and got them in five-hundred-kronor notes too. She could now use her money as she wished, and nobody would suspect her. She raised the wine glass, closed her eyes and drank. Life immediately looked much brighter.

Chief Inspector Petterson and Strömbeck sat in front of the computer, each with a cup of coffee. The press release about the paintings having been found had been issued to the media and everybody thought the case was now solved. However, here at the police station they knew better. The paintings were still missing and every attempt at analysing the joke with the pram had failed. The police had been fooled yet again. Chief Inspector Petterson didn't have much faith in the idea that the article would lure the criminals into the open, but as the situation was now, they must try everything they could. Without knowing what he was looking for, Petterson stared at the surveillance film from the entrance to the National Museum and saw how a man with a peaked cap let go of the double pram.

'Just look at this. He plonks the pram down as if it was a sack of potatoes. No wonder it collapsed.'

'But I don't see why. It could hardly be to destroy any leads,' said Strömbeck.

In the film images you could clearly see how the pram juddered, landed at an angle and ended up deformed. A few seconds later, Martha Andersson and her younger friend Christina appeared together with two museum visitors that you couldn't see the faces of. With considerable effort they pushed the pram into the lift and closed the lift doors. Then they turned round and walked towards the entrance. Judging by the images, they were very pleased with themselves. Petterson looked at that sequence time and time again and suddenly it said 'click'. My God, if Martha Andersson and her friend were involved in this, then they ought to be the *real* paintings.

'Strömbeck. I think we should make another visit to the National Museum. Believe it or not, I think the mystery has already been solved.'

'You mean—'

'There's no time to talk. Come on now!'

A little while later, the two police officers stood together with museum director Tham down in the storage area. They stared at the crying girl and the skipper with his sou'wester.

'Just think, almost everybody in Sweden has these paintings on their walls,' said Petterson and he pulled out his penknife.

'We don't,' said the museum director with a grimace.

Petterson started to carefully cut into a corner of the frame and soon could make something out.

'Now then, look here!' he said, and worked the canvas frame back and forth until the crying girl was at an angle. 'There's a painting underneath. Look!'

'So there is – Monet!' the museum director whispered. 'I can't believe this.'

Ten minutes later, Petterson had also uncovered the Renoir painting.

'Renoir!' The museum director snuffled.

'That's that! We have solved the case!' said Petterson author-itatively. He straightened his back and folded his penknife. 'Now you must make sure that you get proper alarms for the museum, so that we can avoid this sort of thing in the future.'

'Alarms are expensive. Our budget is too small,' the museum director complained.

'Then you will have to make sure that you are given a bigger budget,' answered Petterson.

On their way up in the lift, the atmosphere was oppressive, but, just as the lift doors opened, the museum director plucked up courage.

'As for our funding, Chief Inspector, if the ransom money can be found, the ten million, I mean, then we could—'

'The ransom money?' Petterson came to a halt.

'Yes, the money the museum paid to the villains with the help of the Friends of the Museum.'

Petterson held on to the door frame to steady himself. Oh, heavens above! He had completely forgotten about that ransom. The investigation could not be closed at all.

'Of course. We are still busy working on that angle. I'll have to get back to you,' he mumbled and rushed off. On his way down the steps, he turned to Strömbeck.

'Damned nuisance that the director mentioned the ransom money now. One is never allowed to be really pleased.'

'She is right, Petterson. The money is still missing.'

68

'What's this?' Brains put the newspaper down, but picked it up again. On his way to afternoon tea at Martha's, he had caught sight of the evening paper and had taken it in with him. Now he wished that he hadn't seen it. With a creased brow, he skimmed through the article.

'"Big security van robbery. No leads",' he read out loud. 'Martha, my dear, I'd been thinking that we'd have a bit of peace and quiet, but—'

'What's the matter?'

'The Yugoslavs –'

'What is it? Tell me calmly and clearly.' The window was open and she went to close it. Then she got out her knitting. Judging by the look on Brains' face, he had a lot to talk about. The cardigan was not quite finished; she always found it hard to fit the arms and the back piece together but now was the perfect opportunity to settle down to her knitting and listen to Brains' news.

Brains cleared his throat.

'You know that bank robbery that Juro was planning? We talked a bit about it at Asptuna. Instead of shooting with machine guns, I suggested a security van robbery where they would anaesthetize the people in the van. And look at this!' Brains pointed at the article. 'They've done just like I said. They got hold of twenty million. Twenty million! It must be Juro!'

'Well, I never. Juro?' Martha put her knitting aside, got up and started to make some coffee. When the water boiled, she poured it into the coffee pot, put out some cups and filled a little bowl with chocolate wafers. She served Brains. Then she sat down on the sofa again and if Brains hadn't snatched away her knitting needles at the last second, she would certainly have sat on them. She put the yarn over her finger and started knitting again. 'But Brains, what's worrying you? You can't be convicted for your good ideas, can you?'

'No, it's not that. Juro said he would hide the post bags in Djursholm and then lay low a while until the heat was off. But the bags won't be there for ever. If we're going to strike, we must do so *now*.'

'Hmm, so it's time again?' Martha mused, and munched an entire wafer all at once.

'For the *ultimate crime*, yes, and for that we need the money under the mattress. We must invest.'

When Martha had complained that the bed in her room was too hard, Brains came up with the idea that she could hide Dolores's money in there. He had loosened a plank, and between the springs and the base of the bed he had put duvet covers, nappies and pillowcases stuffed full of banknotes. Then he had nailed the plank back in place and, strangely enough, the bed had become more comfortable. But now they needed some cash. Brains clasped his hands together on his tummy.

'To fetch the Yugoslavs' money, we need a van to transport the loot in.'

369

'Why not a taxi? Nobody would suspect an ordinary taxi.'

'Better still, I vote for a people carrier. One of those with room for eight or nine people and where you can stand up inside – which would be good for Anna-Greta who finds it hard to bend down. They have a wheelchair ramp too. We can walk straight in with the Zimmer frames and load up what we want.'

'I'm beginning to get the picture. Twenty million, you said? That would be a lot of post bags.'

'On the Internet selling sites you can buy people carriers. A Toyota or Ford Transit, for example. There's plenty of room in them.'

'So we've got to invest to be able to commit new crimes? I'm not sure about that; we aren't businessmen. It was simpler with paintings,' said Martha.

'Perhaps, but this feels more substantial,' Brains said.

'We would avoid the cultural responsibility with this type of heist, of course.' Martha put her cup aside and picked up her knitting again. 'You know what? It's high time we called in the others.'

Brains beamed.

'That's what is so nice about you. You always understand.'

After dinner, the League of Pensioners gathered together for a hastily summoned meeting in Martha's room. When they had all got their cloudberry liqueur, Martha started speaking:

'It's about a robbery. The first question is whether we want to risk our place in Diamond House. If we do this, we'll probably have to stay abroad for several years.'

'That doesn't sound very pleasant,' said Anna-Greta and immediately thought about Gunnar.

'Unless we can arrange false identities, of course. Nowadays you can buy a new name and a national identity number, did you know that?' Christina said, having read a crime novel that was called *Not You – the Stolen Identity*.

'Oh, can you indeed? Then I'm on board,' said Anna-Greta, and Rake nodded in agreement.

'The bank and others who are affected will be compensated,' Martha went on.

'The bank? Is that necessary?' protested Rake. 'I don't want to give to those who steal from others.'

'But unless everybody is satisfied, it wouldn't be the perfect crime, would it?' said Martha.

'The *ultimate* crime,' Anna-Greta corrected her. 'So we are going to do such a kind of robbery that the bank won't be hurt by it. Have I understood this correctly?'

'Not really. We aren't the people who will do the robbery. It has already been done. We shall simply fetch the money,' Brains clarified.

'You always make it sound so easy,' Anna-Greta said with a sigh.

'Of course there'll be risks. Nothing ventured, nothing gained, right?' put in Rake, and he fiddled with the new cravat around his neck. This time he had one in silk.

There followed a several-hour-long discussion about the future, and after two bottles of liqueur and when everybody had had their say, each and every one of them had acquired very rosy cheeks.

'To think that finally we are going to steal again,' said Christina. 'Delightful. And I was so scared that the rest of my life would be boring. Now they should see me in Jönköping.

Incidentally, do you think they'll write a book about us in the future?'

'Absolutely,' Rake reassured her. 'People love reading about real events.'

They all smiled and, despite it being so late in the evening, they had to sing a few songs. They were thoroughly enjoying themselves when suddenly the door was wrenched open.

There stood Nurse Barbara.

'What on earth do you think you are doing! You'll wake up the whole house. You ought to have turned off your lights long ago.'

The five of them stared at each other. Nurse Barbara?

'But where is Katia?' Martha stuttered.

'She has been moved. Diamond House is now entirely my responsibility.'

69

Since Katia had been sacked, nothing was the same. The girl had written a letter to thank them for the last few weeks, and she had said that she was sorry she had been forced to leave them. The League of Pensioners lamented the fact too, because nobody, absolutely nobody, wanted to return to how things had been before.

During Katia's reign at the retirement home, the old people who lived there had regained their zest for life. Now they were seething with defiance, and Nurse Barbara got nowhere with them. When she said it was time to go to bed, they didn't obey, and when she tried to lock the doors, they stood in the way and called for more staff. It the food didn't taste good, they complained loudly and refused to eat it, and more and more of the pensioners asked for the key to the gym. A lot of them questioned their medication, and only when they were completely convinced would they take their pills. When Nurse Barbara was so insensitive as to try to cut down on the coffee drinking to only two cups a day, they knocked over the coffee pot. So while the League of Pensioners were fully occupied with planning new crimes, everything at Diamond House was going to rack and ruin. Martha saw what was happening and treated every-body to her fruit pastilles.

Nurse Barbara stared at the elderly residents through the glass partition and listened absentmindedly to the cackle out there. Anna-Greta played her records, Dolores was singing, and two of the old guys were snoring. Now it was a bit calmer, but earlier in the day there had been such a lot of noise and bustle that she had very nearly lost control of herself. In the new retirement homes, she would make sure that she got an office with a door to close and with a window onto the yard, not in towards the lounge like here. As soon as they bought the new retirement homes, she and Ingmar could administer them together and everything would be better. Then he should give her more freedom so that she could reorganize, and make everything better. They needed more staff, that was unavoidable, but Ingmar held back. On the contrary, he wanted to make further cuts. She pondered this. Immigrants were, after all, good at looking after their own relatives. What if she could get them to work here without pay? That would lower their costs even more. Ingmar would love her for that suggestion; he wanted big profits and quick results. Regardless, for now she would have to try to appease the oldies with friendly words. She got up and went into the lounge.

'What lovely weather we've got today, haven't we?' she started off.

'Yes, we want to get out into the sun. And have better food. Not listen to a load of promises and empty talk. You can't fool us,' said Henrik, who was ninety-three, giving her the finger. Nurse Barbara went back into the office. It was calmer there.

*

374

'You know what? She won't be able to put up with this much longer,' said Martha a week later when she heard Nurse Barbara's heels echo in the corridor. 'Even Dolores hisses at her.'

'Let the awful woman be. As long as things are chaotic here, she won't care about what we are up to,' said Brains, putting his paintbrush down. Like the others, he had started painting and was now really keen on it. Half-completed canvases were leaning against the wall, and he had spilt paint all over the floor. He leaned back and admired the painting in front of him. The canvas was covered with thick layers of paint and was very modernist. 'Oh, it's such fun to paint,' he went on. 'A pity I didn't start up earlier.'

'It smells of oil paint everywhere. Can't you use another type of paint?' Martha wondered.

'Not for our purposes,' said Christina. 'You can do a lot with oil. I told Barbara that we had named our little artists' group "Competent Oldies". She didn't answer, just glared at me.'

'And another thing, did you know that she had gone back to three cups of coffee a day?' Anna-Greta interposed.

'Has she indeed? She's trying to ingratiate herself with us. Anyhow, soon we can ignore her. It's time we were off,' said Rake.

'With the people carrier,' said Martha. 'Think what we could fit in that – paintings, post bags and entire ATMs, if we wanted.'

'And the Zimmer frames!'

Martha and Brains looked at each other and smiled. For every new adventure they planned, they felt all the better. What stimulated them most of all was new challenges. Any day now, they would put their plan into action.

70

'This certainly wasn't what we had in mind when we applied to the Police College!' Inspector Lönnberg sank his teeth into the hamburger and looked out through the windscreen. It was raining; it had been raining every day for the last few weeks. A greasy sliver of tomato had fallen onto his trousers and he knocked it off onto the floor of the car. 'Now we've been sitting outside this damned old folks' home for several days without anything happening.'

'But something has happened – they got a cat,' said Strömbeck. He popped a portion of tobacco under his gum. 'Unless I'm mistaken, you were the one who suggested we should shadow them. OAPs in a retirement home . . .'

'Not me. It was orders from above. One of Petterson's brilliant ideas. Incidentally, you smell of tobacco. Couldn't you try another brand?' Lönnberg opened his mouth wide and some bits of pickle landed on the seat. He brushed them off too, and threw a glance at Strömbeck. The man never seemed to need to eat anything, he lived on nicotine. That tobacco and nicotine chewing gum. On the other hand, it had been even worse before, because then he had smoked cigarettes. Then he really did stink. But Inspector Lönnberg liked Strömbeck – he was reliable. He had a wife and two kids and when he was at home he seemed to help with everything. He belonged to that new generation of men who changed nappies and did the cooking. Lönnberg himself was brought up according to the old adage that it was the man who decided. The woman should be at home, have children and keep house. Why had they changed that? As soon as he had told his girlfriends that they would be housewives, his relationships had started to go wrong. A long time ago he had given up the idea of getting married, and he was happy with his life, his garden and his books. Above all, he lived for his work and at the moment he was frustrated with these old people. He had got nowhere with them, and, quite honestly, didn't know how he should handle the situation. But since they might lead him to the missing money, he couldn't give up. He had never believed the story that the banknotes had blown off the Finland ferry. These old people were cunning, and he could feel in his bones that they had hidden the ransom money somewhere.

It had been worse than any of the previous times he had brought Martha in for questioning. Petterson made no progress with her at all. Dressed in a well-fitting two-piece suit with a matching scarf and shoes, Martha came into the interrogation room. She had smiled encouragingly all the time and assured him that she hadn't seen the money, but that she would do all she could to help him. If she heard or saw the tiniest thing that was suspicious, she would immediately get in touch. He was certain that she was laughing behind his back. In the end, the boss had decided to put a watch on them all. Petterson assumed that the pensioners were 'goalkeepers' for a criminal organiza- tion, and that sooner or later the police would discover their secret links. Criminals usually used social outcasts or the local drunkards, but using elderly pensioners like this was perhaps a new trend.

Inspector Lönnberg looked at the hamburger in his hand, did a quick calculation, and popped the rest of it into his mouth. A shower of salad and mayonnaise dropped onto his trousers. He swore, pulled out his handkerchief, and wiped it all onto the floor. Then he turned to Strömbeck.

'The League of Pensioners, what contacts could they have with the underworld?'

'I've no idea who they cooperate with. But they were proud of the art robbery.'

'Hell, I'm getting fed up with this. Shadowing somebody with a Zimmer frame . . .' Lönnberg tried to loosen a bit of salad that had fastened between his teeth.

'That's why the boss has called this Operation Undercover. He said nobody must find out what we're doing.'

'Proper villains are more substantial, so to speak,' said Lönnberg.

'Yes, then it's real police work. But this? The last few days we have followed them to the chiropodist five times.'

'And the public reading at the library.'

'Don't forget the water gymnastics and the religious services.'

'What if they've had secret meetings with somebody? We really do have to shadow them across the board,' said Lönnberg.

'But what were you thinking of when you ordered back-up to go to the Eros Rosen Massage Centre? Next time we'll be accused of procuring!'

'But –' He turned silent. Martha Andersson and her two lady friends had come out of the retirement home closely followed by the two elderly men in their group. They stood there on the pavement as if they were waiting for something. He prodded his colleague.

'Listen, Strömbeck. Something fishy is going on. I can feel it in my bones.'

'Last time, they drank tea at NK, then they took some roses to a grave in the Forest Cemetery, and then it was time for their usual foot massage. What suspicious activity do you think they can be engaged in now?'

A green people carrier approached, slowed down and stopped right outside Diamond House. A light-haired man in his fifties jumped down from the driver's seat, opened the door and let down the ramp. The three ladies went in with their Zimmer frames, followed by the two men.

'Five elderly people get into a people carrier. Now, Lönnberg, we've got them. They'll certainly be going to rob a bank,' said Strömbeck.

Lönnberg pretended not to hear the irony, but put his hands on the steering wheel. When the driver had put the ramp up again, closed the back doors and got back up into the driving seat, Strömbeck pulled out his binoculars.

'Now they're off. We'll follow them.'

'Roger, you're the boss.'

'But drive carefully so they don't see us.'

'Hell, sure. I won't use the blue light.'

The green people carrier rocked its way forward while the windscreen wipers worked at full speed. The five had affectionately named the van The Green Menace, and were all very pleased with it. Martha was the only one who wasn't in the best of moods. She had backed the van into a parked handicap vehicle outside Diamond House which had led to something of a tumult. After various diplomatic euphemisms, Christina had suggested that they should ask Anders to drive instead, and the others had mumbled and muttered so much that finally Martha had let him take the wheel. Martha knew that this was probably for the best. Rake and Brains had – in a physical sense – long since passed their best-before date, and when it came to heavy lifting it would be good to have Anders along with them, but, even though he was Christina's son, Martha was not sure they could rely on the boy. He seemed so young – forty-nine. Could he deal with this? Or what if they got hold of the twenty million and then he drove off with it all? Then they wouldn't just have lost *half* the loot, but *all* of the loot. Martha had tried to console herself with the thought that a trusted civil servant like Anders would not steal. Then she thought about their own backgrounds and became worried again. Regardless, now it was too late to change anything, because Christina had let the cat out of the bag and Anders had understood that the five of them were planning new crimes.

'Don't you have any conscience at all?' he had asked.

'That is just what we do have,' Christina explained, and then she told him about the *ultimate crime* and the Robbery Fund.

'The Robbery Fund, Anders, my dear, is important,' she had said. 'We who have built up this country want to be comfortable in our old age. We are not real villains, you see. We are helping out where the state has failed to do what it should. We are only borrowing a bit from the rich, and giving it to the

380

needy. Yes, you know, people that the state is saving money on – widows, the old and those who are sick longer than the politicians have decided is reasonable.'

Then Anders had hugged Christina and said that he was proud of her, after which he had pointed out how boring and meaningless his civil service job was, but that by helping the elderly he felt he could do some good. Indeed, that is how Anders happened to become a handyman for the League of Pensioners. Martha accepted this, and thought it was wise to maintain contact with the younger generation so as not to stagnate the group. However, he could never become a proper member; he was going to be paid for his work. They had also decided that they would administer the Robbery Fund themselves.

'I'll be in charge of that bank account,' said Anna-Greta with her glass-breaking voice, and then there wasn't so much to add.

Anders hadn't been able to refrain from spilling the beans to his sister. Emma, in turn, had rolled her eyes and said that their mother seemed to be getting younger and more daring every day. Martha had heard every word when the brother and sister stood smoking on the street outside Diamond House.

'From now on, I will take better care of Mother,' said Anders.

'Me too,' Emma agreed.

When Martha had heard this, she agreed to let Anders join in. At the evening meeting that same day, they realized he was needed.

'Large detached houses in Djursholm are awkward. The wine cellar is nearly always in the basement down some steps. So it would be great if we can get some help,' said Brains.

'And the post bags are bound to be heavy,' Rake filled in.

'Besides, it is important that we get the *entire* loot with us. We can't keep on losing half of what we steal all the time. It just costs too much,' said Anna-Greta.

'It costs too much to lose half of the loot from a robbery?' Martha repeated, somewhat perplexed. 'Can something cost too much if you don't actually own it?'

'Don't start up again, this isn't the time for philosophy,' Rake sighed.

'I think it'll be good to have Anders with us,' Christina interposed. 'It will give us a contact in Sweden who can look after our things while we live abroad. I'm sure there will be lots that must be arranged here at home.'

Martha agreed with that, because as soon as the five had got their money, they were going to fly to the West Indies. They had made that decision a few days earlier. Anna-Greta had already booked the flights and a hotel on the Internet, as well as arranging all the necessary papers. How she had managed that was more than Martha could fathom, because they ought to be in the criminal register. Then she realized that the system would certainly have weeded them out because of age. So there were some benefits to being old.

A car in front sounded its horn, and Martha wanted to do the same, but then she remembered she was in the passenger seat and wasn't driving. It was Anders who was steering the rocking van in towards the centre of Djursholm and not her. After he had changed to a lower gear, and driven past the library, he continued straight ahead and then turned to the left beside the lake path. Martha looked out. They drove past several large, luxury detached houses, each one seeming larger and more magnificent than the other. Then they drove past a bay and up a slope.

'Here it is,' said Anders. He turned right and parked the van at the side of the road. It had become silent in the van, and they were all filled with the solemnity of the moment. Rather cautiously, they studied the house.

'Skandiavägen, that's the right address. I can't see any lights in the window,' said Brains. 'The mother-in-law must have gone away, like Juro said.'

'It looks completely empty,' Christina whispered with a shaky voice. 'But do you really think they have hidden the post bags here?'

'We'll observe first before we strike,' Martha said.

'If anybody comes across us, we'll simply say that we thought this was the Crown Retirement Home. Isn't that what you said, Martha?' Rake wondered.

'Yes, right. The house is as big as an institution. The Crown sounds perfect. Did you bring your picklock with you, Brains?'

'Yes, and some extra cellar keys. People often have the fanciest locks you can imagine, but forget the cellar.'

'And the alarm?' Christina wondered.

'You know that. It's my speciality,' Brains answered.

'Right then, let's go in,' said Christina, putting on a black scarf. If you wore black you couldn't be seen so easily – that was the first thing she had learned at Hinseberg. Now she looked as if she was going to a royal funeral. The only thing missing was the mourning crêpe.

'Wait, Brains, Rake and I will check the house from the garden first,' said Martha. 'Then – when the coast is clear – we'll go down into the cellar.'

'Yes, that was the plan.'

'OK, then?' said Brains, who thought it was unnecessary to remain sitting in the people carrier too long. 'Everyone ready?'

The very same moment that Martha opened the door, a car drove up the slope. The dark blue Volvo seemed to glide forward and slow down just after it had passed the people carrier.

'That's done it,' Martha said.

71

'Well, that's one for the book. Those damn pensioners got into the people carrier with their Zimmer frames, but are now leaving it without them. They haven't even got walking sticks. Didn't I tell you they were shady types?' Inspector Lönnberg pointed at the oldies in the half-dark.

'Now don't get excited, Lönnberg. You never know with these pensioners,' said Strömbeck. 'Park on that track to the left and slam the car door when you shut it. It will seem normal. Then walk up the slope while I sneak after them.'

'OK, but be careful. It's dark.'

'All the better, then they won't see me.'

'But don't forget the pitfalls. This time of year you could sprain your ankle on winter apples.'

'I won't see what I slip on until afterwards, will I?' Strömbeck muttered. He wound his scarf an extra time round his neck, put up his collar and, bent low, sneaked towards the house. At first he didn't see anything, but when his eyes had grown accustomed to the dark, he could make out three black silhouettes. If anyone here was risking a bad fall, then it was these three, he thought. Perhaps they'd end up with a fractured thigh, every one of them. He went closer. The oldies were not sneaking around. They were walking as if they were going to visit somebody – although it was perfectly obvious that nobody was at home in the house which had no lights on at all. Strömbeck got into a good position behind a fir tree and peeped between the branches. The three walked slowly round the house and now and then looked up at the windows before approaching the entrance and ringing the bell. When nobody answered, they made their way to the cellar entrance.

One of the men fumbled with the lock, but then Strömbeck didn't see what happened. He plucked up courage and nipped in through the gate. Once inside the grounds, he caught sight of a greenhouse. That ought to be the perfect vantage point.

Martha stared up at the enormous luxury villa which towered above her like a fairy-tale castle. What if the villains were sitting inside with the lights turned off and waiting to ambush them? Wasn't there something fishy about that dark blue Volvo? Perhaps it was owned by the people living here – but in that case wouldn't they have driven into the yard? What if it was the police? Or the Yugoslav mafia? Were they going straight into a trap where they would be caught red-handed? Martha shivered in the dark. This was all beginning to be a bit too much to keep track of.

'Psst!' Brains put his hand on her shoulder. 'I've forced the lock, now I've only got to deactivate the alarm. Can you fetch Anders with the trolley?'

'What about the Zimmer frames?'

'Bring them too.'

Martha buttoned up her coat. Dear, oh dear, what a feeling in her tummy. Now they were in it for real. They could still say that they had gone to the wrong house, but as soon as they took the post bags they would be in trouble. If anyone saw them, then that was it! They still had a few minutes to abort the whole project – but, no, they had, after all, dreamed of the *ultimate crime* for so long. She took a very deep breath and hurried off to the people carrier. There, she took out her Zimmer frame and signalled to the others to join her. Anders was first out, and when he reached the cellar door he opened up his luggage trolley.

'Where are the bags?'

'They are down there,' Brains whispered and pointed down the cellar steps. 'They look like ordinary ten-kilo bags. Carry them up one at a time. Then we can each take a bag on the Zimmer frame.'

'What if they collapse like the pram did?' said Martha.

'Pah, you didn't buy them on the Internet.'

Anders hurried down the steps.

'I hope he is as competent as Christina claims,' Martha whispered.

'Oh yes, he is strong,' Brains noted.

'That isn't the same thing,' said Martha.

After a few moments, Anders' grunts could be heard from down in the cellar, and he managed to lift four bags before he came back up the steps, panting.

'I'll take three on the trolley and you can help with the fourth one,' he said, and put a bag on Martha's Zimmer frame. Just as he had done that, Martha thought she saw somebody in the greenhouse.

'There's somebody there!'

Anders stopped in his tracks.

'We'll withdraw slowly to the people carrier as if we hadn't seen anything,' he said.

At that point, the shadow in the greenhouse moved and then rushed out. The apparition ran in their direction with its arm stretched out as if holding a gun. Anders speeded up, and Martha and Brains found cover behind a tree. The man got closer, but when he cut across the lawn he fell.

'He must have tripped over the compost,' said Brains.

'Or an apple,' Martha said.

The League of Pensioners quickly withdrew to the people carrier, while Anders ran ahead with the trolley. But it was dark and there were a lot of apples, and when the trolley hit something, the post bags fell off.

There go our millions, Martha thought while she tried to get her bag to the people carrier, gasping as she did so. The ten kilos bumped up and down in her Zimmer frame basket in a worrying manner, and she was afraid she would lose the lot. If the bag fell onto the ground, she wouldn't have the strength to pick it up again. Then Brains came to her aid, and at last they reached the people carrier. The Green Menace stood there with the rear doors open and the wheelchair ramp lowered, so you only had to drive straight in. But Anders was taking his time and Martha thought that he had laid his hands on the money and done a runner. Or he had ended up in a scuffle with the man who had tripped. Indeed, a lot of thoughts flashed through her mind before Anders finally came running up. She froze where she was.

'Where are the bags?' she asked and stared at the empty trolley.

'I'll explain. We must rush. Get in!'

He shooed them into the people carrier, retracted the ramp, closed the rear doors and nipped into the driver's seat.

'Where are the bags?' Martha asked again, but didn't receive an answer. Anders turned the ignition key and accelerated as he turned into the road and drove off. Not until they had got some distance did he turn around.

'How many bags did you get with you?'

'One, that's all,' said Brains. 'Where are yours?'

'To think that you've bought a big people carrier to transport one sack of potatoes,' he said. 'Expensive transport.'

'What do you mean?'

'That wasn't a wine cellar, but a *potato cellar*,' he said. 'I've got a cold, but you ought to have noticed. The smell, I mean. They were *sacks of potatoes*.'

'Must have got the wrong address,' Brains tried to explain it.

'The man on the lawn, then, who was that?' Martha wondered.

Anders started laughing so heartily that he could barely hold the steering wheel. Nobody heard what he said. Not until his third attempt did he succeed.

'The man said he was from the police. The Great Potato Robbery . . .'

Now they all roared with laughter and started speaking at the same time so that Martha had to call them to order.

'Perhaps the sacks of potatoes were just a red herring?'

'You and your red herrings,' Rake muttered.

'No, the raid that Juro planned might have gone wrong,' said Christina in such an authoritative tone that everybody listened. 'You know those colour ampoules that the banks have nowadays? The Yugoslavs might have robbed the security van, but then got red dye all over the banknotes.'

'Blue dye,' Anna-Greta corrected her.

'Then they would have had to throw everything away. That's why there were no post bags in the cellar. That could be the explanation.'

'And the potatoes?' Brains wondered.

'Just a few sacks put by for winter.'

'But Juro won't give up so easily,' Brains said.

'Perhaps not, but there aren't so many security vans nowadays,' Christina went on. 'I ought to have thought of it before. That type of robbery is old hat. Now there are smarter ways. Incidentally, there is a car behind us. A Mercedes.'

'Christina might be right,' Brains chipped in. 'They talked a lot about security vans in the nick, but the people who had been convicted had been in prison many years. They can have missed the latest.'

'I think that Mercedes is actually following us,' Martha interrupted them.

They were silent for a few moments, and then they all turned round. It was hard to see in the dark, but you couldn't mistake the headlamps and when they passed a street lamp they saw that the car was grey.

'Well, we are in Djursholm, after all. Mercedes cars are just as common here as bicycles in Copenhagen. Perhaps it would be stranger if we *hadn't* seen a Mercedes,' Anna-Greta pointed out.

They were satisfied with that answer and on the way in to the city the subject changed to their journey. Now they wouldn't have any money for it.

'Pity, I was looking forward to travelling abroad,' said Christina, then she sneezed. She always seemed to be catching colds, but the black clothes had been rather thin.

'Regrettably, we will have to cancel our tickets and hotel reservations,' said Anna-Greta. 'But that's no problem with the help of the Internet.'

'A good thing, Anna-Greta, that you can take it like that. We shouldn't regard this as a failure, but rather as a full-scale rehearsal,' said Martha. 'We have experienced lots of new things.'

They all agreed with her, and when they reached the retirement home they were very tired but no longer so disappointed. Martha got out of the minibus, and when she heard the faint sound of an engine she turned round. For a moment she thought she glimpsed the grey Mercedes, but when she looked again she couldn't see it. She must have imagined it all.

The next morning, they were sitting there with their minds elsewhere and drinking coffee, when Brains suddenly rustled the newspaper a bit more than usual.

'Now here's something, have you seen this?' he said and opened the pages of the paper flat so that all could see: BIG SEIZURE AFTER FAILED ROBBERY. BANKNOTES UNUSABLE.

'What did I tell you!' Christina exclaimed and clapped her hands in delight.

'Probably best we go into my room,' Martha signalled and got up. The others followed after her. Once installed on her sofa, Brains read aloud from the newspaper. The article was about a security van that had been robbed and the discovery of a pile of post bags at a recycling centre. The notes had been dyed blue and were impossible to use. They all looked at Christina.

'Well, it seems you were right,' said Brains. 'And it could

have been Juro. Weird that he should make a mistake about something so simple.'

'Even villains can miss out on modern developments. Just like the man on the street who thinks he can do everything and knows everything,' said Martha.

'That type of person never learns anything new,' Brains agreed.

'The guards in the vans have special security cases nowadays. That's what they said on the radio this morning,' Christina went on. 'The cases have built-in ampoules containing dye. The slightest shaking of the ampoule and the dye sprays out. And there's a GPS. You can't take those cases outside the area they are pre-programmed for. If you do, the GPS notes it, and sends an alarm.'

They all turned round and gaped at Christina. After her stint in prison she had become really interested in crime. She was the sort of person who really immersed themselves in a subject. If she became interested in gardening, she would only talk about plants, and if her interest switched to art, then it was only paintings that mattered. Now she seemed to have settled on crime. Complicated crimes.

'GPS and ampoules with dye. Then you've got to fool the system. Perhaps you can do it with cold. If you freeze the whole thing,' Brains thought aloud.

'It's only in Southern Europe they still use the old security cases,' Christina said. 'We could go down there.'

'The prisons abroad aren't as nice as the Swedish ones. No, I've got another idea. Instead of stealing money that has already been stolen, we commit the robbery ourselves,' said Martha.

A deathly silence followed, and nobody dared to look anybody else in the eye. Martha had put into words what all of them – in secret – had been thinking: should they go the whole way and become *real* robbers?

'You mean . . . ?' Christina rocked on her chair.

'Big-time robbery is actually serious,' said Anna-Greta. 'We'd be taking the step from being nice painting kidnappers and people who intended taking money that had already been stolen, and become big-time robbers ourselves. Is this really in line with the philosophy of the League of Pensioners?'

'How else are we going to fill the Robbery Fund? As long as we don't hurt anybody, and give the money to a good cause, I can't see that there is such an enormous difference.'

'"It is more beautiful to hear a string that snaps than never to draw a bow,"' declaimed Christina who, despite having switched to detective stories, still remembered her Swedish classics.

'But how can we carry out a big-time robbery?' Rake wondered. 'Five oldies can hardly storm into a bank with drawn pistols. This sounds difficult, that's for sure.'

'All professions have become more complicated. And more boring too,' Anna-Greta added. 'When I worked in a bank there were no computers. I used to count banknotes as quick as a magician, and nobody could do sums in their head as fast as me. Now those skills just don't count for anything. Everything is on computers. You just press your mouse.'

'Please, Anna-Greta, can't you just say computer?' Rake interposed.

'Well, whatever,' Martha went on. 'We can't really think other people are going to commit our crimes for us. We must think up something ourselves.'

'So what are we going to do?' Brains wondered.

'I don't know. But when you least expect it, help is at its closest,' said Martha.

And believe it or not, so it was.

72

The five of them were interrupted just as they were discussing the exact time for the big robbery. Without warning, Nurse Barbara stepped into Martha's room and said that everybody should immediately go to the lounge. When they asked why, she was already halfway out the door.

'The damn woman.' Rake made a face. 'She could at least have said what it was about.'

They had barely arrived in the lounge and noticed the flowers on the table before Barbara clapped her hands, climbed up onto a chair and said:

'Now we are going to celebrate, my friends.' She was a bit unsteady on her heels.

'My friends? That's going a bit far,' Rake muttered.

'Thanks to a donation from Dolores, we are going to have a big party here tomorrow. This is the fifth anniversary of Diamond House and right in time for the jubilee we have some other news too.' Nurse Barbara's face broke into a wide smile. 'After long negotiations, Director Mattson has bought two retirement homes which will be part of a new organization. Yes, Director Mattson will describe this to you at a meeting later today, but I can already tell you that the new retirement homes will be amalgamated with Diamond House. Everything will be organized in a new company and Director Mattson and I will be on the board. This is indeed something we simply must celebrate . . .'

'For you perhaps,' said Martha.

'Nurse Barbara has said that we are going to have a big party,' Dolores chipped in, and everybody turned towards her. She bent down over her shopping trolley and dug around among the blankets while she hummed to herself. Then she pulled out some five-hundred-kronor notes and held them up for all to see. 'This is for the party, and there is more here if it should be needed.'

'Oh no,' groaned Christina and Anna-Greta simultaneously. Brains went pale, Rake hiccupped, and Martha felt her tummy cramp. If the police found out that five-hundred-kronor banknotes were circulating at the retirement home, they would search the place again. It wouldn't take them many minutes to discover that the numbers were the same as those of the notes on the ferry that had 'blown away' and before long, the hiding place under Martha's bed would be revealed.

'Oh dearie me, things are getting hot,' said Martha.

'They are indeed. We must act NOW,' Brains whispered.

'I'll immediately book tickets and the hotel,' said Anna-Greta.

Martha got up, and while the murmur got louder inside the lounge she went up to the window to think. They must be off as soon as possible, but they hadn't finished their preparations for the next coup. A robbery must be prepared down to the tiniest detail. She looked out. A car slowed down and stopped a little further down the slope. A dark blue Volvo. She looked up and down the street, but the grey Mercedes she had seen earlier had disappeared.

The party at the retirement home started at four in the afternoon. Nurse Barbara thought that was for the best since, as usual, she considered that everybody should be in bed by eight.

'She can never relax, can she?' said Martha. 'Children are allowed to stay up longer when there's a party.'

'Some people have to have strict rules to feel good,' said Brains.

'But at her own party . . .' Martha sighed.

When they had dressed up for the party and Brains had come to fetch her, Martha glanced out of the window again. There was the grey Mercedes.

'Brains, have you seen it?'

'Wait, I forgot my specs,' he said, but when he returned the car had driven off. Instead, the dark blue Volvo from the day before had parked down the slope.

'First there was a grey Mercedes here, and now there's a dark blue Volvo. Why?' Martha wondered.

'Everybody has a Volvo like that.'

'But that Volvo has a towing bracket and double rear mirrors.'

'The police would hardly keep a watch on a retirement home, would they? It must be somebody else,' said Brains. 'What if—'

The door opened, and in came Rake.

'What are you doing? Everyone's waiting.'

'We're coming,' said Brains but as soon as Rake had left the room he turned to Martha again. 'You know what, I'm beginning to feel afraid. If that was Juro who failed with the van robbery, then he must quickly get hold of money some other way. I think he wants to pump me for everything I know about locks and alarms. They are tough guys, that lot. What if he has worked out that I'm living here, and he is the person sitting in the grey car?'

Martha slipped her hand into his.

'But the Mercedes isn't there any longer. You can relax. Now we must hurry because Anna-Greta has promised that we shall sing.'

She took his hand and led him out into the lounge where they joined the others in the choir against the short wall. Martha pulled out her tuning fork, sounded a tone and then they all started singing old Swedish favourites, before letting Rake finish off with 'Towards the Sea'. However, when Anna-Greta then indicated that she would like to sing 'Childhood Faith', a capella, the others said it was time to get seated.

Then a fanfare was heard and the lights were dimmed.

'Take a seat, everybody,' Nurse Barbara urged, and soon after that two waiters came in with a shellfish and salmon paté on a bed of dry ice. It lay in a large porcelain platter which was decorated with salad leaves and dill. When the ceiling lights suddenly changed to blue, it all looked very magical.

'Goodness, that is quite something,' said Martha. 'Dolores seems to have been very generous.'

'With our money,' Martha added.

'Can you see that carbon dioxide snow? Not something you want to dip your fingers into. That is really cold and can freeze most things,' said Brains.

After a while the lights were turned on again, and Barbara,

wearing an evening gown with a plunging neckline, started to hand out streamers and party hats. *Evidently she isn't so stingy after all*, Martha thought. *Perhaps she has learned her lesson.* Then champagne was served, and when everyone had been given their glass, Director Mattson got up and proposed a toast.

'To the future!' he said, and looked down into Barbara's cleavage.

The main course consisted of roast turkey with fancy potatoes and haricots verts, and everybody rubbed their eyes, wondering if it was really happening.

'This is almost like a Nobel Prize banquet,' said Christina.

'All that is lacking is the prize money,' Anna-Greta neighed.

The murmur got louder and the elderly residents enjoyed themselves, though many of them wondered whether they were dreaming. When Dolores got up and with clasped hands thanked her son for the money, everybody knew they were at the retirement home as usual. After her little speech, the lights were dimmed once more, a wall of smoke spread out and the two waiters appeared again. Accompanied by music and pulsating disco lights, they served raspberry sorbet and chocolate sauce in small dishes decorated with lemon balm. Except for the fact that the disco lights triggered two epileptic fits, everything went off well. When it was getting near eight o'clock, Nurse Barbara clapped her hands.

'My dear friends, it is getting late. It will soon be time to withdraw.'

'We're not going to do that at all,' the oldies called out in one voice, and before she could say any more Director Mattson got up.

'This evening is a very special evening,' he started off. 'First and foremost, we would like to thank Dolores for treating us to this party, but I also have an announcement.'

'Probably more staff cuts,' Martha mumbled.

'Nurse Barbara told you earlier today that we have amalgamated with two other retirement homes but that is not the only thing we are celebrating. Nurse Barbara and I have got engaged.'

'Oh, it's like that, now I see. This way you don't have to pay for your own party, you misers,' Martha muttered to herself.

The door opened and in came the two waiters with a strange machine which blew out bubbles. While the transparent, glittering bubbles danced around in the disco light, Martha and Brains sneaked a look at Dolores's shopping trolley. This party must have cost a packet, and it was only a matter of time before Dolores reached deeper into the trolley and discovered that the rest was just newspaper. Martha leaned up close to Brains.

'We ought to act tomorrow, or at the very latest at the end of the week.'

'I know. It might be possible, even though we haven't had time to prepare properly. We have Anders, after all . . .'

They retired to her room and while the night settled they sat with pen and paper and drew up plans.

'I don't think anybody has ever seen a robbery like this before,' Brains finally said with a voice that vibrated with pride.

'Nor me,' Martha said, and she smiled.

73

Nurse Barbara thoughtlessly walked straight into Martha's room without knocking.

'Never do that again,' Martha hissed and got up.

'Goodness me, what on earth are you doing?' Barbara gave a start and looked all around her. The whole retirement home was chaotic nowadays, but the rooms of the choir gang were particularly disordered. Inside the room, the entire choir gang sat and painted. On the sideboard and the coffee table there were oil paints, paintings, frames and a roll of transparent cling film; the floor was covered with empty tubes of paint with the tops unscrewed. An easel had fallen across the sofa, and Brains was standing next to it mixing paint in a bucket. Christina was busy putting thick layers of paint on an enormous painting, and Anna-Greta was adding the finishing touches to a little rectangular painting. It seemed as if she had tried to depict some silver coins in light, grey colours, but it looked more like biscuits. While she painted, she hummed an old popular song to herself.

Nurse Barbara took a deep breath, and then exclaimed: 'Whatever are you up to?'

'Developing as artists,' Martha answered and wiped her face

– already covered with splashes of paint – with the back of her hand.

'Perhaps you could do some watercolours instead?' said Nurse Barbara in at attempt to be positive. Director Mattson had advised her not to forbid this and that, but rather to cajole and use friendly words.

'Watercolour? I've done that for such a long time,' said Christina nonchalantly. 'You see, watercolour has its limitations. Now we are experimenting with oil paint.'

Yes, Barbara could see that. Large abstract paintings were leaning against the walls and chairs, and if it hadn't been for all the cling film, the floor would have been destroyed long ago. She had a closer look. The paintings were joyful and rich in colour, but for the life of her she couldn't make out what they depicted.

'Yes, indeed, art . . .' was all she could say.

'We're having sooo much fun, you know,' Martha exclaimed. 'We're hoping to have an exhibition. Perhaps we could exhibit here at Diamond House too? We've already formed an art club: Old People are Capable – Artists Too.'

'Oh, I see. I'm sure it will turn out well. For now we must clean the room up. It really can't look like this.'

Almost immediately, she regretted the sentence *It really can't look like this*, but on the other hand, that was exactly what she thought. With a deep sigh, she fled into her office and closed the door. After the party she had thought it would be easier to get everyone on her side, but the opposite had happened. Not only had the oldies been doing whatever they wanted, but they were also pushing for more parties – and now the choir gang wanted to exhibit their paintings at Diamond House. She put her hand on her brow. She would have to console herself with the knowledge that finally she had manoeuvred Ingmar where she wanted him. They were going to get married, and even though he had postponed the wedding, they would very soon be looking after three retirement homes together. He would think he was in charge of it all, but no. Her plans were considerably more ambitious than that. The wedding was only the first stop on the way to her dreams.

Martha put her paintbrush down on her lap and threw a glance at the closed door.

'Nurse Barbara didn't dare stay in here. One should feel sorry for her for not being able to enjoy life. And if she had had the slightest inkling of what we were doing, she would have had a heart attack.'

'Yeah, next stop Las Vegas,' said Rake.

'No, the West Indies,' Anna-Greta interposed. 'They don't have any extradition agreements. You can be sent straight home from the US. It will have to be Barbados, but that only takes ten hours, and I've found the most luxurious hotel imaginable there.'

'That is all well and good, but first we are going to Täby, aren't we?' said Martha. And then they all became quiet, because they knew what was waiting. Before they committed their crime, there was one more thing they must check. How the ATM money dispensers in Stockholm actually worked.

The Green Menace yet again made rocking progress on the roads, and with the radio at full volume they drove round to the various ATMs in the northern and western suburbs of Stockholm. The people carrier stopped in Sundbyberg,

Råsunda, Rinkeby and Djursholm and at each stop they clambered out with their Zimmer frames, took some money out, and then went on their way again. Sometimes Rake and Brains left the vehicle, sometimes Christina and Anna-Greta, but they all did their bit with the same concentrated thoroughness. In fact, they were so concentrated on their task, that they didn't notice the dark blue Volvo that was shadowing them. Not even Martha, who was making detailed notes, noticed anything. No, they only had eyes for ATMs and alternative escape routes.

When they had completed their final reconnaissance trip to Täby, they filled the tank at the Q8 petrol station and returned to Diamond House. After a long afternoon nap, they packed for the journey, went through all the details with Anders, and toasted to the success of their project with cloudberry liqueur. This time it was for real. This was to be their first *advanced crime*, albeit in a friendly manner, but nevertheless.

Martha slept like a log that night and dreamed of a successful coup and how she shared out the money to all. Indeed, she even managed a short dream about a successful fraud, and at seven o'clock she woke up bright and alert. Exciting dreams always put her in a good mood.

A good day for a robbery, Martha thought the following afternoon when they approached Täby centre. It was not raining, but the sky was grey and gloomy as it tended to be in that part of Sweden early in December. They were lucky with the weather. The temperature had not sunk below freezing yet, and none of them needed to worry about icy roads and pavements. It was hard enough anyway to walk nice and calmly when you were intending to steal fifteen to twenty million.

'Look, it's turning in there.' Martha put the blinkers on to turn left, changed to a lower gear and followed the Loomis security van at a distance. As they needed two drivers this time, Martha had got her chance to drive too. Anders was in charge of a rented car with a trailer, while she sat behind the wheel of the Green Menace. It wasn't every day that a people carrier shadows a security van, she thought.

'The ATM in Täby centre will be first. Just as we thought,' said Brains, when the van slowed down and turned off to the right towards the car park area.

'I hope it looks the same here as it did yesterday, so that Anders can drive in with the trailer. Everything must work perfectly,' said Martha.

'Don't you worry. One trailer or one people carrier more or less – nobody will care about that. People here are fully occupied with their own doings.'

'But what about the freezers?'

'We're going to a party or a recycling station. If somebody stops us, we say what seems most likely. Although the best thing is not to say anything at all.'

Martha slowly followed after the security van. People on their way home from work hurried across the asphalt looking straight ahead of them and nowhere else. *What a wretched life, such stress*, she thought, but here too were row upon row of shops on several storeys. That could make anybody dizzy. No little stores with a door that went ding-dong, or shop assistants who recognized you. No, not here. Young people today would think she was fibbing if she told them that in the old days the assistants knew you, and knew everything about your parents.

'Martha, you *are* keeping an eye on the Loomis van?' Rake gave her a gentle prod.

'Of course I am,' she said and blushed. He was right. She ought to be concentrating more. Now it was on its way to the ATM and the driver didn't seem to care about the people all around. Anyhow, most of them had finished shopping and were hurrying home in the cold. It was Friday, after all. It would be Friday evenings that people longed to get home to their families and celebrate the end of the working week. *Enjoy yourselves*, Martha thought, *but we are going for the jackpot!* What they were doing was on a grand scale, much bigger than anything they had attempted before. She hummed to herself and felt full of confidence when suddenly she discovered the car in the rearview mirror. A dark blue Volvo. That same moment, she realized it wasn't a coincidence. She looked quickly behind her, asked Brains to hold the steering wheel, and then with her right hand she managed to ease a carton of galvanized nails out of her purse belt. If they were police, then she wasn't just going to give up. She was prepared.

Inspector Lönnberg changed to a lower gear. He gave Strömbeck a tired look and shook his head.

'What the hell are they playing at? They seem to be busy with ATMs today too.' He nodded towards the people carrier. 'Evidently it wasn't enough with ten ATMs yesterday. Now they're going to Täby again. Weren't they there yesterday? I just don't get this!'

'And they withdraw money everywhere. Each time they totter up with their Zimmer frames although they don't need them. I wonder what on earth they are up to. Shall we force them to pull over?' Strömbeck wondered, and popped a portion of tobacco under his gum.

'Yes. You know what? It's bloody well time we did that. It feels as if they're making a fool of us. I reckon we should ignore Petterson's instructions. Let's stop them!' said Lönnberg and immediately felt much brighter. He had long since tired of shadowing the five pensioners and he was really pissed off with them.

'I've got an idea,' said Strömbeck. 'We'll set up a police control at the entrance to the parking area, so that they won't be able to get near the ATM.'

'Although if you think they're going to steal something, shouldn't we wait until they've committed the crime?' Lönnberg asked.

'You always pick on details. OK, if you want. I'm feeling ravenous at the moment. I must get a hot dog first. There's a kiosk over there, shall I get you one too?'

Lönnberg hesitated, but he was hungry too. He had a good look around, and decided that the situation was under control.

'OK, then, but look sharp about it. We mustn't lose sight of them. If they're going to commit a crime, then we must be there, right?'

'It'll only take a minute,' said Strömbeck.

Inspector Lönnberg slowed down and stopped, and Strömbeck quickly nipped out of the car.

Martha looked in the rear-view mirror again. The blue Volvo was nowhere to be seen. Perhaps it was just one of all those people from Djursholm who drove a Volvo; she might have been mistaken. Regardless, she must be very observant.

Nothing could be allowed to go wrong now. Then she caught sight of the Volvo again. Double rear mirrors. So it was the police! Quickly and without slowing down, she wound down the side window and let the carton of galvanized nails fall onto the road in front of the dark blue car. This was purely a cautionary measure, but she thought it was best to be on the safe side. Attention to detail always paid off in the end, and they had prepared themselves as best they could.

The previous day they had timed the security-van deliveries around the suburbs, and noted how long it took for the guards to walk in and out with the security cases. Above all, they wouldn't make the same mistake as the villains they had recently read about. Those crooks had rented a crane and yanked out the entire ATM machine. However, that wasn't where the money was kept, it was next to it.

Martha didn't lose sight of the Loomis security van, and felt the same tingle in her tummy as that time they had robbed the spa in the Grand Hotel. What were a few personal valuables compared to this? A big-time robbery like this could even render them a *four-year* sentence and *none of them* wanted to end up behind bars again. The Princess Lilian suite had spoiled them.

'Do you think they suspect the people carrier?' Christina asked for the third time from the back seat.

'Well, I've never read of any similar robberies,' said Martha.

'That's what is so neat about it,' Rake butted in. 'The police don't have any old crimes to compare with, and then they won't suspect anything. Believe me, this is going to go well.'

'Here's the first ATM that the Loomis van is going to fill,' Anna-Greta informed them. 'They ought to have nine full security cases left in the van. Every case contains four cassettes with five hundred thousand kronor each. That will make almost nineteen million. We can live well on that for a long time.'

'Now, now, first we must pay you back for the stay at the Grand Hotel—' Martha started.

'Yes, that was most annoying,' Anna-Greta interjected. 'I tried to freeze the account, but they had already processed the payment.'

'Well, for unforeseen costs in the future we might have to reckon on journeys, hotels and expenses. The rest will go to the Robbery Fund, I promise,' said Martha.

'Shush, look,' Brains cut her short. 'The van's in position.' He lifted Anders' extra mobile phone with the pay-as-you-go card and punched a quick key. When he heard the signal at the other end, he turned the phone off. He didn't need to do more than that. Anders knew what to do. The guards slowed down in front of them, stopped beside the ATM and got out. Martha stopped, still a bit away, but didn't turn the engine off. The guards opened the back doors, took out a security case, locked the doors again and went into the bank. They didn't even look around.

'Right, we're off,' said Rake. He opened the door of the people carrier and got out.

'With you,' said Brains, and he too got out. Martha saw how they crept up to the security van, glanced all around and set to work. Brains dealt with the alarm and Rake with the back doors. If everything went according to plan, Rake ought to be able to press the resin with metal shavings into the lock. When the guards closed the doors next time, they would shut – but not properly. Then the five of them could strike. In the end, everything depended on Rake being successful. They had, after all, only tried the trick on their own people carrier.

'Where's Anders?' Brains whispered when he got back into the people carrier again. 'I phoned him. He ought to be here now.'

'He's not going to let us down, is he? Christina promised that if he helped us he would get an advance on his inheritance now,' Martha replied.

'Don't you worry! I believe in Anders,' said Brains. 'He'll probably want to join us again—'

'Now listen, we'll pay him as agreed. I mean, he can't be a member of the League of Pensioners,' Martha protested.

When the two security guards had swapped the cases behind the ATM, they took the old case, opened the back doors and put it inside. Then they locked the doors, and went and sat in the front. The back-door lock hadn't engaged properly, which they hadn't noticed because Brains had sprayed the camera lens and disconnected the alarm. Martha quickly put the people carrier into first gear, accelerated and then went straight into fourth gear which stalled the engine and the Green Menace came to a halt diagonally in front of the Loomis van. While she pretended to start the engine again, Christina, supported by Rake, tottered up to the van's driving seat side and knocked on the window. She had a dark wig, was heavily made-up and smiled with plastic fangs from Buttericks joke shop. Rake, for his part, had a light beard and wig and looked much younger than he was. When the driver rolled down the side window, he discreetly went round the van to the other door.

'The engine has stalled. Could you possibly help us?' Christina asked, and pointed at the people carrier. Meanwhile, Anna-Greta came alongside with a bunch of flowers drenched in ether.

'This is for you,' she smiled kindly and pushed them in through the window and right into the faces of the guards. Then she jammed her walking stick under the door handle and secured it with her Zimmer frame. The guards attempted to back away from the window but Rake had already squirted Instant Glue into the lock. The next moment, Christina poured the entire contents of the ether bottle onto the driver's seat and just managed to get her hand in through the gap in the door and roll up the side window, before the men turned round. Then she slammed the door hard and pushed her Zimmer frame back into place.

'Now you've no possibility of getting out,' she mumbled proudly and became almost disappointed when she saw that the guards had already become unconscious. Then Anna-Greta quickly retrieved her stick and the Zimmer frame and returned with Christina to the people carrier. Brains and Rake moved to the back doors of the Loomis van, and, when Anders drove up with his trailer, they had already managed to ease it open.

'The simplest things cause the most difficulties,' said Brains and chipped away the resin with the metal shavings.

The trailer was loaded with two freezers filled with carbon dioxide snow and a box of paper streamers. Balloons had been tied to the sides of the trailer, and in one corner there was a large poster proclaiming: Congratulations! Anders jumped up onto the trailer and opened the freezers, and while the white carbon dioxide mist ran down from them Brains and Rake fetched the first two security cases. They placed them carefully on Rake's Zimmer frame.

'Easy does it, so we don't trigger the mechanism,' Brains urged them, but Rake walked softly and safely towards the trailer on his seaman's legs. After which Anders – who was wearing thick gloves – lowered first one and then the other case into the freezer and put some ice on top. When they had got eight of the cases into the freezers and turned round to fetch the last one, Martha suddenly called out.

'Hurry up. We must be off.' She pointed at a group of men in suits and carrying briefcases who were coming towards them. The men were talking loudly and were rapidly approaching.

'We'll just manage the last one,' Brains said, and Rake hurried off. This time, too, they succeeded in getting the case into the carbon dioxide snow and just managed to close the back doors of the Loomis van before the suits got to the trailer.

'You can't park here,' one of them said, and kicked the wheel.

'Be careful!' Martha shrieked, almost in falsetto, but Anders was quicker. He pressed the lids of the freezers shut and gave a wide smile.

'Hen party! What a lovely surprise she's going to get, the bride,' he said and winked at them. 'Never get married,' he added. Then he gave each of them a balloon before getting back into the car. He slowly engaged first gear and drove off. Martha gaped at this and thought that perhaps he wasn't so hopeless after all. Together with Brains and Rake, she hurried into the people carrier again, and when the men had closed the doors off they drove.

'Now we're on our way,' Anna-Greta's satisfied voice could be heard. 'They should have seen this at the bank.'

Martha pulled out from the parking area and followed Anders out from the district and then towards the E4 and Arlanda airport.

'Amazing, it worked!' Rake called out.

'Mind you, we aren't on the plane yet,' said Martha, accelerating.

It wasn't until they were approaching Sollentuna that she noticed the car behind them. It was a grey Mercedes.

74

'Why the hell did you have to go and get a hot dog? Now we've lost them again,' Lönnberg hissed while he looked out across the parking area. It was almost dark and he couldn't see the taxi-bus. Such a large vehicle ought to be easy to make out, but it was green, of course, an awkward colour at this time of year.

'Now, now, you had a hamburger and you spilt all that ketchup on the driver's seat. Above all, you could have kept your eyes open. You should never run over something lying in the road. Least of all a little carton.'

'But damn it! How was I to know that that somebody had dropped a carton of nails?' Lönnberg muttered.

'A hundred galvanized fluted nails that'd pierce any tyre,' Strömbeck said to make it clearer. 'Lucky we had a spare wheel with us.'

'That's enough. End of subject. We've got to find the oldies.'

'All we need now is for them to do something daft. Then I'd apply for retraining. New career,' said Strömbeck.

'Me too,' said Lönnberg, starting the car and putting it into first gear. 'But I don't think we need to worry. They'll have gone to the chiropodist this time too.'

'Hang on, you don't usually find those inside ATMs.'

Lönnberg pretended not to hear, accelerated, and completely forgot to look in the rear-view mirror. If he had done, he would have seen the jack and all the tools lying in the road.

Martha breathed deeply a few times and pressed the accelerator harder.

'What shall we do? The Mercedes is following us.'

'Oh Christ, the Mercedes? Any car but that!' said Brains, who immediately realized what it was about. The grey Mercedes outside Diamond House . . . that was what he had been worried about. Juro and his brothers – they had followed him. At first, perhaps, they only intended borrowing him for technical consultations, but then they had probably understood what was in the offing. Timing the visits to the ATMs, loitering outside Täby, test driving with the trailer the day before. Juro and his mates knew exactly what it was about. Fifteen to twenty million . . .

'The Yugoslavs,' he mumbled. 'And Anders, who's on his way to the barn.'

'Oh Lord, I think they're going to force us off the road,' said Martha.

'Phone Anders and say we'll be late. Meanwhile, we can try to shake them off,' Christina suggested.

'We'll all be getting a good shaking,' said Martha. 'No, hang on, I know –' she said and made a sudden U-turn.

Rake gave a curse and almost fell off his seat.

'What the hell? You and your driving . . .'

'What in the name of Heaven are you doing?' Anna-Greta cried out.

'Next stop Danderyd Church. I've got an idea,' said Martha.

415

It wasn't as though they could object, because she was already going at full speed hunched over the steering wheel. 'We're in for a rough ride!'

'Yes, that's what I'm afraid of,' Rake grumbled.

When the old medieval church came into view on one side, Martha changed to a lower gear and took the next exit from the motorway. The engine was screaming and Brains hoped that the people carrier was going to cope with this. You never knew whether to trust Internet purchases. He glanced in the rear-view mirror, but the Mercedes was still after them. He also caught sight of a familiar car. A dark blue Volvo.

'No, not that too. Now we've got two cars chasing us!' he groaned. Martha checked the rear-view mirror.

'The mafia and the police. That really is—' She made a sharp turn in towards the church.

'But Martha, you've gone the wrong way. Stop! We should be on the way to Arlanda!' Christina squealed, confused.

'Didn't you say that we should shake off our pursuers?'

'With a people carrier? Don't say you're going to lower the ramp too,' groaned Rake.

'But why are we going to the church?' Anna-Greta gasped and hung on to the door handle for all she was worth.

'We'll go inside and pray,' Martha answered and slowed down.

'Not that too,' Rake sighed.

Martha braked and the car came to a halt.

'I'll drop you off here and park the people carrier a bit further away. Take the Zimmer frames and walk slowly into the church. When you get to the alter, you make the sign of the cross.'

'Like hell I will,' said Rake.

'Well, pick up a psalm book, then. Walk slowly and dignified as if you were going to a religious service. Don't forget that we are old and confused. It we take things calmly then we will look innocent and nobody would think we are up to anything suspicious.'

'But the mafia and the police. We can't damn well—' started Rake.

'Out with you. Hurry up!'

'Two cars are chasing us and you make us go into a church,' Brains sighed.

'I'll explain later. Into the church now. This is going to work out OK, and as soon as we're done we can continue to the airport. But don't forget the Zimmer frames.' Martha shooed her friends out of the people carrier and closed the door. Then she parked as close to the church as she could.

'Oh crikey, now I give up,' said Inspector Lönnberg when he saw the people carrier turn off towards Danderyd Church. 'When finally we find them again, they're on their way to church. No way am I bloody well going to sit through a church service.'

'But what are they doing there? Sermons and that sort of stuff, that's only on Sundays,' Strömbeck reflected.

'They will be confessing their sins.'

'Unless they're after the church silver, of course.'

'Look, it's past six o'clock. Our shift has finished. I reckon we should push off,' said Lönnberg. 'I've had my fill of trailing those people carrier carcasses.' He eased up on the accelerator and looked longingly towards the city.

'You can't say that. We must carry on following them. Who knows what they might have been up to since we lost them in Täby. What about all the ATMs they visited yesterday?' said Strömbeck.

'Perhaps the word ATM features in one of their crosswords. Ah, come on, relax. Let's push off.'

'No, not until we have been relieved. Otherwise Petterson will blow his top,' Strömbeck insisted.

He doesn't bloody need to know that we've nipped away, Lönnberg thought. 'OK, if you want. It won't take a minute to check them.' He changed gear, turned off towards the church and drove into the car park outside.

'If they've stolen something, the money ought to be in the people carrier, oughtn't it?' Strömbeck said.

'Hang on, just look over there. They're going into the church with their Zimmer frames and all.'

'Let 'em be. But we are going to search the people carrier. You never know. We might catch them red-handed,' said Lönnberg. He had made up his mind, so that was how it was going to be. The two policemen went up to the driver's side and knocked on the side window.

'Police!'

Martha wound down the window.

'Well now, good afternoon, good afternoon to you,' she said with a smile. 'My, oh my, what fancy uniforms you're wearing today.'

To his horror, Lönnberg discovered he was blushing. He leaned towards her.

'We'd like to check the vehicle. Please open the back doors,' he said.

'But goodness gracious, are you looking for smuggled goods? That is exciting. I'll open it straight away. Do you want me to lower the ramp?'

'No, thank you, we'll manage,' Strömbeck muttered.

'If you find anything nice, couldn't you give it to me? The pension, you know. It doesn't stretch so far nowadays.'

Strömbeck was just about to answer when the police radio sounded an alarm signal. He stopped and looked towards the Volvo.

'Lönnberg, there's something on the radio!'

'Oh, hell, an alarm. Run and check, and I'll carry on here,' said Lönnberg. 'This time I'm not going to give up. Now I'm going to nail them.'

Determinedly, he walked round the people carrier and yanked open the back doors. A walking stick, a pair of support stockings and some incontinence pads fell out. He climbed in and started to look around but was interrupted by Strömbeck who came running back.

'Lönnberg! There's been a big robbery . . .'

'What was I saying? Now we've got them. I bet you—'

'But can't you see? There's nothing at all in here. They can't have stolen *invisible* banknotes, can they?'

That very same moment they heard the familiar sound of a diesel engine in a Mercedes. The two policemen looked up. The car was going slowly as if the driver was looking for something.

'Well, now, look there! A grey Mercedes. What if it's the Yugoslavs?'

'Perhaps that's what the alarm is about.'

'Smart of them to withdraw to a church. I'll check the registration number.' Strömbeck ran back to the Volvo again and turned on the computer. After a few moments clicking, he gave a whistle and jumped out of the car.

'You were right. It is Juro, damn it. Forget the pensioners, let's check the Mercedes instead,' he said.

'Oh, great, real villains. This is more like it!' Lönnberg slammed the back doors shut, mumbled an apology to Martha and ran after Strömbeck. They jumped into the Volvo, drove up to the Mercedes and braked to a halt beside it. Strömbeck got out and knocked on the side window. The driver lowered the window.

'Can we have a look at your driving licence, please? Strömbeck asked.

'Of course.' The driver pretended to be looking for it, but instead engaged first gear. With a roar, the car shot off.

'Bloody hell!' Strömbeck screamed and threw himself back into the Volvo.

'We'll follow them,' Lönnberg shouted and pushed the accelerator to the floor. 'Now we'll nail them.' *A bit of action at last*, he thought. Now, finally, they would have something sensible to do.

75

Martha saw the dark blue Volvo start off in pursuit of the Mercedes.

'There now. That worked a treat,' she said with a happy smile when she saw the two cars disappear at high speed in the direction of the motorway. 'That was close. When Lönnberg came inside the people carrier, I thought we were finished. Even though Anders has the money, he could have found some traces of our crime.'

'It happened so quickly. We had hardly got in through the church doors,' said Christina, making herself comfortable on the back seat.

'Yeah, all we had to do was turn round and go back to the people carrier,' said Anna-Greta. 'But you order us around like cattle.'

'Yes, can you explain this? I haven't a clue what's happening,' said Rake.

'Didn't you see? They were the same cars that have been outside Diamond House. Every time the dark blue Volvo turned up, the grey Mercedes vanished. The Yugoslav mafia recognized the police and that was why they drove off. If we drove in here to the car park, I thought they would catch sight of each other and leave us alone. And it worked. Now we can continue in peace.'

Brains gave Martha an admiring look. How did she manage it?

'Just think, we got rid of *both* the grey and the dark blue car,' said Christina.

'He up above has helped us,' said Anna-Greta, rolling her eyes and looking up at the ceiling of the people carrier.

'No, it was Martha,' said Brains.

'Now, now, I know that of course, I was just joking,' said Anna-Greta and then she started singing her favourite old pop song, which she sang time and again the whole way to Sollentuna. Martha drove at more than 100 kph and it wasn't until they left the motorway and turned down the little unpaved road that she slowed down. Anders should be waiting for them with all the money – if he hadn't done a runner with the loot, of course. Martha had seen how well he had arranged everything concerning the robbery, and had begun to change her opinion of him. There *ought* not to be any need for her to be worried, but . . . She looked at her watch. If everything went according to plan, then they would have time to fetch the money and make it to the last evening flight. To be on the safe side, Anna-Greta had booked with a proper airline. They didn't want to risk one of the low-price flights, and it was important for them to know that they would get to the right destination and not be thrown off the plane because of a shortage of seats. While Martha drove, she thought about everything that Anders had to do. Had he actually done it all? Now the thoughts came back: could they really trust him? In less than half an hour, she would find out.

*

Anders looked at the security cases one last time and raised the axe. Then he stopped. Was the temperature really cold enough? As soon as he had arrived at the barn, he had connected the freezers to the electricity supply. It was best to check how many degrees they had reached now, so that he didn't spoil everything. The cases must be completely frozen and the ampoules of dye be minus 20 or colder. The carbon dioxide snow was great stuff, but it took time to freeze something, and to be on the safe side, he decided to wait a little longer. He looked at the door out of the corner of his eye. It was weird that Christina and the others were taking so long. The League of Pensioners ought to have been here ages ago. As long as they hadn't got caught in a routine traffic-police check, or had a puncture or had been involved in something else, he thought. That could ruin everything. It had all happened so fast that they didn't have any plan B. So the plan they did have simply *must* work. At the same time, he didn't dare phone them. Maybe the police were waiting at the other end ready to trace the call. Best to lie low.

He paced back and forth in the barn a long while until he couldn't stand it any longer. He had to get those banknotes out. He fetched the axe, spat on the palms of his hands and grabbed hold of the handle. By now it all ought to be frozen, and the GPS would be out of action . . . just as long as the ampoules didn't contain linseed-oil dye, because that didn't freeze, but the banks would certainly use old, cheap artificial dyes, he was certain of that. Cautiously he approached the first security case, took aim with the axe and, with a powerful swing, smashed the ampoule. He waited. Listened. Nothing happened. Not a trace of dye seeped out. Then he dared open the case and felt a wave of joy when he saw the banknotes. Encouraged by this, he took out the next case too, but stopped when he heard a vehicle approaching outside the barn. He ran his fingers through his hair, straightened his back and took a few hesitant steps towards the door, where he stopped to listen. He was still cautious so he waited until he heard three knocks, followed by a pause and then two quick knocks. Oh, thank God, they were here now. He slid the lock aside and pushed the door open.

'Everything under control?' Brains wondered and stepped right in.

Anders nodded. 'And the vacuum cleaner?'

'The girls have arranged it. Where are the paintings?'

'In the car. Hang on.' Anders opened the car door and lifted a large painting out. 'Now I hope that your calculations are correct. Four layers of five-hundred-kronor notes on a sixty-five by ninety-five canvas. That's not much.'

'Right, but Christina's two canvases are larger. You know, she had to do something bigger than ever before.' Brains grinned.

'Yes, and then we've got all the other canvases as well as the paintings you are taking as hand baggage. I just hope the cling film works.'

'It did at Diamond House. If the paintings get more or less distorted, it doesn't matter, does it? It's modern art.'

'Now please, we have work to do.' Martha cut them short, brandishing the vacuum cleaner. And her tone was so sharp that everyone knew that now they were in a hurry. While the three ladies sucked the banknotes out of the security cases, the men carefully peeled the first layer of cling film off the canvases. A few cracks appeared in the oil paint and the odd click of paint slipped off – mostly on Christina's oil paintings where the paint was almost as thick as the tubes of oil paint had been – but on the whole everything went even better than expected. Brains and Rake placed the layer of paint on a bench, and returned to the painting. Now the canvas had been exposed, except for a few extra layers of cling film they had put on the previous day.

'Christina and Anna-Greta, now it's your turn,' Brains called out.

The ladies came forward with a bag full of five-hundred-kronor banknotes and laid them in an evenly thick layer on top of the canvas. Martha secured them with a thin plastic net before adding the next layer, and in that way spread several layers of banknotes across the entire painting before sealing it with cling film and gluing the corners. Not until then did Rake and Brains put the layer of paint back in its original place, and fix it in place with quick glue so that the painting looked like an ordinary picture again. Christina had suggested using a stapler, but at the last minute they realized that the staples would show up on an X-ray. While they worked away, Anna-Greta's eyes glistened with pleasure. She liked being surrounded by all these banknotes, and she had never seen as many as these during all her days at the bank.

They laboured away, silently and calmly, but it was a fiddly job getting everything right and they soon got tired. Martha had brought along coffee and sandwiches, and after a little break when they discussed customs procedures, metal detectors and various types of X-ray equipment, they continued with their work. Just before half past eight in the evening they were ready, and they all looked very pleased with themselves – except for Christina, who thought her painting had been messed about.

'It can't be as thick as that. You have destroyed the expression.'

'The expression?' Rake wondered.

'Yes, the message I want to convey with the painting.'

'Well, don't worry. We'll take the banknotes out when we arrive, and then everything will look fine again.'

'But I want my painting to look good.'

They all squirmed with embarrassment until Martha spoke up.

'Christina, dear, the great masters were never satisfied with their works,' she ventured. 'We understand you.'

With that, Christina did actually calm down.

When they had carried the paintings into the Green Menace, Anna-Greta suddenly stopped.

'Oh my God! There wasn't room for all the banknotes,' she noted, disappointed. 'At least a million is left.'

'Well, Anders must get a little something,' Christina quickly retorted. 'He is going to administer us. And Emma, she—'

'Do you call one million "a little something"? One million for paper and stamps?' said Anna-Greta almost reaching thunderous tones.

'But we promised to pay for Gunnar's journeys too, didn't we? That will cost as well,' said Brains.

'Oh yes, that's right. Yes, we had decided that.' Anna-Greta was silent a few moments, but then exploded: 'Oh my God, we've forgotten something!' she exclaimed, and put her hands over her face. 'The money in the drainpipe!'

'Forgotten? No, not at all,' Martha reassured everybody. 'I'll tell you later, but now we must be off to the airport. Into the people carrier with you.'

They all realized that time was short and they climbed into the people carrier. It took a little longer than usual because the paintings were in the way, and they had to squeeze past. When

Anders was about to close the back doors, he hesitated, pointed at the works of art, and grinned.

'The League of Pensioners strikes again!'

'Old people are capable,' Anna-Greta snorted, accompanied by a happy murmur from the others. Martha wound down the window.

'Sorry to be leaving you with the dreary work still to do,' she said, and started the people carrier. 'But, like we said, you'll get paid. Thanks, anyhow, and give Emma our best greetings.'

'I will do, and I'll cover your tracks and take the vacuum cleaner and the freezers to the recycling station,' said Anders.

'Ah, poor boy,' said Christina. 'Come across and visit us so we can repay you as well as Emma. What are you going to do with the Green Menace?'

'Like we agreed. We'll leave it at the drop-off point outside the Arlanda terminal,' said Martha, winding up the window again. 'Then nobody will pay any attention to it until about a week has passed, and by then we will be far away.'

'Unless I fetch it before then,' Anders mumbled.

'Right then, off we go,' Brains said.

'No, hang on a second,' said Christina, and she got out of the people carrier again. She put her arms round Anders. 'Now take care of yourself, my boy, and give Emma some of the money too. Don't forget to say hello to her and little Malin from me.' She pushed a bundle of notes into his hand. 'This is a little advance, and remember that you and Emma will be even richer if you wait for all of your inheritance. If you don't use that million properly, then you won't inherit anything at all. Nothing!'

'Yes, Mother, yes. I know.' Anders smiled and gave her a hug.

*

When the five arrived at Arlanda all of them were feeling very tense. So far, everything had gone well and now they didn't want to trip on the finishing line. They tried to keep calm and walk in a slow and dignified manner up to the cluster of ticket machines. They had no problem with getting the tickets printed, because they had all practised pressing the buttons on those horrid, impersonal machines, and now they even succeeded in getting the machines to give them the baggage tags too! Their suitcases were the correct weight and as they were all labelled with stickers proclaiming 'Old People Are Capable', they were greeted at the check-in desk with a smile, and that, too, went smoothly. Then they had the paintings.

'Do you think they will let us go on board with this?' Christina wondered, and pointed at Anna-Greta's abstract painting which looked like a woman seen from behind, with a rosette and tangled hair. In this painting, their friend had slapped on a great deal of paint to hide lots of banknotes. The work of art was not exactly of a high class. To put it bluntly, it was dreadful. Anna-Greta saw her friends' hesitant faces.

'This is not about what a painting looks like, but about whether the picture is the right size for hand baggage.'

To be honest, the other paintings weren't much better, but they were colourful, well-packed and not a centimetre over the maximum allowed.

'Ah, that would be special baggage,' said the girl behind the check-in desk, and she arranged it. When she saw Martha's rectangular work of art, she became uncertain.

'I don't know about that,' she said.

'This is very fragile and means a lot to me,' said Martha, with a tremble to her voice as she patted the frame on the outside

428

of the paper. She had put several layers of paint on the canvas and then slashed through it all with a palette knife like a genuine Fontana. It would make it easier to get the money out, she reckoned.

'You're going to Barbados, I see,' said the girl behind the desk.

'Yes, to Bridgetown. That's where we are going to have our exhibition.'

'Oh, how nice. And you are flying business class, I see. I'll ask the air hostesses to take care of the painting. It's nice for pensioners to paint. Without artists, society would lose its soul.'

'We've already lost ours,' Martha mumbled.

A little while later, when they were going through security, it wasn't quite as easy as Martha had hoped. The guards immediately discovered a palette knife that she had hidden in her purse belt and so she was abruptly stopped. Then they started to feel the paper around the painting, and look hesitant.

'What's this?' one of the guards wondered with an authoritative voice.

Prevention is better than cure, Martha quickly realized, and she ripped off a corner of the paper and pointed at the label on the corner of the frame.

'See that? *Storm of Roses*, it's called. It's the best I've ever done.' This wasn't a lie, because she had never painted before. Admittedly, you couldn't see any sign of roses, but Martha thought it was a good name. The many 'clumps of paint' hid lots and lots of banknotes.

'I'm not sure we can let this through,' said the guard.

'Tell me you like it. That would please me so much,' Martha appealed to him, and patted the painting with one hand. 'Please!'

Then she was waved through, and shortly afterwards, Brains, Rake and Anna-Greta also went through. But when it was Christina's turn, the light turned red.

'Ooops!' she gasped, and looked unhappy.

'We will have to put this through the X-ray once more,' said the guard.

'Oh my goodness,' said Christina, and the others stared. Rake stood there nervously moving his weight from one foot to the other, Anna-Greta was completely silent, Brains raised his eyebrows, and Martha felt her knees tremble. Considering the circumstances, their friend seemed remarkably calm. Quickly she tore off the paper wrapping, pulled out the round, red drawing pins from the painting, and gave the guard a wide smile. 'Perhaps I went a bit far here, but this painting is rather special. It's called *Brass*, you see. Unfortunately, I forgot the drawing pins.'

The security guards stared at the pile of red drawing pins and didn't know what to think. One of them reached out and picked up something else from the table.

'What about this, then?'

'Ah, my nail file. Is that where it was? I must have dropped it.'

Then, with a gesture of resignation, the security guards waved her through. The League of Pensioners sighed with relief.

'Why did you do that, Christina?' Martha wondered a little later when they were going towards the gate.

'I was just testing the apparatuses. We're going to commit some more crimes, aren't we?'

★

430

When the huge airbus had lifted from the runway and the lights had been turned on in the cabin again, Martha ordered a bottle of champagne. Then she pulled out two sheets of paper.

'I'll just do what we agreed, so that we can post the letters when we arrive.'

'Right, let's drink to that,' Brains agreed, and held up his glass.

'Hang on a moment. Let me write first.'

Martha's handwriting was a bit shaky, but while the others started sipping their champagne and encouraged her with joyous acclamation, she put together the following letter:

> To the Government that can carry out something without being voted down.

At this point she was interrupted by Rake, who thought that she should add 'parliament' too, because they lived in a democracy. Anna-Greta raised her voice and said that they ought to add something about how the money must bypass all the bureaucracy. Martha did as they said, and then went on:

> The 'Friends of the Elderly' association has, at its lawfully convened annual general meeting, decided to annually donate money to those in need. The money can only be donated for the purposes listed below.
>
> All retirement homes shall be renovated and equipped to at least the same standard as the country's prisons. In addition, there should be access to computers, hairdressers and chiropodists. Pleasant outings and humane care are a requirement.

Every old people's home shall have a proper kitchen with competent staff where the food is prepared on site with fresh ingredients. A whisky before dinner and wine or champagne with dinner shall be served to those who so wish.

The residents shall have the freedom to come and go as they please, and to decide themselves what time they shall get up and go to bed.

A gym with training equipment shall be open for all the residents, and the retirement home shall provide a coach.

Everybody shall be able to drink as many cups of coffee as they like, and cakes and biscuits shall be served to those who so wish.

Nobody is allowed to become a politician in a position of power before they have done an internship at a retirement home for at least six months.

The association's committee has created a fund for deserving causes [she meant the Robbery Fund, but of course she didn't spell that out] and will decide when and to whom donations will be made. Decisions of the committee cannot be appealed against. Every donation is free of tax.

Martha formulated the letter so that a copy could be sent directly to the media – that way the letter would not be forgotten.

'And don't forget the money for our friends at Diamond House,' said Christina.

'No, but first we must sign the declaration,' said Martha and she held out the paper. They all signed it with their own names, and that didn't matter, of course, because they had all such illegible signatures that they would have made every doctor green with envy. When they had done this, Martha put the letter into an envelope and licked the flap.

'Then we've got our friends at Diamond House,' Christina reminded them again.

'Yes, but excluding Nurse Barbara,' they all said with one voice.

'Naturally, I am thinking about the others. What about a kitty with specific amounts for outings, parties and fancy dinners at the Grand Hotel?'

'They must have the celebration special too,' Christina said.

They all agreed on that, and Anna-Greta offered to fill the kitty every month. When they nodded, she looked most satisfied and raised her glass.

'Cheers then, comrades! Well, now, that still leaves the money in the drainpipe,' she said and neighed in delight.

'Perhaps not quite. Shouldn't we pay back the donation from the Friends of the Museum?' Christina wondered.

The others thought about this a while, before Christina spoke out.

'Of course. We will increase the amount a bit so that they will be able to afford a better exhibition than that Sins and Desires.'

'I thought that was rather good,' said Rake.

'We'll give them two million a year and then we will still have money left so that we can play at the casino in Las Vegas,' said Martha.

'Great,' they said with one voice until they realized that they were on the way to Barbados.

They all fiddled about with their champagne glasses.

'Pah, never mind. We'll fly to Las Vegas from the West Indies,' said Anna-Greta. 'That can surely be arranged.'

'Excellent, then that's sorted,' said Martha. 'Now all that remains is our letter to the police.' She pulled out the second sheet of paper and wrote down the text they had all immediately agreed on:

To the Police in Stockholm –
Dear Police,
We have been able to observe your hard work at close quarters, and would therefore like to support you. Go to the Grand Hotel in Stockholm and seek out the drainpipe outside the Cadier bar. Loosen the pipe and you will find a pair of tights full of money. We are donating the contents to the Police Pension Fund. You were right. All the money hadn't blown away. Good luck in your future work.
     Best regards,
     The League of Pensioners
     P. S. You can keep the tights.

When that letter too was finished, and Martha had licked the envelope, Brains poured out some more champagne.

'Here's to us – we who are trying to make as many people as possible happy!' he said.

They all nodded and raised their glasses. They could begin their new life abroad with a good conscience. A new adventure was awaiting them! In the unlikely event that they should want to return home again, they had arranged for new identities to be ready and waiting for them. Anna-Greta had already bought some good names on the Internet.

434

Epilogue

Inspector Strömbeck was sitting in front of his computer and checking CCTV images from Stockholm's surveillance cameras. He was looking for photos of a grey Mercedes that should have passed the cameras the previous week. Although they had reacted quickly and driven their dark blue Volvo so fast that the needle on the speedometer was at max, they had lost the Yugoslavs. Strömbeck swore and reached out for the bar of chocolate on his desk. He had started to console himself with sweets – what else could he do? Not only had he failed to nail the Yugoslav mafia, but he had also lost the pensioners.

He glared at the letter on his desk. He had been surprised when he had received a letter from the West Indies by snail mail, but he would never have imagined that somebody could taunt a police authority so. The oldies had suggested that he ought to look for the money in a pair of tights at the Grand Hotel. Down a drainpipe! He swore again, crumpled up the letter and threw it into the waste-paper basket.

Grateful Acknowledgements

While writing *The Little Old Lady who Broke All the Rules (Kaffe med rån)*, I have had a lovely group of people who have helped and supported me.

They include Inger Sjöholm-Larsson, who has read and provided encouragement from the very first embryo to the finished book, and Lena Sanfridson, with whom I bandied the first ideas some years ago, and who subsequently served as a source of inspiration and a sounding board throughout the journey. My grateful thanks also go to Ingrid Lindgren for reading the chapters at the express speed in which they were written, giving encouragement and making sensible observations. Likewise to Isabella Ingelman-Sundberg, who has supported me from the very start.

Thanks, too, to Susanne Thorson for your time and valuable comments, Kerstin Fägerblad for always reading and encouraging me however unpolished the manuscripts I send you, and Fredrik Ingelman-Sundberg for pepping me up, reading and supporting me.

I am also grateful for support and comments from Magnus Nyberg, Micke Agaton, Gunnar Ingelman, Britt-Marie Laurell, Åke Laurell, Ingegerd Jons, Helene Sundman, Anna-Stina

Bohlin, Bengt Björkstén, Karin Sparring Björkstén, Agneta Lundström, Anna Rask, Mika Larsson, Erva Karlgren and Eva Rylander. I am pleased that you took the time to give me your wise comments! The help I got from you has meant a lot.

I would like to say a very special thank you to Barbara von Schönberg, who has been an invaluable force and a source of joy when it came to realizing this book.

Many are they who have helped me with valuable information, and I would like to thank the director of the Sollentuna remand prison, Hanna Järl Källberg, Lina Montanari, and the Grand Hotel, who have guided me during my research for the book. A warm thank you!

At the Forum publishing house I have enjoyed pleasant cooperation with Adam Dahlin, Viveca Peterson, Lisselott Wennborg Ramberg, Anna Käll, Sara Lindgren and Annelie Eldh.

Author Q&A with
Catharina Ingelman-Sundberg

1) How would you describe The Little Old Lady Who Broke All the Rules?
It is a book about five people, all over 70, who become tired of the way society treats them. They leave their care home in a bid to launch new careers as thieves because they have noticed that prisoners are treated better in jail than the elderly in old people's homes!

2) Why did you decide to write about a group of friends living in a care home?
I get so frustrated when I read about harsh savings on elderly care. These older people have built today's society and made it possible for many of us to have a good life. But then when they are 'past it' they are treated very badly. This is just not on. So while this book is full of humour, it is also a strong protest against a society that has forgotten human values. I wanted to highlight this issue and make people think about the care of elderly citizens.

3) Who is your favourite character in the League of Pensioners?
Actually, I love them all. Martha is my central character, of course, and I identify with her, but I like Brains very much, too, as well as Anna-Greta, Christina and Rake. So, you see, it is difficult to single out just one of them . . .

4) Can you see yourself becoming like Martha as you grow older?
Yes, or perhaps I might be even more outrageous! But I'd like to think that I would eat more healthily – and not steal so much!

5) Do you have a favourite moment in the book?
My favourite moment is when the League of Pensioners steal the paintings at the National Museum – and the end of the book too.

6) Do you have any favourite novels?
I enjoy feel-good novels. I also read Dickens, Oscar Wilde and many other English authors. I love English films, too, and the wonderful sense of humour that English people have!

7) What do you enjoy most about being an author?
Honestly, it gives me the freedom to plan my own time and do what I want, where I want.

8) The Little Old Lady Who Broke All the Rules has sold to 17 countries so far and has been published under several different titles. Can you tell us what the other titles are and what they mean?
The original Swedish title is *Kaffe med Rån* which translated means 'Coffee and Robbery'. Some countries have followed the Swedish title, i.e. the Icelandic version *Kaffi og Rán*. The

German title is *Wir fangen gerade erst an* (We've Only Started Now), the Italian title is *La banda degli insoliti ottantenni* (You Cannot Trust the 80 year olds), the Norwegian title is *Svindel og multelikør* (Crookery and Cloudberry liqueur), the Spanish title is *La Bolsa o la vida* (The Money or Your Life) and the Dutch title is very much the same – *Je geld of je leven*.

I love the English title, *The Little Old Lady Who Broke All the Rules* because it says exactly what the book is all about. A group of elderly people who break all the rules – with Martha as their leader. And then I identify with the title personally as well!

9) How does it feel to have written an internationally bestselling novel?
Absolutely fantastic! I am so happy with the response I have had from readers.

10) What do you hope readers will take away from reading about Martha and the gang?
I want them to take care of the old, take care of each other, to remember human values and most of all to enjoy life.

Coming soon . . .

The Extra Ordinary Life of Frank Derrick, Age 81

J. B. MORRISON

Frank Derrick is eighty-one. And he's just been run over by a milk float.

It was tough enough to fill the hours of the day when he was active. But now he's broken his arm and fractured his foot, it looks set to be a very long few weeks ahead. Frank lives with his cat Bill (which made more sense before Ben died) in the typically British town of Fullwind-on-Sea. He watches DVDs, spends his money frivolously at the local charity shop and desperately tries to avoid the cold callers continually knocking on his door.

Then a breath of fresh air comes into his life in the form of Kelly Christmas, home help. With her cheerful resilience and ability to laugh at his jokes, Kelly changes Frank's extra ordinary life. She reminds him that there is a world beyond the four walls of his flat and that adventures, however small, come to people of all ages.

Frank and Kelly's story is sad and funny, moving, familiar, uplifting. For fans of *The Unlikely Pilgrimage of Harold Fry* this is a quirky, life-affirming story that has enormous appeal. And it's guaranteed to make you laugh.

ISBN: 978-1-4472-5274-0

Prologue

I'm eighty-one.

I'm probably supposed to be saying that a lot now.

Ooh, look at you. And how old are you?

I'm eighty-one. That sort of thing.

Sometimes not even waiting to be asked.

I'm eighty-one.

Proudly offering the information at every opportunity, like when I was five years old.

Perhaps I should wear a badge. Like the ones you get stuck on the front of a birthday card. An eighty-first birthday card – if such a thing exists. Do they even make those? Eighty, maybe, but eighty-one? Maybe I could hang some balloons with '81' printed on them above my front door. But there's probably no market for eighty-first birthday balloons either. I'll just have to keep saying it.

I'm eighty-one.

Come inside. Have a seat. Why don't you talk down to me like you did when I was a child? See how my faculties are. Talk to me in a loud baby voice. Get me to fill in a form. Better still, you fill it in for me. Just get me to sign it. I'm probably too blind to read any small print. Sell me things I don't want. Look around for antiques. Case the joint.

I'm eighty-one.

Come and have a go, if you think you're hard enough.

1

On Frank Derrick's eighty-first birthday he was run over by a milk float. He would have preferred a book token or some cuff-links, but it's the thought that counts.

The milk float was travelling at about five miles an hour when the milkman somehow lost control of the slow-moving vehicle, mounting the narrow pavement and coming to a stop, with the wheels of the milk float in the air, on the low stone wall at the front of someone's garden, sending crates of milk, empty bottles, cartons of cream and a few dozen eggs sliding off the back and onto the pavement.

Aside from making a mess of the garden of one of the expected big hitters in the upcoming Villages in Bloom competition, the milkman hadn't done Frank any favours either. He was underneath the vehicle. The only part of his body visible to the outside world was his right arm, sticking out from underneath the milk float, his palm facing upwards, still holding on to the pint of milk he'd just been to Fullwind Food & Wine to buy. It was exactly what the scene really needed – more milk. The upended milk float, protruding pensioner's arm and the steady stream of dairy produce floating down the gutter at the side of the road was like a spoof news story waiting for a punch line at the end of an episode of *The Two Ronnies*.

Frank was in hospital for three days. He had concussion, a broken arm and an acute fracture of one of the metatarsal bones in his left foot.

'Like the footballers get,' the doctor said. 'Do you play football?'

'Not any more. Not with this metatarsal injury.'

'Well, anyhow. It should respond well to some fairly simple self-care techniques. RICE therapy.'

'Ice therapy?'

'No, rice.'

'I don't like rice. Never have.'

'No. RICE. It's an acronym. Rest, ice, compression and elevation.'

'An acronym?'

'That's right.'

'Like the stroke one?'

'Like the stroke one,' the doctor said. 'I'll find you a leaflet.'

Frank also had a broken toe – the one next to his big toe, the little piggy that stayed at home, which was also his prognosis: to stay at home. He had a few cuts, some tyre marks and bruising, and a face like squashed fruit. He looked like one of those horrific newspaper photographs of a mugged pensioner.

'One or two of these cuts on your face may scar,' the doctor said.

'When you get to my age every cut is a scar.'

Frank's right arm was in plaster from the wrist to just past his elbow. They'd set his arm at an angle. Like in a cartoon. His arm would be stuck in a curve for at least six weeks. He looked like he was permanently trying to shake hands with everyone. If you'd sawed his arm off at the shoulder and thrown it, it would have come back.

Before he left hospital Frank had to take the Mini Mental State Examination to check his cognitive state. A young and exhausted-looking doctor in a striped shirt with a plain collar and sweat patches under just the left armpit pulled up a plastic chair next to Frank's hospital bed and flipped open an A4 pad of paper.

'Right, Frank,' he said. 'This test is a standard test. Some of the questions are probably going to seem a bit easy and some of them less so. Are you ready?'

The doctor asked Frank what year it was, what season, what month and the date and day of the week. Frank got them all right – although the doctor didn't say so. He just wrote stuff down and asked another question.

'What country are we in?'

'England.'

'What city?'

'Technically, it's a town.'

'You seem quite angry, Mr Derrick.'

'I was run over by a milkman. How's your day been?'

'Yes. I see,' the doctor said.

'I just want to go home before I catch MMSE.'

'That stands for Mini Mental State Examination, Mr Derrick. That's what we're doing now. I think you mean MRSA.'

'What does that stand for?'

'Deep breath,' the doctor said and he took a deep breath. 'Methicillin-resistant Staphylococcus aureus.' He smiled, pleased with himself as though he'd successfully pronounced

449

the name of that famous Welsh railway station. 'Now, shall we get to the end of the test?'

The doctor asked if Frank knew where he was and the name of the hospital and what ward they were on. Frank only passed on the name of the ward. The Mastermind trophy was as good as in the bag; he was picturing a place for it on the mantelpiece next to three porcelain penguins he'd never really liked that much. He was convinced the middle one was plotting a coup.

'Now, Frank, I'm going to name three objects and I want you to repeat them back to me and try to remember them, okay?'

Frank nodded. It hurt his head.

'Apple, pen, table,' the doctor said.

'Apple, pen, table.'

The doctor asked Frank to spell WORLD backwards and Frank said something about how it certainly was a backwards world. The doctor asked him to subtract seven from a hundred and then seven from the answer and to carry on doing so till he told him to stop. Frank made it as far as fifty-one and was a bit disappointed when the doctor said that was enough. He'd never been great at maths and thought that maybe the bang on the head had actually done him some good.

'Can you tell me who the Prime Minister is?'

Frank told the doctor who the Prime Minister was and that he thought he was an idiot and that he, for one, had definitely not voted for him. The doctor said that wasn't important.

'Oh, but it's very important.'

'Great,' the doctor said, but he didn't mean that it was great at all and he skipped a couple of questions to make the test end sooner. He wanted Frank to go home as well. The doctor wanted to go home. Everyone in the hospital wanted to go home. Who wants to be in a hospital?

'Can you remember the three objects I asked you to name earlier?' the doctor said.

'You mean the apple, the pen and the table?'

The doctor pointed at his wristwatch and asked Frank what it was.

'It looks like quite a cheap wristwatch.'

The doctor wanted to punch Frank. If it wasn't so frowned upon in his profession, perhaps he would have done.

There were a few more questions and a couple of more physical tests, including folding a piece of paper and then unfolding it again and writing a sentence on the piece of paper. Frank wrote, 'Can I go home now please?'

Later that day he was discharged from hospital. As the porter wheeled him to the lifts a nurse handed him a walking stick that he'd tried to leave behind when she'd given it to him earlier and a carrier bag containing his carton of milk. The milk had been out of the fridge for three days now and it was warm and probably turned into cottage cheese or clotted cream. Frank thanked the nurse and planned on leaving the bag in the ambulance on the way home.

After the accident Frank's daughter offered to immediately drop everything and fly back from America to look after him but Frank said there was no need, she had far more important things to do, she had her own life to live, her own family to look after, he'd be fine, it didn't even hurt that much, it was too far, don't be silly, it would cost too much, all that kind of bollocks. What he really wanted her to do was hang up the phone and get a cab to the airport.

'Let me at least arrange for somebody to come in and look after you,' she said.

'I can look after myself.'

'Let me do some research online. Make a couple of phone calls. Just to see what the options are.'

'Really, there is no need. It will cost a fortune. I'm fine. I've had worse hangovers.'

'Dad.'

'Don't you have crime reconstruction shows in America? They'll tie me to a chair and steal my pension.'

'Dad.'

'They'll use my water tank as a toilet. Actually, that might be plumbers.'

'Let me at least look into it. For my peace of mind, Dad. I don't want to worry about whether you've got enough food or if you've set fire to the house making toast.'

'Do you realise how much work I've put in to keeping people out of my home? Word will get out. If I let Robin Willams in a dress come inside to strap me to a chair and steal my antiques, I'll have a queue of boiler insurance salesmen and equity release people halfway up the road.'

'Dad.'

'I'll have to get a revolving door fitted. I'm sure there'll be somebody in the queue willing to sell me one. And once I've let in all the people who want to get inside my flat, what about all the people who want to get on top of it? That queue will stretch for miles. You'll be able to join the back of it without leaving California.'

It was true. People were keen to get on Frank's roof. His flat had something that there weren't a lot of in Fullwind-on-Sea:

452

stairs. Fourteen of them. Making him the go-to guy for stair-lift companies, window cleaners, gutter clearers, chimney sweeps and roofers. Hardly a week went by without him having to make his way down those fourteen stairs to answer the door to a man sucking his teeth and shaking his head.

'You do realise your roof is about to fall off?' Teeth suck.

'Your chimney is listing to the left.' Head shake.

'Have you seen how bunged up your guttering is?' Teeth suck. Head shake.

Maybe his roof *was* about to collapse, but if he did let some-body up there, he wouldn't be able to see what they were doing without walking fifty yards up the road with a pair of strong binoculars. He'd have no idea if they were actually fixing any-thing. They could be reading the newspaper or having a nap, or simply counting to fifteen thousand and then climbing back down to suck their teeth a bit more before presenting him with a bill for a million pounds.

Frank carried on telling Beth why he didn't need any help and about not wanting strangers in his home and she didn't interrupt. She let her dad complain because she knew it would make him feel better about the inevitable outcome – which was giving his daughter what she wanted. In this case, she wanted her dad to be safe and well.

He ranted a bit more and then he said, 'I'm not going to tidy up. I'm not lighting candles and brewing fresh coffee.'

'Of course not.'

The following day a man with an annoying whistle from the care company screwed a key safe to the outside wall of Frank's flat. He put a front-door key inside the safe and programmed Frank's birthday into the combination lock. Three days after that, in the middle of one of the hottest springs since records began, less than a month after Frank had finally got round to putting the fairy lights and tinsel back in the loft, Christmas came to Fullwind-on-Sea.

extracts reading groups
competitions books new
discounts extracts extracts discounts
competitions
books new events
events books
extracts
new titles reading groups
interviews
events extracts
discounts
new books events
events new

www.panmacmillan.com

discounts extracts discounts
extracts events reading groups
competitions books extracts new
reading groups
events
books